T0209178

NOT BY MIGHT

NOT BY MIGHT

BOOK EIGHT

AL LACY

Multnomah® Publishers

NOT BY MIGHT
published by Multnomah Publishers, Inc.

© 1999 by ALJO PRODUCTIONS, INC.
International Standard Book Number: 9781601420053

Cover illustration by Vittorio Dangelico
Design by D2 DesignWorks

Scripture quotations are from
The Holy Bible, King James Version (KJV)

For information:
MULTNOMAH PUBLISHERS, INC.
POST OFFICE BOX 1720
SISTERS, OREGON 97759

Library of Congress Cataloging-in-Publication Data:

Lacy, Al.
   Not by might/Al Lacy.   p.cm.—(The angel of mercy series:bk. 8)
   ISBN-13: 978-1-601-42005-3
   I. Title. II. Series: Lacy, Al. Angel of mercy series: bk 8.
PS3562.A256N68   1999   98-44008
813'.54—dc21   CIP

146655433

*For Steve Curley, my friend and brother in Christ,
who really knows how to supervise the production of
terrific book covers!
Thank you for doing such a great job.
I love you, Steve.*

EPHESIANS 1:2

Not by might, nor by power,
but by my spirit, saith the LORD of hosts.

ZECHARIAH 4:6

PROLOGUE

MEDICAL HISTORIANS HAVE termed nursing "the oldest of the arts and the youngest of the professions." None in the medical profession deny that nursing is an art form. As such, it has gone through many stages and has long been an integral part of human society's development.

I have found it interesting in my study of medical history that nursing first becomes continuous with the ministry of the Lord Jesus Christ when He came to earth. Pre-Christian records of nursing are quite fragmentary. Records of nursing, however, from the early Christian workers to the present day are continuous.

Our Lord's story of the Good Samaritan, and His compassion on the sick, infirm, and dying when he walked this earth have left an indelible imprint on the medical profession. His ministry of love and compassion transformed not only society at large, but also the development of nursing.

The organization of nursing as a profession stems historically from our Lord's earthly ministry and the lessons He left behind. This legacy epitomizes the idea of true altruism, first initiated by Jesus as He moved among a suffering humanity, and then by His early followers.

The word *altruism* comes from the Latin *alter,* meaning

"other." Altruism, therefore, means caring for *others*. True altruism was taught by the Lord Jesus in word and deed, and was picked up from Him by His followers. This birth of Christian idealism would forever have a deep and powerful influence on the art of nursing.

In my stories about nurse Breanna Baylor—now Breanna Baylor Brockman—the art form of nursing is combined with another art form, the western novel, which is uniquely an *American* art form.

Beginning well over a hundred years ago with the dime novels of Ned Buntline and Prentiss Ingraham, the western novel was later given permanent literary stature by Zane Grey, Max Brand, Luke Short, Ernest Haycox, Louis L'Amour, and others. Their works were mirrors of the times and places in which they lived.

To this author, the Old West was a captivating, exciting, romantic place. Having been born and raised in the Rocky Mountain region of Colorado, it is part of my heritage. As a Christian author, with my love of good westerns and fascination for the medical profession, I have combined the two art forms of nursing and westerns with biblical principles and the gospel of Jesus Christ in my Angel of Mercy novels.

It is my earnest desire and fervent prayer that my readers will enjoy this latest effort, *Not by Might*.

1

THE LATE AFTERNOON sun splashed brilliant light above a long-fingered cloud bank in the azure Colorado sky.

Outlaw Pete Dawson sat on a towering rock shelf high in the majestic Rocky Mountains, peering through his binoculars as he made a slow sweep of the surrounding forests of blue spruce, aspen, and birch that stretched southward toward the snowcapped peaks of the San Juan Range.

Less than fifty yards away, the jagged sides of the mountains dropped off sharply from the high snowfields into jumbled heaps of multishaped boulders. Sheer rock ledges hung over dark, shadowed canyons.

It was mid-July, but at the altitude where Dawson sat, snow was packed deep in uneven crevices, shaded by trees that had struggled to root themselves at this level where the oxygen was so scarce.

The outlaw lowered his binoculars and looked back toward his cohort, Dick Nye, who was perched on a rock ledge some two hundred yards away. Nye gave Dawson a wave, signaling that he could see no unusual activity on the trail below.

Both men could look down and see the fancy cabin they and the other gang members had built last year for their boss, Duke Foster. Just to the east of the cabin was Monarch Pass, and to the north, a short distance away, Dead Man's Canyon.

Far below to the west, the foamy Gunnison River twisted through heavy timber on its downward plunge through the dark gorge known as Black Canyon. From there it wended its way to the valley floor, where it would veer north to eventually spill into the mighty Colorado River.

Dawson lifted his binoculars again and focused on the porch at the front of the cabin. Duke Foster; his younger brother, Chick; Jim Felton; and Acton Huxley were lounging there, enjoying the view.

As Dick Nye looked through his binoculars, sweeping the area around the only accessible trail to the cabin, he saw movement. He sat up straight and concentrated on the spot, then grinned as he zeroed in on a huge male grizzly emerging from the murky shadows to stand in dappled sunlight at the edge of the trail. The bear rose up on his hind legs, eyes flickering, nostrils quivering.

"Hungry, big fella?" Nye said in a low tone. "Well, don't be comin' up here. I don't intend to become grizzly food."

Nye lowered the glasses and flicked a glance to his co-sentry. Dawson had spotted the grizzly, too. He looked at Nye, waved the "bear" signal, and put the binoculars back to his face, studying the bear's outer coating of silver hair and the deep brown fur beneath.

Suddenly, the enormous beast sniffed the air, snorted, and wheeled about. With a smooth, fluid movement, he disappeared into the inky forest.

An hour passed.

Dick Nye yawned as he watched the sun ease its way down the western sky. He happened to glance toward Pete Dawson and saw him wave and point toward the trail. Four riders were coming up the mountain at a slow pace.

The riders were gang members Web Crispin and Layton Patch, and two men Duke had just recruited into the gang. Duke had met Mel Skinner and Isaac Gerton in Durango several months ago. They would replace the two gang members killed during a stagecoach holdup near Pagosa Springs.

Dawson and Nye turned toward the hideout and waved a prearranged signal, which caused Duke to lift his cane in the air.

The co-sentries wanted to hurry down so they could meet the new men, but their shift wasn't up until after sundown. Some sharp lawman might have followed the four, or just might have found the trail to the hideout on his own. Duke took no chances. He had men posted on the two lookout points every day, from dawn till dusk.

At the cabin Duke Foster, his brother Chick, and the others greeted the new men as they stepped onto the porch behind Web Crispin and Layton Patch. Skinner and Gerton had a hard look about them, just like Duke and the others.

Duke leaned on his cane, favoring his right leg, and reached out to shake hands with the new men, then introduced them to Huxley, Felton, and Chick. As always, when the brothers were seen together, someone commented on how similar they looked. This time, Mel Skinner said that Chick was just a younger version of his big brother. Chick grinned as he nodded his head in agreement.

"Take a seat, Mel…Isaac," Duke said as he gestured toward a group of wooden chairs.

Jim Felton shuffled his feet and said, "C'mon, Chick. Since it's our turn to cook supper, we'd better get started."

The others took seats when Duke did, and Duke told Skinner and Gerton that the two men on sentry duty would come down when dusk fell. Then he brought up some rob-beries he was planning and explained his strategy to the new men. Skinner and Gerton were amazed at how carefully and thoroughly Duke planned his jobs. They discussed the upcom-ing robberies until dusk began to fall.

The aroma of frying venison was wafting from the kitchen windows as Dick Nye and Pete Dawson appeared at the edge of the deck with two strangers between them who had been relieved of their guns.

Duke leaned heavily on his cane as he rose to his feet.

"Boss," Dawson said, "we saw these fellas comin' up the trail just as we reached ground level. They say they've been sent to you with a message from Harold Sheetz."

A smile spread over Duke's rather homely face. "Oh? You boys come from Harold, eh? If this is true, you'll know the code word."

"We sure do, Mr. Foster," said the older of the two. "Leavenworth."

Duke laughed. "Okay, boys. Give 'em back their guns. They're the real thing, all right." Then he said to the pair, "You fellas got names?"

They told him their names were Bob French and Kyle Munson. French looked to be several years older than Munson, who was in his midtwenties.

"You boys hungry?" Duke asked.

French and Munson looked at each other, then Munson said, "We can't stay, Mr. Foster. Thanks anyway, but we have to head back right away."

"All right. What's the message from Harold?"

"He wants you to come to his house in Denver as soon as you can. He has some real good news for you. He said to bring four or five of your boys with you."

"So what's the good news?"

"We don't know, sir. Harold didn't tell us. We only work for him occasionally. He hired us to come up here and give you the message."

Duke pushed his hat low over his face and scratched the back of his head. "Okay, fellas. You tell Harold we'll be there a day behind you, and we'll come at night."

French and Munson swung into their saddles and soon were out of sight.

"Well, boys," said the boss, "let's eat."

As soon as they sat down around the table, Mel Skinner said, "This Harold Sheetz, boss, who is he?"

"A very good friend of mine," Duke said, who at fifty was showing gray at the temples. "I did a ten-year stretch in the federal pen at Leavenworth, Kansas, for armed robbery in Missouri and Kansas. Harold was a guard there. Early on, Harold and I secretly became friends. He served as a messenger between me and the boys who made up my gang at that time. All of those boys except Acton here are gone now."

Acton Huxley was chewing a mouthful of venison. He smiled, showing bits of meat in his yellow teeth.

"So when I was paroled and got back on the outlaw trail, I paid Harold handsomely for what he'd done for me all those years while I was locked up."

Skinner and Gerton nodded.

"Harold was a trusted employee of the federal government. When an opening came up at the federal building in Denver two years ago, they offered Harold the job. He and I have kept in touch since I got out of prison, so I knew about his move to Denver. I'm not sure exactly what Harold does, but part of his work is in connection with the chief U.S. marshal's office. I've got a feelin' this good news has somethin' to do with information he's picked up in Brockman's office."

"Brockman?" said Gerton. "Who's he?"

"The new chief U.S. marshal."

"Somethin' happen to Duvall?"

"He retired. This guy John Brockman was installed by President Grant a couple months or so ago."

"I see. Hadn't heard about that."

"A bell's ringin' in the back of my mind about that," said Skinner. "Ain't this Brockman guy the one they used to call the Stranger?"

Duke nodded. "That's him."

"And we won't tangle with him, either. Right, big brother?" said Chick.

"For sure. Man's almost superhuman. We'll be plenty careful not to get him on our trail. I have a cousin who saw this Stranger face off up in Wyomin' with that big-time gunfighter Tate Landry. He told me Stranger made Landry look like molasses in January at the North Pole when they drew against each other. Said Stranger was like a well-oiled machine. His gun was in his hand and spittin' fire before anybody saw him move."

"Landry…" Skinner mused. "I heard it was a preacher who took him out."

"Correct," Duke Foster said. "Our Chief U.S. Marshal John Brockman is also a preacher." He chuckled. "Most preachers I've seen are sorta sissified. But this Brockman is one tough cookie." He drained his coffee cup, plunked it on the table and said, "Anyway, Harold Sheetz and his wife moved to Denver a couple years ago. She died last year. He lives by himself in a two-story house right there in town. We'll just go see what this good news is."

Chick looked across the table at his brother. "So who're the four or five boys you're takin' with you, Duke?"

The gang leader grinned. "Well, little brother, you always go wherever I go. And since Web, Mel, and Isaac have just had a long, hard ride, and since Acton's lumbago's been givin' him some trouble, we'll take Pete, Layton, Dick, and Jim with us. We strike saddle at dawn."

It was a cool night in Denver when Harold Sheetz heard the knock at his back door. He laid aside the newspaper he was reading and hurried down the hall to the kitchen. He slid the bolt and opened the back door, immediately recognizing his friend Duke Foster by the light of the lantern on the kitchen sideboard. The men behind Duke were obscured in shadow.

"Duke, ol' pal!" Sheetz said. "Come in! Come in!"

Duke stepped inside, shook Harold's hand, then introduced his men as they filed in behind him.

Harold Sheetz was a few years younger than Duke but had more silver in his hair. "Sure is good to see you again, Duke," he said. "Let's put your horses in the barn; then we'll talk."

A few minutes later, the federal employee and the outlaws sat around the kitchen table. Harold poured drinks, took a gulp from his own glass, and said, "Okay, Duke, here it is. I learned something a few days ago while in the chief U.S. marshal's office that I knew would interest you."

Duke swallowed the stinging whiskey and said, "I'm all ears."

"I think you're aware that we've got a new chief U.S. marshal here."

"Yep. John 'The Stranger' Brockman. Replaced Sol Duvall just a few weeks ago."

"Right. And are you aware of who is executive administrator of the U.S. marshal's office in Washington?"

Duke Foster's features hardened. "Yeah," he breathed hotly. "Chet McCarty."

Chester B. McCarty had tracked Duke fourteen years ago and cornered him at the stockyards in Wichita. Duke resisted arrest and McCarty shot him in the right leg, shattering the bone. Duke went to trial and was sentenced to ten years at Leavenworth. He hated McCarty for taking ten years of his life and for giving him a limp he would carry to his grave. He owed him.

Sheetz grinned evilly and said, "Duke, you're gonna have your chance to get even with McCarty."

A glint lit up Foster's eyes. "How's that?"

"He's comin' to Denver."

"Yeah? Why...when?"

"McCarty's got to do some planning with Brockman. The ever-increasing population west of the Missouri River is bringing more lawbreakers and troublemakers with it."

Sheetz laughed at his stab at humor, and the gang members joined in. Then Sheetz said, "Brockman's force of deputy U.S. marshals in offices all over the Western District, including here in Denver, is worn thin."

Layton Patch chuckled. "That's good news in itself."

"Yeah, and McCarty is coming to Denver on assignment by President Ulysses S. Grant to look into relieving Brockman's load. They want to establish another chief U.S. marshal's office to oversee the offices in California and the northwest territories."

"Too bad those badge-toters are havin' such a hard time," said Dawson. "Tears my heart out."

Sheetz emptied his shot glass, wiped his lips on his sleeve, and said, "McCarty will arrive in Denver next Tuesday, July 23 ...four days from now. He's staying until Thursday. His train leaves at nine o'clock Thursday morning."

"Mm-hmm," said Duke, scrubbing a hand across his mouth and stroking his heavy mustache. "Do you know what hotel the snake-bellied rat is going to stay in?"

"The Westerner. That's where nearly all the government officials and other dignitaries stay when they come to Denver."

Duke nodded silently, still stroking his mustache. "Okay. Then Chick, I want you to take these other boys to the Westerner tonight and get yourselves some rooms. I'll stay here with Harold."

"All right," Chick said. "What's the plan?"

"I'm thinkin' on it."

"Sure, Duke. We'll all be real quiet while you put it together in your mind."

A few minutes had passed when Duke said, "Okay, I've got it. The reason I want you boys to get rooms at the hotel is because we're gonna kidnap McCarty."

The gang members nodded, listening raptly.

"I want the hotel personnel to get used to seeing your faces around there before McCarty arrives and checks in. That way, they'll suspect nothing when you get ready to grab him. You don't want to try it when he's with his badge-totin' pals, especially Brockman. You'll have to grab him on Wednesday whenever he comes back to the hotel for the night. When you check in, use fictitious names, of course, and make up a story about who you are and why you're in town for a few days."

"We can handle that," Chick said.

"I have no doubt of it, little brother. That's why I'm puttin' you in charge of the kidnappin'. You figure out how to grab him and not be seen."

Chick gave his brother a lopsided grin. "Consider it done."

"So what are we gonna do with this McCarty when we kidnap him, boss?" asked Jim Felton.

The look in Duke Foster's gray eyes seemed to come from the rugged crags of malice and evil. Through clenched teeth, he hissed, "Make him suffer. We'll take him to the hideout and close him in a small cubicle in the back corner of the barn. He'll be my prisoner. He sent me to prison for ten years. I'll send him to prison in a tiny wooden cell for the rest of his miserable life."

"Hey, that'll teach him, boss!" Dick Nye said.

"And that ain't all," said Foster, grinding his teeth. "McCarty shot my leg up so I'll be a cripple till I die. Well, he's gonna get a taste of his own medicine. He'll rue the day he ever pinned on a badge and came after Duke Foster!"

At the same time Foster and his men were meeting with Harold Sheetz, John and Breanna Brockman were sitting in the porch swing of their country home some nine miles southwest of Denver.

The full moon was clear-edged and pure against the black velvet of the star-spangled sky. John and Breanna held hands as they kept the swing in motion.

Countless crickets were giving their nightly concert, and the rush of the nearby South Platte River came to their ears as background music.

Just as John turned to look at Breanna in the silver hue of the moon, the night breeze ruffled her hair and blew tiny blond wisps across her lovely forehead. "The Lord sure did a beautiful job when He made you, sweetheart," he said softly.

She smiled and squeezed his hand. "Aren't you the flatterer," she said modestly.

"It isn't flattery, it's fact. You are absolutely the most gorgeous female the Lord ever made."

"You could get a lot of votes against that, you know. All husbands feel that way about their wives."

John chuckled. "Poor blind fools. Of course, it's best that they don't really know that it's John Brockman who got the most beautiful one."

Breanna reached up and pulled his head down, planting a warm kiss on his lips. "You just keep thinking that, darling."

"I don't think it," he said flatly. "I know it."

Breanna kissed him again, then laid her head against his shoulder. Looking toward the stars, she said, "Thank You, Lord, for giving me this wonderful man. Truly I am blessed beyond measure."

"I'm the one who's blessed, Breanna darling."

"Let's not argue tonight, sweetheart," she said. "How about a moonlight walk?"

"You're on."

They stepped off the porch and strolled up the lane between the long double row of cottonwoods. The breeze rustled the leaves, adding to the pleasant night sounds.

"John," said Breanna, "I'm sure you're looking forward to seeing Chet McCarty again."

"I sure am. We got quite well acquainted when I was in Washington."

Breanna recalled how much her husband had talked about Chet McCarty when he returned from his trip to Washington, where he had been officially commissioned by President Grant as chief U.S. marshal of the Western District.

"I'm so glad something is being done in Washington about the load on your shoulders, darling," Breanna said. "I know it was heavy for Chief Duvall, but just since you took over his job there's been a marked increase of crime out here in the West. The need for deputy U.S. marshals has increased with it, but the number of men keeps dwindling."

John thought how true her words were. He was responsible for eleven U.S. marshals' offices all the way to the west coast, and every office was sadly understaffed, including his own. At present, the staff of thirty-one deputies working out of the Denver office was spread very thin. Washington had promised him more deputies as soon as possible.

John had two deputies recuperating in their Denver homes from gunshot wounds. Two others had been buried in the past month. Right now, every available man was on assignment out of town except two—young Deputy Billy Martin, who manned the front desk at the office, and Deputy Dave Taylor, who was kept on call to assist John in case of emergencies in and around Denver.

John was glad to have Taylor, who had been town marshal of Sheridan, Wyoming, for several years. Dave had decided to become a federal lawman three years ago and was sent to beef up the staff of then Chief Marshal Solomon Duvall.

"Maybe Chet will have something more definite to tell me about new deputies when he comes," said John.

Soon they reached the main road and turned around. As they headed down the gentle slope that led to their house and outbuildings, Breanna said, "I'm glad, at least, darling, that you haven't gone outlaw-hunting yourself very much since we got married. But I fear you will if Washington doesn't hurry and send you some new men."

"I'll have to. Can't let the bad guys take over the country." He paused, then said, "It's been so good that we've had time together, and your nursing hasn't taken you away a whole lot."

"Yes," she said, noting a falling star. "Oh, look, John! See it?"

"Mm-hmm. Some tail on that one."

Of late Breanna had been dividing her time between working at Mile High Hospital and the office of Dr. Lyle Goodwin, who had been her sponsor for some time as a visiting nurse. Since marrying John on June 4, Breanna had taken fewer traveling jobs, though she had not cut them out completely.

When they neared the house, Breanna said, "How about we tell our boys good night, John?"

They moved past the house and approached the barn and corral. Ebony, John's black gelding, stood in the corral, his coat shining in the moonlight. He nickered when he heard them approaching.

Instantly, Breanna's black stallion, Chance, whinnied and came out of the shadows at the rear of the corral.

Both horses stuck their long faces over the top rung of the split-rail fence, waiting to be petted. John patted Ebony's neck; then the horse bobbed his head and whinnied at Breanna, wanting some attention from her.

"Ebony's jealous," said John. "You'd better pet him a little."

Breanna laughed as she used her other hand to rub Ebony's muzzle. Instantly, Chance made a deep nickering sound and nudged Ebony away with his shoulder. Ebony whinnied a complaint, but Chance was a bit larger, and Ebony already knew by experience that moving Chance away from Breanna was an impossibility.

John reached over the fence and patted his horse. "It's all right, big boy," he said. "Daddy loves you."

"Well, Mommy loves him, too," said Breanna, "but we don't want to start a fight here, do we?"

John reached over with his free hand and rubbed Chance's head. "I owe you a lot, ol' pal…even my life."

Just over a year ago John had found Chance running in the wilds of Montana, leading a pack of wild horses. The big untamed stallion had allowed John to ride him out of a forest fire in which John was hopelessly trapped.

Breanna hugged the stallion's neck. "Thank you, once more, Chance, for saving Daddy's life. If it hadn't been for you, he would have burned to death."

Chance nickered affectionately, and Ebony joined in, getting himself another few strokes from the beautiful lady.

"Well, honey," said the tall man, "it's getting late. We'd better head for the house."

2

UPON ENTERING THE house, John and Breanna went directly to the kitchen. Their custom since the day they were married was to read a chapter of the Bible aloud at the kitchen table and discuss some portion of it before retiring for the night.

For the past three nights they had been reading in Zechariah. They alternated reading a verse apiece in chapter 4, and when they had finished, John said, "Verse 6 is a powerful one, honey. Let me read it again: 'Then he answered and spake unto me, saying, This is the word of the LORD unto Zerubbabel, saying, Not by might, nor by power, but by my spirit, saith the LORD of hosts.'

"Of course, in the context, here, God is speaking to Zerubbabel. You remember that he was in the line of David and, according to the Book of Ezra, was called Sheshbazzar when the Jews were in captivity in Babylon, both under Nebuchadnezzar and Cyrus. Zerubbabel is listed in the genealogy of Jesus in both Matthew and Luke."

"I remember that," said Breanna.

"Well, Cyrus appointed Zerubbabel governor of the Jewish colony when he allowed the Jews to return to their own land, and when they got to Jerusalem, the first thing Zerubbabel set about to do was to rebuild the temple. You will recall that immediately there was opposition from the enemies of God, and for a while it looked like Zerubbabel would never get the temple rebuilt. But during this trying time the Lord sent his message to Zerubbabel through Zechariah, telling him that the temple would indeed be rebuilt, but it would not be accomplished by the might nor the power of human flesh, but by the Spirit of God."

Breanna smiled. "And it was!"

"That's right. Ezra chapter 6 tells all about the house of God being finished in the sixth year of King Darius's reign, and it tells of the great celebration by the Jews when the new temple was dedicated. Most certainly with all the opposition, the finishing of the temple could only come by the hand of the Holy Spirit Himself."

"For sure," said Breanna. "And the words 'Not by might, nor by power, but my Spirit, saith the LORD of hosts' teach us a basic truth about our God and His mighty work in salvation, and His mighty work in the lives of His born-again children. When God gives His great salvation to repentant sinners, there is nothing mortal involved. They are not saved by the might nor the power of man; the great work of regeneration is done by the Holy Spirit."

"Mm-hmm," John said. "And so it is when He works His mighty wonders in the lives of His born-again children; it is not by the might nor power of human flesh, but by His precious Holy Spirit."

"Wonderful truth," said Breanna. "That way, when He saved us, and when He works His wonders in our daily lives, He gets all the glory."

"Amen," said John, closing his Bible. He reached across the table and took both of Breanna's hands in his, then said, "Let's just give Him our praise and glory right now."

Breanna smiled at him and bowed her head.

On Tuesday, July 23, Chief U.S. Marshal John Brockman and Deputy Dave Taylor stood on the platform at Denver's Union Station as the big engine chugged to a halt with bell clanging and steam hissing from both sides.

The two lawmen remained some distance from the train and looked on while people who were meeting friends and loved ones crowded close to the passenger cars.

Unbeknownst to Brockman and Taylor, Chick Foster stood a few paces down the platform, eyeing them and waiting to get a look at Chester B. McCarty. Duke Foster's hatred for the lawman had gotten into Chick's system, too. He was glad Duke had given him the task of kidnapping McCarty. It made him feel good to know he would have an important part in helping his brother get revenge for the ten years in prison and his crippled leg.

For a moment, Chick let his gaze rest on the chief U.S. marshal. He was awed at the sight of the man who had long been known as the Stranger, a man who was loved by decent, law-abiding people and hated by outlaws. Chick Foster didn't exactly hate him, but he hated what he stood for. Lawmen made life miserable for men like him and his brother. Chet McCarty had certainly dealt his brother a great deal of misery.

As Dave Taylor stood beside his tall, broad-shouldered boss, he felt proud to be associated with him. John Brockman, when traveling the West as the Stranger, had made a name for himself as he made his mark against outlaws and lawbreakers. Many who had dared go up against him now lay six feet under, while a great host of others languished in prison cells. Unlike most chief U.S. marshals, Brockman was known to leave his desk at times and go in pursuit of outlaws. Up to now, Taylor had not had the pleasure of riding after outlaws with Brockman, but he hoped the day would come soon when it would happen.

"Ah, there he is, Dave!" said Brockman, heading for the third coach, where a rugged-looking middle-aged man was stepping down from the rear platform.

It took Chet McCarty only seconds to notice the man who stood out from the crowd because of his height. A smile worked its way across his florid face as he and Brockman came together. "John!" said McCarty, setting down his bags and extending his hand. "Good to see you!"

"You too, sir," said Brockman, clasping his hand in a firm grip. "Did you have an enjoyable trip?"

"Yes, I did. I love the wide-open spaces out here in the West."

John turned to his partner. "Mr. McCarty, I want you to meet one of my deputies, Dave Taylor."

McCarty and Taylor shook hands, greeting each other amiably; then Brockman said, "I assume this is all the luggage you have."

"That's it."

Dave moved quickly, picking up both pieces of luggage. "I'll carry these for you, sir."

McCarty thanked him and followed John out of the station to the parking lot. Dave hurried past them, placed the small pieces of luggage in the rear of the buggy, and untied the reins while his superiors were boarding.

Moments later the buggy wheeled out of the lot and headed down the broad, dusty street.

26

᠅

Before the lawmen left the depot, Chick Foster had mounted his horse. Now he sat staring after the buggy. When it passed from view, he touched heels to his horse's flanks and trotted the opposite direction. Moments later, he swung from the saddle at the small corral behind Harold Sheetz's house, led the horse through the gate, then headed for the back porch.

Duke and his other men were sitting around the kitchen table, playing poker, when Chick walked in. Duke looked up. "Well? Did he get here?"

"Yep. Brockman and one of his deputies met him. Saw McCarty lift his hat once, and you're right, big brother. He's got a head full of carrot red hair. 'Course, it's got some gray mixed in with it, too."

"Been a while since I seen him," grunted Duke. "I'll be glad when he's limpin' around that little cubicle we're gonna build him in our barn."

Dave Taylor swung the buggy off Sixteenth Street onto Blake Street and headed for the Westerner Hotel. While the buggy rolled along, Brockman and McCarty talked about the situation in the western part of the country of so few federal lawmen compared to the ever-increasing number of outlaws.

"I know you're wondering if I have any good news about reinforcements for your office and the other eleven offices out here, John," said McCarty. "I can't give you any exact numbers or exact dates, but we're definitely making headway on the problem. We've got men out in towns all over the West, talking to town marshals, their deputies, and county sheriffs and their deputies. Many are showing real interest in becoming federal lawmen. Should have more information for you within a couple more months. We'll talk more about it tomorrow."

"Fine, sir," said Brockman.

McCarty turned to Taylor. "That federal badge looks good on you, Dave. I assume you were a lawman elsewhere before you went to work for the federal government. Tell me about yourself."

"Well, to begin with, Mr. McCarty," said Dave, "I'm from Missouri. Born and raised in Kansas City. My first job as a lawman was as one of five deputy marshals under Kansas City town marshal Jake Gibbs."

"Oh, sure. I met him once several years ago. Good lawman."

"Yes, sir. I started under Marshal Gibbs when I was twenty-one. He taught me a whole lot about being a lawman during the eight years I worked under him. I believe I proved myself to him because when the chairman of the town council in Sheridan, Wyoming, contacted him, asking if he had a man he could recommend to become their town marshal, he recommended me."

Brockman chuckled. "It was just the opposite, Dave. I heard that Jake Gibbs recommended you so he could get rid of you!"

McCarty laughed. "You suppose that was it, John?"

"Oh, I'm sure of it. Dave's worthless as a deputy U.S. marshal, so I figure he must have been worthless all along."

Dave's face flushed. "Aw, c'mon, Chief. I'm not that bad."

John reached around behind McCarty, patted Dave's shoulder, and said, "Sure you are! That's why I keep you around. I like 'em ba-a-ad!"

All three men laughed, then McCarty said, "So you went to Sheridan from Kansas City and became the town marshal."

"Yes, sir. I was there five years, and I kept hearing how desperately the government needed deputy U.S. marshals, so three years ago I applied for the job by mail to Chief Duvall. He checked my record both in Sheridan and Kansas City, and hired me. I enjoyed working under Chief Duvall, and under Chief Brockman, since he took over." A big grin captured his mouth. "Ah…that is, until today!"

There was more laughter as the Westerner Hotel came into view.

McCarty said, "I suppose there's a Mrs. Dave Taylor?"

"Yes, sir. Prettiest little thing you ever saw. Her name's Nyla."

"Any children?"

"Oh, yes. Dave Jr., who's almost fourteen; Elizabeth, who is twelve; and Nellie, who is nine."

"Sounds like you've got a nice family."

"That I do, sir."

"I'll put in with that," said John. "Dave has a wonderful wife and three precious children."

Taylor swung the buggy up in front of the Westerner, then carried the two bags inside while Brockman was checking McCarty in at the front desk. When McCarty's bags had been deposited in his second-floor room, the three men returned to the buggy, and Taylor drove to the federal building on Tremont Street.

Taylor dropped the two men off and drove the buggy down the street to the hostler's. He was unaware of a tall, slender man with a low-slung gun on his hip who had just pulled up to the hitching rail across the street. The man dismounted and set cold eyes on Taylor.

Moments later, Dave Taylor came out of the hostler's office, his badge glinting in the sunlight, and headed toward the federal building. He greeted the few people coming toward him on the boardwalk and whistled a nameless tune as he picked up his pace.

Suddenly a tall, lanky form jumped out in front of him from between two buildings. He pinned Taylor with his cold, rancorous eyes and let his hand hover over the butt of the Colt .45 on his hip.

Taylor instantly recognized gunhawk Zeke Patton. His mind flashed back to a hot August day in Sheridan some four years ago when he put outlaw Nick Patton under arrest. Patton had been wanted in two states and four territories for murder. His younger brother, Zeke, was with him, but at that time had no criminal record.

Zeke had looked on while Nick told Taylor he wasn't going to prison and then went for his gun. Taylor outdrew him, putting a bullet in his gun arm. Later, Zeke was at the hanging. Fierce hatred shone from his eyes when Marshal Dave Taylor pulled the lever of the gallows, dropping Nick to his death with one arm in a sling and the other tied behind him.

Taylor had not seen Zeke since that day, but he'd never forgotten the hateful look in the man's eyes. Taylor had heard about Zeke making a name for himself on the roster of top gunfighters. He knew by the men Zeke had drawn against and put down that he was plenty fast...faster than Dave Taylor would be.

Dave eyed the hand that hovered over the holstered gun, then raised his line of sight to meet Patton's frigid gaze. "Been a while, Zeke," he said.

Patton's voice was emotionless as he said, "Yeah. Long enough for my brother's body to turn back to dust in the grave."

Ignoring the bold reference to Taylor's execution of his brother, Dave said, "So I hear you're a big-name gunfighter."

"I've taken out a few of the better-knowns."

"New Mexico, I understand."

"Mostly. I get around some. Was passin' through town and stopped to wet my whistle. Happened to see you goin' into the hostler's back there."

People had begun to collect within earshot of the two men.

Dave could feel the venomous hatred pulsating inside Zeke Patton. He dared not show the fear crawling up his backbone. "So you decided to stop me and say hello."

"Not exactly. I stopped you so I could settle the score. You put Nick in his grave. I figure to do the same to you. But I'll let you draw first."

"Fool thing to do, Zeke. Just get back on your horse and ride. You aren't blind, so you can see this badge on my chest. You gun me down, you're in a heap of trouble with the federal government."

"I don't really care about that," Zeke said evenly. "I'm gonna kill you, but I'll let you go for your gun first. Go ahead. Draw."

"You like living as much as Nick did. Even if you kill me, Zeke, this badge won't die. It will come after you on another man's vest. You can't take on the federal government. You'll end up dead like your brother, or with a bullet through your heart. Don't do it."

Little points of light gleamed in Patton's eyes as he swore at Taylor and went for the gun on his hip.

At Denver's Mile High Hospital, nurse Breanna Baylor Brockman stood in conversation with receptionist Mabel Trotter.

"So have you had any word from Iron Hawk and Silver Moon, honey?" asked Mabel.

Breanna smiled at the thought of her Cheyenne Indian friends whom the Lord had given her the pleasure of leading to Him. "They were at our house a few weeks ago, only for an hour or so. They are very happily married, and they told me of other Cheyenne who have come to know the Lord since I was at their village."

"Wonderful!" said Mabel, who was a dedicated Christian.

"I hope to return to the village and—"

Breanna stopped speaking when she saw Sheriff Curt Langan and Deputy Steve Ridgway carrying a man through the front door. "Excuse me, Mabel," she said and rushed toward them.

Breanna's eyes widened when she recognized Deputy Dave Taylor, one of John's best deputies. He had taken a bullet in the chest and was unconscious.

"I'll take you to one of the operating rooms," she said, leading the way.

Breanna knew Dave and Nyla Taylor well, and concern captured her heart. "What happened?" she asked over her shoulder as they rushed down the hall.

"He met up with a gunslick who's been carrying a grudge against him," said Ridgway.

As they passed the nurses' station, Breanna called to two nurses behind the counter. "Marsha! Susan! We need one of the doctors, quick! We'll be in operating room 3! Hurry!"

Langan and Ridgway were puffing from exertion as they followed Breanna into the operating room. She pointed to the operating table and said, "Lay him right here," then dashed to the large window on the side of the room, pulled the drapes back to allow the sunshine in, and hurried back to the table.

Sheriff and deputy stepped back to let Breanna go to work.

"Will you gentlemen help me get his vest off, please?" she asked, lifting Taylor's head.

As soon as the vest was removed, Breanna ripped the shirt from around the wound and did a quick examination.

"Oh no!" she gasped.

"Real bad?" asked Langan.

Without looking up, she said, "The slug is dangerously close to his heart. Removing it and keeping him alive at the same time are going to be very difficult."

The door swung open, and Dr. Hugh Cameron, a recent addition to the hospital staff, rushed in. He glanced at the two lawmen and moved up beside Breanna.

Breanna looked at Cameron. "Sheriff Langan and Deputy Ridgway just brought him in, Doctor. This is Dave Taylor, one of my husband's deputies. The slug is very close to his heart."

Cameron leaned close, scrutinizing the wound. Shaking his head, he wiped his brow and said, "This is one for Dr. Carroll."

Though the hospital now had three other physician-surgeons, Dr. Cameron, like the rest of them, had the utmost confidence in Dr. Matthew Carroll, who was also chief administrator of the hospital.

Breanna felt the same way about Carroll's expertise, apart from the fact that he was married to her sister, Dottie.

"Dr. Carroll is in surgery," Breanna said. "He should be about through. I'll go see."

Just as she stepped into the hall, she saw the door of operating room 1 swing open. A nurse came out, and Breanna rushed to her.

"Thelma, is Dr. Carroll finished in there?"

"Yes. He's getting cleaned up. Mary will stay with the patient for a while."

Breanna hurried to the room where doctors and nurses washed up after surgery.

Dr. Carroll was drying his hands when Breanna burst

through the door. Looking around, she saw that they were alone, and said, "Matt, one of John's deputies is in operating room 3 with a bullet lodged dangerously close to his heart. Dr. Cameron is with him, but he said this is one for you, and I agree."

Carroll laid the towel aside. "Let's go."

As they hurried down the hall, Carroll said, "Which deputy is it, Breanna?"

"Dave Taylor. You've met him."

"Oh, yes. So it's bad, eh?"

"Yes."

Breanna was on Carroll's heels as he rushed into the room. He nodded at Langan and Ridgway, then stepped up to the operating table beside Dr. Hugh Cameron, who was doing what he could to stay the flow of blood from Dave Taylor's chest wound.

"I felt it best that you handle this one, Doctor," said Cameron.

Carroll nodded, and while he examined the wound, he said to Curt Langan, "Sheriff, what happened?"

"You've heard of Zeke Patton?"

"The gunfighter?"

"Yes. He showed up in town a little while ago and ran into Deputy Taylor on Tremont Street. I was in the gun shop, and through the window I noticed a crowd gathering in the street. I stepped out just in time to see Patton draw on Deputy Taylor and put him down. Someone had alerted Steve, and he was coming on the run when Patton drew and fired."

"I saw the whole thing, Dr. Carroll," put in Ridgway. "As soon as the shot was fired and Deputy Taylor went down, Sheriff Langan called for Patton to drop his gun. Patton then made his final mistake. He swung his gun on my boss. The sheriff put a bullet through his heart."

"People on the street made sure I understood that Patton forced the fight," said Langan. "They said Taylor warned Patton that he would be in deep trouble if he shot a federal officer. Patton cursed him and went for his gun."

Carroll shook his head and said, "I hope the day comes when this kind of thing doesn't happen on our streets, Sheriff."

"Can't come too soon for me."

Carroll turned from the patient and said, "Breanna, prepare Deputy Taylor for surgery. I want you to assist me."

Dr. Cameron looked relieved as he said, "I have a patient to see, Dr. Carroll. If you should need my help, please send for me."

"Thank you," said Carroll. "I will."

Mabel Trotter looked up from her desk as Sheriff Langan and his deputy came from the hall into the lobby. "How's he doing, Sheriff?" she asked.

The lawman paused. "I can't really tell you, ma'am. Dr. Carroll is doing the surgery."

"Well, that puts him in the best of hands."

As Langan and Ridgway neared the door, they saw through the glass that a young woman was approaching. Steve rushed ahead and opened the door.

The young woman was quite pretty and had long, dark brown hair. She glanced at his badge, smiled, and said, "Thank you, Deputy."

Ridgway grinned. "My pleasure, ma'am."

As the lawmen walked toward their horses, Steve said, "Did you notice how she smiled at me, boss?"

"That's nothing," quipped Langan. "The first time I saw you, I laughed out loud!"

Mabel greeted the young woman approaching the reception desk.

"I'm Natalie Fallon, ma'am," came the reply. "Dr. Matthew Carroll hired me by mail to join the nursing staff here at the hospital. He knows I was to arrive this week. May I see him?"

"Dr. Carroll is in surgery right now, Miss Fallon, but our policy is for new nurses to see our head nurse first. Her name is Mary Donelson. She just finished assisting in surgery and isn't in her office yet. I'll take you there. I'm sure it will only be a few minutes until she joins you."

"That will be fine. Thank you."

Breanna had the patient prepared, but before Dr. Carroll began probing for the slug, he said, "Breanna, Dave's life hangs in the balance. One slip on my part could be fatal for him. Let's pray and ask the Lord for His help."

John Brockman and Chester McCarty were in John's office discussing papers McCarty had laid on the desk, when there was a tap on the door.

"Yes, Billy!" called Brockman.

The door opened a few inches. "Chief, Sheriff Langan is here to see you. He says it's urgent. Dave Taylor's been shot."

Dr. Carroll and Breanna were laboring over the wounded deputy U.S. marshal when they heard the door open and close quietly. Breanna, who was facing the door, said, "It's Mary, Doctor."

"Come in, Nurse Donelson," said Carroll, without taking his eyes off his work.

Mary moved close. "I was just told about Deputy Taylor, Doctor. I understand it's quite serious."

"Yes. Bullet lodged very close to his heart."

"What do you think?"

"If I can remove the bullet without causing damage to his heart, he'll be all right. It's a touchy situation. Can't tell you any more than that."

"All right. I was told that Sheriff Langan and Deputy Ridgway are going to advise Chief Brockman and Mrs. Taylor. They will no doubt be in the waiting room when you're finished."

"Thank you," said Carroll. "We've had prayer about it here, but if you get a minute, please pray for the Lord's hand on mine."

3

As Mabel Trotter and Natalie Fallon drew near Mary Donelson's office, a weary-looking Stefanie Langan walked toward them. Mabel paused at Mary's open door, noting that the head nurse wasn't there yet, then turned and smiled at Stefanie.

"Hi, Stef, you just got out of surgery, didn't you?"

"Yes. I was with Dr. Goodwin in number 2. Took longer than we expected, but the patient is doing well."

"Good. Your husband was just here."

"Oh?"

"I'll explain after I introduce you to our newest nurse. Stefanie Langan, this is Natalie Fallon."

"Glad to meet you, Natalie," said Stefanie. "Welcome to Mile High Hospital. Where are you from?"

"Chicago."

"I see. Well, I'm sure you'll like the drier air here."

"Stefanie is a C.M.N. like you, Natalie," said Mabel. "She also happens to be our head nurse's daughter. You saw her husband, Denver County Sheriff Curt Langan, and his deputy when you came in."

"Oh, yes. I did notice their badges."

"So why were Curt and Steve here?" asked Stefanie.

Mabel explained what she knew about Deputy Taylor being brought in with a bullet in him, and that Sheriff Langan and Deputy Ridgway had carried him in.

"Is it a serious wound?"

"I think so. Breanna was at my desk when they brought him in. She took one look at him and hurried them to an operating room. Dr. Carroll is doing the surgery, with Breanna assisting."

"That's good. Is Nyla here yet?"

"No, but I'm sure she will be soon."

Stefanie sighed, wiped a hand across her brow, and said, "I'm going home. That long surgery wore me out. I need to get some rest before my three children get home from school this afternoon. It was nice to meet you, Natalie. We'll see each other again in these halls, somewhere."

"I'll look forward to it," Natalie said warmly.

Stefanie put a hand on Mabel's arm. "Honey, when Nyla comes in, tell her I'll be praying for Dave."

"Will do," Mabel assured her.

As Stefanie moved down the hall toward the lobby, Mabel said, "Here, Natalie. Come on into Mary Donelson's office and sit down. She should be here soon."

Natalie took a step inside, commenting, "Must be a pretty heavy load for Stefanie, having to work this job, be mother to three children, and wife to the sheriff."

Mabel smiled. "Well, she only works part time here at the hospital. It would definitely be hard for her if she had to work a regular shift all the time. She did work full time until she and the sheriff adopted three children several months ago. Now she's mainly mother and housewife. Oh, here's Mary."

After introductions were made, Mary said, "Dr. Carroll gave me your file, Natalie. I've been expecting you. Welcome to

Denver, and to Mile High Hospital."

"Thank you, ma'am. I just met your daughter a couple of minutes ago. She's lovely, and I can see where she got it."

"Why, thank you," said Mary, smiling. "Stefanie is a sweet girl, and I'm very proud of her."

"You certainly should be. Mabel was telling me about Stefanie and her husband adopting three children."

"It's a big task, but they are precious, well-behaved children."

"I'll see you both later," said Mabel. "Gotta get back to my post."

As Mabel walked away, Mary invited Natalie to sit down, then took a file from a cabinet and said, "You're from Chicago, I believe…"

"Yes, ma'am."

Mary opened the file. "Well let's see what else we have here about you…"

Stefanie Langan passed through the front door of the hospital and saw Chief U.S. Marshal John Brockman hurrying along the boardwalk from downtown, and Nyla Taylor, almost running, coming from the other direction.

John waited for Nyla, and as they turned off the board sidewalk toward the hospital, Nyla began to cry. John was trying to encourage her as Stefanie ran and threw her arms around her weeping friend.

"What can you tell us, Stefanie?" John asked.

Moving along with them, Stefanie kept an arm around Nyla and said, "I don't know very much. I was working with Dr. Goodwin in surgery when they brought Dave in. All I know is that Dr. Carroll is doing the surgery with Breanna assisting."

"Oh, but he's still alive!" sobbed Nyla.

"Yes, honey. He's still alive. I'll go in with you."

Nyla wiped tears. "But weren't you leaving?"

"I was, but I changed my mind. I'm staying with you till the surgery is over."

Mabel was talking to a hospital visitor at her desk when Stefanie, Nyla, and John entered the lobby. Stefanie gave Mabel an "everything's under control" wave, and they kept moving.

As they reached the hall, Stefanie said, "Mom wasn't in her office a couple minutes ago, but she might be now. Let's check. If she is, she might know how the surgery is going."

Mary ran her gaze down the first page of Natalie's employment application. "I see you received your medical training at the University of Chicago School of Medicine."

"Yes," Natalie said, nodding.

"And you worked at the University Hospital there for three years after graduation."

"Mm-hmm."

"And I assume you—" Mary looked up to see her daughter standing at the open door with an arm around Nyla Taylor, and John Brockman just behind them.

Stefanie stepped through the doorway. "Excuse us, Mom... Natalie...but I need to ask a question. Do you know how the surgery is going on Dave?"

"I was in there before Dr. Carroll and Breanna started," Mary replied, "but I haven't been in since."

"Do you know how serious it is, Mrs. Donelson?" Nyla asked.

"Very serious. The bullet is in his chest, but that's all I can tell you. When I was in the operating room, Dr. Carroll was too busy to give me any details. The nurse who told me about Dave's wound also told me that Dr. Cameron was the first doctor to examine Dave. He turned the surgery over to Dr. Carroll. Stefanie, if you can find Dr. Cameron, he can tell you the extent of the wound."

Stefanie patted Nyla's shoulder as she said, "Do you have any idea where Dr. Cameron is, Mom?"

"No, honey. Sorry."

"All right…we'll find him."

Mary set compassionate eyes on Nyla Taylor and said, "When I left the operating room I took a few minutes in the nurses' lounge to pray for Dave…and to pray for Dr. Carroll."

"Thank you," Nyla said quietly.

"Come on, Nyla," said Stefanie. "Let's go find Dr. Cameron."

Mary watched as Stefanie guided the teary woman down the hall with her arm around her, and the tall man walked beside them.

As she turned back to face Natalie, the young nurse said, "I like that, Mrs. Donelson."

"What's that, dear?"

"Your taking time to pray for the man in surgery and for the surgeon's hands. I also like that black Book I see on your desk."

Mary glanced at her Bible, then met Natalie's soft gaze. "You're a child of God, aren't you, Natalie?"

"Yes, ma'am. Born again and washed in the blood."

"Wonderful! We have several nurses on staff who are Christians. My daughter is one of them."

"I could tell that."

"You haven't met Dr. Carroll yet," said Mary, "but he is also a Christian."

"Really?"

"He sure is. And the nurse who's assisting him right now is a Christian, too. Her name is Breanna Brockman. She's the wife of the tall man with the badge you saw with Stefanie and Nyla. John is chief U.S. marshal here in Denver, and a preacher of the gospel, too. Breanna is responsible for bringing Sheriff Langan, Stefanie, and Deputy Sheriff Steve Ridgway to the Lord. Not to mention a number of others here in Denver. She's quite a witness for Jesus."

"This is marvelous!" exclaimed Natalie. "I'm so happy to learn that my head nurse is a Christian, that the chief administrator of the hospital is a Christian, and that some of the nurses are, too. I'm certainly looking forward to meeting Breanna. Praise the Lord!"

"And I'm glad to know that you are one of us, dear."

In operating room 3, Breanna administered more ether to Dave Taylor, who had started to wake up during the surgery. He was now resting quietly once more.

Dr. Carroll's brow was beaded with perspiration. As Breanna laid aside the ether-soaked cloth, she picked up a small towel from the instrument cart beside the operating table and dabbed the sweat from his forehead, then went back to cleaning blood from around the incision.

As the doctor probed for the .45-caliber slug, Breanna automatically picked up a longer pair of forceps from the cart just as he started to ask for them.

A slight smile curved Dr. Carroll's lips as he handed her the shorter pair of forceps and she slapped the longer pair in his palm. Grasping the retractors, which were already in place between the blood vessel clamps, Breanna widened the surgical field to give him a better view of the wound.

"What are you smiling about?" she asked.

"You."

"Me?"

"Mm-hmm. You so often anticipate my next move when you're assisting me in surgery. You really ought to go back to school and become a doctor, Breanna. You'd make a great surgeon."

"Thank you, dear brother-in-law," she said, "but need I remind you that I want to cut back on my medical work and spend more time just being a wife to John? I would love the challenge of becoming a doctor, but I won't pursue it."

Carroll probed the wound carefully, holding his breath to help steady his hand. As Breanna looked on, she could sense his uneasiness about the delicate task at hand. They both knew that one slip of the hand could end Dave Taylor's life.

Stefanie found Dr. Hugh Cameron at the nurses' station on the second floor and introduced him to Nyla Taylor, explaining that she was wife of the deputy who was in surgery.

Nyla's cheeks were wan as Stefanie said, "Mrs. Donelson told us you were the first of the hospital's doctors to examine Deputy Taylor when my husband and Steve Ridgway brought him in."

"Yes, I was."

"We haven't been able to find out just how serious the wound is, nor the exact nature of it…"

"Mrs. Taylor," Cameron said, turning to Nyla, "we need to get you off your feet. Let's go down to the surgical waiting room and sit down. Then I'll explain it to you."

There was no one else in the waiting room as Cameron led

them in and they all sat down. The doctor pulled up a chair and sat directly in front of Nyla, who was between Stefanie and John Brockman.

"Mrs. Taylor," said Cameron, "I won't beat around the bush. Your husband's wound is very serious. The bullet is in close proximity to his heart."

Cameron went on to explain in detail the danger involved in the attempt to remove the slug.

Nyla's lips quivered as she said, "Oh, Stefanie, I don't know what I'll do if Dave dies! You're a lawman's wife, too. We live with this every day of our lives, wondering when some outlaw will shoot our husbands. I thought I could handle it, but now that Dave's lying in there on that operating table, at the edge of death…I can't stand it!"

She broke into sobs, and Stefanie took her in her arms and held her tight. John looked on, feeling helpless.

When Nyla's sobbing subsided, Stefanie said, "Honey, I know this is very hard for you. But let's not give up. Dave's going to come through this. And when he recuperates, he'll be right back out there doing his part to make the West a safer place to live. You've shown Dave ever since you married him that you're right there at his side to encourage him in his chosen line of work. I've done the same for Curt. It's no easy thing to know the badge our husbands wear is a target to outlaws. But where would society be if our husbands, and all those men like them who wear badges, suddenly quit? We'd be prey to every heartless, greedy no-good who ever decided to live by the gun. Is it right to say that every lawman should remain single and never marry because of the strain it would put on his wife?"

Nyla looked at Stefanie through her tears and said, "No. That wouldn't be right. I'm sorry. Right now, I'm not thinking too well. I—"

"Mrs. Taylor," cut in Dr. Cameron, "Dave's wound is a very serious one, yes. I won't minimize it. But let me also say that I excused myself from doing the surgery because I feel Dr. Carroll is much more qualified to perform it. In my opinion—and it is shared by everyone in this hospital—your husband is in the hands of the best surgeon in the business. And I might add, he's in the hands of the best surgical nurse in the business."

"That's right, Nyla," said Stefanie.

"And not only that," said John, "Dave's also in God's very capable hands."

Nyla bit down hard on her quivering lips and nodded. More tears spilled down her cheeks.

"Tell you what," said John. "I'd like to take a moment right now to pray for Dave. And for Dr. Carroll and my wife as they work on him."

"Oh yes!" cried Nyla.

Stefanie held Nyla tightly as John prayed, asking God to guide Dr. Carroll's capable hands and the hands of Breanna. His own voice quivering, John asked the Lord to spare the life of his deputy and to give him back to Nyla and the children.

When Mary Donelson and Natalie Fallon had discussed Natalie's service at Chicago's University Hospital and the experience she had received there, Mary said, "There's nothing in your file to indicate why you chose to come to Denver, Natalie."

"It was because of my mother's health. Mom has consumption. She's a widow, Mrs. Donelson."

Mary nodded solemnly.

"Mom's name is Marie. The doctors in Chicago told her she should move to Denver's high, dry air. I knew about the hospital here and about Dr. Carroll. So I wrote and asked him if he needed any nurses. He sent a wire the same day he received my letter. After he received information from my school and from the hospital where I was working, he wrote me and said the job was mine if I wanted it."

Mary nodded at her and smiled.

"Mom and I arrived here the day before yesterday. We're living in a boardinghouse over on Glenarm Street. She seems to be doing better already."

"Well, that's good news."

"Mom's a Christian, too, Mrs. Donelson. And so was Dad."

A look of sympathy shone in Mary's eyes as she asked, "How long has it been since your father went to heaven, honey?"

Natalie's countenance dimmed. "Four years. Dad was a doctor in La Moille, Illinois, a small town west of Chicago. For nineteen years he was the only doctor in a radius of thirty miles. He literally worked himself to death, Mrs. Donelson. No matter what time of day or night someone needed him, he was always there. Many times he went night after night without sleep, just because he was so needed by the people of the area."

Mary reached across the desk and patted Natalie's hand as her eyes misted and deep lines furrowed her brow.

"Dad was only forty-three when he died," Natalie said, sniffling. "He was a healthy man and would have lived out his natural life if he hadn't worked himself into the grave. One day he collapsed just after delivering a baby in a farm home. He hadn't slept for seventy-two hours. His heart just gave out."

"I'm sorry, honey," said Mary. "I can see you loved your father very much."

"More than I could ever put into words. I've told myself ever since that I would never marry a country doctor. I watched what Dad's deterioration and eventual death did to

Mom. I'd never go through a thing like that, Mrs. Donelson. Never."

"I understand, dear," said Mary, patting her hand again. With that, she closed the folder. "Well, let me take a few minutes and go over some of our rules, regulations, and procedures around here."

Natalie dabbed at her tears with a hankie, and said in an attempt at lightness, "I guess every place has to have those."

After explaining the hospital policies, Mary told her to report for work the next morning on the day shift, then turned her over to a nurse who would lead her on a tour of the building.

Mary watched Natalie walk down the hall, then hastened to the surgery waiting room and entered to find her daughter sitting beside Nyla, holding her hand.

"Any news?" Mary asked.

Stefanie patted Nyla's back and said, "After Dr. Cameron explained what he knew about Dave's wound, he had to get back to work. And John had to leave because he has an official here from the U.S. marshal's office in Washington. But he did stay with Nyla long enough for me to go into the operating room to see what I could find out. Dr. Carroll said that so far everything was all right, but it was going to take quite some time to get the slug out and repair the damage."

Mary sighed. "Well, praise the Lord it's going well. I'm sure John was glad to hear that."

"He sure was. He said he would come back late this afternoon to check on Dave."

Nyla took a shuddering breath. "Stefanie, you need to be home when your children get out of school. If the surgery is still going on whenever you need to leave, you just go."

Stefanie shook her head. "I'm not leaving you till I know

Dave is out of surgery and is okay. My kids know that if I'm not home they are to go to the neighbor's house next door. Sometimes I get tied up here at the hospital and can't always make it home by the time Jared, Susie, and Nathan arrive. It'll be fine. I'm not leaving you."

Nyla stroked Stefanie's cheek. "You don't know how much this means to me."

Stefanie reached up and squeezed Nyla's hand. "I hope it never happens, but maybe someday I'll need you to stay with me in a situation like this."

"I hope it doesn't happen, either, but if it should, I'll be here."

Breanna mopped Dr. Carroll's forehead as he clenched his jaw. He had the slug gripped in the pincers of the forceps deep in Dave Taylor's chest and was ready for the delicate removal.

Breanna laid the cloth aside, gripped the retractors, and said, "All right. Let's get it out."

The heart next to Carroll's forceps thumped in a steady rhythm. This was the crucial moment.

The doctor's hands began to tremble.

Breanna stabilized the retractors as best she could, then carefully gripped his wrists, steadying his hands. "All right, Dr. Matthew Carroll," she said with a level tone. "You can do it. Remove…the…slug."

Tension mounted as Matt slowly inched the slug out of Dave's chest. When it was free, Breanna let go of Matt's wrists and said, "You did it, Doctor. You did it!"

Matt breathed a sigh of relief as he dropped the deadly slug into a metal pan and wiped sweat from his brow. "Not without God's help and yours, dear sister-in-law!"

Breanna smiled. "All right. Let's repair the damage and get him closed up."

As they began the task, he said, "Breanna, they don't come any better than you. Thanks for steadying my hands."

"My steadying your hands wouldn't mean a thing if those weren't the most talented surgical hands west of the Mississippi River."

4

MARIE FALLON SAT at the front window in the room's most comfortable overstuffed chair and watched the people pass by on Glenarm Street. She and Natalie had decided on a second-story room in the boardinghouse so Marie could look down on the street. Until her health improved a great deal, she wouldn't be leaving the room, so living on the second floor posed no problem for managing the stairs.

On her next birthday, Marie would turn forty-six, but her rail-thin body, sunken cheeks, and the dark circles around her eyes made her look much older. Her graying hair was pulled straight back into a bun, which added to her aged look, but she insisted on wearing it that way so Natalie wouldn't have to take time to fuss with it. When Natalie started her job tomorrow, she would have enough to do without worrying over her mother's hair.

Marie kept her Bible open on her lap to read while periodically glancing down at people on the street. The afternoon was warm. She had asked Natalie to lift the big window a few inches before leaving for the hospital, so she could have some fresh air during the day.

A soft breeze toyed with the curtains as the rattle of wagons and the sound of horses' hooves blended with the grinding of metal-rimmed wheels on the hard-packed street. She picked up parts of conversations as people passed by on the boardwalk.

When Marie finally closed her Bible and laid it on a small stand next to the chair, she poured herself some water and said, "Thank You, Lord, for bringing us to this beautiful part of the country. I'm not coughing nearly as much as I did in Chicago. Already I'm feeling a bit stronger, too."

Her attention was drawn to the street when she heard the sound of Natalie's voice near the front door of the boarding-house. A young man was tipping his hat to her and introducing himself.

Marie could make out her daughter explaining that she was a nurse and had been hired at Mile High Hospital. She would start on the day shift at seven o'clock the next morning. The young man welcomed her to Denver and said he hoped she would like it here.

Natalie explained about her mother and how the Chicago doctors had told her to move to Denver. Even as she spoke, Natalie's line of sight drifted upward. When she saw her mother, she gave a tiny wave.

Natalie then said something to the young man, and he looked up, lifted his hat, and said, "Hello, Mrs. Fallon! Welcome to our fair city!"

Marie waved to him and smiled.

Natalie and the young man exchanged a few more words that Marie couldn't make out; then he touched his hat brim and walked away.

Moments later the young nurse entered the room and closed the door behind her.

"How are you feeling, sweet mother of mine?"

"Not too bad," came Marie's reply, accompanied by a slight smile. "I've only coughed a little since you left."

"Wonderful!" Natalie bent down and kissed her mother's forehead. "You're going to do just fine here."

"So how did it go at the hospital?" Marie asked.

Natalie told her all about Mary Donelson, Stefanie Langan, and Mabel Trotter, and how welcome they had made her feel. She went on to tell her of so many on the hospital staff being Christians, and what a sweet person the head nurse was. She explained that Dr. Matthew Carroll was tied up in surgery the whole time she was there, but that Mary Donelson had told her he was a Christian. She no doubt would get to meet him tomorrow.

Marie's pale lips curved upward as she said, "I heard you tell the young man down there that you are to start on the day shift tomorrow, and you have to be there at seven o'clock."

"That's right," said Natalie, glancing out the window to the street below.

"He seemed quite friendly."

"Hmm?" Natalie said, turning back toward her mother.

"The young man down there."

"Oh. Yes. He is very friendly. But then, I'm finding everyone in this town very friendly."

"What's his name?"

"Who?"

"The young man down on the street."

"Oh. Ah…Ted Myers. He works for his father, who owns a furniture store over on Arapaho Street."

"He seemed very nice."

"Yes. He's very nice."

"Good-looking, too."

Natalie picked up the pitcher of water from the stand and said, "I'll freshen this for you."

As she headed for the kitchen area, Marie said, "Honey,

you've got to let go of—"

"Please, Mom," Natalie cut in quickly, "I've told you I don't want his name brought up. He's gone. He's out of my life, and that's that."

"But he's not out of your heart," countered Marie.

Natalie was silent as she worked the pump that brought water from the well beneath the boardinghouse. She carried the full pitcher back into the parlor area, set it on the stand, and said, "There you are, Mother. Cool, fresh water."

Marie looked up at her. "Honey, the only way you're going to get him out of your heart is to meet some other young man. Like the one down on the street."

"Mom, I don't even know if Ted Myers is a Christian. We only talked for a moment, as you saw."

"I didn't mean him in particular. I meant one like him, but of course, a Christian. You've got to get on with your life, honey. It's only natural that you fall in love with some fine young man, marry, and raise a family. Just because things didn't work out between you and—you and the young doctor— doesn't mean you have to be an old maid."

"I know, Mom. I know. It's just that—"

"You're still in love with him. Maybe instead of ridding yourself of his memory and trying to get him out of your system, you should swallow your pride and see if you can find him."

Natalie shook her head. "He wouldn't want me now. Besides, he's probably married. Could we talk about something else?"

"All right. Let's talk about your new job. It sounds like you're really going to enjoy working at Mile High Hospital."

✧

After six hours of performing surgery on Dave Taylor, Dr. Carroll knotted the last stitch, and Breanna placed a bandage over the incision and tied it in place.

She then removed the ether-saturated cloth from Taylor's face and said, "You've done a marvelous job, Doctor. He's lost so little blood, in spite of the long surgery. Dave's going to make it, isn't he?"

"Barring some unforeseen complication of some kind, he's going to live."

Breanna closed her eyes in relief. "Thank You, Lord Jesus. Thank You."

The door from the hall opened, and Mary Donelson came in. "Is he all right?" she asked in a low tone.

Dr. Carroll gave a weary nod. "He's fine. It was touch-and-go for a while, but as I told Breanna, barring any unforeseen complications he'll be just fine."

"Praise the Lord!" exclaimed Mary.

"As soon as I wash my hands, I'll go out and tell Nyla," said Carroll.

"John's back, Doctor. He's going to be very glad to hear the news about his deputy."

"That's for sure," said Breanna. "Well, I'm going to clean this place up. Mary, would you tell John I'll be out in about twenty minutes, please?"

"No, honey. You just get yourself washed up and go out to your husband. I'll have someone else clean up in here. You've been at this operating table a long time. Go on, now."

"That's telling her, Mary," said Carroll. "If someone didn't sit on my sister-in-law now and then, she'd work herself to death."

Breanna chuckled. "Dr. Carroll, you're a worrywart. Hard work never killed anybody."

A smile graced Mary's lips as she said, "Well, nonetheless, you're not going to clean up after this surgery. Go on. Get yourself washed up and go to your husband." Then Mary disappeared through the door.

"I guess you got the message," Carroll said.

"I did. Let's go wash up."

The door opened again and two orderlies entered, pushing a cart. Doctor and nurse looked on as Taylor was transferred expertly from table to cart, then wheeled out to be taken to the recovery room, where a nurse would stay at his side.

Moments later, when Carroll and Breanna entered the waiting room, Mary was there, along with Stefanie, Nyla, and the chief U.S. marshal.

Brockman's face beamed as he reached out to curl an arm around his wife's waist and said, "Mary told us the good news, Doctor. Praise the Lord."

Tears of joy pooled in Nyla Taylor's eyes as she rose to her feet and said, "Dr. Carroll...Breanna...thank you for your magnificent work."

Both doctor and nurse flashed her weary smiles.

"This was a tough one," said Carroll. "Like I told Nurse Donelson, it was touch-and-go for a while, but thanks be to God, we were able to get the slug out without damaging his heart. All around, it was a difficult surgery to perform, but Dave is doing as well as can be expected for what he's gone through."

"How long will he have to be in the hospital, Doctor?" Nyla asked.

"At least three weeks, so we can keep him under constant observation."

"And if he's well enough to go home in three weeks, Doctor," said John, "what's your estimation of when he can come back to work?"

"If all goes well, Chief, he'll be back on the job in about three months."

"When can I see him?" asked Nyla.

Carroll rubbed his angular chin. "You might as well go on home, Nyla. Breanna had to give him ether not very long before we finished. He'll be out at least another hour, and even when he wakes up, the nurse who is with him will sedate him. I understand your wanting to see him, but right now what he needs most is complete and absolute rest without interruption. Best thing is for you to come back in the morning."

"All right, Doctor. I want to do what's best for Dave."

Tears of joy and relief were shed as John Brockman gathered everyone in a circle and offered praise to the Lord for sparing Dave's life.

As thank-yous and congratulations were going around, Breanna asked John if he and Chet McCarty were able to accomplish what was needed for the day. John assured her they had and would pick up tomorrow where they'd left off.

"Are you still planning for us to take Mr. McCarty to dinner at a restaurant tonight?"

"Yes, and he's quite eager to meet you. I left him at the hotel and said we'd pick him up by seven, if possible…or I'd get a message to him if there was some complication here."

"What about tomorrow night? Has anything changed?"

"No. Since Pastor Bayless changed this week's midweek service to Thursday night so that the missionary could come and present his field to the church, everybody we want to invite can come to dinner."

"Did you already tell Mr. McCarty about tomorrow night?"

"No, honey. I figured you'd like to offer the invitation yourself."

Breanna smiled. "Okay. I'll just do that."

As the group was breaking up, Breanna spoke to Mary, asking if she could see her in private for just a moment.

John chatted with Dr. Carroll while Breanna talked to Mary on the other side of the room. After a moment, Breanna was back. She slipped her hand into the crook of John's arm and said, "All right, Chief Brockman. We'll make a few stops to offer dinner invitations on the way home; then we can head for the house. I need to freshen up and change clothes. Then we'll take your big-brass boss to dinner."

Chester B. McCarty opened the door of his hotel room and smiled at the man who towered over him.

"Hungry?" John asked.

"I think I could put a good meal in the coffer," McCarty said with a chuckle. "Is the surgery over?"

"Yes, sir. Deputy Taylor is going to be all right."

"Wonderful. Is your wife with you?"

"She's down in the lobby, anxious to meet the top gun of the country's marshals."

"Well, let's not keep the lady waiting!"

They were unaware of malicious eyes that watched them walk down the hall toward the stairs.

Breanna, who was seated on an overstuffed couch in the lobby, rose to her feet when she saw her husband and a red-haired man walking toward her.

"Sweetheart," John said, "I want you to meet Chet McCarty."

Breanna blinked, shook her head, and said, "Darling, this can't be Chet McCarty."

Both men looked puzzled.

"Of course it is," said John, frowning slightly.

An impish gleam flashed in her sky blue eyes. "But John, you told me he was ugly, that his eyes were different colors, and his ears stuck out so bad if he ever got in a high wind, they'd lift him like wings."

McCarty laughed. "So that's what you told her, John!"

"N-no sir. I—"

Breanna giggled, causing both men to burst into laughter.

"John, this is some woman you married!" said McCarty.

Feeling somewhat relieved, John said, "Breanna, you little scamp! You might have gotten me fired!"

McCarty chuckled. "No way, John. A man who's smart enough to marry a little lady like this will never be fired. Commended, yes, but never fired!"

As he spoke, the executive administrator of the United States Marshal's Office stepped to Breanna and took her hand, bending over it and lightly kissing it. "Madam Brockman, it is my distinct pleasure to make your acquaintance."

As he released her hand, Breanna said, "And it is my pleasure to meet the man to whom my husband is responsible, sir."

John looked at the ceiling, then said, "All right, Miss Charmer, let's go feed the man to whom I'm responsible. Right now I am responsible to see that he has his evening repast."

During the meal, Chet McCarty was curious to learn how John and Breanna had met. Both of them told the story, filling him in on the details of how John appeared, seemingly from out of nowhere, on a stormy day in Kansas to save Breanna from being trampled to death by hundreds of stampeding cattle.

They had both realized they had strong feelings toward each other, but they were separated for some time until finally the hand of God brought them together. A short time later, they were married.

When conversation at the table began to dwindle, Breanna said, "Mr. McCarty, John and I have made plans about feeding you tomorrow evening."

McCarty smiled. "I will look forward to it with great anticipation, m'lady. Where will we be dining tomorrow evening?"

"At our house."

"Oh, really?"

"Wait till you get a taste of Breanna's cooking, sir," said John. "This little gal is the best cook in the West!"

Breanna blushed. "Oh, John, don't tell him that. He'll expect too much; then he'll be disappointed."

McCarty chuckled. "I doubt that."

"We've also invited some other guests," said Breanna. "You know Solomon Duvall, of course."

"Yes. He was in the office this afternoon for a few minutes. It was good to see him again. So he's to be at your house for supper tomorrow night?"

"Yes, along with our Denver County sheriff and his wife, and my sister and her husband, Dr. Matthew Carroll, who is chief administrator of Mile High Hospital. I've already made arrangements for the Langan children and the Carroll children to eat supper with Mary Donelson, who is the head nurse at the hospital. She also happens to be the Langan children's grandmother."

McCarty's brow furrowed. "But even without the children, Mrs. Brockman—"

"Please call me Breanna."

"But even without the children, Breanna, isn't preparing this meal too much for you, since you work at the hospital?"

Breanna smiled, brushed at her blond locks, and said, "I

asked Mary if I could work a half day tomorrow so I could have the afternoon off to prepare supper. She agreed whole-heartedly."

McCarty shook his head. "John, I'll say it again…this is some little lady you married."

John grinned as he said, "And don't I know it!"

Harold Sheetz began building a fire in his kitchen stove while Duke Foster, Pete Dawson, Layton Patch, and Dick Nye watched.

"You boys hungry?" asked Sheetz, who had only been home from work a few minutes.

"Hungry enough to eat an elephant," spoke up Patch.

"Well, if you and one of your pals will jump in and help me, we'll eat a lot sooner."

"We can do that," said Dick Nye, rising from his chair. "Come on, Layton."

The back door opened, and Chick Foster and Jim Felton entered the kitchen.

Duke eyed them. "So what do we know?" he asked.

"McCarty's in room 12, big brother," Chick said. "The rest of us are in rooms farther down the hall. We'll be able to watch McCarty real close."

"Good. Now we need to talk strategy."

"I've got it all figured out," Chick said. "Since we don't know where McCarty might spend tomorrow evening, we'll just be in our rooms with one of us watchin' for him to come back for the night. The later the better, so we can do this unseen and undetected."

"Okay," Duke said. "We'll hope it's that way. Go on."

"Here's what I figure," Chick said. "We'll wait till McCarty's in his room, then I'll knock on his door while these other boys are pressed flat against the wall beside me. I'll pretend to be an admirer of the U.S. Marshal's Office. I'll tell him I found out he was in town and sure would like to meet him, and would appreciate a few minutes of his time."

"Then what?"

"Well, if he invites me in, I'll club him on the head real quick. If he doesn't, I'll signal these boys, and together we'll coldcock him. Sound all right so far?"

Duke grinned as he leaned forward on his cane. "I have no doubt you can pull it off, little brother. Go on."

"Well, when we've got McCarty in dreamland, we'll take him down the back stairs of the hotel, put him in the wagon Harold has provided us, and head for here. The whole bunch of us will be long gone with McCarty as our prisoner before anyone knows he's missin'."

Duke scratched his head. "Okay. Now, what if you have people showin' up on your floor while you're kidnappin' McCarty?"

Chick gave his brother a reassuring grin. "Don't worry about it, Duke. We'll handle it. That's what you pay us for, isn't it?"

"Yep."

"Well, we like our pay. We'll take care of anybody who sticks his nose in."

"We sure will, boss," said Dawson. "Don't you fret none. We know what capturin' this dude means to you. We'll handle it, no matter what."

Duke eased back on his chair and laughed. "You boys have made me a happy man. At last I'll have the revenge I've wanted for fourteen years! Payback time is gonna be a whole lot of fun!"

Meat was sizzling in a skillet on the stove, and the room

filled with its aroma. Harold Sheetz stepped close to the table with a big fork in his hand and said, "Duke, I don't mean to throw cold water on all this happiness, but have you considered the possibility that by abducting a federal man—especially the top man in the U.S. Marshal's Office—that you're going to bring the federal government down on your head? Don't you think it would be better to just quietly kill him and hightail it out of town without McCarty weighing you down? That's more what I had in mind when I wanted you to know McCarty was going to be in town."

Duke guffawed. "The government hotshots don't scare me! We'll have a plenty good head start on 'em. Besides, it'll be at night, so nobody'll see us. We'll be deep into the Rockies before they even know McCarty's gone. A good deal of the time we'll be travelin' on gravel roads this side of Monarch Pass. There'll be no way to track us. I appreciate your concern for our well-being, Harold, but it's McCarty who's gonna suffer."

Harold pulled at an ear. "But you'll probably have John Brockman on your trail. He isn't gonna take lightly having his boss-man kidnapped. Brockman's got some kind of sixth sense when it comes to tracking."

"Well, I'd rather not tangle with that guy they call the Stranger," said Duke, "but on the other hand, he's only flesh and blood like the rest of us. We ain't got no reason to shake in our boots because of him. A bullet through his head will take care of him. He'd just better not get too close to the Duke Foster gang!"

5

ON WEDNESDAY MORNING, a few minutes past seven, Breanna Brockman had just given medicine to a patient and was exiting the room when she saw Mary Donelson walking toward her with a lovely young lady in a nurse's uniform.

"Breanna!" called Mary. "I have someone here I want you to meet!"

Holding the medicine tray in one hand, Breanna smiled and said, "Looks like we have us a new nurse."

Mary introduced Natalie Fallon to Breanna, explaining that she was from Chicago and had been hired by Dr. Carroll through the mail.

"Welcome, Natalie," said Breanna. "Did you get your schooling at the University of Chicago School of Medicine?"

"Yes, I did. And I worked three years at the University Hospital after receiving my C.M.N."

"You can't beat that for good experience," Breanna said.

"Mrs. Brockman…"

"You can call me Breanna, honey."

"All right. Breanna, Mrs. Donelson tells me you are a Christian."

"Why, yes. And that must mean you are, too!"

Natalie nodded. "And it's wonderful to come here and find

that I have so many Christians to work with. I'm so excited about it!"

Mary spoke up and told Breanna about Natalie's mother, explaining that they had come to Denver for Marie Fallon's health.

"I'm sure your mother will do better here than in Chicago, Natalie," Breanna said. "I've seen many people come to Denver from the humid areas back east and from down south. Their suffering has eased, and some of them have seen tremendous improvement."

"I'm encouraged," Natalie replied. "Mom's already coughing less and sleeping better."

"Well, praise the Lord for that."

"I do praise Him, with all my heart."

"I'd love to meet your mother," said Breanna.

"We'll just work on that," Natalie said with a smile.

"Breanna," Mary said, "I know you're only working till noon today, but I'm going to put Natalie with you for the morning. You can help show her the ropes. I'll put her with someone else this afternoon."

"That's fine with me. I'm mixing powders in the pharmacy and delivering them to patients right now. I can use some help."

"All right," said Natalie. "Let's go."

Mary smiled as the two young women hurried down the hall together. She knew Breanna would be a strength and a blessing to Natalie.

While grinding medicines with mortar and pestle, Breanna and Natalie talked about the Lord. Breanna invited Natalie to attend First Baptist Church, telling her what a wonderful pastor they had in Robert Bayless.

Natalie's eyes sparkled as she said, "I can't wait to pay your church a visit. Maybe if Mom gets to feeling better, I can bring her, too."

"We'd love to have her," said Breanna, putting a strong twist on the pestle.

There was a moment's silence in the pharmacy as they both ground powders, then Natalie said, "Mrs. Donelson tells me you're actually a visiting nurse."

"Mm-hmm. Not as much as before John and I married, which was on June 4 of this year. I still do some traveling, but I want to be a good wife to my husband and spend more time at home. When I'm here, I split my time between working at the hospital and working for my sponsoring physician, Dr. Lyle Goodwin, at his office. That way I can be at home in the evenings with John."

"I saw your husband yesterday," said Natalie. "Tall one, isn't he."

"He's that, all right."

"And quite handsome, I might add."

"Thank you," Breanna said with a smile.

"Is it hard, being married to a lawman?"

"It has its moments of difficulty, but this is what God wants for John, so I pray daily for the grace to stand by his side."

"Mrs. Donelson told me he's also a preacher."

"Yes. Some have dubbed him 'The preacher with a gun.' He's an excellent preacher, but he feels the Lord's work for him is to help make the West a safer place to live."

The two nurses delivered medicine to the patients, and while they were in the hall between rooms, Natalie told Breanna about her father being a small-town doctor in Illinois.

As they headed back toward the pharmacy to grind and mix more medicines, Natalie said, "Mom and I literally watched

Dad work himself to death while being poorly paid by his patients. That is, when they paid him at all."

"I see," said Breanna, grinding steadily. She sensed the bitterness in Natalie for having lost her father at such a young age. Changing the subject, she asked, "Is there a young man in your life?"

Natalie was slow in replying, but finally said, "No, Breanna. Not now."

"But there used to be?"

"Ah…yes. There was once."

Breanna noticed the change in Natalie's expression. "Oh, honey, I'm sorry. I guess I treaded where I had no business."

"No, it's not that. You're only showing interest in me, which I appreciate. The young man who used to be in my life was a medical student at the University of Chicago School of Medicine at the same time I was. We…we were quite serious about each other, but when he decided he wanted to be a doctor in a small rural town somewhere, I…I broke it off."

"Oh? Because of what happened to your father?"

"Yes. I didn't want to go through another experience like I did with Dad. And I sure didn't want to be his wife and suffer like I saw Mom suffer. No thank you!"

"So, how did your young doctor take it?"

"Not too well. He was brokenhearted, and I hated doing it to him, but I had to. His mind was set on being a country doctor, but I'm not going to be a country doctor's wife."

Natalie looked at Breanna to see her reaction, but Breanna kept on grinding powders. She took a deep breath and said, "I take it you think I was wrong for not marrying him."

"I can't judge you, honey," said Breanna. "Maybe you didn't have the strong, deep, marrying kind of love in your heart for him."

"Or I wouldn't have broken it off?"

"Something like that."

Natalie took a deep breath, then said, "He told me if I really loved him I would marry him and help him follow his dream."

"There's a lot to be said for that. But I can't judge you, Natalie. I haven't walked in your shoes."

The mist returned to Natalie's eyes. But this time tears formed and began to spill down her cheeks.

"Were you actually in love with him?" Breanna asked.

"Yes...I was."

"But not anymore?"

"That's right," Natalie said, grinding the medicine with vigor. "I'm over him now. I've lost all track of him. He's out of my life. No doubt he's following his dream somewhere and has found a young woman to marry who doesn't mind seeing him work himself to death." She suddenly let go of the pestle and brushed at the tears on her cheeks.

Breanna poured her mixed powders into a cup for blending with water, looked at Natalie, and said, "Tell me I'm wrong, honey."

Natalie sniffed. "Tell you you're wrong about what?"

"Tell me I'm wrong when I say you are not over your young doctor. Tell me I'm wrong when I say you are still in love with him."

Natalie blinked against the new supply of tears welling up. She poured her mixture into a cup and set the mortar down. Turning to face Breanna head on, she said, "All right. I can't tell you you're wrong. I am still in love with him." She sniffed again. "But I'll get over him, Breanna."

"How long ago did you break it off?"

"Two years. Two years and two months."

"I take it he's a Christian."

"Yes. A fine one. He always treated me like a queen. But it still wouldn't have worked out, Breanna. There was no way I was going to change my attitude about being married to a small-town doctor, not after what I saw my mother go through—watching Dad die a little at a time while faithfully caring for his patients, and having a bit of herself die at the same time."

Breanna put her arms around Natalie and said, "The Lord has a plan for your life, honey. If you'll let Him, He will work it out."

Natalie clung to her and said, "Oh, Breanna, I'm so glad Mom and I came here. And I'm so glad the Lord has given me Christians to work with...like you. Thank you for being so kind and understanding."

It was almost noon when John Brockman and Chet McCarty arrived at Mile High Hospital.

Mabel Trotter was busy talking to a nurse when Brockman and McCarty moved past her desk. John caught her eye, smiled, and waved.

"Excuse me, Wanda," Mabel said to the nurse. "Chief Brockman!" she called out.

John halted. "Yes, Mabel?"

"Were you wanting to see your deputy?"

"Yes. I want to find out how he's doing."

"His condition is still serious, sir, and Dr. Carroll is not allowing any visitors except Mrs. Taylor, who's with him now. I'm sure Breanna could give you the latest information."

"All right. Do you happen to know where she is?"

"No, sir. But someone on either floor can tell you, I'm sure."

John and McCarty headed down the hall for Mary Donelson's office. Before they got there, John saw Breanna come out of the pharmacy with the young lady he had seen in Mary's office the day before.

Breanna flashed her husband a warm smile as they drew up. "Hello, darling. Hello, Mr. McCarty. John, I would like you and Mr. McCarty to meet our newest nurse, Natalie Fallon."

Both men greeted Natalie, then John said, "I saw you yesterday in Mrs. Donelson's office. Welcome to Denver, Miss Fallon."

"Thank you."

"Breanna," John said, "we'd like to find out how Dave is doing before I take you home."

"He's resting well, but Dr. Carroll is not allowing any visitors yet."

"That's what Mabel said. She also said Nyla's with him."

"Yes."

"Could you go into the room and have Nyla come out? Mr. McCarty would like to speak to her, and so would I."

"Sure. Would you like to take the elevator?"

"Elevator?" echoed McCarty. "The hospital has an elevator?"

"Sure does," said John. "It's equipped with ropes on a pulley so even one of the nurses can use it."

"Well, isn't that something? I've seen elevators with those rope pulleys in a couple of hotels in the Washington area, but I didn't know hospitals were using them."

"Makes it a lot easier to get patients in wheelchairs from floor to floor," said Breanna, "and to move surgery patients up and down on carts. So which do you gentlemen prefer?"

"I think we can climb the stairs," said John. "Okay, Mr. McCarty?"

Natalie trailed along as they climbed the stairs to the second floor and moved down the hall to Dave Taylor's room. Leaving the other three in the hallway, Breanna entered the room and closed the door behind her.

Nyla was seated on a straight-backed chair next to the bed. Dave was sound asleep.

Stepping close, Breanna whispered, "John and Mr. McCarty are in the hall. They would like to speak to you."

"All right," said Nyla, rising from the chair.

Breanna looked down at Dave's pale features. "He still seems to be resting well."

"Yes. I'm thankful for that."

Breanna opened the door for Nyla, then followed her out, closing the door.

"Mrs. Taylor," McCarty said, "I want to tell you how sorry I am that your husband has been shot. From what Chief Brockman tells me, Dave is an excellent deputy. Be assured that we in the Washington office deeply appreciate a man of his caliber and are proud that he wears the badge of deputy U.S. marshal. We'll be pulling for him, that he will have a swift and complete recovery."

"Thank you, Mr. McCarty," said Nyla. "I'll tell Dave what you said. It will mean a lot to him."

"He means a lot to us, ma'am. I wish we had a thousand more just like him."

Nyla blinked at the tears threatening to fill her eyes. "Thank you, sir. And thank you for coming by."

"My pleasure, ma'am."

Nyla turned to John. "Chief Brockman, thank you for your prayers on Dave's behalf. Please don't quit praying for him, will you?"

"I sure won't...for many reasons." John grinned, then said,

"One reason is that I need Dave back on the job."

"He'll be eager to get back."

"I'll check on him later," said John.

As Nyla reentered the room, Breanna said, "John, I have a couple of quick things to do. I'll meet you and Mr. McCarty in the lobby in about five minutes."

Natalie stayed at Breanna's side as they hurried downstairs and headed for the pharmacy.

"Breanna," she said, keeping pace, "thank you for letting me work with you this morning. I hope Mrs. Donelson pairs us up lots of times."

"I'm sure she will," said Breanna.

They entered the pharmacy and put things away as they had found them. There was one cup of mixture left to be taken to a patient. Natalie said, "I'll take this to Mrs. Barker, Breanna. You go on now."

"All right, Natalie. Thank you."

Natalie placed the cup on a medicine tray, and as they moved into the hall, she said, "Breanna, your husband is such a nice man. Where did you find a big, handsome fellow like him?"

Breanna gave her a wide smile and headed for the lobby. "I'll never tell!"

Natalie laughed, and they parted.

At the Westerner Hotel, Chick Foster descended the stairs from the second floor and approached the desk.

"May I help you, Mr. Harrison?" the desk clerk said, smiling amiably.

"Possibly. I noticed that the people who were stayin' in room 9 at the head of the stairs checked out earlier this mornin'."

"Yes, sir."

"Since I'm going to be here a little longer, I was wondering if it would be possible to get that room."

"Is there something wrong with room 16, sir?"

"Oh no. Of course not. It's just that I think I'd like the view from room 9 better."

"I see," said the clerk, opening the registry book. "Looks like that'll be no problem."

Duke Foster and the rest of his gang were lounging in Harold Sheetz's parlor, talking about the upcoming kidnapping of Chet McCarty, when they heard the back door open and close. Seconds later Chick appeared, carrying a small box. "Okay, boys," he said, "here's a fresh supply of cartridges for everybody."

"Where you been?" said Duke. "Certainly it didn't take you a half hour just to buy cartridges."

"I took a little stroll back to the hotel."

"What for?"

"Well, I had a little brainstorm on the way to the gun shop. I got to thinkin' it'd be easier and quicker to take McCarty tonight when he returns to the hotel if we were in room 9, since McCarty's in room 12. I got the room changed."

"What if he comes in the back door?" spoke up Jim.

"Why would he do that? He'll probably be with Brockman durin' the evenin'. Why would Brockman deliver him to the alley?"

Jim shrugged. "Just tryin' to think of everything."

Duke chuckled. "I appreciate it, Jim, but chances are pretty slim that McCarty will come in the back door. Go ahead, little brother."

"I'll be in my socks," said Chick. "Pete, Dick, Layton, and Jim will be in my room with me. When McCarty passes my door, I'll slip up behind him real quietlike and crack him over the head with my gun barrel. We'll carry him down the hall to the back door, down the stairs to the alley, and dump him in the wagon."

"I like it, Chick," said the gang leader. "That's better than your original plan of knockin' on his door to get at him. I'm glad you were able to get room 9."

Chick rubbed his hands together. "Won't be long, big brother, and you'll have that dude at your mercy."

"Yeah, and he ain't gettin' no mercy from me!"

That evening, Solomon Duvall arrived at the Brockman home with Curt and Stefanie Langan, and right behind them the Carroll buggy rolled into the yard. Breanna stood on the front porch to greet them, with the door open behind her.

As the silver-haired Duvall stepped from the buggy and helped Stefanie down, he sniffed the air deeply and said, "Breanna, whatever we're having for supper sure smells good!"

As the sheriff was tying his horse to one of the hitching posts, he said, "Smells like fried chicken, mashed potatoes, brown gravy, hot bread just out of the oven, and creamed corn."

Breanna laughed. "Okay, Sheriff Langan, tell me who the spy is!"

"Spy, nothing! It's just that I've eaten at your house enough to know the particular scents that come from your kitchen. Am I right?"

"Yes, you are. That's some kind of sniffer you've got there!"

Matt and Dottie approached the porch, and Matt said, "Makes no difference what's in Breanna's oven. One thing's for sure, it's always going to be good!"

Dottie, who strongly resembled her sister, made a mock

pout and said, "Sis, I don't think I'll ever be able to match your cooking."

Breanna stepped off the porch and hugged her, saying, "Nonsense, honey. You can already cook circles around me."

Solomon Duvall eyed the sisters, noting that this evening Dottie's hair was styled exactly like Breanna's. If he didn't know there were two years between them in age, he would swear they were twins.

"Everybody come on in," said Breanna, her arm around Dottie's waist. "John and Mr. McCarty will be here any minute."

Even as she spoke, the familiar rattle of a buggy came from the lane. Everyone turned to see John and the man from Washington, D.C., approach the house.

Introductions were made, and McCarty ran his eyes between the sisters. "You two don't happen to be twins, do you?" he asked.

"Not quite," replied Dottie. "One of us is two years older than the other."

Breanna laughed. "And we're not telling which is which!"

McCarty said, "And I'm not going to press the issue. It's dangerous business to touch on a woman's age!"

The group had a good laugh, then John led everyone inside.

While they were eating, Chet McCarty looked at the two sisters and said to John and Matt, "Those two look so much alike. Do you husbands ever get them mixed up?"

John laughed. "Never have, Mr. McCarty. And the reason is, that as beautiful as Dottie is, Breanna is even more beautiful!"

"Oh no," said Curt Langan. "Here we go again!"

McCarty frowned. "What do you mean?"

"We've all heard this argument before, sir. Matt and John have gone round and round as to which of them has the most beautiful wife."

Dottie and Breanna blushed as they exchanged glances.

John laid his fork down, wiped his mouth with a napkin, and said, "Actually, there's no room for argument. Breanna is the most beautiful woman in the whole world. That settles it."

The chief administrator of Mile High Hospital shook his head, swallowed a mouthful of mashed potatoes, and said, "No, no, John. Dottie is the most beautiful woman in the world. I'll grant you that Breanna is very beautiful, but Dottie still has the edge on her."

Curt Langan held up both palms. "Wait a minute, gentlemen! With all due respect, the most beautiful woman in all the world is seated next to me—Stefanie Langan!"

It was Stefanie's turn to blush.

When the good-natured laughter had died down, Chester McCarty said, "There is no reason for this argument to continue. I'll settle it. The most beautiful woman in the whole world lives at 222 West Cherry Street in Washington, D.C. Her name is Verla McCarty!"

Breanna giggled and said, "Now, gentlemen, on that note, we beauties at this table humbly request that the arguing come to a halt."

"That's right!" agreed Dottie.

"Amen!" said Stefanie.

With a serious manner, Solomon Duvall looked across the table at Brockman and McCarty and said, "What progress has been made toward relieving our chief U.S. marshal in Denver of his load?"

McCarty set his coffee cup down. "John and I have worked out all the details for establishing the U.S. marshal's office in San Francisco as a chief U.S. marshal's office. This will relieve John of the responsibility for all of California and the northwest territories."

"And who have you chosen to head up the San Francisco office?"

"We put our heads together on that and decided on the deputy who has already been heading up the office—Jack Donner."

A smile spread over Duvall's wrinkled face. "Good. I was hoping you'd do that. Jack's a good man and deserves the promotion."

"I've already wired President Grant about our choice," said McCarty, "along with our choice of San Francisco for the chief's office. I'll meet with him as soon as I return to Washington, and get the wheels rolling."

Duvall nodded. "And what about more men for the Denver office? We're hurting bad here, especially losing the men we have in the past few weeks—Dave Taylor being the most recent one."

"I'm working on it. And when I get back to Washington, I'll concentrate real hard on sending a deputy to take Taylor's place."

"I'm glad to hear that, Mr. McCarty," spoke up the sheriff. "Steve and I try to help out as much as we can when John runs short, as we did for Chief Duvall. But the outlaws are getting more numerous. The Denver office really needs more deputies badly."

Matt Carroll said, "Well, I'm very glad to hear that John's load is going to be eased, Mr. McCarty."

Other subjects were introduced around the table, and soon everyone was pushing their empty plates away.

Breanna looked around the table. "I hope all of you saved some room for dessert."

Matt grinned. "And what is that, Breanna?"

"My special oatmeal cookies."

The doctor's eyes lit up. "Hallelujah! Mr. McCarty, just wait till you sink your choppers into one of these cookies."

Solomon Duvall wiped his mouth with a napkin and said, "I've eaten at this table a few times, Breanna, but I haven't had the pleasure of eating your oatmeal cookies yet."

Dottie and Stefanie poured fresh coffee around while Breanna set two platters of cookies on the table. Soon, both McCarty and Duvall were smacking their lips and declaring how delicious the cookies were.

When the enjoyable evening came to a close and the guests were gathering at the front door, Breanna disappeared for a few minutes, then came back bearing two paper sacks stuffed with oatmeal cookies.

"Chief Duvall…Mr. McCarty…since both of you liked my cookies so much, I'll give each of you a sackful to take along."

As the guests walked out onto the porch in the moonlight, Curt Langan said, "John, Chief Duvall rode out with us. We have room for Mr. McCarty, too. We can deliver him to his hotel if you'd like."

"I appreciate that, Curt," said the tall man, "but there are still a few loose ends we need to wrap up. We were planning on doing that during the ride back into town. But thanks, anyhow."

"Okay," Langan said, nodding.

The women hugged each other good-bye, and soon the buggies were rolling up the lane toward the road.

"See you in a little while, sweetheart!" John called back to Breanna.

Breanna gave a jaunty wave.

6

As JOHN BROCKMAN guided the buggy to a halt in front of the Westerner Hotel, a wagon stood waiting in the alley near the back staircase, hitched to a pair of fast horses.

Chet McCarty glanced at John in the soft yellow glow of the street lamps and said, "When I talk to the president, I'll let him know all we've discussed, John." Sliding from the buggy seat, he added, "Good night. See you in the morning."

"Yes, sir. I'll be here in plenty of time to get you to the depot. Good night."

McCarty moved across the boardwalk and entered the hotel lobby. When the door shut behind him, John wheeled the buggy around and headed back up the street.

All was quiet on the second floor. Layton Patch stood at the door of room 9, peering through the small crack that gave him a limited view of the top of the stairs and a short length of the hall. He was listening intently for the sound of footsteps mounting the stairs.

Chick had removed his boots and was in his stocking feet. The gun butt felt slick in his hand. He swore as he transferred the gun to his other hand and rubbed a sweaty palm down his pants leg.

"What's he doin', bein' out so late?" he hissed to his cronies.

Dick Nye and Pete Dawson were seated on a small couch, and Jim Felton was sitting on the edge of the bed.

Dawson snickered, keeping his voice low. "Maybe Brockman threw a big party for him."

"Yeah," said Nye. "Maybe he won't be in till dawn!"

"I don't know what you guys see that's so funny about this," Chick grated angrily. "This ain't no game we're playin'!"

Patch looked away from the door and glanced over his shoulder. "Chick, you need to relax a little. McCarty'll get here. And when he does, he's our prisoner. You just stay ready."

Chick glared at him. "Don't tell me how to do my job, Patch! I'm ready! And I don't need you to—"

"Hey, guys!" Felton said. "Let's not fight amongst ourselves. I know this is nerve-rackin', but stay cool. We're gonna get McCarty for Duke, and Duke's gonna reward us big. You wait and see."

Chick took a deep breath, then set his gaze on Patch. "Sorry, Layton. I'm a bit uptight."

"I'm sorry, too, Chick," said Patch. "We're all uptight."

"Just hang on, boys," put in Dick Nye. "Like Jim said, it's gonna turn out all right. Pretty soon we'll be hightailin' it outta town with ol' carrottop bound, gagged, and unconscious in the back of the wagon."

At the Sheetz house, a nervous Duke Foster paced from wall to wall in the parlor, leaning heavily on his cane. Harold Sheetz was seated in an overstuffed chair, watching him.

Mumbling to himself, Duke growled, "What's takin' 'em so long? Somethin's wrong. I just know it. Somethin's gone awry."

"You don't know that, Duke," said Sheetz levelly.

"Well, McCarty's not gonna stay out all night," argued Duke. "It's after ten o'clock. I think he got back to the hotel but somethin' went wrong. Harold, I tell you, if Chick and them guys mess up, I'll—"

"Get a grip on yourself, Duke," said Sheetz, rising from the chair. "Your boys aren't going to let you down."

"But what if they did? They get caught, and it'll bring the law right here to your doorstep! We'll both hang!"

Harold laid a steadying hand on Foster's shoulder. "Don't fret, Duke. There's no need to panic. I've got a good feeling about this. Chick and the boys will pull it off."

Foster wiped a hand over his sweaty brow. "I sure hope you're right, pal. I sure hope you're right."

As John Brockman's buggy passed under a street lamp, something in the seat beside him caught his eye. The sack of oatmeal cookies! *Chet had forgotten Breanna's cookies!*

He slowed the horse, then shook his head and snapped the reins, mumbling, "No…I'll just give them to him in the morning."

He turned the corner and started down the dark street, then shook his head. "No, he may want to pack them in his luggage. I'd best take them to him now."

Chet McCarty walked through the deserted hotel lobby and headed for the stairs. He caught sight of the night clerk in his peripheral vision and went over to the desk. "Hi, Jerry. In for a long, boring night, eh?"

"Looks like it, Mr. McCarty," said the small, thin man, as he laid down the book he was reading. "I don't really mind, though. It gives me a chance to catch up on my reading."

"Well, readers are leaders, they say," commented McCarty. "What are you reading?"

"It's a historical novel. Tells about the gold rush in California back in 1849. There weren't as many men who struck it rich as I thought. Lots of them gave up and went back home. Others stayed and toughed it out, but never got rich. It was probably only about 20 percent of them who got rich."

"I've heard that," said McCarty. "A lot of those men died in the goldfields, too. Fought and killed each other over the gold."

Jerry Hinson nodded. "That's how the book depicts it."

Turning away from the desk, McCarty said, "Well, good night, Jerry."

"Good night," replied the clerk, then called after him, "I hope you get a good night's sleep, Mr. McCarty."

"You can count on it," McCarty said over his shoulder, and started up the stairs.

In room 9, Layton Patch widened the crack a little and turned his ear toward it. "Hey, guys!" he said in a hoarse whisper. "McCarty's comin'! I just heard the clerk at the desk call him by name!"

Chick wiped sweat from the palm of his gun hand and rushed to the door. Peeking past Patch, he whispered, "I can hear him comin' up the stairs! Move back, Layton!"

Patch tugged at the gun belt on his hip and stepped back.

Pete Dawson wore a wide grin as he said, "Duke's gonna love us for this, guys! He's gonna love us!"

Downstairs, behind the desk, Jerry Hinson was once again wrapped up in his book when he heard the front door open and saw the tall, wide-shouldered chief U.S. marshal enter, carrying a brown paper bag.

"Hello, Chief Brockman. What can I do for you?"

Brockman leaned over the counter and said, "Jerry, I let Mr. McCarty off a few minutes ago in front of the hotel. My wife gave him this bag of cookies after supper at our house tonight. He left them in my buggy. I assume he's already gone upstairs?"

"Just went up, sir. If you hurry, you can catch him before he gets to his room."

"Okay. Thanks."

Chet McCarty fumbled in his pocket for the skeleton key as the door to room 9 swung open without a squeak and Chick soundlessly rushed toward him.

Layton Patch stood in the doorway with the other gang members looking over his shoulder. Their nerves were tight, and they were ready to spring into action.

Suddenly, Patch saw a dark figure coming up the stairs.

John Brockman hurriedly topped the stairs, carrying the sack of cookies. By the vague light of two low-burning kerosene lamps midway down the hall, he saw the stocking-footed man raise the butt of his gun to strike down McCarty.

"Chet!" shouted John, whipping his gun out of its holster. "Behind you!"

McCarty turned just as Chick brought the barrel downward. It missed his head and struck his shoulder a glancing blow, but the impact was enough to knock him off his feet.

Chick pivoted, cocking the hammer of his gun.

"Drop that gun!" Brockman shouted at Chick. He saw the door of room 9 swing open and another man come out with a drawn revolver.

Chick ignored the command and lined his weapon on Brockman, giving John no choice but to fire. The flash of gunfire ripped through the dim light of the hallway, and a roar of reverberating sound filled the second floor of the hotel.

Chick caught the bullet in the middle of the chest. The impact of it momentarily lifted his feet off the floor; then he went down flat on his back.

John flung himself sideways just as Patch's gun roared. The bullet left its breath on John's ear as it whizzed by and chewed into the wall behind him.

The second blast of Brockman's .45 merged with the roar of Patch's gun, and Patch staggered backward from the wallop of the slug, falling against Jim Felton, who was on his heels. Felton shoved Patch's body aside and drew a bead on Brockman.

John's weapon roared again. The slug struck Felton on the left side of his chest, spun him in a half circle, and slammed him against the wall beside the door.

Pete Dawson and Dick Nye swung the door shut with a bang and locked it.

John moved to the crumpled form of Layton Patch and saw that he wasn't breathing. He picked up Patch's gun and tossed it across the hall. He then stepped to Jim Felton, saw that he was still alive, and also kicked his gun down the hall.

McCarty was on his feet now. He leaned over, checked the skid of Felton's gun, and picked it up.

"Stay back!" John called to him. Then he flung himself belly down on the floor, facing the door to room 9. "All right, you two in the room! Throw down your guns and come out! I am Chief U.S. Marshal John Brockman, and you are under arrest!"

Two shots were fired from inside the room. Both bullets

chewed holes in the door at chest level and found lodging in the wall on the other side of the corridor.

Doors were opening all along the hall. McCarty waved off the curious onlookers, telling them to stay in their rooms and keep their doors locked.

Gun smoke hung in the hallway as John shouted again, "You two in the room! Give it up! Open the door, throw out your guns, and come out with your hands in the air!"

A single shot rang out, the bullet ripping through the door and splintering very close to the other two holes. John unleashed two quick shots through the door. He was down to one live cartridge. He broke the Peacemaker open, spilled out the empty shells, reloaded it from his gun belt, then snapped it shut and waited.

For a few seconds there was only silence, and then he heard a window inside room 9 slam down on its sill.

John leaped to his feet and said, "They've gone out the window! Wait here!"

"I'll keep it under control," McCarty responded.

John bolted to the stairs and went down two and three steps at a time. He noted that Jerry Hinson was gone as he plunged out the front door.

Brockman stood on the boardwalk and listened for any telltale sounds, but the street was deserted. Cautiously, he moved out far enough to where he could see the window of room 9. The window was down, and the street lanterns showed him how the two men had escaped. They had jumped to the hotel balcony, which ran along the front. From there it was only a ten-foot drop to the ground.

John scanned the street, tuning his ears, but there was no sound of any kind and no movement. He knew the two men could not have gotten far, but he would not pursue them. They could be hiding in the deep shadows along the street, and he would be a perfect target in the yellow light of the street lamps.

The best thing right now would be to see if any of the gunmen upstairs were still alive. If so, John might be able to squeeze some information out of him. Somebody was out to capture Chet McCarty. If they had wanted to kill him, they could have taken him out easily with a bullet. But by the actions of the man who was about to clobber him on the head, they wanted him alive. Who were they? And why did they want McCarty?

John hastened back inside the hotel. When he entered the lobby, Jerry was still nowhere in sight. Heading for the stairs, he told himself Jerry had no doubt gone to Deputy Sheriff Steve Ridgway for help. Steve lived much closer than Sheriff Curt Langan.

Dick Nye and Pete Dawson laid their backs against the rear wall of the hardware store two blocks from the hotel. The alley was almost pitch black.

"What...do we...do...now?" said Nye, gasping for breath. "We can't go back...and face Duke...without bein' able to tell him who's dead up there in the hotel...and who's alive."

"For sure," replied Dawson, his chest heaving. "I'd rather not have to face Duke at all, but we owe it to him. We can't just run away."

"He ain't gonna blame us like he's gonna blame Chick," said Nye. "It was Chick's plan."

"Yeah. And did it ever go awry."

"Since we know that was Brockman in there," said Nye, "I'm afraid all three of our boys are dead."

"Me too. But we've got to know before we break this to Duke. He'll want answers."

"Let's go back down the alley and hide in the shadows between the two buildin's across the street from the hotel. We'll sneak up close to the street and watch what happens over there at the hotel."

When John Brockman reached the top of the stairs, he found Chet McCarty kneeling over one of the outlaws.

The man was still conscious.

"What about the other two?" John asked.

"Both dead. I didn't hear any shots. The window-jumpers get away?"

"Yes. Apparently they climbed onto the balcony then dropped to the ground. I didn't see hide nor hair of them. No way to chase them in the dark. What have you learned from this one?"

"Nothing. He won't even make a peep."

Brockman knelt on Jim Felton's other side, pulled back his vest, and examined the chest wound as best he could in the soft light. "Doesn't look too good, fella," he said. "You're losing blood plenty fast. I've seen a lot of gunshot wounds in my time. I doubt you've got more than a few minutes to live."

Felton gritted his teeth. "Tryin' to scare me, are you, Brockman?"

"So you know who I am. Did you hear me identify myself to your cohorts who ran into the room?"

"Nope. I must've been out then. But I know who you are."

"How about telling me who you are?"

Felton only gave him a cold stare.

"Look, fella," said John, "I'm not fooling you. You aren't going to make it. Blood's flowing out of this wound like a river, and I've got a feeling it's filling your lungs. Why don't you—"

Felton started to contradict Brockman, but when he opened his mouth to speak, he coughed and his body spasmed. The spasms were followed by blood filling his mouth and trickling from the corners.

"You're about done for, mister," said John. "Why don't you do the decent thing before you die and tell us who you are, who you work for, and why he or they wanted to lay hands on Mr. McCarty?"

The look in Felton's eyes showed his fear of dying and what might come afterward. Nodding, he licked his lips. "All right." He coughed again, and more blood appeared at the corners of his mouth. "My...my name's Jim Felton."

"Sounds familiar," said John. "There's a wanted poster on you, I'm sure."

"Yeah," he said through pain-clenched teeth. "I...I run with the Duke Foster gang."

"Duke Foster!" exclaimed McCarty. "He's somewhere around here?"

Felton nodded.

"You know Foster, Mr. McCarty?" asked Brockman. "I've known of him for years, but I wasn't aware he and his gang were in Colorado."

"I know him," McCarty said flatly. "About fourteen years ago—as a deputy U.S. marshal—I chased him across Missouri. Ran him down in Kansas City. Tried to arrest him peacefully, but he decided to shoot it out. I shot him in the leg and shattered a bone. Left him a permanent cripple. He did ten years at Leavenworth. I'd heard that he was back leading his gang, and robbing and killing in Missouri and Kansas, but I wasn't aware he was in Colorado, either."

Felton, wanting to come clean before he died, sent a glance at the lifeless form of Chick Foster down the hall and said,

"The first man you killed, Chief Brockman, is Duke's younger brother, Chick."

"I see. And this other guy?"

Felton ran his weakening gaze to the body that lay only inches from him. "That's Layton Patch."

John looked at McCarty. "He's wanted, too. Robbery and murder."

McCarty nodded.

"And who are the ones that got away?" queried Brockman.

"Dick Nye…Pete Dawson."

"Mmm-hmm. I know those names, too. Same thing. Robbery and murder."

The outlaw's body spasmed.

When he settled down again, John said, "Felton, you're doing a good job. Now, I want to know what Duke Foster was going to do with Mr. McCarty."

Felton swallowed hard. His voice was weaker when he said, "Duke has a burnin' hatred for Mr. McCarty because he crippled him for life and sent him to prison for ten years. He says he 'owes' him."

Brockman looked at McCarty.

"The model criminal mind," said McCarty. "He would never admit that he got what he deserved."

"No," said Brockman. "We lawmen are the bad guys. We should just let the robbers and killers rob and kill, and look the other way."

McCarty nodded. "I remember the venomous look Duke gave me that day in the Kansas City Courthouse after he was sentenced to Leavenworth. He was led away on crutches. If ever I saw naked hatred in a man's eyes, I saw it then. I was the bad guy for chasing him down and arresting him."

Felton began speaking again. "Duke wanted to kidnap you,

Mr. McCarty, so he could take you to his hideout in the mountains, cripple you permanently, then make you his prisoner for the rest of your life."

John shook his head. Figuring Duke would be somewhere in or near Denver at the moment, he said, "Felton, where is—"

Jim choked on the blood in his throat. It took him several minutes to stop coughing. The pain was taking its toll on his mind, and it showed in his glassy eyes.

Leaning close, John said, "Felton, where is Duke hiding?"

The dazed outlaw thought Brockman was asking where the mountain hideout was located. He licked his lips and said in thick-tongued response, "It's a big, fancy cabin. High in the Rockies on…on the west side of Monarch Pass. Dead…Dead Man's Canyon is close by. Cabin's in a wide notch, with trees on two…sides. It—"

"No, Jim. That's not what I was asking. Is Duke somewhere in or around Denver right now?"

Rapid footsteps sounded on the hotel stairs. Someone was coming up fast.

John gave McCarty a "don't-let-anyone-interrupt-right-now" look.

McCarty rose to his feet and met Deputy Sheriff Steve Ridgway and Jerry Hinson at the top of the stairs. Shaking his head, he said in a low tone, "Give it a minute! John's getting information from a dying outlaw."

Ridgway nodded, planting his feet. McCarty turned back, and Ridgway looked on from where he stood.

Felton was in another coughing spell. When he stopped coughing, John said, "Tell me where Foster is, Jim."

The dying outlaw worked his mouth with effort, but coughed again, choking on the scarlet fluid in his throat. He gasped and went still, his eyes staring vacantly toward the ceiling.

John sighed and looked up at McCarty. "He's dead."

McCarty nodded solemnly.

Brockman closed Felton's sightless eyes, then swung his gaze to Ridgway. "Thanks for coming, Steve. We had us a little shoot-out."

"So I was told by Jerry," said Ridgway as John stood.

Brockman and McCarty filled Ridgway in on what happened and what they had learned from the dying outlaw.

Steve rubbed his chin, saying, "Sheriff Langan has mentioned Duke Foster a time or two. Pretty mean cuss, I understand."

"To put it mildly, yes," said John.

"Well, I'll go get the sheriff out of bed. I'm sure he'd want to know about this incident tonight. Those two who got away have no doubt gone to wherever Duke Foster is hiding."

"If Duke doesn't already know about his foiled plan," said Brockman, "he will soon. We've got to do everything we can to keep him from getting away."

"Right. And we'll help you all we can, Chief."

"I know you will," said John. "And I appreciate it."

As he headed for the stairs, Ridgway said over his shoulder, "As soon as I alert the sheriff, I'll get one of our friendly undertakers out of bed. Can't leave these bodies lying here in the hotel."

"I'm grateful for that," said Jerry from the staircase. "I'm sure our guests will be, too."

"Be back shortly," Steve said.

People were gathered at the bottom of the stairs. As Ridgway reached them, they started asking questions. Hurrying toward the door, he said, "Excitement's all over, folks. You can go back to bed now."

Doors began opening along the hall on the second floor

again, and faces were showing in the dim light.

"Shooting's all over, folks," John called to them. "Everybody stay in your room. Get yourselves a good night's rest."

Almost in unison, the doors shut.

Jerry moved on up the stairs, carrying a paper sack. Holding it up, he looked at John and said, "Chief Brockman, I found Mr. McCarty's cookies lying down here a ways on the stairs. You must have dropped them when the shooting started."

John grinned at Jerry, then glanced at Chet McCarty.

"My oatmeal cookies!" gasped McCarty. "How could I have been go forgetful! I'm getting worse the older I get."

As McCarty's fingers closed around the neck of the sack, John said, "Boss man, you'd better be thankful you did forget them. That's what brought me back to the hotel."

McCarty's face turned pale. Scrubbing a hand across his mouth, he drew a deep breath and said, "That's one time my forgetter saved my hide, John. If you hadn't come back, I'd be Duke Foster's prisoner right now."

7

THE GRANDFATHER CLOCK in the parlor chimed eleven times. Breanna Brockman paced the floor as she prayed. John should have been home over an hour ago. What was keeping him?

This is the load a lawman's wife carries, she thought, her mind running to Nyla Taylor sitting by her husband's hospital bed.

Breanna had adjusted to her role as a lawman's wife as much as a woman could adjust, but the icy hand of fear on her heart when her man didn't come home on time was another matter.

She could stand it no longer. Hurrying up to the master bedroom, she changed from her dress into a split skirt for riding. She took her .36-caliber Navy Colt revolver from a drawer, broke it open, and checked the loads. Snapping it closed with an adept twist of her wrist, she stuck the gun under her waistband and hurried down the stairs.

Chance and Ebony were standing in the center of the corral in the moonlight. Upon hearing her approach, they trotted to the gate, nickering.

"Chance, my boy," she said, opening the gate and passing into the corral, "we're going to saddle up and go look for Daddy."

Across the street from the hotel, Dick Nye and Pete Dawson waited in the deep shadows between two buildings.

"There he is again!" said Pete, elbowing Dick.

They had seen the slender man with a badge on his chest enter the hotel a short while earlier, alongside the desk clerk. Now the young lawman was leaving. He was almost running as he disappeared down the street.

"I'd think if any of our boys were still alive, they'd have brought a doctor by now, wouldn't you?" said Nye.

"Yeah, I'm sure they would. Brockman killed all three, you can bank on it."

"I never liked the idea of comin' into Brockman's territory, anyway. The man's uncanny. Sure didn't take him long to put down Chick, Layton, and Jim. We'd have been better off to leave McCarty alone."

"Yeah," said Dawson, "but you know Duke. He's got a hatred inside him toward McCarty that won't quit. He just had to get his paws on him."

"Well, he ain't gonna get his paws on him now."

Fifteen minutes passed.

Studying the spot where he had last seen Ridgway, Nye said, "Where do you suppose that deputy went?"

"Probably to bring the undertaker," mumbled Dawson. "I really liked those guys. And now they're dead, sure as anything. Duke's gonna be hot about Brockman killin' Chick."

"Yeah. You're right about that. I wish we didn't have to be the ones to— Hey, there's another badge-toter! Prob'ly one of Brockman's deputies."

Sheriff Curt Langan was running on the dirt street alongside the boardwalk. When he reached the front of the hotel, he bounded across the boardwalk and plunged through the door.

A few hotel guests were still gathered at the bottom of the stairs, talking about the shooting, when Langan passed through the lobby and headed upstairs. When he reached the top, he saw John Brockman placing a corpse next to two others on the hallway floor in front of room 9.

Langan, looking a bit sleepy, eyed the dead men and said, "What did you gentlemen have here, another Gettysburg battle?"

"Not quite," said John, "but it was bad enough. One of them lived long enough to spill the beans on Duke Foster."

"That's what Steve told me. Except he didn't live long enough to tell you where Foster is at the moment."

"Right. All we know is that he's somewhere in or near Denver."

Langan pushed his hat up and scratched the back of his head. "That covers plenty of territory. There's not a lot we can do. Steve said two of them got away—Dick Nye and Pete Dawson."

"Yes, and they've probably hightailed it back to wherever Foster is staying. About all we can do is spread the word around town with Foster's description, and the descriptions of Nye and Dawson. Ask folks to keep an eye out for them."

"I'll start the wheels on that in the morning," said Langan, "but we're probably going to be too late. Duke and those other two will no doubt make a run for it."

Brockman pointed to one of the outlaws. "Before he died, that one right there gave me the location of Foster's hideout. West side of Monarch Pass, near Dead Man's Canyon. As you know, I'm short on deputies. But as soon as I can, I'll get somebody on Duke's trail or go after him myself."

"I'm going to get you more help as soon as I possibly can, John," spoke up McCarty. "I've made you that promise, and it stands."

"I appreciate that, sir," said Brockman. "But until then, we'll just work with what we've got."

Nye and Dawson watched as a hearse pulled up in front of the hotel and the undertaker and the slender young deputy they had seen twice before got out. Both men went inside the hotel.

Moments later, through the lobby windows, the outlaws saw a few hotel guests collected to one side as they watched two men—John Brockman and the undertaker—carrying a sheet-draped body out the door. Right behind them came two more men with another sheet-draped body.

Some of the people followed them out and stood on the hotel porch. Nye and Dawson listened to the talk and learned that the second pair of men were Sheriff Curt Langan and his deputy, Steve Ridgway. Then came a third pair—Chet McCarty and the desk clerk Jerry Hinson—with the last body.

While the bodies were being placed in the hearse, Nye turned to Dawson and whispered, "I dread it, but we gotta tell Duke that all three are dead."

"Yeah. My stomach's already upset. Let's go."

Suddenly they heard pounding hooves and noted a big black stallion carrying a blond woman. She drew rein and stopped at the hearse.

They watched Brockman rush to her and soon learned that the lady was Brockman's wife.

Nye and Dawson hurried down the alley to the end of the block, crossed to the next block, and continued on. When they were far enough from the front of the hotel, they dashed across the street and worked their way down the dark alley to the place they had stashed the wagon earlier. Climbing aboard, they drove

it slowly and as quietly as possible to the far end of the block, then headed through the dark streets toward Harold Sheetz's house.

Fear prickled Pete Dawson's skin like a rash as he pulled the wagon to a halt near the barn. His mouth was dry as he said, "Okay, Dick. Let's get it over with."

"I'd rather face every man I've murdered than do this," said Nye, alighting from the wagon.

"That'd be quite a few dead men," Dawson said, chuckling without humor. "How many have you murdered for Duke?"

"Six."

"Br-r-r-r. I wouldn't want to face a half dozen men I'd murdered if they could come back from the dead."

"Well, they can't, so I guess my analogy was a bit extreme."

They moved through the backyard. Lanterns burned in almost every room of the house. As they stepped up on the back porch and Pete knocked on the door, they could hear voices inside.

The sound of heavy footsteps came toward the door; then a shadow appeared behind the curtain covering the door. Harold Sheetz swung the door open and ran his gaze over their faces, then looked behind them. "Where's the rest of them and McCarty?" he asked. "Duke's in the parlor, and he's plenty upset."

"Well, he's gonna be a whole lot more upset in a few seconds," said Dawson. "Everything went wrong."

"What do you mean?"

"Let's go in. You can learn about it at the same time Duke does."

Duke was on his feet as they entered the room. Ejecting a string of profanity, he demanded to know what had taken them so long...and where was McCarty? And where were Chick and the other two?

They exchanged glances, then Nye said, "I'll tell him."

97

"Tell me what?" boomed Foster, spraying saliva.

"You'd better sit down, Duke," said Nye.

Foster's eyes bulged. "Sit down? Why?"

A cold chill lodged in Dick Nye's spine, and he wanted to turn and bolt for the door. His throat felt as if an iron band were around his windpipe.

He forced his voice to function. "Duke, everything went wrong," he said hoarsely.

Harold Sheetz stood motionless, looking on.

"What do you mean, 'everything'? You mean you didn't capture McCarty?"

"No, sir. We didn't."

Duke's neck flushed red, and the color worked its way up to his face. "Well, what happened? Where's Chick?"

Nye looked at Dawson, whose features were pinched and white. Turning back to Duke, he said, "Chick's…uh…Chick's dead, Duke. So are Jim and Layton."

Harold Sheetz took an involuntary step backwards.

It took a few seconds for Nye's words to sink into Duke's brain. Then he staggered back a few paces and flopped to a sitting position on the couch. All the blood had seeped out of his face, leaving a colorless mask. "H-how? Wh-what happened?"

Looking around for some chairs, Nye and Dawson each picked one up and sat down in front of a stunned Duke Foster.

Fumbling for words, Nye told Foster what had happened at the hotel, and Pete Dawson filled in at times when Nye's nervousness caused his mind to go blank.

Duke's first emotion was sadness for the loss of his brother, and he finally broke down and wept. His body was racked by shudders, and tears flowed down his cheeks as he repeated Chick's name over and over.

When his initial grief subsided, anger began to take over as

he spoke the name of John Brockman, knowing it was he who had killed Chick and the other two gang members.

Soon, anger had turned to wrath. Duke's face was almost purple, and the muscles in his jaws were flexing as he spat the words, "Brockman! He's gonna die, that's what! He's gonna die! I'll get even with him if it's the last thing I do! I'm gonna kill that low-down skunk with my bare hands!"

Harold Sheetz approached the man with caution, saying, "Duke, I know how you feel, and I can't blame you for hating Brockman, but I'd suggest you think over trying to kill him. Not only will he be hard to get to because of his position as chief U.S. marshal, but the man himself has a reputation for being hard to kill. Many men have tried it, and now they lie six feet under. We've heard tonight how he took out Chick, Layton, and Jim. They're dead. He's alive. I don't want to see you get killed while trying to lay your vengeance on him."

Duke was quiet for a moment, staring at the floor. Smoldering resentment showed in his eyes as he ran his gaze to Sheetz and said evenly, "Brockman's got to die, Harold. He killed my little brother. I'll never rest until he's dead, and I want him dead at my own hand."

"But Duke—"

"I know, I know," cut in Foster, throwing up his hands. "I'm a cripple. I'm not in his league when it comes to fightin'. What I mean by my own hand is, I'll be satisfied when Brockman's dead by the hand of the man I send to kill him."

Harold shook his head. "Well, your hired killer better be plenty good at it, Duke, or he's a dead man."

"I'll worry about that, Harold," said Foster, swinging his gaze to Nye. "Dick, how would you like to pick up an extra twenty thousand dollars?"

Nye grinned. "I could always use that kind of money. The

most you paid me for takin' care of those other six guys I've done in for you is five thousand."

Foster chuckled evilly. "Yeah, but none of them was John Brockman. There'll be more risk."

"A lot more," said Nye. "We'll need a plan. I mean a foolproof plan."

"Agreed. I wouldn't want it any other way. I want you alive and Brockman dead. And after you've done it, I'm sending you to Washington to take out Chester B. McCarty. However, first things first. It will take some time to work out a foolproof plan, but we'll stay right here with Harold till it's done." Turning to Sheetz, he said, "That okay, Harold?"

"Of course. You gotta lay low, that's for sure, and you want to stay in Denver so you can work out your plan to put Brockman six feet under."

"We'll have to lay low all right," said Foster. "Brockman's got three dead men with Wanted posters on every one of 'em. It won't take him long to find that they're part of our gang. He may figure out that we've been settin' up this thing from close by. So we'll have to stay right here in the house."

Foster turned to Sheetz and said, "Harold, this plan will come together only if you fill us in on everything that's goin' on at the chief U.S. marshal's office."

"You bet. Like you said, Duke, it'll take some time. But the right situation will come along, and when it does, you can have your vengeance on the dude who killed your little brother."

"I knew I could count on you, Harold. Eventually I'll learn of somethin' that'll put Brockman in a position vulnerable to Dick's killin' talents, and the great Chief U.S. Marshal John Brockman will die!"

✣

John and Breanna lay in each other's arms with the pale moonlight shining through their bedroom window.

"John, darling," Breanna said softly, "I'm so thankful the Lord protected you in that gun battle tonight. Every day I pray so hard that He will keep His mighty hand on you."

John had not told Breanna about the bullet that almost hit his ear in the shoot-out. It was over, and he was alive and untouched. Why scare her with the reality of how close death actually had come to claiming him?

"I appreciate your prayers, honey," he said. "Thank God for the protection of the Holy Spirit. It's like we were discussing the other night about Zechariah 4:6. I'm alive after that shoot-out tonight not by mortal might, nor by human power, but by God's mighty Spirit."

The next morning, John Brockman was at his desk going over some reports from deputy U.S. marshals who headed up some of the other Western District offices. It was just an hour from the time he was to pick up Chet McCarty at the hotel and drive him to Union Station.

There was a familiar knock at the door.

"Yes, Billy!" he called.

Billy Martin opened the door a few inches. "Chief, Stu Morrison and his men just returned. He would like to see you."

Brockman didn't like the look in Martin's eyes. John had sent Deputy Stu Morrison and a band of five other deputies to track down a large gang of train robbers. "Something wrong?" he asked.

"Well, sir, it's good in one way, but bad in another. Stu will tell you all about it."

"Send him in."

Brockman rose to his feet and offered his hand as Morrison came in. "Billy tells me you've got good news and bad news for me."

"Yes, sir."

"Sit down," said Brockman, gesturing to either chair that stood before the desk.

When both men were seated, Brockman said, "Let's hear it."

"The good news, sir, is that we came back with six members of the Cullen gang in handcuffs, and we left seven dead ones after we had a shoot-out with them just outside of Goodland, Kansas. One of the dead was Jake Cullen."

"That is good news," said Brockman. "The railroad companies will be happy to hear that the Cullen gang is out of business." The chief paused. "I know the bad news has to be that we suffered some casualties, so I'll make it as easy on you as I can, Stu. How many killed?"

Morrison swallowed hard and cleared his throat. "Ah…one, sir. Bill Nevins."

Brockman's brow furrowed. "Oh no. And Bill's got two children."

"Yes, sir. Deputies Art Banks and Breck Hamby are at the Nevins home now, advising Mrs. Nevins of Bill's death. They took her pastor with them."

Brockman nodded. The furrows in his brow deepened. "How many wounded?"

"Two, sir. Deputies DeWitt Granshaw and Red Varick. I'm pleased to tell you that both only have flesh wounds."

"Well, I'm glad for that."

"Granshaw and Varick are at the hospital, and we took Bill's body to the undertaker's before coming here."

John closed his eyes and rubbed the lids gently. "I'm thankful that the rest of you got back without a scratch, but I hate to lose Bill…and I'm sorry about DeWitt and Red. I'll go see Donna Nevins, then I'll drop in on my two wounded men at the hospital. That is, after I deliver a certain Chester B. McCarty to Union Station so he can catch a train."

Morrison's jaw dropped. *"The* Chester B. McCarty? Executive administrator of the U.S. Marshal's Office in Washington, D.C.? That Chester B. McCarty?"

Brockman nodded. "That one. I've got some good news to tell you men. I want all of you to get some rest this morning, but I'll need to call a meeting this afternoon. Let's say three o'clock. Will you let Banks and Hamby know, in case they aren't at the Nevins house when I get there?"

"Sure will, sir."

"Had a little excitement at the Westerner last night involving McCarty. I'll tell you all about it at the meeting."

As John drove McCarty to the depot, he told him about Stu Morrison and his men breaking up the Jake Cullen gang. McCarty was glad to hear of the gang's downfall but was sad to hear that one deputy had been killed and two wounded to bring it to pass.

Shaking his head, he said, "This cuts your force even more, John. Wish I could send you a whole battalion."

"I wish you could, too."

"Anyway, I'm going to do everything I can to strengthen your ranks."

"I know you'll do what you can, sir."

With Chet McCarty on the train, John made his way to the Nevins home, where he joined with the family's pastor in doing what he could to comfort the widow. Deputies Banks and Hamby had already left.

From there, John drove to the hospital.

Just as the chief U.S. marshal was tying the buggy horse to a hitching post in the hospital's parking lot, he saw a wagon coming down the street with the team at a full gallop. The wagon careened off the street as John was approaching the front door of the hospital and skidded to a halt a few feet from him.

On the seat was a young woman who was obviously about to give birth to a baby. She was doubled over with labor pains.

Her husband—looking wildly nervous—jumped out of the wagon, saying, "Hold on, Jenny!"

When his feet touched ground, he turned his right ankle and howled, going down on one knee.

John rushed to him. "You hurt bad, fella?"

"I don't think I broke it, Mr.—" His eyes found the badge. "Uh…Chief. But I think it's sprained pretty bad."

Jenny was moaning and gritting her teeth, still bent over.

"What's your name?" asked John.

"Les Osterman, sir."

"Well, Les, you stay right here, and I'll get Jenny inside, if it's all right with you."

"Yes, of course. Thank you. I'm not going anywhere."

John went to the other side of the wagon and laid a hand on the young woman's shoulder. "Little lady, your husband said it would be all right if I carry you into the hospital. He's hurt his ankle. I'm sending help for him."

Pain evident in her face, Jenny Osterman nodded. She cast a worried look at her husband and leaned toward John.

Cradling her in his arms, he hurried away, calling back, "Hang on, Les. Help will soon be on the way!"

Breanna was in surgery with staff physician Dr. Malcolm Watts while Watts sewed up Deputy Marshal DeWitt Granshaw's left side where a bullet had ripped through at a depth of half an inch. Granshaw was awake and enduring the pain.

The door opened and Mary Donelson entered. "How's it going, Doctor?" she asked, moving close to the surgery table.

"Just fine. We'll be done in a few minutes. Something you need?"

"No. I just wanted Deputy Granshaw to know that Chief Brockman was here to see him."

Breanna's head came up. "Oh, Mrs. Donelson. You mean that tall, dark, handsome man who walks in my dreams?"

"That's the one," said Mary, chuckling. "Since Deputy Red Varick is already taken care of and in a room, Chief Brockman is visiting him. He said to tell his beautiful wife and his wounded deputy that he'd be back shortly."

"I'll look forward to seeing him," said Granshaw. Mary started toward the door, paused, and said, "Oh, Breanna…your husband will have an interesting story to tell you."

"Really?"

"Mm-hmm. He almost had to deliver a baby outside the front door of the hospital."

Breanna raised her eyebrows. "You're not kidding me, are you?"

"No. He can tell you all about it."

"I'll want to hear it."

John Brockman was outside surgery when Mary stepped into the hallway.

"It'll be a few more minutes, Chief," she said.

"Okay. I think I'll go look in on Dave Taylor."

"Sorry, but Dave isn't seeing visitors yet, Chief."

"No?"

"He's still having a tough time, and Dr. Carroll will only allow Nyla in there with him."

Concern showed in John's gray eyes. "Has he taken a turn for the worse?"

"No," said Mary, shaking her head. "It's not that. Dave sustained a pretty bad wound. Any time a person is torn up as much as he was near the heart and in the chest, it takes some time to get over it. We have no doubt he'll be as good as new when he gets all healed, but it's going to be a rough few days getting him on the path to recovery."

"Any idea when I might be able to see him?"

"I can't really say. It's up to Dr. Carroll. But I can guess. I'd say give it a try in two more days."

"Will do. In the meantime, when you go in there, you tell him I'm still holding him before the Throne."

"I sure will."

The door to the operating room opened, and Breanna emerged, holding a bundle of bloody towels. "Oh, hello, darling," she said. "You'll be able to see DeWitt in about five minutes."

"I'll wait," he said, obviously drinking in her beauty with his eyes.

Breanna blushed and flicked a glance at Mary, then hurried away.

Moments later, as John stood over DeWitt Granshaw, Dr. Watts said, "He'll be fine after sufficient recuperation time, Chief."

John smiled down at his deputy and said, "How long will that be, Doctor?"

"Three weeks should do it; maybe a little less."

Breanna reentered the room and moved toward her husband.

"I'm sorry, Chief," said Granshaw. "I know you're already short of men."

"You don't have anything to be sorry for, DeWitt. You were just doing your duty."

"Hard to lose Bill Nevins," said Granshaw.

"Bill Nevins?" said Breanna. "He wasn't—"

"Yes," said John. "He was killed at the same time DeWitt, here, and Red Varick were shot."

"Oh, I'm so sorry. Poor Donna…and those precious children."

"I went to see her before coming here," said John. "Her pastor is with her."

John patted his deputy's shoulder and said, "You did an excellent job, DeWitt. You get some rest. I'll check on you later."

Granshaw managed a lopsided grin. "Thanks, Chief."

Turning to Breanna, John said, "Well, I've got to get back to the office."

She stepped into the hallway with him, and when the door closed behind them she said, "Mary tells me you almost had to deliver a baby at the front door of the hospital."

John grinned. "Came close. I'll tell you the story tonight. The young father found me when I was coming back to see DeWitt. They've got a bouncing baby boy."

"That's nice. And my big handsome husband helped."

"A little."

John glanced back at the door to the operating room. "I hope DeWitt and Red heal up as the doctors predict."

Breanna touched his arm tenderly and said, "Darling, I know this loss of three more men comes as a hard blow to you. But I feel certain that Mr. McCarty will find a way to send you a good number of men. They'll be here soon."

John took hold of her shoulders and looked deep into her eyes. "Thank you, my sweet, for always being such an encouragement to me."

She warmed him with a smile. "I think that's what wives are for."

Looking in both directions down the hallway, John planted a kiss on the tip of her nose and said softly, "You are without a doubt the most wonderful woman in all the world."

Breanna reached up and caressed his cheek. "As long as I am in your eyes, Chief Brockman, that's all that matters."

8

AT THREE O'CLOCK, Chief U.S. Marshal John Brockman met with Deputies Stu Morrison, Art Banks, and Breck Hamby. He commended them for a job well done in bringing down the Jake Cullen gang and explained the reason for Chester McCarty's visit to Denver.

Brockman then told them about the shoot-out the night before at the Westerner Hotel.

"Chief, what can we do to help find Duke Foster?" Stu Morrison said, leaning forward in his chair.

Brockman rubbed his chin. "I can't keep you gentlemen in town very long. There are outlaws to pursue. However, I'm going to have you work with Sheriff Langan for a day or two. Langan's due here any minute. He started the ball rolling this morning by putting out word all over town on Foster, Nye, and Dawson, along with their descriptions. People in Denver know to be on the lookout for them. We also need to work the surrounding areas, since we don't know where Foster might be holed up."

At that instant, there was a knock on the door. Deputy Billy Martin let Sheriff Langan in, and as he shook hands with the deputies, Brockman said, "I was just explaining to the men that you had already gotten the word out on Foster and his two cronies. If you think you've got the town covered, Sheriff, I'm going to send these men out to the surrounding areas and let them ask questions of farmers and ranchers. Maybe somebody out there has seen the gang."

"Good idea," Langan said. "Steve Ridgway and I will make sure every merchant in town has a description of those three, and we'll alert the railroad and stagecoach people, too, just in case Foster should try something cute."

Brockman nodded. "It's good to leave no stone unturned, although I think Duke will head for that mountain hideout once he can get clear of the Denver area."

"You're probably right, but like you said, leave no stone unturned."

"Okay," said Morrison, rising to his feet. "Let's go turn stones. I'll work it out systematically, Chief, so we don't overlook anybody. I figure to work the farms and ranches in a twenty-mile radius. The three of us ought to be able to cover it in a couple of days."

"Sounds good," said Brockman, also rising to his feet. "Go to it."

"We've got about four hours of daylight left," said Breck Hamby. "Let's see if we can come up with something by dark."

Two days passed. Shortly after darkness fell on the second day, John Brockman met with his three deputies and Sheriff Curt Langan. Morrison, Banks, and Hamby had talked to someone on every ranch and farm in a twenty-mile radius and come up empty. Langan and his deputy had covered every shop and store in town. No one had seen anyone answering the description of Foster, Nye, or Dawson.

Brockman eased back in his chair, ran his gaze over the faces of the four men seated before him, and said, "Duke and his pals probably left the other night right after the shoot-out. The place to find them is their hideout in the mountains."

Langan sighed. "Seems that's what happened. They're sure nowhere to be found around here."

"I'm glad Felton told me where the cabin is located," commented Brockman. "Shouldn't be hard to find."

Light came into Langan's eyes. "Foster doesn't know that Jim Felton told you how to find the hideout, does he?"

"No, he doesn't."

"So they won't know anybody's coming to the cabin at Monarch. Be easy to surprise them."

One of the deputies stirred. "You want us to ride for Monarch Pass, Chief?"

John shook his head. "Can't spare you for it, Stu. I've got to send all three of you after a gang of bank robbers who are robbing and killing in northern New Mexico. I've promised Washington for two weeks that I'd send men as soon as I had them available. I must send you fellas to New Mexico tomorrow."

"Then what about Foster?" Hamby asked.

"Looks like I'm going to be the man to go after him."

"By yourself, sir?" Art Banks said, his eyebrows arching.

"I don't like it that way either, but it may come to it. McCarty promised to send me a man to take Dave Taylor's place as soon as he could. I'll have to give it a little time and see if he can come up with one. If he does, that deputy and I will leave for Monarch Pass shortly after he gets here. I'll get Sol Duvall to sit in for me here at the office."

The next day, when the sun was lowering toward the Rockies, John Brockman left his buggy in the parking lot and headed for the front door of the hospital. He was there to pick up Breanna but had come a little early to check on Dave Taylor and visit DeWitt Granshaw and Red Varick.

"Hello, Chief Brockman," Mabel Trotter said. "You're early today."

"I'd like to see Dave Taylor, if I could, and I want to check on my other deputies, Mabel. Do you know if Dr. Carroll has given permission for Dave to have visitors yet?"

"Not that I know of, sir, but you can go up and see. Mrs. Taylor is with him."

"All right. And do you know where my wife might be?"

"It so happens that I do. Dr. Goodwin came in a few minutes ago saying that he needed to talk to her. Right now they're in Mrs. Donelson's office."

"Okay. I'm going to Dave Taylor's room, and then to look in on my other two deputies. If Breanna comes out of the office before I get back, please tell her where I am."

"I sure will, Chief."

Hurrying up the stairs, Brockman decided to look in on Granshaw and Varick first. He spent a few minutes with each deputy, then headed down the hall. Both Granshaw and Varick were improving and would leave the hospital the next day.

The door was closed to Dave Taylor's room. Brockman looked around for a nurse, but the hallway was unoccupied. Mary had said he should try to see Dave in two days. Time was up, and there was nobody in sight to ask. Shrugging his wide shoulders, he tapped lightly on the door.

He heard soft footsteps and then Nyla opened the door and smiled at him. "Hello, Chief Brockman."

Just over her shoulder John saw nurse Natalie Fallon leaning over Dave, putting a thermometer in his mouth.

"How's he doing?" John asked Nyla.

"Somewhat better. But don't quit praying for him."

"Oh, I won't do that. Can I come in and see him?"

Nyla cocked her head. "Well-l-l, Dr. Carroll hasn't lifted the ban on visitors yet."

John lifted his hand, making a space between his thumb and forefinger, and asked, "Just for this long?"

Nyla turned to the nurse. "Miss Fallon, could the Chief U.S. Marshal of the whole country west of the Missouri come in for a little tiny minute?"

Dave looked toward the door and said around the thermometer, "Id woul' he'p me if he coul' come id."

Natalie smiled, then nodded at Brockman. "Okay. But just for a tiny minute."

As John approached the bed on the opposite side from Natalie, Dave raised a shaky right hand.

Natalie removed the thermometer as John gripped Dave's hand gently.

"Glad to see you, Chief," Dave said weakly. "Thank you for coming."

"I'd have been in here a lot sooner if the boss man in the head office of this hospital had let me."

"I know. Nyla told me."

"So how are you feeling?"

"He should be feeling better, Chief," said Natalie. "His temperature is down to an even one hundred. It was much higher earlier this afternoon."

"I am feeling better," said Dave. "Not 100 percent, but better."

Natalie grinned. "One hundred percent won't come for at least another day, Dave!"

John chuckled as he said, "I'm glad to know there is at least some improvement, Dave. Breanna and I have been praying for you."

"Thank you, Chief."

Natalie looked down at her patient. "Well, Deputy David Taylor, I must move on. My shift is almost over. God bless you. I'll see you in the morning."

"Before you go, Natalie," said John, "I'd like to pray. Since he's your patient today, and you're a Christian, I'd like you to thank the Lord with us that Dave is finally showing some improvement."

"Of course," said Natalie. "I'm honored that you would include me."

When John closed off his prayer, tears were coursing down Nyla's cheeks. Natalie put her arms around her and held her tight. "God is good, isn't He, Nyla?"

Nyla sniffed and nodded.

Natalie patted her back gently and said, "I've got to see another patient before time to go home, so I'll excuse myself." Having spoken, she quietly slipped out the door.

John looked down at Dave. "I need to go in just a moment, too. Thought you might like to know that Chester McCarty and I—with President Grant's permission—have worked out a plan for the San Francisco office to become a chief U.S. marshal's office. It will oversee California and the northwest territories."

"Oh, that's good, Chief. That'll relieve you of a lot of responsibility."

"He's going to send us some new men soon, too."

At that instant, the door opened and Dr. Carroll entered. Forming a mock scowl on his face, he said gruffly, "Now, look here, Chief Brockman. I haven't yet given the order to allow visitors for this patient."

"But you were about to, weren't you, Doctor?" said John.

"Well, I was going to if I found him feeling up to it."

"I'm up to seeing my boss, Doctor," Dave said, meeting his gaze.

A grin broke over Matt's face. "I just talked to Nurse Fallon. She told me how much better you feel, and that your temperature is coming down."

"So you're not throwing me out, brother-in-law?" John said.

"Hardly. In fact, I'm glad you're here. Dave speaks so well of you I know it's good therapy for him to see you."

"You're right about that, Doctor," said Dave.

"I agree," spoke up Nyla. "Dave has a light in his eyes he didn't have until Chief Brockman came in."

Carroll pulled back the covers. "I want to check your bandage, Dave."

All was quiet while the doctor looked under the bandage, studying it for a long moment, and then probing gently with his fingertips. When he finished, he tied the bandage in place and put the covers back. "Looks good, Dave," he said. "The healing process is beginning."

"That's good news, Doctor," said Nyla.

"Sure is," agreed John. "Well, I've got to find my wife and head for home. I'll check on you again tomorrow, Dave. Take care of yourself so you'll heal fast. I need you."

When John opened the door, Breanna was standing there.

"Oh, hello, sweetheart," he said warmly. "Are you ready to go home?"

"Mm-hmm. After I find out how Dave's doing. I know he doesn't need too many people in the room at one time, so I waited out here."

Matt looked past John and said from Dave's bedside, "He's showing some definite improvement, Breanna. The Lord is answering prayer."

"Praise His name!" she responded.

"Can you come in for a minute, Breanna?" asked Nyla. "Dave and I would like to talk to you."

Breanna smiled at her husband and stepped into the room. She put an arm around Nyla's waist and looked down with compassion on Dave. "What did you want to talk about?"

"We just want to thank you for stopping by the room so often as you're doing your duties in the hospital," said Nyla. "We know you have plenty to do already without taking the time to look in on Dave. It means more to us than we can ever tell you."

That's right," said Dave. "And I want to thank you for praying for me. I know you and the chief pray for me together, as well as separately. Please know that Nyla and I love you for it."

"You're one of my husband's favorite deputies, Dave," said Breanna. "We both appreciate the good job you've been doing since John became chief U.S. marshal. He needs you, so hurry and get well."

John helped Breanna into the buggy seat, kissed her hand, and moved around to the other side.

"Darling, you're such a romantic," said Breanna.

"What do you mean?"

"I don't imagine one husband in a thousand kisses his wife's hand like you so often kiss mine."

"I can't speak for those other husbands," John said softly, "but you are the queen of my life. Queens get their hands kissed, don't they?"

"Oh, John. I love you so much."

The tall man started the buggy across the parking lot and turned onto the street. As they headed south, he said, "Mabel told me you and Dr. Goodwin were having a conference in Mary's office."

"Mm-hmm."

"I suppose he wants to send you on an assignment?"

"Mm-hmm. And I think it's one I should take."

"So where are you going?"

"Empire."

"Oh, really?" The small town of Empire, Colorado, was some thirty miles west of Denver in the mountains. "What's the job?"

"A young mother almost died giving birth to her first child yesterday. The town's physician, Dr. Rex Rawlins, wired Dr. Goodwin this morning, telling him about the young mother's close call with death. He explained that the baby is doing all right, but that the mother is having some serious complications."

"I see."

"Since there is no hospital in the mountains and the mother is in no condition to travel, Dr. Rawlins asked Dr. Goodwin to send one of his visiting nurses, preferably one with a great deal of experience. The sick woman will need the best care possible."

John turned and looked at her. "Dr. Goodwin knows where to find the best nurse for the job. Do you have any idea how long you might be gone?"

"There's really no way of knowing, darling. It will depend on how well the lady responds to treatment."

"So you're going tomorrow, I suppose."

"Mm-hmm. I'll head out early on Chance. If I leave at sunup, I should be to Empire before noon."

"Well, you're not riding up there alone. I'll escort you."

"Darling, there's nothing to be afraid of. There are no Indians between here and Empire. And I'll have my revolver with me."

"No way, sweet stuff. We'll go by Sol's house right now. I'll ask him to oversee the office for me tomorrow. You're not riding up there alone."

"John, I'm not a child. I'll be fine. You need to be here on the job."

"The job will still be here when I get back. And I know you're not a child, but you are my wife. The issue is settled. I'm escorting you to Empire."

Breanna chuckled and playfully punched his shoulder. "You're the most stubborn man I know, John Brockman."

He gave her a sidelong glance and a slanted grin, then said, "The Lord gave you to me, beautiful lady, and I'm going to take care of you."

Though it was the middle of the summer, there was a slight chill in the air at daybreak as John and Breanna prepared for their ride to Empire. Breanna wore a high-necked white blouse, a corduroy divided skirt, and boots. She stood by the corral gate, stroking Ebony's long nose while John saddled Chance at the barn door. Chance kept looking at his mistress and nickering, showing his jealousy over the attention she was giving Ebony.

John led Chance to the gate, carrying Ebony's bridle. "Here's your jealous boy, Mrs. Brockman," he said. "Better give him some attention before he decides to take a bite out of Ebony."

Breanna took the reins in her hand, and John turned his attention to Ebony, slipping the bridle over the horse's head. He fit the bit into Ebony's mouth, then buckled the bridle on snugly and led him to the barn door to saddle him.

Breanna opened the corral gate and led Chance out. The

gray of the new day was brightening the eastern sky as she looked westward and swept her gaze along the shadowed sloping fields that led to the foothills of the Rockies. In the distance were the dark blue mountains whose shoulders swept upward into snowcapped spires that seemed to touch the sky.

Gripping the reins, Breanna said, "Let's walk you a little before we begin our ride, boy."

She led the huge black to and fro along the corral fence. She was delighted with his gentleness. Actually, he didn't need to be led. Chance followed his mistress like a pet dog, rubbing his black muzzle against her. She returned to the gate as John was leading Ebony out.

John took a few seconds to tie Breanna's small piece of luggage and her black medical bag to the back of her saddle; then they mounted and headed westward. Moments later, they came to the gurgling South Platte River. They crossed at a relatively shallow spot where the water barely touched the bottoms of Breanna's boots.

Periodically, both John and Breanna glanced behind them as they rode toward the foothills. Long lines of pink fire ran level with the eastern horizon, and a bank of scattered clouds to the east was turning a beautiful shade of rose.

To the west, the sky was rapidly losing its gray look and turning more blue every minute. Soon the sun rose behind the two riders and kissed the snowy peaks high above them. The sight was exhilarating. As the sun rose higher, it blazed out the darkness between the ridges ahead of them, giving fresh, brilliant color to the broad sweep of the land.

As the morning progressed, Chance and Ebony carried their riders into the high country, skirting rushing streams and passing under towering evergreens. The sweet smell of pine filled the air.

It was almost eleven o'clock when the small town of Empire came into view, nestled among aspen, birch, and lofty pines that swayed in the breeze.

Empire's business district had only one street, and it was exactly one block long. The false-fronted buildings were clapboard, with signs above the doors. Some signs were faded and weatherworn, and others were bright-colored with bold lettering.

Small frame houses and log cabins were intermingled on the side streets. There was a red schoolhouse at the east edge of town, and a white church building with a steeple at the west end.

As John and Breanna turned onto Main Street, John pointed with his chin and said, "I see the doctor's shingle...up there on the right, beside the hardware store."

"Yes, I see it," said Breanna. "Dr. Rex Rawlins, M.D. Takes a dedicated man to come to a small community like this, when he could set up his practice in a large city and make more money."

People along the street watched the man and woman on the pair of large black horses. When John and Breanna met their gaze and smiled, the people smiled back.

They drew up in front of the doctor's office and dismounted. John wrapped the reins of both horses around the hitching rails, took Breanna's hand, and led her across the boardwalk.

A couple of elderly men were sitting on a bench in front of the hardware store. "Good morning, gentlemen," John said.

"Good morning," said the one who looked to be the youngest. "Please pardon my friend, here. He's deaf."

John nodded, and opened the door. When they stepped inside, they saw a silver-haired woman at the desk. She looked to be in her midsixties. Her eyes widened when she saw the badge on John's chest, and she said, "Good morning, folks. I'm

Isabel Mullins. Dr. Rawlins is with a patient at the moment, but he can see either or both of you as soon as he's finished."

"Ma'am," said the tall man, "I'm John Brockman, and this is my wife, Breanna. She's here by assignment from Dr. Lyle Goodwin in Denver."

"Oh! Yes, of course," said Isabel, pushing her chair back and standing up. She studied John's badge for a moment, then said to Breanna, "I didn't realize our visiting nurse was the wife of the chief U.S. marshal in Denver! Welcome to both of you."

"Thank you, ma'am," said Breanna. "My husband will be heading back down to Denver momentarily. He rode along to escort me here."

"I see. Well, I'm mighty proud to make your acquaintance, Marshal Brockman."

"It's my pleasure, ma'am."

"Please...sit down," said Isabel. "The doctor shouldn't be much longer."

When the Brockmans were seated, Isabel looked at Breanna and said, "Have you known of Dr. Rawlins before now?"

"No, I haven't," said Breanna. "But I must say, I admire him for coming to Empire."

Isabel nodded. "He is quite the young man. He's only in his midtwenties...just two years out of medical school. Did you know or know of Dr. Eugene Hooper, who had this office before?"

"No, I wasn't even aware there was a doctor's office in Empire until Dr. Rawlins's wire came to Dr. Goodwin yesterday."

"I see. Well, Dr. Hooper had this office for some fifteen or sixteen years. He brought Dr. Rawlins here to work with him as soon as Dr. Rawlins graduated from medical school. Dr. Hooper was getting up in years and knew he would have to

121

retire, which he did, just three months ago. As planned, Dr. Rawlins took over the practice. Dr. and Mrs. Hooper now live in Michigan, where they had originally come from. The people of this town and area absolutely love Dr. Rawlins. As you'll see, he's a very warm and likable person. Knows his stuff, too."

"That's good," said Breanna. "I'm sure I will enjoy working for him."

The door of the inner office opened, and a beefy man in his early fifties appeared, followed by a handsome young man with angular features and sand-colored hair. The latter wore a white frock over his white shirt and tie, and a stethoscope dangled from his neck.

Rawlins noticed the couple seated in front of Isabel's desk, gave them a smile, then said to his patient, "You be sure to take those powders every day at breakfast time, George." Then he said to his assistant, "Isabel, we need to set up an appointment for George."

"All right, Doctor." She opened her appointment book. "This same time a week from today all right, Mr. Wilson?"

"Be fine," said the patient.

As George Wilson went out the door, Isabel said, "Dr. Rawlins, this lady is your visiting nurse, Breanna Brockman, and this gentleman is her husband, Chief U.S. Marshal John Brockman."

Rawlins greeted them warmly, saying he had heard of the new chief U.S. marshal in Denver. He added to Breanna, "Mrs. Brockman, I appreciate so much that you're here. You are highly recommended by Dr. Goodwin. And I'm impressed that our visiting nurse is married to a man of such distinction."

Breanna sent a sly look to her husband. "See? I told you this is how people look at you."

John's features tinted. "I'm just a man trying to do a job."

"And doing it quite well, sir," said the doctor. "I've been told that you not only wear a badge, but that you preach a good sermon."

"Now and then I get a good one out," said John.

"Don't let him kid you, Doctor," said Breanna. "I've never heard him preach one that wasn't excellent."

"Sounds like you might know what a good sermon is, Doctor," said John.

Rawlins grinned. "Well, sir, let me put it like this. To me it's a good sermon, no matter what the subject, if it exalts the Lord Jesus Christ, declares that the new birth is necessary for salvation, and shows Jesus as the only way to heaven."

Breanna clapped her hands together. "I'd say we have a born-again doctor here, John!"

"And a born-again assistant, too!" put in Isabel.

"I'm glad I'll be working for a Christian doctor," said Breanna. "And I'm glad he has such a sweet Christian assistant!"

John cleared his throat gently. "Well, honey," he said to Breanna, "I'd love to stay and have some fellowship with these good people, but I need to head back." He turned to Rawlins. "I assume she has a place to stay, Doctor."

"Yes. She'll be staying in the home of her patient, Rose Anderson. Rose's husband, Ray, is a coal miner."

"Do they have a barn and corral for Breanna's horse?"

"No, sir, but we have a hostler. We'll put her horse there."

"Fine," said John. "Nice to meet you, Doctor…and nice to meet you, Mrs. Mullins. And best of all, it's nice to know that we're all in God's family."

"Amen," said Rawlins. "It's been an honor to meet you, Chief. God bless you!"

"And God bless both of you."

Breanna followed John outside. Before he mounted, he took her in his arms and held her close for a moment, then kissed her soundly. "Wire me when you're ready to come home, sweetheart. I'll ride up and escort you home."

"I could escort myself, darling, but since you are so stubborn about it, I'll wire you."

John grinned. "I'm stubborn about it because I love you so much, and I want you safe at all times."

"And I love you for it," she said.

John kissed her again, then swung into the saddle. "I'll miss you."

"I'll miss you, too," she said softly.

John nudged Ebony into a trot. When he reached the end of the street, he drew rein, turned, and waved.

The sun glistened on Breanna's hair as she waved back, saying in a whisper, "I love you, my darling."

She felt a pang of loneliness when he disappeared around the corner.

9

BREANNA BROCKMAN INDEED found Dr. Rex Rawlins to be a warm and likable man as they got acquainted.

After some time, he said, "You're probably wondering why we don't rush over to the Anderson home right away."

"Yes. I expected that we would be going soon."

"Rose has been in a great deal of pain, and I had to administer a heavy sedative about two hours ago. She won't be awake for at least another two hours. Let me explain Rose's situation. I believe Dr. Goodwin informed you this was her first child."

"Yes."

"I knew she was going to have some trouble delivering because of her body structure, so I was prepared. I had the Chamberlen forceps at my fingertips when the delivery began. As usual in a case like this, I had to put the forceps on the baby's head and do the delicate removal in conjunction with her contractions."

Rawlins explained in detail the complications Rose had suffered during the delivery and that she had been having a great deal of abdominal pain since. He could find no reason for it, except for the difficult delivery. He thought the pain would subside within a couple of days but wanted to have an experienced nurse with her until she was much improved.

"I'm happy to be here, Doctor," Breanna said. "I'll watch her very closely, I assure you. How is the baby?"

"He's fine. Although using forceps can result in disaster to the baby if not used properly, they were vital in this birthing."

"Have you studied the history of forceps, Doctor?" Breanna asked.

"Not in any detail. I know they were invented by Dr. Peter Chamberlen of Great Britain, in the seventeenth century, and that Chamberlen was the official physician to Queen Anne, wife of King James I."

"Right. It was Dr. Chamberlen who delivered their first son, Prince Henry. It's interesting to me that at first the medical world adamantly condemned the use of Chamberlen's forceps because of the damage that could be done to babies at childbirth when used by doctors and midwives with unskilled hands. In…I think it was 1693, it became illegal in Europe for a midwife to use forceps, and in order to obtain or keep a license to practice medicine, a man had to purchase a pair of Chamberlen's forceps and demonstrate that he could use them skillfully."

"I hadn't heard that," said Rawlins. He chuckled as he said, "Maybe I need to keep you around for a good while. You could teach me some medical history!"

Breanna laughed. "I doubt I could teach you much, Doctor."

Rex Rawlins guided Breanna down the street while she led Chance. After they boarded the horse at the hostler's, they walked toward the Anderson home, which was on the north side of town, two blocks from Main Street.

"I haven't asked the baby's name, Doctor."

"Donald. They're calling him Donnie."

"And I assume his weight and measurements are normal?"

"Quite."

"And you said his father is a coal miner."

"Yes. The mine where he works is just three miles due north of town. Ray has stayed home with Rose and Donnie the past two days, since the birth. He doesn't get paid when he's not working, so he's grateful that you're coming to stay with Rose."

"They're having a difficult time financially?"

"Somewhat."

"Well, I realize the normal procedure is for them to pay you for my services, then you pay me."

"Yes."

"Let's not charge them anything."

The doctor looked at her askance. "But you have to make a living, Breanna. You—"

"Please, let's just say that John and I are quite well off financially. Dr. Goodwin pays me when I work at his office, and the hospital pays me when I work there, but I really am not working because we need the money. I'm working because I love what I do. So…let's make it clear to Mr. Anderson that there will be no charge for my services."

Rawlins shook his head. "I've seldom heard of anyone, no matter how wealthy they might be, who doesn't want more money. You are truly an angel of mercy, dear lady. I know Ray and Rose are going to deeply appreciate your kindness and generosity."

"Jesus put it so beautifully, Doctor, as reported by Paul in Acts 20:35, 'It is more blessed to give than to receive.' I'll get a greater blessing out of it than they will."

"God bless you, Breanna," Rawlins said sincerely.

"He does, Doctor, in spite of my shortcomings."

They drew near a humble little frame house that Rawlins pointed out. "They have a spare bedroom for you, Breanna. It's small, but comfortable, and Rose always keeps a clean house."

"The small bedroom is fine, Doctor," Breanna said as they stepped up on the porch. The door opened, and a smiling Ray Anderson said, "I saw you coming, Dr. Rawlins. This is our visiting nurse, I take it."

"Yes. Ray, I want you to meet Breanna Brockman. She is a certified medical nurse and has many years of experience. She is also the wife of Chief U.S. Marshal John Brockman in Denver."

Ray threw up his palms in mock fear and said, "Then I'll have to stop robbing banks, won't I?"

Breanna laughed, and Ray invited them in.

"Rose is still sleeping from that sedative you gave her this morning, Doctor," said Ray.

"I told Breanna she might still be under," responded Rawlins. "I'll get on back to the office and let you two get acquainted. Breanna will take charge of Donnie right away for you, and she'll be here to care for Rose when she awakens."

Rawlins was still carrying Breanna's small piece of luggage, and she carried her medical bag.

Ray said, "Let me have those, and I'll take them back to the spare bedroom. Would you like to see the room now, ma'am?"

"Yes, in just a moment." She turned to Rawlins. "You'll need to tell me about Rose's medication, Doctor."

"I'll take these on back," said Ray.

As he headed toward the rear of the house, Doctor Rawlins said, "There's an ample supply of laudanum on the table beside Rose's bed. You will need to use your discretion as to how much and how often to administer it. I'm sure you are well experienced with laudanum."

"That I am."

"There are also sedative powders to be used in like manner."

"All right, Doctor."

"I'll come back this evening to check on her."

As Ray returned he heard the doctor's last words and said, "Thank you, Dr. Rawlins, for bringing Breanna to us. I know she'll be an encouragement to Rose."

"You're quite welcome," said Rawlins. "Breanna will take good care of Rose and the baby." The doctor flicked a glance at the nurse and added, "There's something you need to know about this dear lady, Ray."

"What's that?"

"She's a very generous person. She has already told me that her services will be free of charge."

Ray looked as if he couldn't believe his ears. "Free of charge? Well, she has to be paid for her work."

"No, I don't," Breanna said levelly. "I know you've had to miss two days' work since Rose began labor, and I know that you don't get paid when you're not at the mine. I want to do this for you and your family, Ray."

Tears rushed to Ray's eyes, and his face flushed. "Ma'am, I don't know what to say. I really don't think it's right that you come here to care for my wife and baby and not be paid for it."

Breanna laid a gentle hand on his upper arm. "It's right if I say it's right. And I say it's right. End of discussion."

"I'm at a loss for words, Breanna."

"You don't have to say anything. I know you appreciate it."

"Well, I have to be going," said Dr. Rawlins. "See you both this evening." He started toward the door. "Breanna, if some emergency should arise, there are neighbors all around who would come running to get me."

"All right, Doctor."

When Rawlins had gone, Ray showed Breanna the room

where she would be staying. His brow furrowed as he asked, "Is it all right, ma'am?"

Breanna found it to be clean and pleasant, and assured him it was fine. Wanting to change into a dress and shoes, she told Ray she needed a few minutes, then she would sit down and wait with him for Rose to awaken.

Ray told her the baby was in his bassinet in Rose's sewing room just off the parlor, then went to the parlor to wait for her.

Breanna reappeared in a dress with a crisp white nurse's apron over it. She had exchanged her riding boots for button-up shoes. Before she could sit down or they could exchange words, the baby began to cry, and Ray sprang up.

Breanna waved him off. "I'll get him."

Stepping into the sewing room, Breanna looked down at little Donnie Anderson and above his cries said, "What's the matter, honey? You hungry?"

Carrying him into the parlor, she cuddled him close to her heart and asked, "Did Rose feed him before Dr. Rawlins gave her the heavy sedative?"

"Yes."

"He's hungry again, which is normal," she said, checking his diaper. "Oops! He needs changing, too. I'll change his diaper; then we'll have to awaken Rose so she can feed him."

When Breanna returned from the sewing room, Donnie was quiet. She cuddled him close and sat down in a rocking chair, facing Ray. "Maybe his worst problem was the wet diaper. We won't bother his mommy till he says he's hungry."

Ray smiled and seemed to relax his vigilance.

Breanna began rocking the chair, and soon the baby's eyelids drooped. "He's going back to sleep, Ray," she said.

"Really? I'd think he'd be getting hungry."

"He will, all right, but with his mother on laudanum, he's

getting some of it, and it will make him groggy and want to sleep more."

Ray focused on Donnie. "Looks like he's asleep already."

"He sure is."

"Do you have children of your own, Breanna?"

"No, John and I only recently married. We haven't started our family yet."

"I see. Had you known Marshal Brockman long before you married?"

"A little over a year."

"And he's only been chief U.S. marshal for a few months, right?"

"That's right."

"There's a little bell that keeps ringing in the back of my mind, Breanna. It seems that somebody told me Denver's new chief U.S. marshal is the man they called 'The Stranger.' Is that correct?"

"Yes, it is."

Ray's eyes showed keen interest as he said, "I've heard so many stories about him. Like…he can draw his gun and fire so fast you couldn't see his hand move. And he's been known to take on five or six husky men at a time and leave them all lying in a heap. And he helps people who are in all kinds of trouble, no matter what it is. I've heard of several people who have been in need of money, and he's given them more than they needed. Is all that true?"

"Every bit of it," said Breanna, still rocking. "I could tell you stories that would amaze you, and some you probably wouldn't believe. I'm married to a wonderful, marvelous, and generous man, Ray."

"And Marshal Brockman is married to a very generous lady, too."

"John and I simply want to share the blessings God has given to us with others who are not so fortunate."

Breanna had prayed before arriving at the Anderson house that the Lord would give her wisdom. If they weren't Christians, she wanted to be used of God to share His message with them. Even while Ray was reflecting on what Breanna had just said, she was praying in her heart for wisdom and Holy Spirit power to witness to him effectively, in love and compassion.

"I remember being told that this John Stranger was also a preacher," said Ray. "Is that so?"

Breanna nodded. "John has the souls of men utmost in his thinking, Ray. Wherever he goes, whether he's preaching in a pulpit or just talking to someone, he wants to be sure they know that Jesus Christ loves them and that He died on Calvary's cross to pay the price for their sins. Ray—"

When a loud moan came from the bedroom, Ray jumped to his feet. "Rose is waking up," he said.

"I'll put Donnie back in his bassinet," said Breanna.

When Breanna came into the bedroom, Ray was bending over his wife, holding her hand and saying, "Honey, our visiting nurse is here."

Rose was a small woman, barely in her twenties. She had a heart-shaped face and big blue eyes. Those eyes were a bit droopy as she looked at Breanna, who had moved up beside Ray.

"Hello, Rose," Breanna said, leaning down so Rose could focus on her face. "My name is Breanna Brockman, and I'm a certified medical nurse. I'm here to take care of you and your new little son."

It was evident that Rose was in pain, but she managed a smile and said, "I'm so glad you're here, Mrs. Brockman."

"You can call me Breanna."

Rose smiled again. "Thank you for coming, Breanna."

"Still lots of pain in your midsection?"

Rose nodded, then asked about Donnie.

"He's doing fine. I changed his diaper a little while ago, and I thought we were going to have to wake you so you could feed him, but he went back to sleep."

Rose licked her lips. "Could I have some water? The laudanum and the sedative Dr. Rawlins gave me make me thirsty."

"I'll get some," said Ray, and hurried from the room.

"Have you been able to feed the baby all right, even though you've been in such pain?" asked Breanna.

"Yes."

"Do you have pain anywhere else, other than the abdomen?"

"No."

"That's good. Now, Rose, I want you to understand that I'm at your beck and call, and I don't want you to ever hesitate to call me when you need me. I'm going to be in here most of the time anyway, but no matter what time it is, or where I might be in the house, please call me when I'm needed."

Rose smiled again. "Thank you, Breanna."

Ray rushed in with a pitcher. While he was pouring water into a tin cup, Breanna leaned down and took hold of Rose's shoulders. "Here, honey, let me raise you up just a bit so you can drink."

When Rose had sipped most of the water, Ray said, "I'll leave you ladies now. There's some work I need to do in the yard, since I'll be going back to work at the mine tomorrow." With that, he disappeared from the room.

"Rose," Breanna said, "I'd like to examine the area where the pain is centered, if you don't mind. Since you're my responsibility, I want to know exactly what I'm working with."

"Of course," said Rose, trust evident in her eyes.

Pulling the covers back, Breanna did a thorough examination, pressing gently as she probed the area and asked questions. Running her fingertips back to the lower left side of the abdominal area, she said, "So this spot right here is the seat of the pain?"

Gritting her teeth, Rose nodded. "Yes."

"By what I feel here," said Breanna, "and by your reaction when I press on the most tender spot...if it were on the right side, I'd say it was appendicitis."

"So that can't be it?"

"No. It's in the wrong place." Breanna grinned. "That is, unless you've got a misplaced appendix."

This made Rose smile again. "Probably isn't that, though, huh?"

"I very much doubt it," replied Breanna, bringing the covers back up. "Dr. Rawlins and I talked about your pain before we got here. He's quite sure the pain will ease a bit each day as your body begins to heal from the ordeal you experienced in giving birth to Donnie."

"He's worth it," she breathed. "I would go through it all again, even if the pain was ten times worse. I've never experienced such joy, Breanna, until Dr. Rawlins laid my newborn baby in my arms."

"The Lord Jesus said something about that, Rose. It's in the sixteenth chapter of John, verse 21. He said, 'A woman when she is in travail hath sorrow, because her hour is come: but as soon as she is delivered of the child, she remembereth no more the anguish, for joy that a man is born into the world.'"

"I...I didn't know that was in the Bible."

Suddenly the baby's cry was heard from the sewing room.

"Well, it sounds like Donnie's hungry," said Breanna. "I'll be right back."

⋏

That evening, Rose was propped up with pillows as Breanna carried a tray of steaming food into the room and set it on the small table beside the bed.

"I told Ray to go ahead and eat," said Breanna, "so I could feed you."

Rose frowned. "When are you going to eat?"

"After I've fed you."

"It smells good, Breanna," said Rose, "and I'm sure you're an excellent cook, but I don't have much appetite."

"Well, appetite or not, honey, you've got to eat. You must keep up your strength so you can feed Donnie, and you must nourish your body so it will heal. You've also got to drink lots of water to help offset the laudanum I'm giving you. Otherwise you'll dehydrate."

"You sound like you mean business, Nurse Brockman," Rose said, a smile tugging at the corners of her mouth.

"I do mean business, lady," Breanna said, making a mock frown line her flawless forehead. "I want my patient to get well."

Rose gave in, and Breanna sat on the edge of the bed and fed her. After a few minutes, Rose said, "When Ray came in here this afternoon while you were tending to Donnie in the sewing room, he told me you're not going to accept pay for being here and taking care of Donnie and me."

Breanna met her gaze. "He told you right."

Tears formed in Rose's eyes, which were almost the same shade of blue as Breanna's. "How can we ever thank you?"

"My thanks will come when I see you rid of the pain and getting better and better every day."

"The world needs more people like you, Breanna," Rose said softly.

"You're so kind," responded Breanna. "Come on, now. You have to eat some more."

Ray was still in the kitchen finishing up his supper when Breanna entered with tray in hand.

"Did she eat?" he asked.

"About half of what I dished up for her."

"Her appetite's not so good."

"No, and I had to get a little tough with her before we got that much down."

"I'm sure she'll eat more when she gets to feeling better," said Ray.

"Of course. The main thing now is to get enough food down her so she can keep up her strength."

There was a knock on the front door.

"I'll get it, Breanna," said Ray. "You go ahead and eat."

While Breanna was dishing up her supper, she heard the familiar voice of the town physician. Seconds later, both men appeared at the kitchen door.

"Hello, Breanna," said Rawlins. "Ray said you just fed Rose and are about to have your supper. I'll go check on her, then come and talk to you. Ray tells me Donnie's doing okay."

"Yes. He's a fine husky boy."

"See you in a few minutes."

"All right, Doctor."

Breanna ate hurriedly but was still not quite finished when Dr. Rawlins returned to the kitchen with Ray on his heels.

"There was no need for me to stay long, Breanna," said the doctor. "Rose is doing quite well, considering what she's been through. You've done a good job giving her just enough laudanum to take the sharp edge off the pain. She tells me you made her eat more than she wanted."

"That I did."

"Good. She also said you've been pouring water down her. And that's good. So, I'll get out of here and let you finish your supper. I'll check on her again about this time tomorrow evening."

The next morning, after Ray had gone to work and Breanna had mother and baby sleeping, she decided to tidy up the house a bit. Ray had said he'd cleaned the house yesterday morning. While following his "cleaning," Breanna had to chuckle, thinking that men just didn't have the knack for keeping a house clean like it should be.

That evening, Dr. Rawlins came by as expected to check on his patient. Rose was still experiencing pain in her left side, but it seemed to be lessening.

Midmorning the next day, Rose awoke to see her nurse sitting in a straight-backed chair, reading her Bible.

When Breanna heard Rose stir, she looked up and smiled. "There's my patient, back from dreamland. What can I get you?"

"I'm a little thirsty."

Breanna laid her Bible on the bed beside Rose and poured her a cup of water from the pitcher on the nightstand.

When Rose had drained the cup, she flicked a glance at the Bible and said, "I've noticed you reading your Bible before. You seem to read it so eagerly."

"I can't get enough of God's Word, Rose. This is the most fascinating and marvelous Book in the world."

Breanna had been praying silently only moments before that God would give her just the right opening to witness to Rose about the Lord Jesus.

"I've read it some," said Rose. "We have a Bible somewhere in the house. It might be in a trunk on the back porch." She winced, and her hand went to her lower left side.

"Hurting?"

"Yes."

"I'll give you some more laudanum. It's been nearly three hours."

After the laudanum had been administered, Breanna sat down beside the bed again. Knowing that within twenty minutes or so Rose would be getting drowsy from the fresh dose of laudanum, she said, "You say you've read the Bible some?"

"Mm-hmm."

"What would you say its main theme is?"

Rose thought on the question. "Well, I'd say it's how to live like God wants us to live. The example and teachings of Jesus are the most important of all that's written in the Bible."

"I agree that the Bible shows us how God wants us to live, honey," said Breanna, "but how we live doesn't affect where we spend eternity."

Rose's face twisted in astonishment. "It doesn't?"

"No. In the Bible we have examples of 'good' people who went to hell, and 'bad' people who went to heaven because they admitted they were bad and got saved God's way."

"Really?"

"Mm-hmm. Thieves are considered to be bad people, aren't they?"

"Of course."

"Do you remember the two thieves who were crucified with Jesus?"

"Yes."

"One of them admitted he was a guilty sinner and cast himself on the mercy of Jesus, and the Lord told him they would be together that very day in paradise. The thief claimed no merit on which to go to heaven, for he had none. He's up there with Jesus right now because he repented of his sin and trusted Jesus alone to save him."

Rose blinked but said nothing.

"Now, honey, you know that the Pharisees were considered by the people of Israel to be 'good' men, right?"

"Yes."

"And do you understand that the publicans were looked down on as 'bad' people?"

"I remember something about that."

"Luke chapter 18 tells about two men who went to the temple to pray…a Pharisee and a publican. The Pharisee self-righteously thanked God that he was not a sinner like other men…like the publican who prayed close by. Now, in his own eyes, and in the eyes of the populace, this Pharisee was a good man and needed not to be justified before God because he was so good.

"The Bible, however, says that all men are sinners before a holy God. It was Jesus who told this story. He went on to tell that the publican very humbly smote his breast and said, 'God be merciful to me, a sinner.' Jesus said it was the publican who left the temple justified before God. Rose, unless we are justified before God, we have to go to hell when we die. We cannot go to heaven without being justified. Let me read you something…"

Breanna noted Rose's eyes. Soon she would be under the influence of the laudanum. Flipping to the book of Romans, she said, "Listen to this. God is talking here to people who have been justified, and He tells us how it happened. Romans 5:8 and 9 says,

'But God commendeth his love toward us, in that while we were yet sinners, Christ died for us. Much more then, being now justified by his blood, we shall be saved from wrath through him.'

"Do you understand? As guilty sinners before God, we can only be saved from the wrath of God through the Lord Jesus Christ, who died for us on the cross, and He justifies us by His blood when we repent of our sin and put our faith in Him and Him alone to save us. We shall be saved from wrath through Him, not our good works or religious deeds."

Breanna elaborated on this for several minutes, wanting to make sure her patient understood the purpose of Christ's blood-shedding death at Calvary.

Rose moved her head back and forth slowly. "I was raised in church, Breanna, but I never heard anything like this. Ray and I were brought up in the same church and have always believed that a person goes to heaven on the basis of how good they live."

"But in the eyes of God, we are not good. Right here in this same book of Romans, it says, 'There is none righteous, no, not one' and 'There is none that doeth good, no, not one.' This is why God's perfect, sinless Son went to the cross and bore our sins for us. He is the only One who can save us. Remember what I read to you a moment ago: 'We shall be saved from wrath through Him.' You must put your faith in Jesus alone to save you, like the thief on the cross did."

Rose blinked again. "I…I just never had this shown to me before, Breanna. It's all so new."

Breanna knew she must be wise and not push Rose too hard. "You're getting drowsy, honey," said the nurse. "I'll be quiet now. You rest and think on what I've shown you. We'll talk some more later."

The laudanum was easing Rose's pain. She smiled and nodded, snuggling her head down into the pillow.

10

IT WAS NEAR noon the next day when Breanna stood over her patient, watching her sleep. A half hour before, Breanna had given Rose a stronger dose of laudanum than usual. The pain was somewhat worse, and the doctor had left it up to her discretion as to when and how much to give her. Cautious but concerned, Breanna had carefully increased the dosage.

As she turned and headed for the bedroom door, she whispered, "Lord, the additional Scripture I gave her this morning...may it do its work in her heart. Help me to be able to talk to Ray, too. Both of them need You, Lord."

Breanna had wanted to feed Rose some lunch before giving her the fresh dose of laudanum, but Rose was hurting too much to eat.

She entered the kitchen to prepare herself a sandwich, but as she started to open the bread box, there was a rapid knock on the front door. She hurried to answer the knock.

When Breanna opened the door, Isabel Mullins was standing there. "Breanna! Dr. Rawlins sent me to get you!" she gasped. "He needs you at his office immediately!"

Breanna saw another woman, in her midfifties, move up to the porch from the side of the house and mount the steps.

"What is it, Isabel?" Breanna asked.

"There was a brawl at the Iron Horse Saloon about half an hour ago. Two men have been cut up fierce with knives. Doctor needs your help to keep them from dying!"

Breanna glanced at the woman who now stood beside Isabel.

"I went next door before coming here," said Isabel. "This is Effie Downing. She knows the Andersons well. She agreed to come over and stay with Rose and the baby."

"That's sweet of you, Effie. I'm Breanna Brockman."

"Nice to meet you, ma'am. How's Rose doing?"

"She's had a slight setback today. Some increase of the pain in her left side. She's asleep right now. I gave her a dose of laudanum a little while ago. The baby's asleep right now, too, with a full tummy."

"All right," Effie said, nodding.

"I have no idea how long I'll be gone, Effie, but if Rose wakes up so she can feed the baby, please see that it's done."

"I will."

"And if Rose's pain should get seriously worse when the laudanum wears off, please send someone to the doctor's office to let me know. I don't want Rose suffering needlessly when there is a way to ease her pain."

"There are other neighbors close by who will help me get the message to you if it becomes necessary," said the small gray-haired woman. "You go now and answer the doctor's call."

To Isabel, Breanna said, "Do you think I'll need my medical bag?"

"I doubt it. Doctor has plenty of supplies and instruments."

"All right. Let's go."

They had started across the yard when suddenly Breanna stopped, pivoted, and said, "Effie?"

"Yes, ma'am?"

"When Rose wakes up, make her drink two cups of water. If I'm gone quite a while, put a cup down her every hour."

A few minutes later, the two women reached the doctor's office. Isabel rushed ahead of Breanna and opened the door to the examining room at the rear. "Dr. Rawlins, here's Breanna."

Breanna's gaze fell on two men who lay on separate examining tables. She could see why Rawlins had called for her. The half-drunk men had both been cut up seriously, but the doctor could only work on one bleeding man at a time.

It was almost four-thirty when Effie Downing and Rose Anderson heard the front door of the house open and close. Seconds later, a weary-looking Breanna Brockman entered the bedroom, ran her gaze from Effie to Rose, and said, "Honey, you look like you're hurting pretty bad."

"She is," said Effie. "I didn't think it was bad enough to send someone after you, but she's hurting quite a bit."

"I'm so sorry, Rose," said Breanna. "How long has it been since you fed Donnie?"

"About twenty minutes. Effie put a dry diaper on him, so he's okay for a while."

"I'll give you some more laudanum right now," Breanna said, moving to the small table that held the laudanum and the sedative powders.

While Rose was downing the medicine, Effie said, "So how did it go with the men who had been cut up in the brawl, Breanna?"

"We were able to get them stitched up before they bled to death. I'll save anybody's life I can, and try to alleviate as much suffering as possible, but I have a hard time feeling sorry for men who get themselves cut up in a drunken brawl at a saloon."

"My sentiments exactly," said Effie. "This world would be a lot better off without saloons and the vile stuff they sell."

"You're right about that," agreed Breanna.

"Well, ladies," said Effie, "if I'm not needed anymore, I'll head on over to my house."

"Thanks for coming, Effie."

"You're welcome, and if you should need me anytime, just holler."

"Thank you."

"And I thank you, Effie," said Rose. "You're a true friend."

"Just want to help if I can," said the gray-haired woman; then she was gone.

Breanna pulled the covers down. "Rose, I want to examine you. I'll do my best not to cause you any additional pain, but I just want to see if I can feel something in there I didn't find before."

Rose nodded, a look of worry on her face.

After several minutes of careful examination, Breanna pulled the covers back up and said, "Nothing's different. I don't like this bit of a setback, but it's not too much out of the ordinary for a woman who has had the problems you did in bringing Donnie into the world. This is your first child, too. You probably won't have this problem with your next one."

"I'd go through it to bring another child into this family," said Rose, "but if I could choose, I'd bypass this type of aftermath."

"Can't blame you for that," Breanna said, patting her shoulder.

They heard the back door close and Ray's voice, calling that he was home. He was disturbed to learn that Rose's pain had grown worse. To encourage him, Breanna explained that this kind of thing sometimes happened when a woman's insides had been torn up some in bringing a child into the world.

When Dr. Rawlins came by for his usual evening visit, he did some probing of the painful area himself. He felt sure Rose's problem would start getting better in a few more days, but if it didn't, he might have to do exploratory surgery. Because laudanum was tincture of opium, and therefore habit-forming, he couldn't keep her on it too much longer.

The scream seemed to come from a great distance as it pierced Breanna's sound sleep. Startled, she sat bolt upright in the bed, blinking at the dull light of the moon filtering through the curtains.

She pressed fingertips to her temples while her senses came to full consciousness; then another scream cut through the night.

Breanna's mind cleared, and she realized the screams had come from Rose Anderson in the next room. Ray had been sleeping on the couch in the parlor, and Breanna could hear his bare feet slapping the wood floor as he stumbled and groped his way toward the bedroom.

Breanna threw her legs over the side of the bed and grabbed her robe as a third scream echoed through the house.

What moonlight was coming through the tiny window was enough to find the partially open door and fling it wide. Ray was trying to calm Rose, who was mumbling incoherently. Little Donnie could be heard crying in the sewing room.

"Ray, I'm here," said Breanna. "What's wrong?"

While Ray held Rose in the near darkness, he said above her mumbling, "She's had a nightmare. Could you light the lantern on the dresser? There are matches in a small dish right next to it."

"Yes. Just a minute."

Rose's mumbles faded into a long, low wail. Then she sobbed, unaware that Ray was holding her.

Breanna found the matches and lit the lantern. Leaving it on the dresser, she moved to the opposite side of the bed from Ray and leaned close, saying above Rose's sobs, "It's Breanna, Rose. It's all right. Ray is right here with you. He's got his arms around you. Tell us what's wrong."

Rose looked into Ray's eyes, suddenly realizing that it was his strong arms around her. Gasping, she sucked in a ragged breath, flicked a glance at Breanna, and said, "Oh, Ray… Breanna…I had a horrible nightmare! I dreamed that a huge black beast had me cornered and was ripping its claws into my side, and— Oh! My side! Breanna, it hurts bad!"

"It's the pain in your side that brought on the nightmare, honey," said Breanna. "Let's get her flat on her back, Ray."

Ray eased his wife out of his arms and onto her back. The baby's shrill cries seemed to fill the house.

"Ray," said Breanna, "would you see to the baby so I can examine Rose's side?"

Without a word, Ray left the room.

"I'll try not to hurt you, Rose, but I've got to see if I can feel anything down here."

Breanna probed the area slowly, methodically. Rose winced each time Breanna's fingers pressed down. When the examination was over and Breanna was pulling the covers back in place, Rose said, "What do you think?"

Ray walked into the room, carrying Donnie. The baby's cries had been reduced to a mild fussing.

"Oh, my baby," Rose said, her mothering instinct coming to the fore. "He's hungry. Give him to me, and I'll feed him."

"But you're hurting bad," said Ray.

"He still has to eat."

"Can you stand the pain long enough to feed him?" asked Breanna. "If you think you can, I'll hold off giving you more laudanum until you're finished."

"I'll feed him first," said Rose.

As Ray laid the baby next to Rose, she said, "Ray, you get back to bed. Four-thirty comes awfully early, and you've got a hard day's work ahead of you."

Suddenly she jerked, doubled up, and let out a cry. Her hand went to her left side.

"That does it," Ray said. "I'm going after Dr. Rawlins right now."

"No, please," said Rose. "I don't want to bother him in the middle of the night. It's…it's easing off now. I'll feed Donnie, and Breanna can give me some more laudanum. If it isn't better by the time this next dose wears off in the morning, I'll let Breanna summon the doctor."

Ray bit his lip. "This worries me, honey. I want something done so you're not hurting like this. What do you think, Breanna?"

Breanna had a suspicion of what was wrong, but she would keep it to herself for now. "Let's do as Rose asks, Ray. You go on to bed and see if you can get some sleep. I'll stay with her while she feeds the baby, and administer the laudanum directly afterward."

Ray nodded reluctantly, then bent down and kissed Rose's forehead, told her he loved her, and left the room.

When Ray awakened at his normal time, he smelled breakfast cooking. Having slept in his clothes, he pulled his boots on and went to the kitchen.

"Good morning," said Breanna while stirring pancake batter at the stove.

"Breanna," he said in a chiding tone, "you haven't slept since I went back to bed, have you?"

"I'll be fine. Nurses have to learn to survive on little sleep sometimes. Goes with the job."

"How is Rose?"

"She's sleeping well right now. And so is Donnie."

"Maybe I should stay home so I can run for the doctor if you need him."

"There's no need for you to lose another day's pay. Effie told me to holler if I needed anything. I promise, if Rose has more pain like we saw last night, I'll summon Dr. Rawlins."

Ray thought a few seconds. "All right. Thank you, Breanna, for being so good to us. I'll eat my breakfast, and head for work."

Breanna was sitting beside the bed, reading her Bible, when Rose began to stir at nine o'clock that morning. The laudanum was wearing off, and she could tell that her patient was in agony.

Within another minute, Rose began twisting and turning in the bed, and soon she was crying out groggily while trying to focus on Breanna's face. "Breanna! Breanna!"

"I'm here, honey. It's bad, isn't it?"

"Yes! Oh, yes! It...really hurts!"

A chill rippled over Breanna's skin. If her suspicions were right, Rose was in trouble. "Look, honey, I'm going to get Dr. Rawlins here. This is getting serious."

"Wh-what do you think it is?"

"No time to explain it," said Breanna. "I'm going to get

Effie to stay with you while I run for Dr. Rawlins."

Rose gritted her teeth as a spasm of pain shot through her side. "What about Donnie? He's got to be fed."

"I took care of him two hours ago. I gave him some of the cow's milk Ray and I used for breakfast. It may give him a tummyache and maybe even diarrhea, but there was no way for you to feed him when you were deep under the influence of the laudanum. You hang on. I'll be right back with Effie."

Moments later, Breanna was back with Effie at her side. Leaning over her patient, who was moaning in misery, she said, "Effie's here now, Rose. I'll be back with Dr. Rawlins as soon as I can."

When Breanna was out the door, Effie sat down beside the bed and took hold of Rose's hand.

"Effie," said Rose, straining to speak, "did she tell you what she thinks is wrong?"

"No, she didn't. She was in too much of a hurry to get the doctor."

Holding her skirt ankle-high, Breanna ran as fast as she could toward Main Street. People watched her with curious eyes when she turned the corner onto Main and headed down the block, running in the dust of the street rather than on the boardwalk.

Isabel Mullins looked up from her desk startled when an out-of-breath Breanna burst through the door and gasped, "Isabel! I need Dr. Rawlins right now! Is he in the back?"

Isabel laid down the pencil in her hand and stood up. "No, he's not."

"Where is he? I've got to get him to the Anderson house, quick! I think Rose has an ovarian cyst. Her pain is almost unbearable. If it is a cyst, as you well know, it could burst any minute. The toxin it releases could kill her."

"Breanna, Doctor is at the Mizpeh Mine, ten miles west of here. They had a cave-in early this morning. All the other doctors in this part of the mountains have been called there, too. I just got word they are pulling men out of the mine one or two at a time. A few are dead, but those who are alive desperately need medical attention."

Breanna pressed fingertips to her temples. "Something's got to be done, Isabel. I can't let her die! It would take too long to ride to the mine and bring Dr. Rawlins back here, even if he could be spared at the cave-in site."

"I agree," said Isabel. "If she's got a cyst on her ovary, and it bursts…"

Breanna looked the woman in the eye. "Isabel, technically Rose is Dr. Rawlins's patient. But he's not available. If she has a cyst, I've got to do what's necessary."

The truth of it showed in Isabel's eyes.

"Tell me," said Breanna, "is Dr. Rawlins of the opinion that an ovariotomy is the only solution in a grave and dangerous situation like this, or is he of the Robert Liston persuasion?"

Isabel looked at her blankly, then said, "Oh, yes. Dr. Hooper spoke of him…he's the famous British physician who calls surgeons who do ovariotomies 'belly rippers.' He says the operation itself is more dangerous than the cyst on the ovary."

"That's what he says. I know that American surgeons are split down the middle on the subject. What was Dr. Hooper's opinion?"

"He believes Liston is wrong…that there is greater danger in not performing the surgery."

"Do you know what position Dr. Rawlins takes?"

"No, I don't. Drs. Hooper and Rawlins never discussed it in

my hearing, and Dr. Rawlins has never mentioned it. Probably because so far we've not had a patient with an ovarian cyst since Dr. Rawlins has been here."

"Well, I think you've got one now. And it's got to come out."

"And you will do the surgery." It was a statement, not a question.

"I have no choice. I hate to go against Dr. Rawlins's position if he's in agreement with Liston, but my brother-in-law, Dr. Matthew Carroll, believes ovariotomies are necessary to save lives, and I'm in agreement with him. I've assisted him and other surgeons with ovariotomies, and if I find that's Rose's problem, I'll have to perform the surgery myself. I've seen women die with ovarian cysts, and I can't let it happen to Rose." She took a deep breath and said, "Oh, I wish Dr. Rawlins were here."

"But he isn't, dear," said Isabel, "and Rose's life may be at stake. You can't wait for Doctor to return. He could be gone a day or two…maybe longer."

A look of resolve settled on Breanna's face as she said, "Isabel, in case it is a cyst, I'll need the necessary instruments and supplies to perform the surgery."

Five minutes later, Breanna dashed outside carrying scalpels, forceps, ether, and other equipment in a cloth sack. She prayed as she ran, asking the Lord to help her if indeed she had to perform the surgery.

Effie was standing over the bed, holding on to Rose's hands, when Breanna came into the room. Breanna knew by what she saw that the pain was greater than ever. Placing the cloth sack on a chair, she stepped up to the bed and said, "Rose, Dr. Rawlins is at the Mizpeh Mine. There's been a cave-in. He's been there since early this morning, and there's no way to know when he might return. I've got to become the doctor here. I'm going to do another examination, but this one will be internal."

Her face lined with pain, Rose said, "What do you think it is?"

"I think you have an ovarian cyst."

Effie's jaw slacked. "If she does, who's going to do the surgery?"

Breanna's features were stony. "First thing is to make the examination."

Rose and Effie exchanged fearful glances.

When Breanna had finished the examination, she didn't have to say a word. Both women knew by the look on her face that Rose needed surgery.

"Are…are you going to do the surgery?" asked Rose, her features tight.

Effie's eyes were transfixed on Breanna.

Leaning close, Breanna said, "Only if you give me permission. Do you understand that at any minute the cyst could burst and send its poison through your body? It's a big cyst, Rose. If it bursts, your chances of living are very slim."

Rose swallowed hard. "There's no other way but surgery?"

"In my opinion, there is far greater danger to let that cyst stay where it is."

Rose grimaced with pain and then nodded. Fear captured her eyes.

"I have much experience in assisting surgeons with ovariotomies, Rose. But I am not a surgeon. If you tell me to proceed, I will do my very best to remove the cyst correctly. If you say to wait until we can get Dr. Rawlins here, I will abide by your wish. But I must warn you, it is my opinion the cyst will burst very soon."

There was a tremor in Rose's voice as she asked, "H-how will the surgery be done?"

"By abdominal section. I will have to remove the entire ovary and the fallopian tube, in case the cyst is malignant."

"But I could die during the surgery, couldn't I?"

"I won't lie to you, honey. Yes, you could. But you could also die a very painful death if the cyst bursts inside you."

For a moment the entire room was silent as a tomb.

Effie and Breanna watched various emotions glide over Rose Anderson's face. Rose tried to swallow the fear that locked in her throat.

"Breanna...

"Yes?"

"I...I want you to do the surgery, but—"

"But what, honey?"

"Before you begin, I want to be saved. I've been thinking over all the things you told me and showed me from the Bible about salvation. I'm a lost sinner, Breanna, and I'm afraid to die without Jesus."

Confusion showed on Effie's face.

"Then let's take care of it right now," Breanna said.

She stepped to the chair where she had left her Bible and moved back to the bed.

A spasm of pain lanced through Rose. She gasped, then relaxed. "Go ahead, Breanna."

Quickly, Breanna went over the gospel, making sure Rose understood that Christ's death, burial, and resurrection were necessary in the eyes of God the Father to provide the one and only way for sinners to be saved.

When Rose acknowledged that she believed it, Breanna said, "All right, listen to these words from John chapter 1. Of Jesus, it says, 'He came unto his own, and his own received him not. But as many as received him, to them gave he power to become the sons of God, even to them that believe on his name.' You do believe that Jesus is the only way of salvation, don't you?"

"Oh, yes."

"You've already admitted that you are lost and need to be saved."

"Yes."

"Then the only thing you have to do to be saved, Rose, is to call on Jesus, invite Him into your heart, ask Him to forgive your sins, and save your soul. Romans 10:13 says, 'For whosoever shall call upon the name of the Lord shall be saved.'"

"Will you help me, Breanna?"

"Of course."

Effie Downing watched in silence as Breanna led Rose to Jesus.

Rose had tears on her cheeks. "All right, Breanna, I'm ready now," she said. "Please proceed with the surgery."

11

Rose Anderson suffered spasms of pain as she watched Breanna preparing for surgery. A small table was used to hold the surgical instruments, the bottle of ether, and cloths.

While Breanna dipped the surgical instruments in wood alcohol to sterilize them, she said to her assistant, "Now, Effie, you will notice I am placing four scalpels in order, each one with a blade a little different in shape."

Effie Downing nodded, paying strict attention.

"When I'm ready to begin, I will simply say, 'scalpel.' You will place the first one in my right hand. During the course of the surgery, I will lay that one aside, say 'scalpel,' and you will place the second one in my hand. In between scalpels one and two, I will ask you for these forceps, which I will use to clamp the bleeding ends of the blood vessels. When I have the forceps in place, I will ask for scalpel number two. A little later, I will ask for number three. Number four is a spare, and I probably won't need it. However, if I ask for a scalpel after you've given me number three, this is the one I want. Understand?"

"I believe so."

"When I ask for a cloth, you hand me one of these off this stack."

"All right."

Pointing to the ether bottle, Breanna said, "I will administer the ether to put Rose under, but after that it will be up to you to do it. You need to watch me closely when I put her under, so when I say to give her more ether, follow the same procedure. My hands are going to be very busy, but I will talk you through it as we go. If there's something you don't understand as we go along, please ask. All right?"

"Yes," said Effie, looking nervous.

"Any questions before we begin?"

"I don't think so. You've made it clear enough. I'm just glad you are doing the surgery."

"Well, I wish it were Dr. Rawlins, but that isn't possible, so it'll have to be me."

Rose jerked and moaned as another dagger of pain went through her left side.

"We're about ready, honey," Breanna told her. "Do you have any questions?"

"No, but I want to thank you for being willing to take on this responsibility."

"I must. Since we have no surgeon here, it's my job."

"And I want to thank you for showing me how to be saved, and for leading me to the Lord."

"That was my pleasure, Rose."

"If I don't make it through the surgery, I know I'm going to heaven to be with Jesus."

From the corner of her eye, Breanna saw Effie blink and wet her lips with her tongue. It was obvious that Effie was a bit mystified about Rose's becoming a born-again child of God.

Though Rose was in much pain, she had a peaceful look about her. "Breanna?" she said.

"Yes?"

"If...if I shouldn't make it, please tell Ray I love him, and that I want him to be saved so he can meet me one day in heaven. And…and tell him to take good care of Donnie. Would both of you make sure Ray knows how to feed Donnie properly?"

Breanna laid a hand on Rose's shoulder. "Honey, listen to me. You are going to make it. The Lord is going to give me wisdom, and He's going to guide my hands. Let me quickly tell you about a very special passage of Scripture."

Rose listened as Breanna briefly told her the story of Zerubbabel and the rebuilding of God's temple in Jerusalem after it had been destroyed. She pointed out that with all the opposition of God's enemies it would have been virtually impossible for Zerubbabel and his workers to accomplish the dubious task.

She then quoted Zechariah 4:6, pointing out that God had told Zerubbabel through the prophet Zechariah that there would indeed be victory in the matter, and that the wall would be rebuilt. The victory, however, would not come by the might or power of mortal hands, but by the Spirit of God.

"And that's the way it's going to be here, Rose," said Breanna. "These mortal hands will wield the scalpels, but you're going to come through this surgery, not by the might or power of Breanna Brockman, but by the Holy Spirit of God."

Rose's pale lips curved in a smile. "This is all so new to me, Breanna, but I believe it."

Breanna took a few seconds to pray aloud, holding Rose's hand.

"Rose," Breanna said in a soft, level tone as she picked up the ether bottle and a folded cloth, "you just relax as best you can. You can help if you'll take deep breaths."

When Rose was under the ether, Breanna said, "All right, Effie. Here we go."

While her heart pounded her ribs, Breanna cleansed the abdominal area, called for scalpel number one, and carefully made the incision. She used the forceps to clamp the bleeding ends of open blood vessels and went after the ovary with the cyst. When it was successfully removed, she also took out the fallopian tube.

Two hours had passed when the nurse-turned-surgeon made the final stitches in the incision. From the sewing room, they heard the baby's cry.

Without looking up, Breanna said, "Effie, will you see to Donnie, please?"

"Of course. I'm sure he's hungry and no doubt needs a changing. I'll take him over to my house and give him some more cow's milk."

"Thank you," said Breanna. "I can take better care of Rose if I don't have the baby to look after. I'll clean up here once I'm finished with the stitches."

"Why don't I take some diapers with me and keep Donnie at my house till I see Ray come home this evening," Effie told her. "Then he won't disturb Rose when he cries."

"That will be a great help, Effie. Thank you."

Breanna could hear Effie talking to the crying baby while she changed his diaper then took him out the door. The loud wails faded and soon were gone.

Moments later, Breanna knotted the final stitch in the incision. Rose was deeply under the ether but breathing steadily. "Thank You, Lord," Breanna sighed. "Thank You."

Breanna cleaned up after the surgery and in an hour had everything back to normal. She sat down beside the bed and watched Rose, who was still resting under the ether.

The sound of the front door opening met her ears, followed by light footsteps. Effie appeared at the bedroom door, holding a sleeping Donnie Anderson, and whispered, "She still under?"

Breanna rose from the chair. "Yes, she'll probably come around in another hour or so."

"Good. I...I need to talk to you, Breanna. Could we talk right now?"

"Of course."

"I'll put Donnie in the sewing room and be right back."

The sun was lowering in the western sky as Ray Anderson turned off the street at a fast pace and headed down the alley toward his house. He was anxious to see how Rose was doing.

Bounding across the backyard, he moved onto the porch and into the kitchen. "Hello!" he called. "The miner is home!"

Having announced himself, he headed up the hall toward the main bedroom. As he reached the sewing room door, he paused and looked in to see if his little son was in his bassinet. Finding it empty, he moved on to the bedroom and stopped at the open door.

Breanna was sitting beside a pale-looking Rose. Both women looked at him and smiled.

"Where's Donnie?" Ray asked, looking around.

"He's next door," said Breanna, rising from the chair. "Effie is taking care of him."

"Oh? How come?" He moved to the bed and bent down to kiss Rose's forehead.

Breanna paused for a moment, then said, "We had an emergency today. Effie was here to help. When it was over, Effie volunteered to take Donnie to her house. She'll bring him home soon."

Lines formed on Ray's brow. "What kind of an emergency?"

Breanna cleared her throat. "Rose had to have surgery."

"Surgery? What kind of surgery?"

"Her pain became much worse, Ray. I feared that she might have a cyst on her left ovary. When I saw her hurting more and more, I did an internal examination. I found that she did have a cyst...a large one. If the cyst were to burst, it could have killed her. There was no choice. The cyst had to come out, along with the fallopian tube."

Ray reached down and took Rose's hand, held it firmly, and looked at Breanna. "Did Dr. Rawlins say she'll be all right now?"

"Dr. Rawlins hasn't seen her."

"What? He hasn't seen her? Who did the surgery?"

"I did."

Ray gasped and let go of Rose's hand. "You performed the operation?" His features were ashen.

"Yes. And I can tell you that Rose will be all right now."

"But...but, Breanna, you're not a doctor! Why would you take it upon yourself to—"

"There was no doctor available, Ray," Breanna said defensively. "There was a mine cave-in at Mizpeh early this morning. Dr. Rawlins, and many other doctors from all over the region, were called up there to save lives."

Ray rubbed his jaw thoughtfully. "We heard about Mizpeh's cave-in over at our mine. But Breanna, you're not a surgeon. Couldn't it have waited till Dr. Rawlins got back?"

"No, it couldn't. Isabel told me that Dr. Rawlins might not be back for a day or two. Maybe even longer. When I did the examination, it felt to me like the cyst was dangerously close to bursting. If I was going to save Rose's life, I had to perform the operation immediately."

Ray's face pinched. "But what if—"

"I have assisted in many ovariectomies, Ray. True, I don't have a doctor's degree, and I'm not a licensed surgeon."

There was an angry edge to Ray's voice as he said, "Breanna, you had no right to take on a task for which you are not trained and licensed. You—"

"Ray!" cut in Rose, breathing hard. "This dear lady saved my life! Tell him about the cyst, Breanna."

Sky blue eyes met Ray's hard gaze. "Ray, when I made the incision and got to the cyst, it was already starting to come apart. If I hadn't done the surgery, Rose would probably be dead by now."

As the words sank in, Ray's countenance changed. Tears filled his eyes. "Breanna, I'm…I'm sorry. Please forgive me. It's just that—"

"I know," said Breanna. "You love Rose, and you don't want anything bad to happen to her. I can understand how you felt, hearing that I had taken it upon myself to perform the operation. But what would you have thought of me if I hadn't tried…if I'd just stood by and let her die?"

"I was wrong to talk to you like that, Breanna," Ray said, sniffing and wiping tears. "Thank you. Thank you for sticking your neck out to save my sweet Rose's life."

"Ray…" Rose said weakly. "You need to know that Breanna explained the danger I was in if the surgery wasn't done, and she explained the danger I faced if she did the surgery. She left the decision up to me. I'm the one who said to go ahead. I'm glad I made the right decision. I'm still alive, and I'm here with you and Donnie. I know I'll get well soon, and we can go on with our lives."

The rugged coal miner found fresh tears in his eyes. Wiping them away, he looked at Breanna. "Forgive me, Breanna. I was out of line."

Breanna smiled. "You're forgiven, Ray. Let's just be thankful to the Lord that Rose is alive."

"Yes. Yes, I am thankful." As he spoke, Ray dropped to his knees beside the bed and took Rose's hand again. "Sweetheart, I'm so thankful I didn't come home to be told you had died."

There was a moment of silence as Rose and Ray looked deep into each other's eyes. Then Rose said, "Honey, my life was saved today, and my soul was, too."

Giving her a quizzical look, he said, "I don't know what you mean."

Though Rose was weak and weary from her ordeal, she told her husband that Breanna had been talking to her for the last couple of days about opening her heart to Jesus and being saved, and that just before the surgery, she told Breanna she wanted to take care of it.

She explained that she had become a child of God by receiving Jesus Christ into her heart, asking Him to save her soul and forgive her sins.

"I want you to let Breanna show it to you from the Bible like she did me. No one has ever shown it to me before. I wasn't aware of how to be saved, nor was I aware that a person can actually know he or she is going to heaven."

Ray glanced at Breanna, who was once again seated on the other side of the bed. "Breanna, please understand that I don't mean to offend you," he said, "but the religion I was raised in is good enough for me."

"But our religion gave no assurance of heaven, Ray," said Rose. "I had no peace that I would go to heaven if I died while Breanna was performing the surgery. But when I did what the Bible says and received Jesus into my heart, I had peace that I'd never known existed. This is not religion, Ray. This is salvation."

Ray thought on his wife's words for a moment. "What I have is good enough, Rose. I can live with it."

"But can you die with it?" interjected Breanna.

"What do you mean?"

"If you had died in a mine cave-in today, as some men did at Mizpeh, would you be in heaven right now, Ray? Or would you be in hell?"

"Well, I hope I'd be in heaven."

"You hope?"

"Yes, ma'am."

"But you don't know it."

"No offense, Breanna, but no one can know it."

Breanna opened her mouth to speak but was interrupted by a feminine voice coming from the parlor. "Hello! Donnie and I are back!"

Ray left Rose's side to take his little son from Effie's arms. The baby looked bright-eyed and happy.

"I understand you assisted Breanna with the surgery," Ray said. "I want to thank you. And thank you for taking care of Donnie."

"My pleasure," Effie said warmly.

"Effie," said Rose, "why don't you tell Ray what happened to you today while I was still under the ether after surgery?"

Effie gladly told Ray that as she stood by the bed that morning when Breanna led Rose to the Lord, her own heart had been convicted that she was lost and needed to be saved. After taking Donnie to her house, she fought against the gospel in her heart, but only for a little while. When she couldn't take the burning conviction any longer, she came back and told Breanna she wanted to be saved.

"Now I know I'm going to heaven when I die, Ray, and I've never had such peace."

Ray rubbed an ear nervously and said, "I'm happy for both you and Rose, Effie, if this receiving of Jesus has helped you, but I believe that a person has to die before he knows if he has lived good enough to go to heaven."

"Ray," said Breanna, her voice filled with compassion, "people don't go to heaven by how well they live. The Bible says salvation is by grace through faith in the Lord Jesus Christ, not of works, lest any man should boast. Grace is unmerited favor. And since salvation is by grace, people who have believed that and received Jesus into their hearts can know, while they are still alive on earth, that they're going to heaven when they die. First John 5:13 says, 'These things have I written unto you that believe on the name of the Son of God; that ye may know that ye have eternal life.'"

Ray's head bobbed. "I never knew these things were in the Bible. It gives me something to think about."

"Good," said Breanna, and let it drop, not wanting to push him too hard.

"Could I have some water, please?" came Rose's weak voice.

While Breanna was giving Rose a drink, Ray said, "Breanna, thank you for saving Rose's life. Thank you for doing the surgery."

"I'm glad I was here to do it, Ray. My only concern now is that Dr. Rawlins will not be angry at me for attempting it, though by every indication, the operation is a success."

There was a knock at the front door. "Hello!" came a familiar voice. "It's Isabel Mullins. I'm here to see about Rose! May I come in?"

It was midafternoon the next day when Dr. Rex Rawlins trotted his horse into Empire and drew up to the hitching rail in front of his office. Weary to the bone, he dismounted slowly and wrapped the reins around the rail, then removed his medical bag from where it was tied at the back of the saddle.

Upon entering his office, he found Isabel at her desk in conversation with a local rancher named Bob Chambers.

"Hello, Isabel," said Rawlins. "Bob."

"Welcome home, Doctor," said his assistant. "You look tired."

"Just a bit," he replied, giving her a slanted grin.

"How'd it turn out up there, Doc?" asked Chambers.

"Well, we got every man out. Six were dead before the rescue team could get to them. Three died after we got them out. But we were able to keep eleven from dying. They're back with their families now."

Chambers nodded. "I'm glad for the eleven."

"So you're waiting to see me, Bob?" Rawlins asked.

"No, sir. Bobby Jr. fell off the hay wagon this mornin'. Broke his arm. That pretty nurse you brought here to take care of Rose Anderson is with him in the back room—"

Rawlins looked at Isabel. "Did the bone need setting?"

"Yes. She's already got that done. She's putting the splint on now."

The doctor nodded. "I'll go see how it looks. Since Breanna's here, who's looking after Rose Anderson?"

"Effie Downing."

"So how's Rose doing?"

"She's all right, Doctor, but there's something I need to tell you."

"What's that?"

"Rose had a large cyst on her left ovary."

"A cyst?"

"Yes. It's gone now."

Rawlins blinked. "Who figured out that she had the cyst?"

"Breanna. The pain became unbearable. Breanna came to

get you about nine-thirty yesterday morning. Of course, you weren't here. She told me she thought Rose had a cyst and that if she did, it would have to come out immediately. So she took the necessary surgical equipment and ran back to the house."

"And?"

"She did an internal examination and found the cyst. It was a big one. She performed the surgery, Doctor, and removed it, along with the fallopian tube. The cyst was at the bursting point when she got in there."

"And Rose is doing all right?"

"According to Breanna she is. I saw her yesterday afternoon, and she looked pretty good for having been through surgery."

"Well, I'll see how Breanna's doing with Bobby, then we'll go see about Rose."

As Rawlins headed for the door of the examination room, Isabel said, "Doctor—"

He paused. "Yes?"

"Breanna is concerned about how you will react to her having done surgery on your patient."

A smile formed on his lips. "She saved Rose's life, didn't she?"

"That she did."

"Then what's to be concerned about?"

"When she came here and learned that you were at Mizpeh, she asked me where you stood on the Robert Liston issue. I couldn't tell her because you've never mentioned it."

"I believe Liston is wrong. What Breanna did is right."

Isabel heaved a sigh of relief. "Good. Go tell her those same words."

The door to the examination room opened, and Breanna came out with seven-year-old Bobby Chambers, whose right arm was in a splint.

"Oh!" said Breanna. "You're back, Doctor!"

166

"Yes, and I think I've been replaced."

"Pardon me?" Breanna's heart began thumping against her rib cage.

"You set Bobby's arm and splinted it."

"Well, Doctor, the boy was in a great deal of pain, and—"

"You did the right thing. Let's take a look at it."

Rawlins sat Bobby down, removed the splint, and examined the arm. While he was doing so, Breanna flicked a glance at Isabel, who smiled at her and nodded.

"Well, Bobby," said the doctor, replacing the splint, "Nurse Brockman did an excellent job on you. Perfect. Most nurses wouldn't have known how to set a broken arm."

The boy was in some pain, but he looked up at the doctor and said, "She's really nice…an' she only hurt me real bad once. That was when she put the bone back like it should be."

"That's good," said the doctor.

Bob Chambers asked what he owed, and Isabel told him eight dollars. The bill was paid, and as father and son prepared to leave, Bob set appreciative eyes on Breanna and said, "Thank you for coming to help Bobby when I knocked on the Andersons' door, ma'am."

"You're welcome," said Breanna.

"Bobby," said the father, "you need to thank Nurse Brockman for fixing your arm."

"He already did, Mr. Chambers," said Breanna. "I got a hug with his good arm in the back room. But I would take another one if he has a hug to spare."

Bobby hugged Breanna's neck again and thanked her. When she kissed his cheek, his face turned crimson.

When Bob and Bobby Chambers were gone, Rawlins turned to Breanna and said, "I understand you're replacing me as a surgeon, too."

Breanna flicked another glance at Isabel, who gave her another mysterious smile. Slowly she met the physician's gaze and said, "It really had to be done, Doctor. I can explain—"

"No need to explain," said Rawlins, laughing. "Isabel just told me all about it. You did the right thing; I don't care what Robert Liston says."

Breanna heaved a sigh of relief. "And you're not upset that I went ahead with the surgery, even though I'm not a doctor?"

"Of course not. Apparently you've assisted in ovariotomies before."

"Several."

"I thought so. Otherwise you wouldn't know what to look for when you saw the cyst. Come on. I want to take a look at your work."

"All right."

As Breanna preceded Rawlins to the door, she looked over her shoulder at Isabel and said, "Now I know what you were smiling about. You already knew I wasn't in trouble."

Isabel released a satisfied smile.

Rex Rawlins drew the covers over Rose Anderson and said, "Breanna, you did an excellent job. The incision was done perfectly, and you've sewn it up like an expert surgeon." He added with a smile, "You really should go back to school and become a doctor."

"That's what I think, too, Dr. Rawlins," said Rose. "If it weren't for her, I would probably be dead."

"You're right about that," agreed the doctor.

"Women doctors are few and far between," said Breanna. "Society will hardly accept them. I'll just stay a nurse."

"I know," said Rawlins, "but I believe that will change as

time passes. It will probably be the twentieth century that sees it, but I think it'll come. He paused and added, "Breanna, I want to commend you for having the courage and the good sense to do the surgery."

"Guess what else happened, Doctor," said Rose, her eyes showing some sparkle.

"What's that?"

"I'm a born-again Christian now."

"Really?"

"Yes! I remember you talking about how wonderful it is to know Jesus, but I paid little attention. Breanna worked on me and gave me Scripture about salvation. She led me to the Lord just before she did the surgery."

"Marvelous, Rose. I'm so happy to hear that. What does Ray think about it?"

"He's a little confused right now but said he's glad for me. Breanna gave him some things to think about, and I'm sure he's doing that."

Rawlins looked at Breanna. "You're quite a go-getter, lady. It's a joy to see someone so eager to win people to the Lord."

Breanna smiled broadly. "Jesus went to the cross for me, Doctor. It's my duty and joy to tell others about Him."

"We need more Christians like you," he said. "New subject, Breanna"

"Yes, sir?"

"Can you stay a few more days to care for Rose until she's past the danger of any unforeseen problems arising due to surgery?"

"I'll be glad to, Doctor."

"Good!" exclaimed Rose.

12

DEPUTY U.S. MARSHAL Palmer Danfield crouched in a thick stand of mesquite scrub as twilight stole across the Texas panhandle. The three outlaws he had been tracking for nearly a week were feeling safe now. Two hundred yards from where Danfield lurked in the brush, they were lighting a campfire on the south bank of the Canadian River, which they wouldn't do unless they figured they hadn't been followed. A campfire could be seen for miles in this country.

Danfield would let them begin their meal and surprise them when they were totally off guard.

Clete Forbes, Alton Hamm, and Rufe Blocker had robbed banks in four towns of the northwest corner of the panhandle, leaving five people dead—three bank customers, a bank officer, and a town marshal. By the time Danfield had been assigned by U.S. Marshal George Frame of the Amarillo office to go after them, they were headed east. He figured they were aiming to cross the border into Indian Territory. But Deputy U.S. Marshal Palmer Danfield had a change of plans for them.

Soon the vault of blue-black sky lightened to twinkling stars, and then night fell over the serene, silent, luminous prairie.

Danfield left his horse tied to a mesquite bush and moved

in on foot. When he was within forty yards of the outlaws, he could hear their chatter and laughter as they prepared supper.

A melancholy, misshapen moon rose to make the starlit night one of deep shadows. As he knelt behind a low, flat rock formation, the face of his wife, Laura, haunted Palmer Danfield. She had died of fever three months earlier. They were married barely more than a year when she was taken from him. Their first child was in her womb when she died, and though he never saw his son or daughter, he felt a double loss.

Danfield allowed his quarry another twenty minutes, which found the outlaws still laughing and chatting as they devoured their supper. It was time to arrest them and head back to Amarillo.

The Texas sun was midway in the morning sky as U.S. Marshal George Frame sat at his desk in Amarillo, poring over a report that had been handed to him the day before by a pair of his deputies. The men had tracked down a gang of horse thieves who had stolen horses from the U.S. Army.

Suddenly Frame became aware of male voices in the outer office. Two of them belonged to the deputies whose report he held in his hand. Another was the voice of the deputy who worked the desk. The fourth voice was quite familiar, and one he had been anticipating.

Frame moved across his office with a spring in his step, opened the door, and saw the muscular form of Deputy Palmer Danfield. "Palmer! Glad to see you back! How'd it go?"

Danfield grinned. "Come over here and take a look, boss."

Frame joined the others, who were looking through the large window onto the street where three lifeless forms were draped over the backs of their horses.

Frame knew he was looking at the bodies of Clete Forbes, Alton Hamm, and Rufe Blocker. He also knew that Danfield would have brought them in alive if he could. "Gave you a fight, eh?"

"Yes, sir."

"Good work, Palmer. I'm glad you're back. I have something very important to talk to you about. Feel up to it now, or would you like to go home and rest for a while?"

"I'm fine. Let's talk."

Frame ordered the desk deputy to see that the bodies were taken to the undertaker, and the outlaws' horses were sold to the hostler. The money from the sale would go to the undertaker for his services.

When Frame and Danfield were seated in the inner office, Frame took an envelope from a desk drawer and said, "Palmer, I have an official letter here from Chester B. McCarty. He's assigning you to the Denver office."

Danfield's eyebrows arched. "Denver, eh? Well, that sounds good. I've long wanted to meet the Stranger."

"You know I hate to lose you," said Frame, "but as we've already discussed, it's been hard for you to maintain your home here in Amarillo, where everything reminds you of Laura."

"Yes, sir."

"I received a wire from McCarty the very day you rode out after those three killers. He explained in the wire that the Denver office has had several casualties among their deputies, and that Chief Brockman needed at least one good man in a hurry. I knew you were wanting to get away from Amarillo, so I wired him back and gave him your name, along with your fine record and outstanding qualifications. So...you're Denver-bound."

"All right, sir. It's fine with me."

"Good. I'll wire McCarty today, let him know you're back, and we'll get the machinery in motion."

Chief U.S. Marshal John Brockman arrived at the federal building a few minutes before eight o'clock on Monday morning, August 5. He greeted Deputy Billy Martin and entered his private office. He had just sat down at his desk when Billy knocked and called out, "Chief, the Western Union messenger is out here."

"Send him in, Billy!"

Denver's Western Union office had three messengers, and John knew them all. This time it was young Tommy Watson who brought the message.

"Good morning, Chief," said Watson, approaching the desk. "I have two telegrams for you. One is from Mrs. Brockman."

"Oh! All right."

Tommy laid both yellow envelopes on the desk and placed a sheet of paper before Brockman for his signature. He signed the paper, thanked Tommy, and flipped him a ten-dollar gold piece.

Tommy's eyes widened at sight of the gold. "Thank you, sir!"

When the door shut, John tore open the envelope from Breanna and read the telegram. Breanna gave a brief explanation of Rose Anderson's condition, explaining that Dr. Rawlins had asked her to stay a few more days, and that she had agreed to do so. The "few more days" would probably be a little more than a week. She loved her husband with all of her heart and would wire him when she was ready to come home.

Laying Breanna's telegram aside and feeling a pang of loneliness for her, John opened the second envelope. It was from Chet McCarty.

✧

Deputy Billy Martin was arranging folders in a metal file behind his desk when he looked up to see Harold Sheetz enter the office with a stack of papers in his hand.

"Hello, Billy," said Sheetz, smiling broadly. "My boss asked me to deliver these to your boss."

At that instant, the door of the inner office opened, and John Brockman appeared. Brockman laid friendly eyes on Sheetz and said, "Good morning, Harold. More papers from your office?"

"Yes, sir."

"I'll take them, Harold," said Billy.

As Martin took the papers, Sheetz said, "Any new recruits coming your way, Chief? I know you're awfully short on deputies."

"You knew Chet McCarty was here, didn't you, Harold?"

"Yes, sir. And Billy told me he was going to send you some replacements for the men you'd lost. That's why I was asking. I was wondering if any were on their way yet."

John looked around to make sure no one was near the open hallway door, then said, "I'll let you in on a little secret, Harold."

Billy Martin's ears perked up.

"What's that, sir?" asked Sheetz.

"I just received a telegram from Mr. McCarty. He's sending me a crack deputy named Palmer Danfield from the U.S. marshal's office in Amarillo, Texas."

"Great!" exclaimed Billy. "At last! Results!"

John smiled at his youthful deputy. "McCarty's telegram said he's working on sending more deputies. Now, this Palmer Danfield…I've heard about him. He's got a reputation for being fast and accurate with his gun. He's tough as nails, and he's very good at tracking and catching outlaws."

"Have you ever seen him before, Chief?" Billy asked.

"No. But I'm sure looking forward to meeting him and having him on my staff." John paused, then said, "In fact, I'm already making plans for him. He's got some loose ends to tie up there in Amarillo, which will take a few days. McCarty said Danfield is scheduled to leave Amarillo on the 8:00 A.M. train for Denver a week from today. He'll be in here the next day at 1:30 in the afternoon."

"So what are your plans for him, Chief?" asked Billy.

"Well, once Danfield arrives, I'm going to take him with me and head for Duke Foster's hideout on Monarch Pass. I'll have Sol Duvall oversee the office while I'm gone."

Harold Sheetz's heart was pounding. He dared not show too much interest, but he casually asked, "Chief, wasn't it some of Duke Foster's men that you shot it out with at the hotel several days ago?"

"Sure was."

"He's got a pretty good-sized gang, doesn't he?"

"Mm-hmm."

"And you're going to his hideout with just one deputy?"

"It's hard to sneak up on a hideout with a band of men, Harold. The element of surprise can give a tremendous advantage. Danfield and I will have that advantage. We'll capture Foster and the rest of the gang and bring them in for trial. Every one of them is wanted for murder, as well as robbery, and without a doubt they'll hang."

Sheetz shrugged. "Who am I to tell you how to capture outlaws, Chief? Well, I've got to get back to the office. See you both later."

As he headed down the hall, Harold's heart beat like a triphammer. He couldn't wait to talk to Duke!

✸

Duke Foster, Dick Nye, and Pete Dawson were in the middle of a poker game when they heard footsteps on the back porch. Nye and Dawson shoved back their chairs and whipped out their guns, cocking the hammers.

"It's me!" called Harold.

He opened the door and found himself looking into the ominous black bores of three revolvers. Nye and Dawson were on their feet, and Foster sat at the table.

"Easy, boys!" Sheetz said, throwing up both hands.

The tense faces of the outlaws relaxed, and the guns were put away.

"We weren't expectin' you, Harold," said Duke. "What're you doin' home at this hour?"

"I just found out somethin' I thought you'd like to know, Duke. Heard it from Brockman's own mouth."

"I'm listenin'," said Foster.

Nye and Dawson eased onto their chairs.

"Brockman knows about your mountain hideout, and he knows it's on Monarch Pass."

Flame showed in the gang leader's dark eyes. "How'd he find that out?"

"I don't know, but he's planning on making a trip up there to capture you and your gang."

Nye and Dawson exchanged glances, frowning.

"You heard him say this?"

"Sure did."

Duke swore and banged the table with his fist. "Who could've told him about the hideout?"

"It had to have been Patch or Felton," Pete said.

"Wh-what? Why do you say that?"

"Simple, boss. There's no question Chick was killed instantly in the shoot-out at the hotel. He took Brockman's slug right through the heart. That means that either Jim or Layton lived long enough to tell Brockman the location of the hideout. Where else could he have gotten it?"

"Makes sense, boss," said Nye. "It had to have come from one of those two."

Foster swore again. His voice rang with anger as he said, "Whichever one it was, he was a dirty rat!" He turned to Sheetz. "When's Brockman makin' this trip to the hideout? I thought he was short on men."

"He is short on men, Duke. But he's got some new cracker-jack deputy coming next week from Amarillo to join his staff. Supposed to be one tough cookie. The two of them are going to sneak up on the hideout. The element of surprise, Brockman said."

"Boss, we've got to let those boys up at the hideout know about this, so they'll be ready for 'em," said Pete.

Duke gave Dawson a hand signal to be quiet.

Silence prevailed for a long moment.

Then Duke looked up at Sheetz. "Harold, you're resourceful. Find out if Brockman knows this new deputy."

"He doesn't."

"How do you know?"

"'Cause the deputy who works the desk asked him that when he was telling us about this new guy coming. Brockman has heard of him, but he's never seen him."

"Great!" Duke exclaimed. "This is the very thing I've been lookin' for! I've just come up with my foolproof plan to kill Brockman." He laughed. "Brockman will never get to the hideout…and neither will his deputy."

"Tell us, boss," said Nye.

Duke looked at Sheetz again. "Harold, you said this deputy's comin' from Amarillo next week, right?"

"Yes."

"Then we've got to intercept him before he gets here. You've got to find out how he's comin'. You know, stagecoach, horse-back, or train."

"He's coming on the train that leaves Amarillo at eight o'clock a week from today, and he'll be in here at 1:30 Tuesday afternoon. Brockman told me that."

Duke grinned. "Well, I'm glad he trusts you."

Sheetz put an innocent look on his face. "Why shouldn't he? I work for the U.S. government."

Foster, Nye, and Dawson laughed.

"So what about interceptin' this hotshot deputy, boss?" asked Nye. "Exactly what do you have in mind?"

"You, Dick."

"Me?"

"You're the meanest, most cold-blooded, most experienced killer who works for me, aren't you?"

Dick looked at Pete. "Well, boss, Pete's plenty mean."

"Yeah, but not as mean as you, nor as experienced at killin'."

Pete grinned. "Yeah, Dick. You're the worst bad guy I've ever known. It's best you do whatever Duke's got in mind."

"Here's the plan, Dick. You're gonna take a train to Amarillo so's you can be there a couple of days before—what's this hotshot deputy's name, Harold?"

"Palmer Danfield."

Duke nodded. "Okay. Dick, you're gonna get to Amarillo no later than Friday. You've never robbed or killed in Texas, so they won't have any wanted posters on you. When you buy your ticket for Amarillo, buy one at the same time to return to Denver on that 8:00 A.M. train on Monday, so you'll be on the same train as Danfield. Got it?"

"Yep."

"You can nose around and maybe get a glimpse of this Danfield, so you'll know what he looks like before Monday."

"I can handle that."

"Then on Monday, you make sure you board the same coach as him. Find a way to make friends with this guy. When night falls, you lure him onto one of the platforms between the coaches. When you return to your seat, this Palmer Danfield will be layin' dead down the tracks. His badge and identification papers will be in your pocket. Understand?"

Nye chuckled evilly. "I got the picture, boss."

"All right," said Foster. "Now, here's how we get rid of Brockman."

Foster explained that since Nye had not been seen in Denver, and since Brockman didn't know what Danfield looked like, Nye would get off the train in Denver, wearing Danfield's badge and gun belt and carrying his identification papers. When the two of them rode for the hideout in the mountains, Dick would pick the right spot and time and put a bullet in Brockman's back.

"I can do it, boss." Nye chuckled again. "With pleasure."

Duke sighed. "I'll have my revenge on Brockman for killin' Chick, and the law won't be comin' near my hideout."

Pete Dawson laughed. "Hey, boss, that's ingenious!"

Foster rubbed his hands together. "Yes! Yes! Yes! Harold, you'll get a bonus for bringin' me all this information. And Dick...you pull this off as planned, and when you get back here—under cover of darkness, of course—you're gonna get an extra fat bonus for your work!"

A gleam came to life in Dick's eyes. He loved money, and he loved to please his boss.

The ecstatic Duke Foster turned to Dawson. "And Pete, you're gonna get a bonus, too, just for bein' part of this gang!"

On Friday morning, August 9, Dick Nye stepped off the train in Amarillo and made his way through the depot to the men's room. He greeted a man who was coming out and was glad that no one else was in there at the time. He was wearing a brand-new pinstriped suit, string tie, moderate-cut Stetson, and shiny black boots. Except for his heavy mustache, he was clean-shaven.

Standing before the mirror, he winked at himself, adjusted the tie, and said, "Dick, ol' boy, if I didn't know better, I'd say you were a very wealthy and prosperous business man."

Pleased with himself for looking so authentic, he picked up his overnight bag and left the depot. He greeted people amiably as he strolled along the main thoroughfare of Amarillo. When he reached the Panhandle Hotel, he entered the lobby and approached the desk.

Moments later, Nye sat on the bed in his room and pulled a leather scabbard from his overnight bag. Sheathed in the leather was a long-bladed bowie knife. He pulled out the knife and turned it toward the sun's rays shining through the window, making the reflection dance on the walls. Then he ran his thumb lightly along the sharp edge. Grinning his malicious grin, he said in a chilling whisper, "This is for you, Deputy Palmer Danfield. Just for you!" Laughing fiendishly, he slipped the knife into its sheath and stuffed it back in the bag.

Moments later, Dick Nye emerged from his room on the second floor, leaving the overnight bag on the bed, and returned to the street. When he reached the nearest corner, he stopped and looked around. The town's business section was four blocks in length. *No sense in wasting time,* he thought as he spotted a middle-aged man coming his direction from across the street.

When the man drew near, Nye put on a warm smile and said, "Hello, sir. May I ask you a question?"

"Of course," replied the man, stopping courteously.

"I'm a visitor here, sir," said the killer outlaw. "I'm looking for the U.S. marshal's office."

"Oh, sure," said the gentleman, making a half turn and pointing behind him. "Across the street and a block down. You'll see the sign when you get past those cottonwood trees. It's between the Amarillo Bank and the Potter County sheriff's office. Can't miss it."

Nye thanked him and headed down the boardwalk, smiling at people and greeting them. He hoped the deputy would be in the office. If he could make himself known to Danfield now, then just happen to be in the same coach on the train, the lawman would be more off guard.

As he approached the Amarillo Bank, Nye smiled to himself. *Pretty smart,* he thought. *They put the bank next door to the U.S. marshal's office, which is next door to the sheriff's office.* He wondered if any bank robbers had ever had the courage to rob the Amarillo Bank. "Would be a challenge," he told himself aloud.

Nye entered the U.S. marshal's office and was greeted by a young deputy who stood behind a small counter.

"Hello," said Nye, faking a smile. "My name is Ambrose Benson. I'm from Denver, Colorado, and I'm visiting a cousin near Amarillo. Could you tell me if Deputy Palmer Danfield is in?"

"Yes, he is, sir. But at the moment he's in conference with Marshal George Frame, who's in charge of this office. They should be through shortly. Would you like to have a seat?"

"I'll do that." Nye went to a small row of straight-backed chairs that stood in the corner.

When twenty minutes had passed, the deputy spoke to Nye from behind the counter. "Mr. Benson, I'm sorry for this delay, sir. Apparently Deputy Danfield and Marshal Frame have more to talk about than I realized."

"It's all right. I'll wait. Thank you."

When an hour had passed, Nye was getting fidgety but didn't let it show. What was taking them so long?

At that moment, the inner office door swung open. The deputy at the counter said in a low tone, "He's coming out now, Mr. Benson."

Nye rose to his feet and forced a pleasant look on his face.

Palmer Danfield made a final remark to his boss, then closed the door and turned toward the front office.

"Deputy Danfield," said the young man at the counter, "there's a gentleman over here who's been waiting to see you."

"Oh. Sure. Thank you," said Danfield. He headed toward Dick Nye, who noted that the two of them were approximately the same size and build.

Danfield extended his hand. "Yes, sir. I'm Palmer Danfield. What can I do for you?"

Meeting his grasp, Nye said, "Sir, I'm Ambrose Benson from Denver. As I told the deputy over there, I'm visiting a cousin who lives near Amarillo, and I wanted to come by and meet you, since you're moving to Denver."

Danfield looked surprised. "Are you with the chief U.S. marshal's office in Denver?"

"Ah...no, sir. But I'm a close friend of Chief U.S. Marshal John Brockman. As you know, I'm sure, the Denver office has suffered some serious losses among their deputies."

"Yes, I'm aware of that."

"Well, sir, John is so excited about your coming to join his staff, he told me about it. Let me say that I'm very excited about it, too. John has had a tough time handling all the outlaws in his territory, and to see him so elated about getting a man of your qualifications and reputation is a joy to me. As long as I'm here in Amarillo, I wanted to meet you, if possible, and be the first to welcome you to the Mile High City."

"Well, thank you. What do you do, Mr. Benson?"

Nye laughed to himself. The fool was swallowing the story. "I own Benson's Clothing Store in Denver. And that's another reason I wanted to meet you today. As a lawman, you will get a 30 percent discount on all clothing you buy from Benson's…and your wife, too, for that matter. And if you have children, the same discount applies."

Danfield's features sagged. "That's very generous of you, Mr. Benson, but my wife died a short time ago. We don't have any children."

"Oh, I'm so sorry. John didn't tell me anything about—"

"He may not have known, sir," cut in Danfield. "Please don't be embarrassed. Anyway, thank you for the offer. I'll take you up on it when I get settled in Denver."

"I'll look forward to it," said Nye, heading for the door.

"Thank you for coming by," Danfield called after him.

"My pleasure."

As he headed back toward the hotel, Dick Nye said to himself, *Palmer Danfield, you won't live long enough to find out there is no Benson's Clothing Store in Denver.*

13

BREANNA BROCKMAN STOOD at the kitchen window in the Anderson house and watched the torrent of rain. Lightning flashed overhead and thunder boomed like cannons on a battle-field as trees cracked in the high wind. It was the third day in a row that heavy rainstorms had come to this small town high in the Rocky Mountains.

Turning from the rain-splattered window, Breanna stepped to the stove and picked up the steaming teakettle, which was just beginning to whistle. She carried it to the table and smiled at Effie Downing, who was coming through the hall door. "Are they still sleeping?" she asked.

Effie nodded and sat down at the table. While Breanna poured the steaming liquid into teacups, Effie said, "I don't understand how Rose and Donnie can sleep through all that racket."

"Well, I'm glad they can," said Breanna, taking the teakettle back to the stove.

"So what do you think, Breanna?"

"Well, it seems to me that Rose is doing well enough that you can look in on her periodically during the days, just to make sure she's all right. Since she's on her feet part of the day now, I think she can take care of Donnie. She'll have Ray here at night."

"Helps a lot since Donnie's been weaned onto cow's milk," said Effie. "I'm glad the little fellow made the transition with so little stomach upset."

"Me, too," said Breanna, taking a sip of tea. She set the cup down and started to say something else, but was interrupted by a loud crack of lightning. The thunder that followed shook the whole house.

"If they slept through that one, they'll really be doing something," said Effie. "You were about to say something, Breanna."

"I was going to say that when this rain eases up, I'll walk on over to the office and tell Dr. Rawlins that you and I discussed it, and we agree that I should head on home. If he's in agreement, I'll go ahead and wire John in the morning. If he can come tomorrow, I'll be gone then. But it may take another day."

They heard Donnie's cry from the bassinet, which was now beside Rose's bed, and both women left the kitchen. When they reached the bedroom, Rose was up with the baby in her arms.

"We were hoping the storm wouldn't waken either of you, dear," said Effie. "But we're not surprised that you're awake."

Rose sat down on the bed and held the baby close to her breast, patting his back and speaking in a soft tone.

When the pounding of the rain on the roof began to lessen and the lightning and thunder eased, Donnie drifted back to sleep.

Breanna extended her arms. "Here, honey, I'll take him. You lie down again."

Breanna placed Donnie in the bassinet, then stood over Rose, who was being tended to by Effie.

Rose set her gaze on Breanna. "Have you decided yet?"

"Mm-hmm. Effie and I talked about it. She says she can

185

look in on you a few times during the day, and since Ray will be here at night, I might as well go home. It'll depend on how soon John can get loose from his job to come and get me. Maybe tomorrow. Maybe the next day."

Rose's lower lip trembled. "I understand, Breanna. And I know it's time for you to go. But I sure am going to miss you."

"I'll miss you, too. But it isn't really like we'll never see each other again. It's not that far to Denver. Maybe someday you and Ray and Donnie can come and pay us a visit."

"I'd like that. You've told me so much about your place in the country. I'd love to see it."

"Maybe I'll just hide in their wagon and come along," said Effie.

You'd certainly be welcome," said Breanna with a warm smile.

"One thing about it, though," said Rose. "If we don't get to see you anymore in this life, Breanna, we'll meet again on that golden shore."

"Praise God for that!" said Effie.

"Amen!" responded Breanna.

The rain was soon down to a light sprinkle. Noting it, Breanna said, "Well, I guess I'd better go discuss my going home with Dr. Rawlins. May I borrow your umbrella, Rose?"

"Of course."

It was still sprinkling when Breanna stepped onto the board-walk in front of the doctor's office.

Rex Rawlins was at Isabel's desk, making notes in a patient's file. He looked up, and his mouth curved into a smile. "Hello, Breanna. Some storm, wasn't it?"

"Mm-hmm. Almost as bad as yesterday."

Brushing raindrops off her dress, she said, "No patients at the moment?"

"No. And no more appointments today. Doesn't mean they won't come pouring in here at any moment, but right now it's quiet. Isabel's cleaning the examining room. Did you want to see me?"

"Yes. We need to talk about my going home."

Rawlins chuckled. "Well, to tell the truth, I was hoping that day would never come. I'd like to hire you as my nurse if we could find some kind of a job for your husband here in Empire."

"Well, since the town marshal's job is taken," said Breanna, "I guess that's out."

Getting a serious look on his face, the doctor said, "So, how soon do you think you should go?"

"Well, sir, it's been eight days since I wired John and told him it would be a few more days. It's probably time to wire him again. I discussed it with Rose and Effie, and they tell me they can handle it in the daytime. And, of course, Ray is home every night. So I think I've worn out my usefulness here. I might as well get home and be useful there."

"Tomorrow? The next day?"

"If it's all right with you, Doctor, I'll wire John in the morning. If he can come right away, I'll be gone tomorrow afternoon. If he can't make it that soon, it'll be the next day."

"Of course. When you know for sure when you're going, I'll make it a point to start looking in on Rose and the baby once a day for a while."

"That would be good, Doctor, just in case something unforeseen should develop from all she's been through."

Suddenly the rain came down hard, pounding on the roof.

"Looks like we're going to get some more," commented

Rawlins, glancing out the window to see people on the street scurrying for cover.

Lightning split the sky, making everything a cold blue-white in flickering waves, then thunder crashed, vibrating the building.

"Doctor…" said Breanna.

"Yes?"

"I'm very concerned about Ray's spiritual state. I've given him the gospel on several occasions now, but he evades the issue. He won't let go of his work-your-way-to-heaven religion, yet he says he wishes he could really know where he's going to spend eternity. I haven't much longer to work on him. Will you—"

"I sure will. I'll take up where you leave off. And God bless you for trying so hard with him."

Breanna sighed. "I'd bring the whole world to Jesus if I could."

"I know you would."

Lightning popped again, and thunder boomed.

Rawlins smiled. "I'm sure you're looking forward to going home to be with your husband."

"Oh, yes. I missed John very much when we were apart before we got married. But it's even harder to be apart now."

Breanna had wondered about the doctor. He'd said nothing about having a wife, so she concluded that he wasn't married. She wondered if there was a young woman in his life.

Rawlins glanced out the window at the pounding rain and said, "I hope these storms let up before you head for home, Breanna. I'd hate to see you and your husband try to ride in weather like this."

Breanna's eyes strayed to a framed diploma on the wall behind the desk. Looking back at the doctor, she said, "I certainly hope we don't have to contend with inclement weather. Maybe it'll get it out of its system for a while after today."

Her gaze went back to the diploma. "I was just noticing, Doctor…you graduated from the University of Chicago School of Medicine."

"Yes," he said, glancing behind himself at the diploma. "In spite of my terrible grades."

"Terrible grades, I'm sure! Tell me if I'm wrong. You graduated in the top ten of your class, didn't you?"

Rawlins's face tinted. "Well, ah…yes."

"Top five?"

"Second, if you must know," he said, grinning.

"I figured as much. We just had a new nurse come to Mile High Hospital who graduated from the nursing school there. In fact, according to the graduation date on your diploma, you and our new nurse had to have been at the university at least partly at the same time. You might know her."

"Maybe. What's her name?"

"Natalie Fallon."

There was dead silence, except for the pounding of the rain on the roof.

The instant Natalie's name came off her lips, Breanna saw the effect it had on young Dr. Rawlins.

Breanna could do nothing but act as if she didn't notice. "Do you know Natalie Fallon, Doctor?"

In the moment it took for Rex to loosen his tongue, Breanna's thoughts ran back to her conversation with Natalie about the young doctor she had refused to marry because he wanted to practice medicine as a small-town country physician.

Rex swallowed hard, and said, "I…ah…yes, Breanna. I know Natalie. We were once deeply in love."

While Breanna was trying to find the right words to use at this point, Rex said, "Natalie's father was a medical doctor, Breanna. He worked himself to death. He was the only doctor in an area too large for one man to handle. But he was so dedicated to his patients that he sacrificed himself to give all of them the proper care."

Breanna nodded slowly. "And when you told Natalie that you were going to set up your practice somewhere in a small country town, she broke off the relationship. She made it clear that she wasn't going to go through what she had seen her mother suffer with her father."

Rex looked a bit surprised. "Yes. Exactly."

"Natalie told me the whole story. She didn't name this young doctor, so until now I had no way of knowing it was you. She said she had no idea where he was, and assumed that by now he was married."

Rex rubbed the back of his neck. "I tried to get her to see that just because her father let his work wear him down till it took his life, it didn't mean I would. But it was like talking to a stone wall. It's in me to serve in a small town exactly as I'm doing, Breanna. God put this ambition in me."

"And I admire you for what you're doing," said Breanna. "You could make a lot more money in a large city."

"If money were my goal in life, I could do that. But people in and around Empire need a doctor. And I'm happy being that doctor. This is where God wants me."

"I have no doubt about that."

"I tried to get Natalie to see that in order to fulfill God's will for my life, I had to serve in a small community. I told her that if a woman loves her husband, she will follow him and stand by him in his chosen profession. But she wouldn't listen. She broke it off. I...I guess it was because she didn't really love me like I thought she did."

"That wasn't it, Doctor."

He looked at her questioningly. "What do you mean?"

"As Natalie and I talked about this unnamed young doctor, I detected that her feelings for him were still very strong. So I asked her if she was still in love with him. She admitted that she was. Then she added that in time she would get over him."

There was a pinched look to Rex's expression as he moved his head back and forth.

"What I think, Doctor," Breanna went on, "is that she feels she must get over you because she figures you're now someone else's husband. The girl walks close to the Lord. She is living a good testimony for Him. And because she's a dedicated Christian, she knows she must not go on carrying a torch for a married man."

The rain was easing up, but Rex Rawlins was unaware of it. His mind was on Natalie, who still held the key to his heart.

"Natalie told me that her young doctor is a fine Christian," said Breanna. "She said you always treated her like a queen. Then she grimly said that marriage couldn't have worked because she would never change her attitude about being married to a small-town doctor."

Rex Rawlins was visibly shaken. His features were pale as he said, "Breanna, I will probably never marry. I couldn't love another woman like I love Natalie." His voice caught, and he was silent for a moment before he said, "It would do no good to make a trip to Denver and try to talk to her. You know how firm she is in her position. I know I'm fulfilling God's will for my life right here in Empire, caring for the people of this town and the surrounding areas. I would be wrong to leave here."

Breanna's heart was heavy for both the doctor and Natalie. Her voice quivered slightly as she leaned closer to him over the desk and said, "Doctor, the Lord is aware of how both you and Natalie feel. I'm going to pray that He will take control of the situation and bring the two of you together. This love within you was put there by the Lord, and He hasn't taken it away to let either of you fall in love with someone else. There has to be a solution, and God can work it out."

Rex chuckled hollowly. "Breanna, your faith is stronger than mine. It would take a mighty big miracle to ever bring Natalie and me together."

A graceful smile adorned her lips. "Doctor, our God is the God of miracles—mighty big miracles. The creation of this gigantic universe was a miracle, wasn't it?"

"It sure was."

"Who did it? Wasn't it the same God who lives in your heart and mine?"

"Yes, of course."

"When Zerubbabel needed a miracle so he could rebuild the temple in Jerusalem, did it happen?"

"It sure did, and I love the way God put it to him: 'Not by might, nor by power, but by my spirit, saith the LORD of hosts.'"

Breanna laughed. "John and I have marveled over that verse a lot lately."

"It's a potent one."

"Yes, and spoken by the same God who performed the miracle. I'm going to pray for just that kind of miracle in your life and Natalie's. I believe He is going to bring the two of you together...not by might, nor by power, but by His precious Holy Spirit."

Rawlins shook his head and smiled. "Breanna Brockman, you're really something, you know that?"

"Just a sinner saved by grace, Dr. Rawlins. A sinner saved by grace with a great big wonderful God who can perform mighty big miracles. Well, sir, I'd better be going. I've got to see about our patient and her baby."

Rex walked her to the door. She picked up the umbrella

and said, "I'll let you know about my departure time after I wire John and hear back from him in the morning."

"All right."

As she started through the door, Rawlins said, "Breanna…"

Pausing, she looked over her shoulder. "Yes, Doctor?"

"You're one in a million."

She smiled and said, "One in a million sinners saved by grace with a great big wonderful God who can perform mighty big miracles. See you tomorrow."

As she lay in bed that night, Breanna said in a whisper, "Lord, I can't believe You allowed Rex and Natalie to meet and fall in love, then pulled them apart. This was Natalie's doing. And yet, I can understand why she feels as she does. It had to have been horrible to watch her father die so young as a result of his ceaseless work.

"They're both such sweet Christians, and I can see what a wonderful couple they would make in the bond of marriage. They both have so much to give in life…and how much better if they could do that giving together. I don't know what it will take to unite them, Lord, but You do. I'm just asking You to perform Your miracle for them in Your own great and marvelous way. And I thank You that You will."

As always before she went to sleep, Breanna prayed for John, asking the Lord to keep him in the hollow of His mighty hand, and to protect him from all harm and danger that he faced as a lawman.

The sky was cloudy the next morning, but no rain fell. There were signs that the clouds might be breaking up, especially in the east where the sunshine was attempting to break through.

Breanna made her way from the Anderson house to Main Street and soon drew up in front of the Western Union office. She was surprised to find the door locked and a sign in the window announcing that the office was closed. A sheet of paper was stuck in the window beside the sign, explaining that the storms had downed the telegraph lines in the mountains, and until they were repaired, there would be no wire service.

Wondering just how long that might be, Breanna decided to talk to the telegrapher. There was a permanent sign above the door that said he lived upstairs.

She went to the back of the building and found the stairs that led to the apartment. Reaching the top of the stairs, she found the door standing open but could see no one in the parlor.

"Hello!" she called. "Anybody home?"

Footsteps answered her question, and a tall, lanky man of sixty appeared. "Yes, ma'am?"

"Sir, my name is Breanna Brockman. I'm a visiting nurse, and I've been here for several days caring for Dr. Rex Rawlins's patient, Rose Anderson, and—"

"Oh, sure! Glad to meet you, ma'am. I'm Barry Stubbins. Folks in town have been talkin' about you, sayin' what a nice lady you are. I'm glad to meet you."

"Thank you, Mr. Stubbins."

"They tell me you're married to the chief U.S. marshal in Denver."

"Yes. I'm sorry to bother you, but I came to the office to send a wire to my husband, and saw the note on the door. I need to know how long you think it will be until the lines are back in service."

"No way to know exactly, ma'am, since I can't send messages to our main office in Denver, nor receive 'em. But I'm sure the company knows the lines are down. No doubt they're workin' on 'em now. We've had this problem many a time before, and it's usually taken 'em about a week to restore service."

Breanna felt her heart sink. "A week?"

"Yes'm."

"All right, Mr. Stubbins. Thank you for the information."

"You're welcome, ma'am."

When Breanna entered the Anderson house, Rose was sitting in a rocking chair in the parlor, holding Donnie. "Did you get the wire sent all right, Breanna?" she asked.

"No. The telegraph lines are down. Mr. Stubbins says it could be a week before wire service is restored."

"Oh, my. I'm sorry, but I won't mind keeping you another week."

Breanna grinned. "Honey, I can't stay another week. I've got to get home. I've decided to go home tomorrow."

"You mean ride by yourself?"

"Yes."

"But I thought your husband didn't want you riding alone...that he wanted to escort you home like he escorted you here."

"Well, that is the way John wants it, but there's no way to contact him, so I'll leave first thing in the morning. I'll be home by noon or shortly thereafter. John will understand when I explain about the telegraph lines being down in the mountains."

Rose's mouth pulled into a grim line. "*If* you get home. Breanna, it's dangerous out there in those mountains. There are wild animals…outlaws…and there could be hostile Indians. You'd better find somebody to ride with you, or wait till the lines are repaired."

"I realize the danger involved, Rose. I've got my revolver in my small bag, and there's a rifle in my saddle scabbard. I know how to use both weapons. John has trained me. God willing, I won't run into any outlaws. I realize in some parts of the mountains the Utes and Arapaho are a problem. But they are farther south. Besides, who would I get to ride all the way to Denver with me?"

"I don't know, but the wild animals, Breanna. Cougars, bears, wolves. I really don't want to see you try it alone."

"Well, as for the wild animals, and the outlaws, too, for that matter, I have an edge: Chance. He's faster than any horse I have ever seen. He can outrun John's gelding, Ebony, and Ebony's faster by far than the average saddle horse. I'm really not afraid to make the trip down to Denver alone."

Rose smiled thinly. "If I can't talk you out of it, I sure can pray for you."

"Now, I don't mind that at all," said Breanna, rising from the sofa. "Tell you what. I'll walk over to the doctor's office right now and tell Dr. Rawlins and Isabel good-bye. I'll be leaving in the morning before they open the office."

Breanna had just left the side street and was heading up Main when she saw Dr. Rawlins driving his buggy away from the office the other direction. Usually when a doctor went out on calls, there was no telling how long it might take. She would delay her departure in the morning long enough to stop and tell him and Isabel good-bye right after they opened the office.

✧

That night in her bed at the Anderson home, Breanna prayed again for Rex and Natalie, asking the Lord to work His miracle in their lives. Life was short, and two people who loved each other as they did shouldn't be wasting time being apart.

When it came time to pray for John, a strange sensation washed over Breanna. She tried to shake it, but it would not go away. Biting her lip, she said, "Dear Lord, I sense that John is in grave danger. Something's wrong. You understand what's making me feel this way, and You know what danger is lurking near John. Please protect him. Keep him in the hollow of Your mighty hand.

"Lord, I know that in the course of his job there's a threat of danger, but there's something churning inside me. Please keep my John safe and from all harm. I'm trusting You to answer my prayer."

It took John Brockman's wife a while to fall asleep, but finally, peace stole over her heart, and she slid into restful slumber.

DICK NYE KEPT himself half-hidden behind a pillar at the Amarillo depot to watch for Deputy U.S. Marshal Palmer Danfield.

The train had three passenger coaches. The first one was coupled to the baggage coach, which was directly behind the coal car. The dining car was coupled to the rear of coach number three, and behind the dining car was the caboose.

The fireman was busy scooping up coal from the coal car and depositing it in the engine's firebox. Flames leaped from the opening with each shovelful.

While observing passengers bidding good-bye to family members and friends, Nye was rethinking his original plan. Instead of boarding the same coach as Danfield, he would take a seat in another coach. He didn't want his mission to fail because Danfield thought it too coincidental that they end up on the same coach. Once he saw what coach Danfield chose, he would board the next one, then find a casual way to run into him.

Little by little the passengers were boarding the train. Noting that it was barely five minutes until time for the train to pull out, Dick Nye was getting somewhat apprehensive. Where was Danfield?

Suddenly Danfield appeared with U.S. Marshal George

Frame at his side. The deputy was carrying a small valise. Since they were coming toward the front of the train, Danfield must have checked his heavy luggage at the baggage coach.

Danfield paused at coach number three, looked inside, and nodded at Frame. They shook hands, and Frame watched the deputy board the coach.

Nye saw Danfield take a seat near the middle of the coach, by a window. When he was settled, he waved to Frame, and the U.S. marshal turned and walked away.

Nye angled himself so his face was not visible to Danfield, then pressed through the crowd just as the engine bell began to ring and the conductor appeared at the rear of coach number three, calling for all passengers to board.

He climbed into coach number two at its rear entrance and took a seat at a window on the same side as Danfield. He'd made the right choice. Danfield would think nothing of it when Ambrose Benson came through on his way to the dining car.

The last passengers boarded and put their luggage in the overhead racks, and the engine whistle blew, joining the sound of the clanging bell. Steam hissed from the engine's bowels, and the big steel wheels spun against the steel of the tracks, sending out showers of sparks. The engine lurched forward, causing the couplings between the cars to thunder; then the whole train was moving.

Nye was alone on the seat, for which he was glad. He didn't like people crowding him.

Soon the train was rolling across the Texas plains in a northwesterly direction. Undulating hills with large patches of knee-high native grass spread as far as the eye could see. In the open areas between the patches were clumps of mesquite surrounded by sagebrush, golden wild zinnias, and wolfberry plants.

After gazing out the window for a while, Nye eased back in

his seat and stretched out his legs. He tipped his hat over his eyes, then touched the handle of the razor-sharp nine-inch bowie knife in its sheath under his suit coat. All he had to do now was figure out how to keep Danfield up late and lure him onto one of the coach platforms. The knife would do the rest.

Soon Nye was lulled to sleep by the steady sway of the coach and the rhythmic click of the wheels beneath him. His sleep was disturbed when the train stopped for thirty minutes in Dalhart, Texas, but once it was rolling again, he went back to sleep.

Hours passed.

Nye stirred from his sleep when the conductor's voice boomed out that lunch was now being served in the dining car. He sat up and stretched his arms, yawning, then rose to his feet as a few people began leaving their seats and heading to the rear of the coach.

Following the other passengers, Nye entered coach number three, preparing himself mentally for his "chance" meeting with the man he planned to kill. His line of sight shot straight to the seat Palmer Danfield had occupied, but Danfield wasn't there.

Probably in the dining car, thought Nye.

The passengers ahead of him were choosing tables in the dining car when Nye spotted Danfield seated at a table about midway in the car. He was alone. The deputy U.S. marshal was facing Nye but didn't see him, for he was reading the menu.

Nye halted at the table and said, "Well, whattaya know! Deputy Marshal Danfield!"

Danfield looked up, and a smile broke across his face. "Mr. Benson! Nice to see you again!"

"I had no idea we would be on the same train, sir," Nye said. "What coach are you riding in?"

"Number three."

"I'm in number two."

Nye was hoping for an invitation to sit down, and it came on Danfield's next breath.

"How about joining me for lunch, Mr. Benson?"

"It would be my pleasure, sir. But I insist on buying."

"Oh, no!" Danfield said with a wave of a hand. "I invited you to sit with me, and I'm very glad for the company. Lunch is on me."

Nye felt a warmth pass through him as he eased onto the chair opposite Danfield. This was working out well. Danfield trusted him. And that would be Deputy U.S. Marshal Palmer Danfield's fatal mistake.

Nye picked up his menu and read it quickly.

The waiter came with a pad of paper in hand to take their order. Both men ordered light lunches.

"All right, gentlemen," said the waiter, "it'll be jis' a minute befo' I come back with yo' coffee, an' about ten minutes befo' I bring yo' food."

Both men nodded, and the waiter scurried away.

"So did you have a good visit with your cousin?" asked Danfield.

"Hmm?" Nye's mind was on the task that lay before him tonight.

"Didn't you say you were in Amarillo to visit your cousin?"

"Oh, yes! My cousin! Yes. Had a nice visit."

"I'm glad." There was a pause, then Danfield asked, "How long have you been in Denver?"

"Since the fall of '62. Yes, sir. It'll soon be ten years."

"Mm-hmm. Then you know ex-Chief Solomon Duvall, I take it."

"Oh, of course. Yes. Fine man."

"Yo' coffee, gentlemen," said the waiter, drawing up to the table.

When the waiter was gone, Nye said, "Marshal, since you're buying lunch, may I have the pleasure of buying you dinner this evening?"

Danfield's face lit up with a smile. "How can I turn down an offer like that?"

"Then we're on for dinner?"

"Certainly."

"I...ah...I like to eat late. I noticed on the menu it said they serve dinner until nine-thirty. Could we eat at nine?"

"That'll be fine," said Danfield. "I'll look forward to it."

Nye felt warm inside again. Palmer Danfield had taken a real shine to Ambrose Benson.

The waiter came with their lunch, and Nye kept Danfield occupied by asking about his experiences in tracking outlaws and bringing them to justice. As he listened, Nye knew for sure that he had a rough, tough, dedicated lawman to deal with. He laughed inside. This made it a challenge, and Dick Nye would rise to the challenge. Palmer Danfield had seen his last sunrise.

When lunch was finished, Danfield said, "I don't have anyone sitting by me on my seat, Mr. Benson. How about joining me and finishing the ride to Denver in my coach?"

Nye would rather not be seen sitting with Danfield in his coach. Tonight, someone sitting close by might wonder where the deputy was when Nye returned to the seat after disposing of him, and start asking questions.

But what could he do? He dare not turn down the invitation to sit with Danfield. Any excuse he came up with would sound lame.

Smiling broadly, Nye said, "Why, that's mighty nice of you, Marshal. I'll go fetch my overnight bag and meet you in your coach."

When Nye sat down beside his intended victim in coach

number three, he asked him for more stories about his pursuit and capture of outlaws. Danfield was happy to oblige. It was midafternoon when the train stopped in Clayton, New Mexico. The engine took on water while some passengers got off and others got on, and after a stop of forty-five minutes, they were rolling again.

An hour later, Danfield had run out of stories, and the conversation diminished. Soon the deputy U.S. marshal excused himself, tilted his hat over his face, and went to sleep.

Dick Nye appreciated the silence. Leaning back and tilting his hat over his face in like manner, he feigned sleep. Actually, he was going over his plan. He chuckled to himself. Palmer Danfield would have lived longer if he had chosen another way to make a living.

The train stopped for an hour at Raton, New Mexico, in early evening, then headed due north for Denver.

At nine o'clock the two "friends" entered the dining car. Nye was glad to see that only a few people were left at the tables.

While they ate, the killer kept his intended victim talking, and when the meal and dessert had been devoured, Nye kept the conversation alive while the waiter continued to bring hot coffee.

By 10:15, there were only two other tables occupied besides that of Nye and Danfield. The other customers soon left.

After a few minutes had passed, the waiter approached the table.

"Gentlemen," he said politely, "I hate to break in heah, but we's gotta close the dinin' car."

"Oh!" said Nye, acting surprised. "I'm sorry, waiter. I didn't realize it was so late. Did you, Marshal?"

"I hadn't noticed, either," replied Danfield. "Sorry."

As the two men headed for the door, Nye's nerves tensed up and his pulse throbbed in the side of his neck. His plan was to take care of Danfield on the platform of the dining car. No one would be coming that way for the rest of the night.

Danfield was walking ahead of Nye. When they stepped onto the platform, the night breeze touched them. Smoke from the engine lifted into the moonlit sky, and sparks rode the breeze a few feet over their heads, cooling and disappearing almost immediately.

The deputy U.S. marshal paused while Ambrose Benson closed the door behind him and squinted to see him in the dark. Danfield said, "Thank you for the dinner, my friend."

"My pleasure," said Nye, pulling the deadly knife from its sheath.

Most everyone in coach number three was asleep as Dick Nye entered and made his way to the seat where he and Palmer Danfield had spent the afternoon and evening together. He was glad that even those who were awake paid him no mind.

He quietly removed his overnight bag from the rack, along with Danfield's valise, and moved swiftly through the front door of the swaying coach. He stopped on the platform and flung the valise off the train as hard as he could throw it. It bounced and tumbled into a shallow gully. He took a deep breath, then stuffed Danfield's gun, holster, and gun belt in the overnight bag.

Nye entered coach number two and returned to his original seat. Just as in coach number three, most of the other passengers were already asleep.

His heart was still pounding as he placed his overnight bag on the seat and sat down beside it. Looking around to make sure no one was watching him in the dim light afforded by the single lantern burning low in the coach, he removed the sheath containing the bowie knife from his belt and placed it in the bag, alongside Danfield's gun belt. He then rose to his feet, placed the overnight bag in the rack, and eased back onto the seat.

The job was done. Danfield's badge was in his coat pocket, along with his wallet and identification papers. His next victim: Chief U.S. Marshal John Brockman. Only this time, it would be a bullet.

Nye was pleased. He couldn't have planned it better if he'd tried. After using the knife on a surprised Palmer Danfield and taking the things off the body that he needed, the moonlight showed him a thicket alongside the tracks. He had flung the body off the platform at just the right time. It rolled into the thicket, where it would not be found for a long time…if ever.

On the same morning that Dick Nye boarded the Denver-bound train in Amarillo, Dr. Rex Rawlins arrived at his office in Empire, Colorado, only minutes after Isabel Mullins had entered.

"Good morning, Doctor," she said in a light tone. "And how is my favorite physician today?"

Isabel had noticed the day before that Dr. Rawlins was not his usual cheerful self. She had not said anything to him about it, but it had bothered her. It was not like him to have that dull look in his eyes, nor to be without his sunny smile. She was hoping that whatever was bothering him had passed. But the dullness was still in his eyes and his features were like gray stone.

Forcing a smile, he said, "I'm fine, Isabel. And you?"

"I'm not so good," she replied, a worried look framing her face.

His brow furrowed. "Aren't you feeling well?"

"Physically, I'm fine, Doctor, but I'm not so good in my soul, because I can see that you're not so good in your soul."

Feigning puzzlement, he asked, "What are you talking about?"

"I'm a mother, Doctor. Mothers develop a sixth sense, and my sixth sense tells me that my favorite physician has something bothering him. Now, out with it! You can talk to Isabel."

"Well, sweet Isabel," he said, trying to sound more like himself, "I just didn't sleep well last night."

"But you were like this yesterday morning, too," she countered.

Rex sighed. "Well, I didn't sleep well the night before, either. Haven't you had nights when you didn't sleep well?"

"Well, yes, but—"

"I'll be fine," he said, gripping her shoulders and looking deep into her eyes. "I very much appreciate your motherly concern, but really, I'm fine. I just didn't sleep well the last couple of nights."

What Dr. Rex Rawlins did not tell his assistant was why he hadn't slept well the past two nights. His conversation with Breanna about Natalie Fallon had surfaced his love for her, brought back the pain of her breaking off their relationship, and had made him miss her terribly. Memories flooded through his mind, and the loneliness he suffered had caused sleep to elude him. He was still very much in love with Natalie and always would be.

Isabel smiled and said, "Do you know a good doctor who can give you some powders to help you sleep?"

He forced a laugh. "No. Could you recommend one?"

Isabel laughed with him and sat down at her desk. From that vantage point, she could see his buggy parked outside at the hitching rail, and his bay mare bobbing her head and swishing her tail. He only left the horse and buggy in front of the office on days he had house calls.

Turning to him, Isabel said, "Doctor…"

"Mm-hmm?"

"I see the mare and buggy parked in front. You don't have any house calls scheduled for today as far as I know. Has something happened?"

"Yes. You know Elsie Chadron?"

"I do. She lives just north of town and has been in on two or three occasions since you've been here."

"Well, last night Elsie knocked on my door close to midnight and told me that her mother, Myrtle Caldwell, is quite ill, and asked if I would go see her this morning. I have never met Mrs. Caldwell, but Elsie said she and her husband were here to see Dr. Hooper a few times some years back."

"Yes, I recall them. If I remember correctly, the Caldwells live about ten or twelve miles due east of here, a mile or so off the trail that leads down to Idaho Springs and on to Denver."

"That's what Elsie said. I'm headed to the Caldwell home right now. You'll have to tell the patients who show up this morning for appointments to come back tomorrow morning. I should be back for my afternoon appointments."

"All right," said Isabel, looking around. "Do you have your medical bag?"

"Yes. It's in the buggy." He started toward the door and said over his shoulder, "See you this afternoon."

"You be careful."

"You sound like a mother."

Isabel chuckled. "Well, somebody has to mother you."

Rawlins took hold of the doorknob, then paused and looked back. "Have you heard anything from Breanna?"

"No, sir."

"Then she must not be leaving for Denver yet. If she comes in, tell her I'll be by to check on Rose sometime this afternoon, and I'll see her then."

"Will do."

Isabel rose from her chair and watched the young doctor stroke the mare's long face, saying something loving to her. Then he climbed into the buggy and drove away. Sitting down again, Isabel said aloud, "Well, Dr. Rawlins, something is eating at you. Whatever it is, I hope the Lord takes care of it soon."

Breanna Brockman was delayed at the Anderson home while treating baby Donnie for colic and was a few minutes later than planned as she tied her small suitcase and medical bag to the back of the saddle.

Rose stood on the porch watching her with tears in her eyes.

Breanna, now dressed in her split skirt, white blouse, and boots, mounted the steps and hugged Rose. As they embraced, she said, "Remember, stay in that Bible every day, and spend time with Jesus in prayer. I'll be praying for Ray. Dr. Rawlins said he would take up where I'm leaving off. We'll see Ray saved. You just believe that."

Rose held her tight. Sniffling, she said, "I do. And Breanna..."

"Yes?"

"I want to thank you again for caring for my soul and leading me to the Lord."

"It's been my joy, honey."

The two women clung to each other for a long moment, then Breanna released Rose and said, "I must go. I have to stop by the office and tell Dr. Rawlins and Isabel good-bye."

Rose kissed Breanna's cheek. "I love you."

"I love you, too," said Breanna, and turned away. Chance snorted as she mounted, and Rose watched her trot away.

Moments later, Breanna left the saddle, wrapped Chance's reins around the hitching rail, and entered the doctor's office.

Isabel was at her desk. She looked up and smiled warmly. "Hello, dear."

"Hello to you, too," said Breanna. "Is Dr. Rawlins in?"

"No, he's not, honey, and I can see by the way you're dressed that you're about to ride for Denver."

"Yes. Will he be here soon?"

"Not till early afternoon, probably. He had to make an unexpected call."

Breanna nodded with an obvious look of disappointment on her face. "Well, I won't get to tell him good-bye. Will you do it for me?"

"Of course, but he's going to be upset. He asked me this morning if I'd seen you. We both assumed you'd be around another day or so."

"I'm sorry. It just worked out this way. Please tell him that it was a pleasure to get to know him and to work with him."

Isabel left her desk and embraced the younger woman, saying she would convey the message to the doctor.

Chance nickered affectionately as Breanna swung into the saddle. She touched his flanks with her heels and pointed him eastward.

Isabel wiped a tear as she watched her ride away and said, "You're quite the young lady, Breanna Brockman. God bless you real good."

Soon Chance and the mistress he adored were weaving their way down the steep trail amid wind-kissed aspen, birch, and towering conifers of varying shades of green.

Rex Rawlins guided the buggy down the winding trail, the sound of the wind's song in the pine and fir that surrounded him. The saw-toothed peaks were bold and rugged, and just below their lofty snowcapped heads were the cool gray crags—majestic cliffs that defied description.

There was a thin haze in the canyons, and fleecy white clouds hovered over the peaks.

Rawlins smiled when he saw a broad-winged bald eagle leave the spire of a rock tower. He watched the bird let the pine-scented mountain winds lift him toward the clouds. The tops of the pines blocked Rex's view of the eagle momentarily, but when he saw him again, the great bird was diving straight down; then suddenly he spread his wings and rode the airwaves toward a female eagle who was rising out of the depths of a canyon to meet him.

The eagle circled her, ejecting a screech, and the two of them flew out of sight together.

Rex thought of Natalie. If only they could be together as husband and wife. He shook his head as if by doing so he could remove such thoughts and ease the pain in his heart. But it didn't work. Natalie's lovely face was still clear in his thoughts.

He remembered his statement to Breanna: *Your faith is stronger than mine. It would take a mighty big miracle to ever bring Natalie and me together.*

Then came Breanna's bold reply: *Doctor, our God is the God of miracles…mighty big miracles. I believe He is going to bring the*

two of you together…not by might, nor by power, but by His pre-
cious Holy Spirit.

Rex drew in a shaky breath and let it out. "Breanna," he
said audibly, "I wish I had your faith."

The buggy rounded a bend, then started down a steep slope
that Rawlins knew was some four miles in length before it lev-
eled off for a while. When he reached the bottom of the slope,
he would make a right turn on another trail, then follow it a
mile or so to the Caldwell cabin.

His mind went to Natalie as the buggy raised and dipped
on the uneven surface of the trail. She had told Breanna that in
time she would get him out of her heart. *Was that just wishful*
thinking, Natalie? he thought. *Is your pain as excruciating as*
mine? Sure, I'd like not to hurt like this either, but the only way
this pain is going to go away is if you tell me you love me and will
marry me, no matter where I have my practice.

Suddenly the mare snorted and nickered, then raised up on
her hind legs, pawing the air and fighting the bit.

It took Rex a second or two to see what had frightened her.

Directly in their path was a large female black bear with two
cuddly cubs at her feet. She had seen the buggy coming and
sensed a threat toward her cubs. Standing erect, her powerful
body rising above the bumpy trail, she snorted and woofed in
anger.

The mare was terrified. She trembled and whinnied, then
squatted slightly, as if preparing to bolt.

"Whoa, girl!" Rex cried, holding the reins taut.

The mother bear ejected a roar that seemed to shake the entire
forest. She took the horse's movements to mean that her cubs
were in grave danger. Abruptly she was a black horror of snarling
teeth and rage. She dropped to all fours, nudged the cubs into the
brush, then released a thunderous roar and charged.

The taste of fear was like copper in Rex's mouth.

The mare screamed as the furious beast drew within thirty yards, and in spite of the doctor's strong arms holding the reins tight, she jerked to the right and bolted.

The sudden lurch of the buggy pinned the doctor to the seat, and within seconds he found himself hanging on to keep from being thrown out. His attempts to slow the mare were fruitless. On and on she galloped, threading between the massive pines and huge ragged boulders that dotted the forest floor.

The mare was running blindly in her terror, and Rex knew that at any moment, the mare was going to take the wagon somewhere only she could go.

Rex's arms felt as if they were going to come off as he pulled steadily on the reins. Low-hanging pine limbs were slapping at the buggy as it fishtailed through the forest.

He raised up momentarily in an attempt to get more leverage on the reins. Suddenly, a limb stung his face and sent him tumbling backward into the small compartment behind the seat. He struggled to bring himself back over the seat. But it was impossible. The speeding vehicle was bouncing high and coming down hard.

Blinking against the smarting in his eyes, he tried with all his might to get over the seat to grasp the reins.

And then Rex saw it coming.

The crazed mare was plunging into dense forest. The trees were too close together to allow the buggy to pass between them. Any moment the buggy was going to slam into the stalwart, ungiving pines. Yet it would be suicide to jump from the buggy at this speed.

In one last attempt to get over the seat, he raised up and lunged forward.

15

REX RAWLINS DESPERATELY reached for the reins as the trees seemed to close in on both sides.

Suddenly the terrified, panic-driven mare veered toward what seemed to be a sufficient opening in the dense trees, but her head struck a low-hanging limb. She stumbled and started to fall. The speeding buggy careened, and the right rear side glanced off a tree, shattering bark. A second later the front wheels hit a fallen tree, hurling Rex from the buggy.

He felt himself spiraling helplessly through the air. As the buggy crashed into a tree, Rex's body connected with something hard. Something seemed to explode inside Rex's head, blasting away all consciousness.

One buggy wheel was still spinning as its shattered frame lay crumpled against the tree. A few feet ahead, the mare lay on her side. Her skull was cracked, but she was still alive. Her sides heaved as she blew painfully. Intermittently, she ejected a shrill cry.

Rex Rawlins lay motionless, his chest rising and falling, but the mare's cries did not penetrate the dark void in his brain.

Some eighty yards to the north was the trail leading to Idaho Springs and on to Denver. Periodically, people passed by on horseback and in wagons and buggies, but the pounding of hooves and the rattling of vehicles covered the sounds of the dying mare.

The first indication Rex had that he was still on earth were the painful cries assaulting his ears. He had the impression they were coming from miles away.

His thoughts seemed to be composed of cobwebs drifting in and out of his mind as if batted by a wayward breeze. Before he could make sense of them, they seemed to dissolve into silken threads that tore as he reached out for them.

The cries. What were they? Why wouldn't his mind clear up? He could feel something touching his face. Was he in some dark dungeon? Had some evil thing captured him…imprisoned him? Was he going to die?

The black-winged thoughts kept coming. Would they torture him before they killed him? Or was this some horrible nightmare carrying him through the haunted dimensions of his mind?

As his mind began to clear, he realized the cries were coming from something…someone in agony. When they stopped periodically, he could hear birds chirping and squirrels chattering.

Rex opened his eyes. Light flooded them, but he could only see things in a blur. He knew now what was touching his face. It was a gentle breeze.

Where am I? What happened? Why—

Another piercing cry assaulted his ears.

He blinked against the blur of light, and now he could see something in motion. There was a strange dance of chaotic images.

Rex blinked again. The dancing images were directly above him. He was lying flat on his back. Tree limbs! Those were the limbs of a pine tree, dancing in the breeze against a blue sky!

The cry came again, but this time it was followed by a whinny.

The mare!

Like the sudden rush of an ocean wave hitting the beach, it all came back. The mother bear protecting her cubs. The mare bolting in terror. The trees whizzing by the buggy. The reins; he was trying to grasp the reins when— The fallen tree. The sound like the crack of a rifle when the wheels hit the tree and the singletree popped, freeing the mare to—

He didn't see what happened to the mare. He was sailing through the air, turning, twisting. Then came the awful sudden stop as his back smashed hard against something. He was falling. The world was whirling and going dark…

Rawlins turned his head at the next sound from the mare. She was beyond his view. But he saw the buggy, or what was left of it.

The mare was hurt and needed his help. Rex gathered his arms to his chest and started to roll over so he could get on his knees, then to his feet.

Something was keeping him from moving his legs. Apparently there was something very heavy lying on them. He tried to raise his head so he could see what was pinning his legs to the ground, but the effort shot pain through his neck.

He twisted his right shoulder, put his right arm under his upper body, and raised up on the elbow. To his surprise, there was nothing touching his legs.

Again he tried to move them, but they were like lengths of dead rope linked to his body.

Cold sweat broke out on his brow. In sudden panic he

managed to sit up. His head felt light, but ignoring it, he put both hands on his thighs and squeezed down hard.

He couldn't feel anything.

Sucking in a deep breath, he moved his hands lower and pinched his knees.

Nothing.

His mind silently screamed against it, and his stomach went sour.

He was paralyzed from the waist down!

His heart pounded wildly as if it were trying to tear itself out of his body.

"No, dear Lord!" he cried. "No! No! No!"

The vertigo in his head was growing stronger. The forest was whirling around him. He could hear the mare whinnying in pain, but the piteous sound began to fade as a dark curtain descended and a black whirling vortex swallowed him.

He fell back hard, his head bouncing on the bed of pine needles.

Breanna Brockman guided Chance down the winding trail, eager to return home to her husband. John wouldn't like it that she'd ridden home alone, but he would be plenty glad to see her, and he would forgive her when she told him the telegraph lines were down in the mountains.

She heard a horse blow, followed by the rattle of a wagon, and presently she saw a rancher and his wife come around a curve in the trail ahead. Though he wore a hat and she wore a bonnet, Breanna could make out their silver hair and knew they were older in age.

A minute later, they were drawing abreast. Both the man and the woman raised a hand in a wave, and Breanna waved back.

"Beautiful horse!" said the woman to Breanna as they met and passed.

"Thank you," responded Breanna with a smile.

"Beautiful woman!" said the old man.

Breanna didn't look back.

"You can notice the horses all you want to, Ralph," she heard the woman say. "But when it comes to women, you keep your eyes straight ahead!"

Breanna smiled and shook her head.

Shortly thereafter, she saw a loaded hay wagon veering onto the main road from a rutted trail off to her left. A man and a small boy were in the seat, and a rider on a strawberry roan gelding moved alongside the wagon. The boy had his right arm in a sling.

Breanna focused on the boy. It was little Bobby Chambers.

At the same instant, the boy pointed to her and said to the man on the roan, "Look, Pa! It's Mrs. Brockman, my nurse!"

Bob Chambers smiled. "Sure enough, son!"

"Grandpa!" Bobby said to the older man who sat beside him. "It's my nurse! She's the one who fixed my arm!"

Bob trotted his horse ahead of the heavily loaded wagon and drew up to Breanna. "Hello, Mrs. Brockman."

"Hello, Mr. Chambers," she said, matching his smile with her own. "It's nice to see you again."

"You making calls for the doctor?" he asked, noting her medical bag.

"No. I'm going home."

"Oh? Are you riding all the way to Denver alone?"

Breanna gave him an affirmative answer, explaining that the telegraph lines had been blown down by the recent storms and she couldn't wire her husband to come escort her.

"Hi, Mrs. Brockman!" said Bobby as the wagon drew up. "My arm's feelin' real good!"

"I'm glad to hear it."

The roan and Chance were checking each other out, muzzle to muzzle.

Bob said, "Dad, I'd like you to meet Breanna Brockman. She's—"

"The nurse who fixed Bobby's arm," cut in the older man. He touched his hat brim. "Glad to meet you, ma'am. I'm Earl Chambers, Bob's dad."

"And I'm glad to meet you, sir," said Breanna.

"We're taking this load of hay into Empire to the hostler, ma'am," Bob said. Turning his head and pointing with his chin, he said, "Our ranch is back that way. The trail we just came in on leads right to it."

"I see."

"Well, Dad…Bobby…we'd best keep moving. Plenty to do when we get back home. Sure nice to see you again, Mrs. Brockman."

Breanna bid them good-bye and moved on. She looked back a few minutes later, and the wagon was out of sight.

Chance carried Breanna on down the trail. A short while later, she was watching two chipmunks chase each other from one birch tree to another when a strange sound met her ears.

She drew rein and listened. Chance tossed his head and looked off to his right as the sound came again. He nickered softly and tossed his head once more.

"What is it, boy?" she said, patting his sleek neck. "It sounds like someone…or something is hurt."

The sound carried to her more clearly, and Chance whinnied and stomped a hoof, looking into the forest to his right.

"It's not a human, boy," she said after hearing the sound for the third time. "But something's hurting back there in the woods."

The painful cry came again, and Breanna picked up a piteous whinny with it this time.

"It's a horse, Chance. It must be injured. Maybe it was attacked by a cougar or a bear. We can't let it suffer. Let's go check it out. You take me to it."

Chance bobbed his head, ejecting a shrill whinny, and moved into the dense forest as Breanna gave him free rein.

On his own, Chance went into a fast trot, and the deeper they went into the woods, the louder was the horse's painful cry.

Abruptly Breanna saw the smashed-up buggy and the bay mare lying on the ground a few yards beyond it. Then her attention was drawn to the man lying flat on his back under a huge pine.

Her body went rigid and her eyes widened in shock when she realized it was Dr. Rex Rawlins!

The mare's cries filled the air, and Chance was whinnying as Breanna quickly dismounted and knelt beside the unconscious doctor. Without touching him, she ran her eyes over his motionless form. He was breathing normally, and except for some red marks on his face, he didn't appear to be hurt.

She glanced again at what was left of the buggy and told herself the buggy had to have been traveling very fast to have smashed up like that when it hit the tree. Rawlins apparently had jumped to spare himself the impact of the collision.

But why was the buggy moving so fast? And why was Dr. Rawlins driving it so deep in the woods where there was no trail?

The mare's whinny evolved into a shrill cry. Leaving the doctor for a moment, Breanna went to the horse. Blood was oozing from a wide split in the front of her head. Bone was showing, and her glassy eyes were protruding from their sockets.

"Oh, you poor thing," Breanna breathed. "What did you do? Hit your head on a low limb?"

Chance nickered from his position near the doctor. The mare released a nicker that sounded identical. She tried to raise her head but found it impossible. Chance gave the same nicker again.

Breanna knew that animals of like kind had a language all their own. The mare had told him something in reply to his query. But only Chance knew what it was.

Breanna bit her lower lip. She wasn't sure what to do. The mare was in a great deal of pain, and her cries were piteous. With her head split open like that, there was little doubt she could live. Should she use her rifle to put the mare out of her misery? But it wasn't her horse. Breanna decided to try to revive the doctor first and ask him what to do with his horse.

Just as she turned back, she heard Rawlins moan and saw his head move. She removed her small canteen from the saddle and pulled the cork as she knelt beside him. His eyes were open but glazed.

Lifting his head with one hand, she put the canteen to his lips and said, "Doctor, it's Breanna. Here, take a drink of water."

Rawlins blinked and tried to focus on her face. "B-Breanna?"

"Yes. Please, drink some of this water."

Rex opened his mouth and Breanna poured the water slowly. He swallowed, then choked and coughed. She eased up, then gave him a few more sips before setting the canteen aside.

The glaze slowly left his eyes, and when he was able to focus clearly, he said, "Breanna…how did you find me?"

"I stopped by your office to tell you good-bye, but Isabel said you had to make a call and had already left. Anyway, I heard the mare's cries from the road. So did Chance. I couldn't go on, knowing an animal was in pain, without seeing what I could do for it. That's when I found you."

Rex licked his lips and said, "Breanna, I'm—I have no feeling from the waist down."

"What?" she gasped. "You can't move your legs?"

"No. I came to— Well, I don't know how long ago. Couldn't be too long. Anyway, when I first came out of it, I couldn't move my legs. At first I thought something extremely heavy was lying on them. But when I was able to look, there was nothing on them. I squeezed my thighs and pinched my knees, but there's no feeling in them at all. I'm paralyzed."

The mare's cries and whinnies kept coming. Rex tried to look in her direction. "Do you know what's hurting her, Breanna?"

"Yes, I just looked at her. Apparently she hit her head on a low limb. It's split open to the bone. She will die, Doctor. I didn't know for sure what to do."

"She's got to be put out of her misery."

"I know. I thought about doing it before you came to, but she's your horse. I couldn't just shoot her and tell you I did it."

"I...I hate to ask you to do it, but I'm in no shape to take care of it."

"Th-that's all right," said Breanna, her heart suddenly feeling like it had turned to lead. "I'll do it."

She picked up the canteen and made her way to Chance. Hanging the canteen back on the saddle horn, she slid the Winchester .44 from its scabbard. Rex watched as she pulled her lips into a thin line and moved toward the mare.

Standing over the suffering animal, Breanna's brow furrowed as she levered a cartridge into the chamber, released the safety, and said, "I'm sorry, girl, but I can't let you go on suffering."

Chance whinnied shrilly. Breanna turned to see him bobbing his head. Was the great stallion who was once the leader of a herd of wild horses actually telling her she was doing the right thing?

Breanna turned back to the mare and looked down at her hands gripping the rifle. Her knuckles were white. She had never had to do a thing like this before. She had once taken an oath to do everything in her power to preserve life. The context of it was human life, of course, but still this suffering little mare was given life by her Creator.

And now, she who had vowed to preserve life was about to end a life. In her work she also relieved as much suffering as possible. There was no choice. She had to stop the mare's suffering.

She heard Chance whinny again, as if urging her on.

She lifted the rifle to her shoulder and lined its muzzle on the mare's head, then took a deep breath and held it. Her heart pounded in her throat as she put her finger to the trigger.

Suddenly the mare made a tiny squealing sound, released a long breath, and her sides went still. Breanna lowered the rifle and bent over the mare, whose wide-open eyes stared vacantly into space. She was dead.

"Oh-h-h, thank You, Lord," Breanna said in a whisper. "Thank You."

When she returned to Rex and looked down at him, he asked, "Can't you do it, Breanna?"

She sighed. "I don't have to. She died just as I was ready to squeeze the trigger."

"Well, thanks be to the Lord."

Breanna returned the rifle to its scabbard and went back to Rawlins, kneeling beside him. "I've got to get you out of here, Doctor, but please tell me what happened."

"I was on my way to make that call. It was to a lady named Myrtle Caldwell, who is quite ill. The Caldwells live a little further east of here. The mare and I unexpectedly came upon a mother black bear and two cubs. The mare was instantly frightened and showed it. The mother bear took it as a threat to her cubs, and charged. The mare wheeled and ran in here, and I couldn't stop her. The buggy hit that fallen tree back there, and I went sailing. That's when I felt like somebody had hit me in the back with a battering ram, and the lights went out. I hit this tree right here, I'm sure."

Breanna was quiet for a moment; then she said, "Doctor, you don't have any sensation in your legs or feet at all?"

"Nothing," he replied. There was anguish in his eyes. "Breanna, my spine must be damaged severely."

"It might be, Doctor, but maybe not. This could just be a temporary paralysis. You know that."

"I realize it could be, but I fear it's permanent."

"Not if God doesn't want it to be permanent. And think of it this way, Doctor. It could have been your head that hit the tree instead of your back. That would have killed you. The Lord wasn't looking the other way, you know."

Rex looked into her eyes steadily. "Breanna, why would He allow me to be paralyzed?"

"Doctor, God's thoughts are above ours. It is not for us to try to reason why He does what He does, or allows what He allows. This is where faith and trust come in. We must have faith that our heavenly Father never makes mistakes, and that He is worthy of our full and complete trust. There is a reason for this."

Rawlins nodded silently, swallowing hard.

"And think of this, Doctor—your mare had to have hit a low tree limb, and she hit it very, very hard. If you could see the way her skull is split open, you'd know what I mean. A blow like that could easily have killed her. I found you because the mare was still alive, and in much pain. Otherwise, I would have ridden on by and never known you were here.

"There were other travelers on the road out there. I met up with some of them. Yet they didn't hear the mare's cries. The Lord let her cry at just the right time so both Chance and I would hear her. Do you see it? If the mare had died, you no doubt would have lain here and died, too. God's not through working in your life, Doctor. You just trust Him."

Rawlins managed a weak smile. "Maybe some of the preacher in your husband has rubbed off on you."

Ignoring his comment, Breanna said, "Now, Dr. Rawlins, I've got to go get help so I can get you out of here and to the hospital in Denver. I'll need a wagon with a mattress in the back so you'll be comfortable, and I'll need someone to help me lift you into the wagon. You just lie here and talk to the Lord. I'll be back as soon as I can."

"I'm sorry to put you to this bother, Breanna."

"Doctor, it's no bother."

"But you need to get home."

"I will. But not until I have you in the hands of Dr. Matthew Carroll at Mile High Hospital. Any suggestions as to where I might borrow a wagon and team, and a mattress?"

"Hostler Bruce Enlow has wagons and teams to rent. Maybe you could get him to come along and help lift me into the wagon. His wife, Lucille, can watch the stable. She does it quite often when he has to be away. I...I wish you could get two men. It's going to be a sticky situation to lift me and put me in the wagon without possibly doing further damage to my spine."

"Yes. Maybe Mr. Enlow will know of someone else in town who would come along. If not, I'll just have to do my part."

"Bruce can probably suggest where you might borrow a mattress."

"All right."

"Tell him I'll pay the bill on the wagon and team rental."

"I'm sure he won't worry about that."

"Would you go by the office, Breanna, and tell Isabel what's happened?"

"I was going to."

"She'll have to cancel all the appointments and send my patients to a doctor in one of the nearby towns."

"I'll tell her."

"And would you ask her to send a doctor from another town to see about Myrtle Caldwell? As soon as possible."

"I will," said Breanna, rising to her feet. "I'll be back as soon as I can."

Rawlins watched her swing up on the huge black stallion and gallop away. Looking toward the sky, he said, "Lord, please don't let me be paralyzed for the rest of my life. I…I don't understand. Why did You let this happen to me? What possible purpose can it serve?"

Isabel Mullins was stunned when Breanna told her what had happened to Dr. Rawlins, and that she was going immediately to the hostler's to rent a team and wagon so she could take him to the hospital in Denver.

Her features ashen, Isabel said, "What can I do, Breanna?"

"I have some instructions from him for you. Other than that, you pray."

Breanna related the doctor's orders to Isabel, then said, "As soon as wire service is restored, I'll let you know how it's going for him."

"I appreciate that," said Isabel, worry adding new lines to her already wrinkled face.

Breanna skidded Chance to a halt in front of the stable, swung from the saddle, and hurried to the office.

When she entered, she found a woman at the worn old desk. "Hello, ma'am. Are you Mrs. Enlow?"

"Yes," the woman said with a smile. "I'm Lucille Enlow. And though we haven't met, I know who you are, Mrs. Brockman. Bruce told me you had left for Denver."

"I did, Mrs. Enlow, but something dreadful has happened. I need your husband's help."

"Oh, I'm sorry. He's gone to Central City. He left only moments after you came for your horse. We had a load of hay coming, so he wanted me to be here when it came, as well as to carry on the business. What's happened?"

Breanna quickly explained about Dr. Rawlins and that she needed to rent a team and wagon. She also needed a man—or even two—to help her safely place Dr. Rawlins in the wagon.

Lucille was sorry to hear of Dr. Rawlins's plight, but explained that they only owned three wagons and teams, and they had all been rented out the day before and wouldn't be returned until tomorrow.

Breanna's nerves tightened. "Mrs. Enlow, do you know who I might go to for help in this? It is imperative that I get Dr. Rawlins to the hospital in Denver as soon as possible."

"Well, let me think, Mrs. Brockman. You might try— Oh, no. The man I was going to suggest isn't in town at the moment, either."

Suddenly Breanna's eyes lit up. "Wait a minute! You did have a load of hay delivered. It was Bob Chambers."

"Yes."

"I met him and his father—along with little Bobby—as

they were coming toward town. Do you know if they went right home after they delivered the hay?"

"Yes, they did. Bob said they had plenty of work to do at home."

"Thank you!" said Breanna, and dashed out of the office. Chance knew by Breanna's hasty stride that he was going to run with her on his back. He snorted as she drew up, and tossed his head. Every muscle in his great body rippled under his shiny black hide.

"Okay, boy," she said as she stepped in the stirrup and swung her leg over the saddle. "Let's go!"

Lucille stepped to the door and watched Breanna gallop the big stallion eastward.

Chance felt the urgency in Breanna. As they left Empire behind and started down the trail, he lengthened into his beautiful stride. The motion of the big stallion was so easy, so smooth, so swift. All Breanna had to do was lean forward over the saddle horn and let him run.

Soon they were approaching the turnoff where Breanna had seen the Chambers hay wagon veering onto the trail earlier that morning. She slowed Chance as they drew near, made the turn, then gave him his head once more.

Like a ghostly black blur, he thundered toward the Chambers ranch.

16

HERE YOU GO, Dad," said Bob Chambers, standing on the ladder against the barn.

Earl Chambers was kneeling on the barn roof. He took the bucket of nails from his son and carried them to the peak of the roof where they had small stacks of shingles placed in a row from one end of the roof to the other.

Bobby was standing with his mother on the ground, watching as his father stepped off the ladder onto the roof and climbed to the peak.

"Papa, could I come up there with you and Grandpa?"

"I told you no already, Bobby," said Mattie Chambers. "It would be too easy for you to slip and fall. You already have a broken arm. Do you want something worse?"

"No, Mama, but I could just sit up there at the top. I couldn't fall then."

"Bobby," said his father as he picked up a hammer, "your mother knows best. It just isn't safe for you to be up here."

"Rider comin'," said Earl Chambers, looking toward the south. "Way he's ridin', I'd say he's in a bit of a hurry."

Bob turned his head and squinted to focus on the horse and rider. "It's not a he, Dad. It's Breanna Brockman. And you're right, she's got that horse moving fast."

Even as he spoke, Bob laid his hammer next to the bucket of nails and started down the gentle slope of the roof. As he stepped down on the ladder, he glanced at the galloping horse and said, "Something's wrong. She should have been halfway to Denver by now."

Bob touched ground and moved up beside Mattie and Bobby as Breanna thundered in. Chance's hooves scattered sod as he skidded to halt.

Remaining in the saddle, Breanna said breathlessly, "Mr. Chambers, I'm sorry to barge in on you like this, but I need your help."

"Certainly," said Bob. "Climb on down and tell me about it."

As soon as Breanna dismounted and started toward them, Bob said, "This is my wife, Mattie." The women exchanged greetings, then Bob said, "What can I do for you, ma'am?"

"It's Dr. Rawlins. He's been injured, and I need to get him to the hospital in Denver. It's his spinal column. He's paralyzed from the waist down."

Mattie gasped. "Oh, no! How did it happen?"

Breanna told them about the bear and the mare bolting into the woods. She needed a wagon to transport Rawlins to the hospital in Denver, and a mattress for him to lie on. She also needed help to lift him into the wagon.

Bob Chambers responded quickly. "Dad and I will hitch up the team and take him to Denver in our wagon, ma'am," he said. "We'll take the mattress off the bed in our spare bed-room."

"I'm really sorry to interfere with your roofing job, Mr. Chambers," said Breanna, "but I appreciate your help...and I know Dr. Rawlins will appreciate it."

"We're glad to help, ma'am."

"That's right," said the elder Chambers. "The roofing job will still be here when we get back."

"Can I go, too, Papa?" asked Bobby.

"No, son. I need you to stay here and take care of your mother. Grandpa and I won't get back till after dark tonight."

"All right," said the boy. "I'll take good care of her."

Rex Rawlins lay on his bed of pine needles, listening to the birds and studying the cottony clouds that drifted above him in the azure sky.

He thanked the Lord for allowing the mare to live long enough so Breanna could hear her cries and come to his rescue.

"And Lord," he said, "I thank You that I didn't hit my head on the tree. Breanna's right. That would have killed me. But...but I just can't be permanently paralyzed, Lord. I can't do my work from a wheelchair. Please. Please give me feeling back in my legs. What will I do if You don't? I'll be a helpless cripple the rest of my life. Somebody will have to take care of me. How will I make a living?"

Rex tried to stay calm, but panic rose within him. Struggling to his right elbow, he sat up and squeezed his thighs.

He could feel nothing.

His breath was coming in short spurts as he pinched his knees. Concentrating on his booted feet, he tried desperately to wiggle his toes. Just the slightest movement or feeling would give him hope.

But there was nothing.

He closed his eyes and said, "Oh, dear God, help me! Help me!" With that, he burst into tears and laid his head back on the ground.

Rex wept for several minutes, then willed himself to stop

crying. "Oh, God," he said, "give me strength. You could have let me hit my head on the tree and die. But You didn't. I'm alive because You want me alive. But Lord, without my legs—"

His words were cut off when the sound of a rattling wagon and pounding hooves met his ears. With effort he raised back up on his elbow. Breanna was on her big black stallion, riding ahead of a wagon. When she veered to one side, he saw that it was Bob Chambers at the reins, and his father sitting next to him. A smile pulled at his lips. "Bless her heart, Lord," he said. "She's brought the right kind of help."

Breanna drew up and dismounted as the wagon rolled to a halt behind her.

She knelt beside the doctor and said, "The hostler was on his way to Central City, so I rode out to the Chambers place. Bob and Earl are going to take you to the hospital in Denver. We've got a mattress in the wagon bed. It'll help cushion the jolts."

Bob and Earl drew up beside Breanna and Rex, carrying two boards six feet long and a foot wide, joined with slats.

Both men spoke words of encouragement to the doctor, telling him they would get him to the hospital as quickly as possible.

"Doc," said Bob, "we've made a pallet so we could load you onto the wagon without putting any pressure on your spine. You can thank this dear nurse of yours for coming up with the idea."

Rex looked at Breanna and smiled. "I've got a whole lot to thank her for, Bob," he said with feeling.

"Well, let's get you in the wagon so we can head for Denver. We've got about twenty-five miles to go from here."

Still on her knees beside Rawlins, Breanna said, "All right, men. I'll roll him onto his side. When I say so, lay the pallet exactly where he had been lying. When it's in place, I'll ease him onto it."

Bob and Earl nodded.

"Now, Doctor," said Breanna, "I want you to stiffen your upper body as much as possible. It will make it easier for me to get you in position. I'm going to take hold of your right arm and your right hip and roll you toward me. Understand?"

"Yes," said Rex. Trying to show as good a spirit as possible, he added, "I still say you should be a doctor. You're doing it exactly as you should."

"Thank you, sir, for your encouraging words. But with the help of these two gentlemen, I'm going to get you to the best and most experienced doctor this side of the Missouri."

"You speak of Dr. Lyle Goodwin, your sponsoring physician?"

"Dr. Goodwin is excellent," she replied, "but I'm referring to the man who is chief administrator of Mile High Hospital."

"Oh, yes. Dr. Matthew Carroll. I've heard a lot about him. I understand he is held in highest regard by the American Medical Association and his peers, even on both sides of the Missouri."

"That's true. And I might add that Dr. Carroll is also my brother-in-law."

"Oh, really?"

"Yes. He married my sister, Dottie."

"I see. Medicine sort of runs in the family then."

"You might say that. All right, Doctor, here we go. Stiffen that upper body…now."

When Breanna felt Rex's upper body tighten up, she gripped his arm and hip and pulled him toward her. "All right, gentlemen. Slide the pallet under him. Make sure the top is about an inch above his head. That will give about the same at his heels."

Bob and Earl did exactly as she said, and when Breanna saw that Rawlins lay evenly on the pallet, she said, "Looks good. Very carefully now…lift him, keeping him as level as you can."

As father and son carried the doctor to the rear of the wagon, Breanna preceded them and watched as they carefully slid the pallet onto the mattress. When it was in place, she said, "Now, if one of you gentlemen would help me into the wagon, I'll turn him so you can remove the pallet."

"How about if we both help you?" said Bob.

Father and son got on both sides of the nurse and hoisted her over the back and into the rear of the wagon. Moments later, the pallet was out from under Rawlins and hung on the side of the wagon bed.

"Now, gentlemen," said Breanna, "I'll need to prevail on you to help me down so I can tie Chance's reins to the rear of the wagon. I want to be by Dr. Rawlins's side while we make the trip."

"You don't need to do that, ma'am," said Earl, heading toward Chance. "I'll tie him there for you."

"Ah…no, Mr. Chambers. You don't underst—"

Chance whinnied and backed away from Earl, shaking his head as the man came close.

Halting, Earl turned and looked at Breanna. "What's the matter with him, ma'am?"

"He will only allow my husband and me to ride him. He thinks that's what you intend to do. He's only been in captivity for a year. My husband found him in Montana. He was leader of a herd of wild horses." She turned to Bob. "If you will help me down, I'll tie him to the wagon and we can head for Denver."

↑

The trail that wound down from the high country was a rough one. Breanna sat beside Rex Rawlins and did what she could to keep him from jostling as the wagon bounced, rocked, and pitched with the rugged terrain.

Breanna reported to Rawlins that Isabel would carry out his instructions and that she would be praying for him. She would also be waiting to hear from Breanna how he was doing when the telegraph lines were repaired.

"She's a good woman, that Isabel," said the doctor. "She's been a widow for ten years, and she lives on the salary I pay her. I hate to think of what's going to happen to her if—" He closed his eyes and sucked in a ragged breath.

Breanna laid a comforting hand on his shoulder. "Doctor, please. You must keep a positive attitude. You mustn't give in to despair."

Fear rode his eyes. "But what if I'm paralyzed permanently? Isabel will not have a job. I won't be able to make a living for myself. How am I going to—"

"Doctor, I realize I'm not lying there as you are. But don't leave God out of the picture. He's still here, and He's still all-powerful. He will have the final say as to whether you stay paralyzed or not."

Rex closed his eyes. "I'm sorry. It's just that…well, I've never been in a helpless situation like this before."

"I understand. But Doctor, our great big wonderful God is the master of all situations, including yours. Don't give up. Keep faith in Him."

Rawlins kept his eyes closed and nodded. "I'm trying. Believe me."

As Bob Chambers carefully guided his team down the

winding trail, Breanna silently prayed for the young doctor. After some four hours, the city came into view with the flat plains beyond to the east.

It suddenly occurred to Breanna that not one word had come from the mouth of Rex Rawlins about Natalie Fallon. He knew she was employed at the hospital.

Breanna wondered how Natalie was going to react when she saw him.

With Chance trailing behind the wagon, Bob Chambers pulled up in front of Mile High Hospital. It was late in the afternoon, but the day shift still had about two hours to go.

"We're here, Doctor," Breanna said. "We'll have you with Dr. Carroll shortly."

Rawlins nodded and tried to smile.

The Chambers men helped her out of the wagon, and as her feet touched ground, she said, "I'll send a couple of orderlies out to get him. Please don't leave until I see you again."

"We'll wait right here, ma'am," said Bob.

When Breanna pushed through the door, Mabel Trotter looked surprised. "Breanna! I didn't know you were back! How did it go in Empire?"

"Honey, I don't have time to talk right now. I've got an emergency on my hands. Is Ma—ah…is Dr. Carroll in the building?"

"As far as I know. I'm sure I'd be advised if he left."

"All right. Thank you."

Breanna rushed down the hallway and made a right turn toward her brother-in-law's office. On the way she would come to the nurses' station and have the orderlies sent out to bring Dr. Rawlins in.

As she drew near the station, she saw Stefanie Langan come from an adjacent room and go behind the counter. Stefanie's line of sight touched her, left her, then came back. "Breanna! You're still in your riding skirt! Did you just get here from Empire?"

"Yes. I'll explain later, Stef, but right now I need two orderlies to carry a man in from a wagon out front. I've got to find Dr. Carroll. Is he in his office?"

"Was a few minutes ago. He and Mom were talking. I'll get Hal and Burt to bring the man in. Should they take him to an examining room?"

"Yes. But Stef, he's paralyzed from the waist down. Be sure they understand that. He had a severe blow to his lower back. No feeling at all in his hips or legs."

"All right. Who is he?"

"He's the doctor in Empire, where I've been working. His name is Rex Rawlins."

"Oh, dear. Paralyzed. That's awful."

"Thanks for your help, Stef. I'll see you later."

Breanna hurried on down the hall. Dr. Carroll's office door was open, and she saw Mary Donelson sitting at a chair in front of his desk. Looking past Mary, Carroll said in a tone of surprise, "Breanna! I didn't know you were due back. I saw John just last night, and he didn't say anything about your coming home today."

"He doesn't know," she said hurriedly. "Hello, Mary. You see, Doctor, the telegraph lines are down from the storms we've had in the mountains, so I couldn't contact John. Listen, I've got an emergency out here."

"What kind of emergency?"

"You know I've been in Empire, working for the doctor there."

"Yes, I can't recall his name. He took Dr. Hooper's practice, didn't he?"

"Yes. Dr. Rex Rawlins. I have him outside in a wagon. He's paralyzed from the waist down. I'll explain it on the way to the examining room. Stefanie is sending Hal and Burt out to bring him in right now."

"All right," said Carroll, rising to his feet. "Mary, we'll work on this matter later. You come with Breanna and me."

As they stepped into the hall, they saw the two orderlies pushing a cart toward the lobby.

Two nurses were just coming out of the lobby. Dr. Carroll paused and said, "Ladies, you just saw the orderlies wheeling a cart toward the front door…"

"Yes, Doctor," said one.

"Would one of you go tell Mabel to send them to examining room 1 with the patient, please?"

"I will, Doctor," said the same nurse as she wheeled about.

"All right, Breanna," said Carroll. "Tell me about Dr. Rawlins's injury."

Mary Donelson took it all in as Breanna explained how Rex Rawlins happened to be thrown from the speeding buggy, how she found him, and her own deduction of his paralysis. She feared the spinal column might be damaged beyond repair, but hoped she was wrong. She added that Dr. Rawlins was a born-again man and had a good testimony in Empire.

They could hear the wheels of the cart coming down the hall.

"It's good to know we're dealing with a Christian," said the doctor. "I'll take a look at him and we'll go from there."

"Doctor, I have to go out and thank the men who made it possible for me to get Dr. Rawlins here," said Breanna. "I'll be right back."

The orderlies were almost to the door when Breanna stepped into the hall. As they slowed to make the turn, she said, "Just one second, fellows."

The orderlies stopped, and Rawlins looked up at Breanna. He was trying to be strong.

"Doctor Rawlins," she said, "I'm going outside to thank the Chambers men for what they did, but I'll be right back. I've told Dr. Carroll the story, and he knows who you are."

Rawlins nodded.

Breanna headed toward the lobby door, and the orderlies wheeled the patient into the examining room.

Doctor Carroll smiled his approval when he noted that Hal and Burt had placed Rawlins on a stretcher board for patients with back injuries. "Good work, boys. Put him on this table over here."

Mary moved close to the table as Rawlins was transferred from the cart.

Looking down at his new patient, Carroll said, "Dr. Rawlins, this is our head nurse, Mary Donelson. And I'm Matt Carroll."

Rex curved his lips in a weak smile. "My pleasure, ma'am. Dr. Carroll, I've heard much about you ever since you took over as head of this hospital. You have quite a reputation. May I say that I admire you very much? Though I'm not happy with the circumstances that have brought us together, I'm glad to finally meet you in person."

Matt's cheeks flushed. "Whatever talents and abilities I have in the medical field have come from the Lord, Doctor. Without Him, I would be nothing. Breanna tells me you are a child of God."

"Yes, sir. Born again and washed in the blood. I'm glad to know that you are, too."

"Now, let's take a look at you," said Carroll. "Breanna said you have no feeling at all below the waist."

"That's right. I'm afraid the spinal column has been severely damaged. Maybe permanently."

Without commenting on Rawlins's statement, Carroll proceeded to examine him.

Breanna had returned, and she and Mary observed as Dr. Carroll first worked on both legs, trying to find any response at all while pressing and squeezing, then running a metal instrument along the bottoms of Rawlins's feet. He then turned Rawlins on his side and slowly pressed along his spinal column from the base of the neck to the tailbone. Next he turned him face down and methodically examined the column again, then spent a good deal of time below the waist in the hip area.

When he finished, he carefully rolled his patient onto his back.

"So what do you think, Doctor?" asked Rawlins.

Carroll's voice was solemn. "Dr. Rawlins, you already know you have a very serious spinal injury."

"Yes."

"I have to be honest with you. It could be that you are permanently paralyzed. However, there may be a way to help you with surgery. But before I go any further, I want the other six doctors in this town to look at you and give their opinions. I doubt we can get them here today."

There was dead silence for a moment. Finally, Rex said, "I appreciate your approach, Dr. Carroll. It's good that you get other doctors to share their opinions. But in your own mind, what kind of chance do I have to ever walk again?"

Carroll drew a deep breath. "I really can't say any more than I already have. I don't want to build up your hopes then have to let you down."

Rawlins's face was gray. "All right," he said in a shaky voice. "All right. We'll see what the other doctors say."

"Breanna," Dr. Carroll said, "you look like you need some rest. You'd better go home now. We'll take care of your patient."

"In a little while," she said. "I'm not quite ready to go home."

"Mary, what's the closest room that's unoccupied?"

"Room 4 is ready, Doctor."

"All right. Send the orderlies back in here. Let's take Dr. Rawlins to room 4. I want you to assign a nurse to come and stay with him. As you can see, he's in a great deal of trauma. I don't want him to be alone."

Mary looked at the clock on the wall. "All right, Doctor. I'll assign one to him through the rest of this shift, then I'll assign another from the night shift, and I'll see to it the third shift supplies him one, too."

"Dr. Carroll," said Rawlins, "you don't need to do that. I'm all right."

"You are not all right, and it's understandable, Doctor," said Carroll. "You know how this kind of situation goes. I'm your doctor, and I say you aren't to be alone until I see you in the morning."

Rex nodded silently.

To Mary, Carroll said, "I'll go with Dr. Rawlins to his room and wait until the nurse you assign him arrives."

Mary headed for the door. "I'll send the orderlies right away, Doctor. And I'll send the nurse to room 4 as soon as I can free one up."

"Wait a minute, Mary," said Breanna. "I'll walk along with you." Then she said to Rawlins, "I'll be back to see you before I leave for home."

As Mary and Breanna started for the door together, Dr. Carroll began to talk to his patient, trying to encourage him.

In the hallway, Breanna said, "Mary, before you assign the nurse to Dr. Rawlins...is Natalie Fallon on duty?"

"Yes, she is. She's working on the second floor. Why?"

"I'll let you send Hal and Burt to pick up the patient first, then I want to talk to you."

Mary eyed her quizzically. "All right. Meet me in my office."

As Breanna walked down the hall, she met up with nurses who were moving about hurriedly, each saying how glad they were to see that she was back. Breanna had hardly sat down in the head nurse's office when Mary arrived and sat down in a chair beside her. "All right, honey, what did you want to talk to me about?"

"Natalie and Dr. Rawlins."

Mary frowned. "Pardon me?"

Breanna told Mary the story of Rex Rawlins and Natalie Fallon. She explained that Natalie had told her about the young doctor but had not named him, and that when she saw the doctor's diploma and asked if he knew Natalie Fallon, it all came together. Now that she knew Rawlins was the young doctor in Natalie's life, and that both of them were still in love with each other, she told Mary that she had informed Rawlins she was going to pray that God would work a miracle and bring them together.

When she finished her story, Mary blinked at the excess moisture that had gathered in her eyes and said, "Breanna, do you suppose this tragedy in the doctor's life is the answer to your prayers?"

"It could be. All I know right now is that I feel strongly impressed that I should ask you to assign Natalie to spend the last hour of her shift with you know who."

Mary sniffed again and brushed away a tear. "I'll do that, but you'll tell her who's in the room first, won't you?"

"Oh, of course. I wouldn't want to hit her with that shock. I want her to know his condition first before she goes in there."

"What if she refuses to accept the assignment?"

"She won't. I guarantee it."

Rising from the chair, Mary said, "I'll go get Natalie. While I'm doing that, will you run down to the room and tell Dr. Carroll it will be a few more minutes before I can supply the nurse he wants?"

"Sure. See you back here shortly."

Breanna was waiting for Mary and Natalie when they came into the office.

"Welcome home," said Natalie. "I didn't know you were back till Mrs. Donelson told me a minute or two ago. She's assigning me to a patient in room 4 who is in a great deal of trauma, but she said you wanted to talk to me before I go in there."

"Yes. I have something very important to tell you."

"All right."

"Natalie, the young man in room 4 has had a very serious injury to his spinal column. He is paralyzed from the waist down. He knows that he may never walk again. Dr. Carroll has told him there may be surgery that can correct his paralysis, but at this point there is nothing certain."

"No wonder he's having trauma. Does he have a wife to help support him?"

"No. He's not married."

"What does he do for a living?"

"He's a medical doctor—the one I went to Empire to help. The horrible thing just happened to him this morning."

"Oh, how terrible! I'll do everything I can to comfort and encourage him. What's his name?"

Breanna glanced at Mary, then looked Natalie straight in the eye. "Remember you told me about the young doctor you are in love with?"

Natalie cocked her head with a questioning look in her eyes. "Yes…"

"I know his name. It's Rex Rawlins."

Deep lines penciled themselves across Natalie Fallon's lovely brow. "How did you find that out?"

"Natalie, the young doctor in room 4 who told me he is still in love with you is Rex Rawlins."

17

NATALIE FALLON'S ENTIRE body felt numb, even as her pulse raced.

Breanna and Mary silently waited for her reaction.

To Natalie, there was no sound at all except the beat of her heart. She ran a dry tongue over her lips and said hoarsely, "R-Rex is in room 4?"

"Yes," said Breanna.

"He's n-not married?"

"No."

"And he told you he's still in love with me?"

"Yes."

Natalie put a shaky hand to her forehead. "You said he's paralyzed from the waist down and may never walk again."

"Yes."

"What happened?"

Breanna quickly explained about the conversation between her and Dr. Rawlins in his office in Empire, when Natalie's name came up. Then she told her about finding him in the woods and bringing him to the hospital.

Natalie ran her stunned gaze to Mary. "So you're assigning me to spend the last hour of my shift with Rex because Breanna told you about us."

"Yes, dear. Do you object?"

Natalie's lips trembled as she said, "No. I want to see him. It's just that it's been so long. And...and he's had this awful thing happen. I don't know if I'm up to it."

"Well, I certainly don't want to put too much on you," said Mary. "I'll get one of the other nurses."

"No!" Natalie was shaking her head. "I want to be the one. I'll handle it with the Lord's help. Th-this is all so sudden. I just need a minute to compose myself."

"Rex needs you, Natalie," said Breanna. "Mary is only doing what I asked her to in sending you to be with him till the shift changes. You have both admitted to me that you still love each other. I felt that maybe you needed to see Rex as much as I know he needs to see you."

"He knows I work here?"

"Yes. I told him."

"But he doesn't know I'm the one who's about to come to his room?"

"No. I think it will be the most pleasant surprise he's ever had in his life. Are you okay with this?"

Natalie nodded as she brushed away a tear.

"Dr. Carroll is in the room with Rex right now," said Breanna. "I'll go tell him the nurse he requested is on her way, and get him to leave the room so you two can have your meeting alone."

"All right. Being alone with him will help."

Mary laid a hand on Natalie's shoulder "You're sure you want to go in there?"

"Yes. I don't know what I'm going to say, but I wouldn't have it any other way."

Dr. Carroll was standing beside Rex Rawlins's bed when Breanna came into the room. Rex was sitting up with a pillow at his back.

"Doctor," she said softly, "the nurse Mary has assigned to this room is on her way. I need to talk to you out in the hall, please. Then I'll stay with Dr. Rawlins till the other nurse gets here."

"Fine," said Carroll. Then he said to Rawlins, "I'll contact the other doctors yet this evening. We'll set up the examination for sometime tomorrow."

"All right, sir," said Rawlins.

When Matt and Breanna stepped into the hall, Breanna whispered, "Come away from the door. I don't want him to hear what I'm going to tell you."

She led him a few steps down the hall, and Carroll saw Natalie waiting for them. He flashed her a friendly smile.

"Natalie is the one who is going in to be with Dr. Rawlins," said Breanna.

"Oh. Good."

"There's something you need to know."

Breanna told Carroll that Rex and Natalie had once been engaged. They had not seen each other for over two years, but both had shared with her in private that they were still in love with each other. She thought it would be good for Dr. Rawlins if it was Natalie who was assigned to his room for the time left in the shift, and Natalie was in agreement.

Matt's heart was touched by the story. Smiling at Breanna, he said, "So you're playing Cupid, are you?"

Breanna shrugged. "Just don't like to see love or time wasted."

Carroll chuckled and said to Natalie, "I hope everything works out between you. Go on in there and take care of the man."

"I need to go in just for a minute," said Breanna, "so I can tell him I'll see him tomorrow. I want to be here when the doctors examine him."

"Okay," said Matt. "See you both tomorrow."

As Carroll moved on down the hall, the two nurses stepped to the door of room 4. "I'll be right back, Natalie," said Breanna.

Breanna stepped up to the bed and said, "Just wanted to tell you that I'll be here tomorrow for the examination, Doctor."

Rawlins smiled weakly. "Thank you for all you've done for me, Breanna. If it weren't for you, I'd still be lying up there in the mountains under that tree."

"I just praise the Lord for the way He worked it out. He does have a way of working things out, you know." Patting his shoulder, she said, "See you tomorrow. Your nurse will be with you in a minute."

Rex was studying her eyes when she turned and headed for the door. She was about to grasp the handle when he said, "Breanna…"

She paused and looked back. "Mm-hmm?"

"I saw a gleam in your eyes."

"A gleam?"

"Yes. Tell me something. Do I happen to know the nurse who's coming in?"

Breanna showed him a bright smile. "Yes, you do." And with that, she opened the door, stepped into the hall, and closed the door behind her.

Keeping her voice low, Breanna said, "He's expecting you."

Natalie's hands were trembling. "All right. Thank you, Breanna, for playing Cupid." She took a deep breath. "Here goes."

Rex Rawlins's heart was banging against his ribs as the door opened and he set his gaze on the beautiful face of the woman he loved. Goose bumps rippled over his skin.

Natalie held Rex's gaze as she stepped into the room and closed the door. She felt tears sting her eyes. She took a faltering step, then stopped as emotion clogged her throat.

"Hello, Natalie," Rex managed to say.

She took another unsteady step. "H-hello, Rex."

All he could do was stare at her with loving eyes.

Natalie's tongue suddenly seemed to freeze to the roof of her mouth as she slowly made her way to the side of his bed.

Neither had ever experienced such an awkward moment of embarrassed silence.

Natalie's lips quivered, but gaining control of her tongue, she said haltingly, "It…it's good to see you. But I wish…I wish it could have been under different circumstances. I feel so terrible because of what has happened to you."

Rex's mind was searching for the right thing to say as another moment of silence prevailed. Finally he said, "God has a purpose, Natalie. I have to trust His wisdom."

"Yes. I'm glad you see it that way. Dr. Carroll is going to do everything he can for you. He's bringing in other doctors."

"He's a good man."

Feeling very much off balance, Natalie said, "You must believe that the Lord is going to let you walk again."

"I'm trying to."

Natalie looked at the water pitcher on the bedstand. "Are you thirsty? May I pour you some water?"

Rex felt no thirst, but to relieve the awkward moment, he said, "That would be fine."

Trying to keep her hands from trembling, Natalie poured him a cup of water. When he took it from her, their fingers touched, and Rex put the cup to his lips and drank.

"Thank you," he said, handing it back to her.

Their fingers touched again, and this time Natalie left it that way for a few moments before placing the cup on the nightstand. "Is there anything I can do to make you more comfortable?"

"Maybe adjust this pillow at my back."

When that was done, Rex said, "You don't have to stand there, Natalie. Please sit down."

She pulled up a straight-backed wooden chair and sat beside the bed.

"Tell me about your practice in Empire, Rex. How did you happen to go there?"

Rex began telling his story and was not yet finished when the door opened and a nurse with silver hair entered.

"Hi, Sylvia," said Natalie, rising from the chair. "Shift change already?"

"Sure is, honey," said the older woman, moving up to the side of the bed. "I understand we have one of our own here. Dr. Rawlins, I'm Sylvia Bennett."

"Glad to meet you, ma'am."

"Mary Donelson tells me you're from up at Empire."

"Yes."

"Nice town. Well, Natalie, you can go home now. Dr. Rawlins is stuck with me for the next eight hours. Of course, you're a lot prettier than I am, but he'll be sleeping some of that time."

Natalie set tender eyes on Rex. "You can finish the story tomorrow. I'll see you then."

"I'll look forward to it," he said softly.

At the federal building, Chief U.S. Marshal John Brockman was putting papers in a desk drawer, getting ready to leave the office, when there was a light tap on the door.

"Come in, Billy!" he called.

The door swung open, and John heard a feminine voice say, "I'm not Billy, but may I come in?"

He was out of his chair in a flash. "Honey, what's going on? Why didn't you wire me?"

Before Breanna could reply, John had her in his arms and was kissing her. She responded warmly, threading her fingers through his hair.

He kissed her a second time, then held her at arm's length and gave her a you've-been-a-naughty-girl look. "Don't tell me you rode down here alone."

"All right, I won't."

Clipping her chin playfully, he said, "All right, Mrs. Brockman. The truth. I want the truth."

Love light shone in Breanna's eyes. "The truth, Chief Brockman, is that we've had some powerful thunderstorms in the mountains, and the telegraph wires are down. There was no way I could wire you that it was time to come for me."

"All right. Keeping to the truth, did you ride down here from Empire alone?"

"Well, the truth is that I did start down alone. My work in Empire was done, and I was eager to get home to the husband that God gave me. However, as it turned out, I made the trip with three men and Chance tied behind a wagon."

John's dark eyebrows arched. "You made the trip with three men and Chance, all tied behind a wagon?"

"No, no. I made the trip with three men—and Chance tied behind the wagon."

John laughed. "The three men...do I know them?"

"You know one of them. Dr. Rex Rawlins."

"Dr. Rawlins? Why did he come to town?"

"He's hurt bad, John," she said, turning serious. "If you'll buy my supper, I'll tell you all about it."

Over a pleasant meal at one of the Brockmans' favorite cafés, Breanna told John the story. When she finished she said, "Am I forgiven now for starting out alone?"

"You're forgiven," he said, smiling at her across the table. "I sure hope Matt and the other doctors can help him. Be a shame for him to spend the rest of his life in a wheelchair."

"I agree. I'm praying the Lord will not let that happen." Breanna took a sip of coffee, then said, "But there is one good thing taking place because of his paralysis."

"Tell me about it."

John was surprised to learn that Natalie Fallon and Dr. Rawlins were once engaged, and was happy to hear that the Lord had made it possible for them to see each other again. He agreed with Breanna that it would be wonderful if they ended up getting married after all.

"We'll sure make it a matter of prayer, sweetheart," he told her.

"Yes, John. Say, I took a moment to stop and see Dave Taylor before leaving the hospital. He's looking much better."

"Yes, praise the Lord. I've been looking in on him every day. He's got a ways to go yet, but he seems to get a little stronger each time I see him."

"So, have you heard anything from Chet McCarty about new deputies for your staff?"

"Yes. It'll be a while before they start coming in a few at a time, but there's a top-notch deputy on his way here from Amarillo right now."

"Oh? That's good. Experienced and proven, eh?"

"Mm-hmm. Name's Palmer Danfield. He's got an excellent service record under his belt. Tough, resourceful, good with his gun."

"So when's this Palmer Danfield supposed to arrive?"

"One forty-five tomorrow afternoon."

"So soon! Good!"

"I'm taking him with me to the Duke Foster hideout on Monarch Pass. We'll head out by three o'clock. Get a good start by sundown."

"Just the two of you?"

"Yes. We'll have the advantage of surprise. Foster's got to be brought to justice, as well as the rest of his gang."

Breanna frowned. "Darling, I sure wish you had more men for this."

John swallowed his coffee and set the cup down. "Sometimes you can have too many men. That's what I meant about the advantage of surprise. It's easier to sneak up on a hideout if there are only two or three of you."

"Well, then, I wish there were another man going with you. Is Sol going to handle the office while you're gone?"

"Uh-huh. I never have to be concerned when he's there."

"It's good that you have him around."

"For sure. Well, I'm fed up."

"I'm fed up, too. Let's head for home."

It was ten-thirty the next morning when Dr. Matthew Carroll stood in examining room 1 at the hospital and ran his gaze over the faces of the six physicians who stood before him. Rex Rawlins lay on the table, and nurses Breanna Brockman and Natalie Fallon flanked Carroll.

"Gentlemen," said Carroll, "I appreciate your willingness to leave your offices to come here and make your examinations. Now that you've finished, let's go to the conference room and talk about it."

Natalie had volunteered to stay with Rex for her entire shift, and would be going back to his room with him. Breanna was going to the conference room to hear what the doctors had to say.

As the doctors filed out the door, Carroll stood over his patient and said, "I'll be back to let you know what we've come up with, once we've talked it out."

"I'll be waiting," said Rawlins, his features a bit pale.

"*We'll* be waiting, Dr. Carroll," said Natalie.

Breanna smiled at her. "Take good care of him."

"I will."

Natalie stood by and looked on while the orderlies carefully transferred Rex from the cart to his bed.

Hal said, "Dr. Rawlins, do you want to lie flat, or should we sit you up?"

"I'll lie flat, thanks. After all those hands and fingers worked me over, I'm a little tired."

"All right, sir. Let's get this pillow under your head."

When the orderlies had left the room, Natalie said, "Now I'll put a woman's touch to this."

Leaning over him, she lifted his head gently and removed the pillow. Using her fist, she punched it until it fluffed up, then leaned down and placed it back under his head. With her face only inches from his, she looked deep into his eyes and said, "How's that?"

"Much better," he replied, holding her gaze. "There's nothing like a woman's touch."

The magnetism they had once known was still there. Natalie kept her face close to his and said softly, "Is there anything else I can do for you, Dr. Rawlins?"

Rex's pulse was racing. "Yes, there is."

"Mm-hmm?"

"A kiss—even just a little one—would make me feel lots better."

For a long moment Natalie's eyes explored his face, then she brought her soft lips down on his. For those few seconds they were carried to another world where there were no hospitals, no paralysis, no broken hearts...no loneliness.

When Natalie pulled away and looked down at him, a single tear gleamed in the corner of her eye.

Rex was still under the spell of ecstasy from her kiss. He looked up at her, feeling his heart reaching for her more than it ever had before.

Wiping the tear away, Natalie said, "Rex, I have never stopped loving you, though I've tried. By now I figured you had met some young woman and fallen in love with her, that wherever you were you were happily married. I knew your utmost desire was to have a practice in a small town somewhere, and I was sure you were fulfilling your dream."

"I was fulfilling my dream in Empire, Natalie," he said, taking hold of her hand, "but it was only half a dream. I've never married because I'm still in love with you. And I always will be."

Natalie felt a rush of hot tears flood her eyes. Gently slipping her hand from his, she reached into the pocket of her nurse's apron and pulled out a handkerchief. She pressed it to her eyes and wept.

Rex reached up and laid a hand on her arm. "Natalie, please don't cry."

Sniffling, she removed the handkerchief from her eyes, looked down at him, and said, "Rex, I've wished a thousand times that I had never broken our engagement. I've laid awake many a night giving myself a mental lashing for being such a fool. I finally resigned myself to the fact that I had made a terrible mistake and would have to live with it the rest of my life."

She broke into sobs, pressing the handkerchief to her face again.

"Natalie, please," said Rex, touching her arm again. "Don't cry."

As she gained control of her sobs, she said, "I'm sorry. It's just that for these two years since I walked out of your life, I have had such pain in my heart. I really tried to suffocate the love I felt for you so it wouldn't hurt anymore. But I couldn't. It's still there, Rex. I love you. Nothing can ever change that."

Patting her arm, Rex said, "Sit down now. Dry up those tears."

It took Natalie a few minutes to stop crying. As she dabbed away the last of the tears, she said, "Let's talk about you. We mustn't despair about your paralysis. It just might not be permanent."

"I try to tell myself it isn't, Natalie, but doubts assail me."

"But the Lord is not short of power, Rex. If He wants you to walk again, He will make it so you can."

"You sound like Breanna. She's got a mountain of faith."

"That she does. When I told her about my young doctor and how I had broken off our relationship but still loved him, she said the Lord had a plan for my life, and if I would let Him, He would work it out."

"And when I told her about us," Rex said, smiling, "she said she was going to pray that the Lord would perform a miracle and let us get back together. And look at us. Here we are. I didn't think I would ever see you again in this life."

"Oh, darling, I just know you're going to walk again. You are. Yes, you are. You just believe it."

"Natalie, thank you for being such an encouragement. Let's take time right now and pray about it. Okay?"

"Of course. Let's talk to the Great Physician. He loves you, and He cares about your life and your career."

As the seven physicians and Breanna Brockman sat around the conference table at Mile High Hospital, Dr. Matt Carroll said, "All right, gentlemen, let me sum up what has been said here. Each of you has given his opinion concerning young Dr. Rawlins's situation, and basically we are all in agreement.

"Without actually opening him up to see the damage, we agree that Rawlins has either a severely damaged vertebral foramen, which is allowing the spinal cord to be pinched, or he could have one or more severely damaged cartilaginous intervertebral disks. If it is the former, the vertebral foramen could possibly be repaired with surgery. If it is the latter, we agree there would be little hope, even with surgery, that he would ever walk again."

Heads were nodding.

Breanna sat in silence, her heart aching for the young physician who had such a promising career in Empire.

"We also agree," Carroll went on, "that Dr. Rawlins's injury could be something else." He ran a palm over his face. "We all know there would be extreme danger if the surgeon who performed the operation was not sufficiently experienced in this field, and highly skilled."

Dr. Lyle Goodwin lifted a hand.

"Yes, Doctor?" said Carroll.

"I might say that if it is a damaged vertebral foramen, that in time, when the swelling goes down and the muscles in the area cease to spasm, there is a possibility that the feeling might come back to his legs. If it did, with proper therapy, he might walk again."

"I agree, Dr. Goodwin," said Carroll.

"Very possible," spoke up one of the other doctors. "However, if it is anything else, surgery must be done."

The others were nodding their agreement.

Dr. Hugh Cameron raised his hand.

"Yes, Doctor?" said Carroll.

"There are seven physician-surgeons in Denver, and we're all present at this moment. If the surgery must be done, which of us will perform it?"

There was an instant rumble of voices, with each of the other five saying he did not feel qualified to perform the delicate surgery.

Carroll set his eyes on Cameron. "Were you volunteering, Doctor?"

Cameron vigorously shook his head. "No, sir! I'm not as well qualified as most of the men here. Whoever does it will be taking on a tremendous responsibility. Even if there is a chance that Dr. Rawlins could walk again, one slip by the surgeon and his chance to walk could be gone forever."

Another doctor said, "Gentlemen, it is my opinion that the senior surgeon among us is best qualified…Dr. Goodwin. If the surgery must be done, I believe he is the man to do it."

Goodwin's face tinted. "No, Doctor, even though I am the oldest here, there is a man who has more experience than I in this field—our illustrious chief administrator, Dr. Matt Carroll."

A chorus of voices agreed.

Matt lifted a hand for quiet. "Gentlemen, we all know the kind of complications the surgeon who does the operation could run into. I am not a specialist. If I found something beyond my knowledge and experience, I could fail the young doctor and cause him to remain paralyzed. Whereas a specialist in the field who has plenty of experience could make the difference.

"Something just came to my mind. A few days ago I was reading in the latest issue of the *American Medical Association Journal* that the prominent Swiss surgeon Dr. Hallet B. Cusing is in this country. Did any of you see the article?"

Only Dr. Goodwin had read it. The others mumbled that they hadn't yet had time to read the *Journal.*

All the doctors, however, knew the name of Dr. Cusing. Living and working in Switzerland, Cusing was Europe's foremost spinal surgeon. Of late, Cusing had made new discoveries in spinal surgery and was famous for his successes.

"Why is Dr. Cusing in this country?" asked one of the physicians.

"According to the article, he came here to lecture in medical schools on the eastern seaboard. The article said that the officials at Bellevue Hospital in New York City were trying to persuade Dr. Cusing to perform spinal surgery on a Manhattan police officer who had fallen from the balcony of a third-story tenement building while attempting to apprehend a burglar. Dr. Cusing was trying to adjust his speaking schedule to do it. He may still be at Bellevue, looking after his patient. I could wire Bellevue and see. If so, possibly I could persuade him to come and take Dr. Rawlins's case."

"I like the idea," spoke up one of the doctors, "but what about the expense? Is Dr. Rawlins able to pay whatever Cusing would charge?"

"I doubt it," said Carroll, "but what is money compared to the young doctor getting his legs back? Certainly something can be done to raise the money."

"I agree, Dr. Carroll," said Lyle Goodwin. "We must not let anything stand in the way of Dr. Rawlins having the necessary treatment. As much confidence as I have in you, I still understand your reluctance to perform spinal surgery. I say you should wire Bellevue Hospital and see if you can contact Dr. Cusing."

"Yes! Dr. Rawlins deserves the best!" said another.

"Do it, Dr. Carroll!" Goodwin said.

Though Breanna sat in silence, she nodded her agreement to that statement.

Every man voiced his opinion, saying they would come up with the money somehow. Dr. Carroll should wire Bellevue Hospital.

"All right, gentlemen," said Carroll. "The wire will be sent within the hour. And I'll keep all of you abreast of the situation."

18

Natalie Fallon was seated next to Rex's bedside when Breanna entered the room.

Natalie let go of his hand and stood up as Breanna moved toward them.

"The meeting is over," Breanna said. "Dr. Carroll will be here in a minute to give you the diagnosis."

"Bad or good?" Rex asked.

"I'll let Dr. Carroll explain it to you. He came up with an idea that could prove to be very good."

The door opened and Matt Carroll entered. He drew up beside the two nurses. "How much have you told him, Breanna?"

"Only that you've come up with an idea. I'll let you fill him in on the doctors' opinions and tell him your idea."

Matt grinned. "I wouldn't have minded if you'd told him."

"I thought it best that he hear it from you."

Matt nodded, then told Rex about the possibility of walking again if the injury was merely a damaged vertebral foramen. If that was the case, surgery would help, but it was extremely risky.

Rex understood the situation and told Carroll he realized the dangers involved in the surgery. "But if I still have no feeling in my feet or legs after the swelling has gone down," he said, "we'll know it's more serious."

"Right. However, we all agreed that this is probably not it. And if we're right, the only way we can know the extent of the damage will be to open you up. At the same time, we must be ready to perform what surgery we find necessary. There can be no delay once you've been cut open. Time is of the essence, Doctor. Your swelling and the resultant spasms will be gone in a day or two. But if surgery is needed, it must be done as soon as possible."

"So what's this idea Breanna spoke of?" Rex asked.

"I'm sure you know of Dr. Hallet B. Cusing?"

"The Swiss spinal specialist. Of course."

"Well, he's in this country on the East Coast right now."

Matt explained that only a few days ago, officials at New York's Bellevue Hospital had asked him to perform spinal surgery on an injured New York City police officer.

"I'm sure Dr. Cusing would stay near his patient for a reasonable amount of time after the surgery," said Matt. "I brought up to the doctors that I would like to wire Dr. Cusing at Bellevue and ask him to come here and take over your case. We all agree that it will take the most experienced eye possible to see the extent of the damage when you are opened up."

Natalie took hold of Breanna's hand and held on.

"Cusing..." Rawlins said, pondering the man's fame.

"Even if by the time he gets here you have feeling in your legs and feet," said Carroll, "we'd all feel better if the top man in the field looks you over. But...if you're still totally paralyzed, Dr. Cusing would be here to diagnose the situation when he opened you up, and he could proceed with the surgery he deemed necessary."

Deep lines formed on Rex's brow. He was looking at the

outline of his lifeless legs and feet under the covers.

"All the doctors agreed that I should wire Dr. Cusing right away," said Carroll. "We need to get him here as soon as possible."

Rex looked up at Dr. Carroll and said, "I appreciate your idea, Doctor. I know Dr. Cusing's impeccable reputation as a spinal expert. But I also know that I can't afford to have him do the surgery, even if he's willing to come. There would be the cost of his transportation from New York to Denver and back, plus his fee. The fee itself could easily run fifteen thousand dollars...maybe more."

"I realize that," said Carroll. "And so do the other doctors. We all agreed that when it comes to comparing money to your getting the use of your legs back, the money is insignificant. We'll do whatever is necessary to raise the money for you."

"Oh, God bless you for that, Dr. Carroll," said Natalie.

"What I need right now is your permission to send the wire to Dr. Cusing," said Matt.

Rawlins pondered it a moment, then said, "Dr. Carroll, raising the money means that somebody has to donate funds...a whole lot of somebodys. I can't let people do that for me. I have great confidence in your skill as a surgeon. If you will be the one to open me up and do whatever surgery you deem necessary, I will be quite comfortable with it."

"I appreciate your confidence in me," Matt said, rubbing his forehead, "but Dr. Cusing is a thousand times more qualified. If I were to do it, there would be no fee. But I might fail you because of my lack of knowledge in the field. We can't let the money be a factor here. I don't know where we would begin to raise funds for Cusing's fee and transportation, but between the other doctors and myself, we'll find a way. If people want to give to the worthy cause, you should let them."

"Dr. Rawlins," said Breanna, "please give Dr. Carroll permission to wire Dr. Cusing. The Lord owns the whole universe. He isn't broke. He can supply the money without inconveniencing anyone."

"You're right, Breanna," said Natalie. "Why don't we just stop right here and ask the Lord to provide the money in His own marvelous way, and trust Him to do it. Then Dr. Carroll can go ahead and send the wire by faith."

"Let's just take it to the Lord right now," said Carroll. "I'll lead us."

Natalie took hold of Rex's hand and squeezed it, then held on while Matt Carroll prayed. He asked God to guide them, provide the funds needed for whatever surgery would be necessary, and to give Rex the use of his legs.

After the amen, Carroll said, "All right, Dr. Rawlins, we've put it all in the Lord's hands. Do I have your permission to send that wire?"

Rex bit his lip. He knew the Lord wasn't going to rain down money from the sky. It would have to come from people. He was having a hard time with the thought of hardworking people sacrificing things they needed in order to give money to him. "Tell you what, Dr. Carroll. I need more time to think on this. Would you give me a day to put my mind on it, and to pray about it myself?"

Carroll did not answer immediately.

Natalie and Breanna exchanged anxious glances.

Finally, Carroll said, "Dr. Rawlins, I'll do as you ask. But we must contact Dr. Cusing before he heads back to Switzerland."

"Just one day. Please?"

"All right. I'll talk to you about it tomorrow morning."

"Thank you, Doctor," said Rawlins, relief evident on his face.

Breanna leaned close. "Is it the money, Dr. Rawlins? Are you concerned that people might be asked to give of their funds so you might walk again?"

Rawlins met her steady gaze. "I just need time to think about this whole thing and to pray."

"I'll be praying, too," she said in a compassionate tone. "The main thing is to see you back in Empire, caring for your patients."

"That's what I want, Breanna," he said, smiling at her. "Thank you again, for all you've done for me."

"It's been a pleasure, Doctor."

"Breanna and I will take our leave now," said Carroll. "Keep him as comfortable as you can, Natalie."

When Carroll and Breanna were gone, Natalie poured Rex a cup of water, and while he was drinking it, she said, "Darling, I love you very, very much."

"And I love you very, very much, too. More than anything in all the world."

Natalie set the cup on the bedstand, leaned down and planted a soft kiss on his lips, then took hold of his hand. "Rex, I was so terribly wrong to refuse to marry you because you wanted to practice your medicine in a small town."

"You had your reasons."

"But my reasons were all wrong. You told me that if I loved you as a wife should love her husband, I would go anywhere with you and be there to help you realize your dream. It wasn't that I didn't love you enough to do that. I simply let my fears override my love. I shouldn't have allowed what happened to Daddy influence me. I should have married you for what you are…not what I wanted you to be."

"I thought about it every day as my heart yearned for you, sweet lady," said Rex. "Sure, it hurt to know that I could love you so much and think you didn't love me enough to overcome your fears. But it didn't change how much I loved you, nor how much I needed you."

Natalie's lips quivered and her eyes misted. "Darling, if you still want me as your wife, I'll marry you right away."

Rex looked at Natalie with loving eyes for what seemed an eternity to her, then drew a deep breath and said, "Darling, I love you with all my heart and would love to marry you, but I can't."

Her face blanched, and she choked out the words, "You can't?"

"Not under these circumstances. I can't let you be burdened with a cripple for a husband for the rest of your life. If God sees fit to leave me paralyzed, I won't be able to carry on my practice. I have no idea how I'll make a living. I simply can't be a burden to you."

"Rex, you wouldn't be a burden," she countered. "I love you."

Natalie drew a shuddering breath and began to weep. "Oh, I wish I had married you when we were in Chicago! We would already be husband and wife now. And we wouldn't be having this conversation. I want to marry you now, Rex! Right now! Even if you are never able to walk again, you can carry on your practice from a wheelchair. I'll work as your nurse and help you."

Tears were streaming down Rex's cheeks. "Natalie, it means more than I can tell you that you love me enough to do that, but…but right now, my mind isn't even functioning normally. Please understand. This is too important an issue for me to properly handle with the duress that's on me."

"I'm sorry, darling. I—"

"No, no," he said, reaching out and stroking her lovely face.

"There's nothing to be sorry about. I love you for what you've just offered to do. But I simply can't deal with it right now. We must carefully consider the implications involved, and this will take some time. So let's not try to work on it right now, okay?"

Natalie nodded, wiping away tears of her own. "I understand, darling. It's just that—well, I let you go out of my life once. I will never let it happen again. Never."

As she spoke, she laid her head on his chest. He held her close, and they wept together.

As Breanna walked down the hall with her brother-in-law, she said, "Matt, have you got a couple of minutes? I need to talk to you."

"Sure. Come on into the office."

When Matt closed the door behind them, Breanna said, "I'm sure Dr. Rawlins's problem is concern that whoever would be contacted to give money for his surgical expenses would give money they couldn't afford. At least for the most part."

"I picked that up, too. And I appreciate that he doesn't want to be burdensome to anyone."

"In your own mind, Matt, where would you go to ask people to pitch in for him?"

"Well, I'm sure we could raise a good portion of it among the doctors who were sitting in that conference room. I thought I might contact the chairman of the town council in Empire. The people know him there, and would no doubt rise to the occasion if they knew their own beloved physician needed funds that might let him walk again."

"Those are your two most natural sources," said Breanna, "but from what I saw a few moments ago, I don't think Rex Rawlins would sit still for it."

"Well, we prayed together, asking the Lord to supply the needed funds. He still must use people, since He doesn't mint U.S. dollars in heaven."

"And that's exactly what He is doing."

"Pardon me?"

"God is using people to supply the funds so Dr. Cusing's fee and transportation costs can be met."

"Don't you mean *will* use people?"

"No. Present tense. John and I will put up the money to pay whatever it costs, Matt. We simply cannot let this opportunity go while Dr. Cusing is in this country. I doubt seriously that he would come back across the Atlantic to take Dr. Rawlins's case. And even if he would, it would be too late."

Matthew was not surprised at Breanna's words. Before John Brockman laid aside his "Stranger" image to marry Breanna and become chief U.S. marshal of the Western District, he had given great sums of money to those in need, leaving behind a silver medallion with a five-point star in the center and a verse around its circular edge: THE STRANGER THAT SHALL COME FROM A FAR LAND—Deuteronomy 29:22.

Carroll was aware that John and Breanna had also given money to people in need since they married. Only Breanna knew the source of John's wealth and the far country from whence he had come to America. Carroll was also aware that Breanna could speak for both of them in money matters. Deeply moved by this show of generosity, he said with relief in his voice, "Thank you, Breanna. If there is any surgeon on earth who can give our patient the use of his legs back, it's Dr. Hallet B. Cusing. Can I go tell Dr. Rawlins right now?"

"Yes, but there is one stipulation. This is to be given anonymously. John will want it that way, too. Just tell Dr. Rawlins that someone with the means, who wishes to remain unnamed, will pay all the expenses to bring Dr. Cusing here, and will meet his fee, whatever it is."

"But he'll know it's somebody connected with the hospital. No one else is aware of what we've talked about."

"No problem. That would take in seven doctors, including yourself, wouldn't it?"

"Yes."

"Then let him wonder who it is."

Matt smiled and shook his head. "You are really something, sister-in-law."

Breanna was about to quip a reply when she saw a familiar face looking at her through the office window that looked onto the hall. She smiled, waved, and headed toward the door. Opening it, she said, "Hello, sweetheart. Your new deputy isn't here yet, is he?"

John grinned at the doctor and said, "Hi, Matt." Then he said to Breanna, "No. I'll come back to say good-bye when he and I are ready to leave about three o'clock. I had a few minutes to spare, so I came by to see Dave Taylor since I'll be gone for a while. A nurse was tending to him, so I only stuck my head in the door and told him I was leaving town for a few days and would see him when I got back. I happened to notice you in here with Matt as I passed the window, and didn't want to leave without stopping to say I love you."

Matt grinned. "John, you're the romantic one, aren't you?"

"Being married to this wonderful female keeps me that way."

"Darling, while you're here, can you spare another few minutes?" Breanna asked.

"Sure. What's up?"

"I'll let Matt explain about Dr. Rawlins's situation, then I'll tell you what I did."

"All right."

When John heard about the diagnosis of the seven doctors regarding Rex Rawlins, and of the possibility of procuring the services of Dr. Hallet B. Cusing, he was pleased. He was also pleased when Breanna told him she had volunteered Brockman money to cover all the costs, and that the Brockmans would remain anonymous.

Putting an arm around Breanna, John said to Carroll, "We're happy to do this, Matt. Get that telegram sent to Dr. Cusing."

Matt thanked them again, and Breanna left the office with John to walk him to the front door of the hospital.

As they walked together, John said, "It sure is good to see Dave sitting up in that chair. Praise the Lord he's doing so well."

"Yes," said Breanna. "Praise the Lord. Nyla is sure happy to see him looking that good."

When they reached the door, John said, "I should be here just before three o'clock, honey. See you then."

Breanna suddenly grasped his hand and said, "John, you remember that I told you last night I wished a third man could go with you on the trip to the Foster hideout?"

"Yes."

"I…I've had a strange feeling about this trip ever since. Like maybe there's some unseen danger lurking on the trail, or something. It's hard to describe it."

John laid a hand on the side of her face. "I'll be fine, sweetheart. I've routed many outlaws out of their hideouts. Besides, on this trip I'll have Palmer Danfield at my side—a tough cookie, and a man with plenty of experience. Don't you worry about me."

Breanna watched her husband head down the boardwalk toward the hitching rail and Ebony. John looked up to the second floor as he was about to mount, and waved—presumably to Dave Taylor.

The tall man swung into the saddle, blew her a kiss, and rode away.

Breanna pushed away the uneasiness she felt about John's trip into the Rockies and decided to see how Rex Rawlins had taken the news that an anonymous donor would foot the bill. Since she was not actually on duty, she would go to Matt's office and wait for him to return.

She had been in the office about twenty minutes when her brother-in-law returned.

"Hi, lady-who-looks-like-my-wife," he said with a smile. "I just dispatched one of the orderlies to send a telegram to Dr. Cusing for me."

"Ah! So our young doctor gave in, did he?"

"Yes. Happily. He and Natalie were both fighting tears when I left his room. You were right, Breanna. Dr. Rawlins was fearful the money would come from bighearted people who had small incomes."

"He's a dear man. It takes an unselfish man to practice medicine in a small town where many of the people can't even pay for his services, and to know he will never make the kind of money the city doctors do."

"You're right about that," said Matt, clearing his throat. "I'm sure glad Denver's not a big city, or people would think Dottie and I were among the elite."

Breanna smiled. "Anyway, I'm glad Dr. Rawlins gave in to let you wire Dr. Cusing. Did he try to squeeze the name of the donor out of you?"

"No. He just said, 'God bless whoever it is.'"

"God has blessed the Brockmans in so many ways," she said. "We could never thank Him enough." She took a deep breath. "Well, Dr. Carroll, I told John before we left the house this morning that once things were settled for Dr. Rawlins today, I'd go on duty. I'll go see Mary and let her put me to work."

At precisely 1:45 that afternoon, the Amarillo train chugged into Denver's Union Station.

When it squealed to a halt, Dick Nye left his seat and stood up in the aisle of the coach, along with the other passengers who were preparing to get off. Some were waving to family and friends through the windows.

With the late Palmer Danfield's gun belt on his waist, his badge on his vest, and his identification papers in his pocket, Nye took the overnight bag down from the rack and got in the slow-moving line filing toward the front entrance of the coach.

Nye had been in situations where he had to keep cool in spite of potential trouble facing him, but none like this. He knew enough about John "The Stranger" Brockman to put his nerves on edge. His masquerade had to be perfect. One slip and it would all be over. Brockman was no dummy, and he was tough as nails. Richard Eugene Nye would have to be on his toes every minute of every hour, and every second of every minute.

As he drew closer to the door that opened onto the station platform and a face-to-face meeting with the chief U.S. marshal, pearls of sweat formed on his brow, and he realized his lips were pressed tightly against his teeth. When the line stopped for a moment, Nye took the time to rub the back of his neck, easing his tension-knotted muscles.

The line started again, and in a matter of seconds the impostor was on the coach platform. He didn't have to search long amid the crowd to find the federal lawman. John Brockman's height made him easy to spot.

Nye set eyes on the tall man, who had focused on Danfield's badge and was threading his way through the crowd toward him. In spite of the tension within him, Nye said under his breath, "Brockman, you don't know it, but you're a dead man."

When Nye left the bottom step of the coach, Brockman was there with his hand extended and a warm smile beneath his well-trimmed black mustache. "Deputy Palmer Danfield," said the chief as they clasped hands. "I'm John Brockman."

Nye felt the power in the man's grip and almost winced as he said, "Glad to meet you, sir."

"I assume you have more luggage."

More luggage! An icy hand clutched Nye's stomach. He had to think fast. "Ah…yes. In the baggage coach." Nye hoped he was right in assuming that the real Danfield had checked larger pieces, since he was moving to Denver. If there were no pieces of luggage, he would blame the railroad for not getting them on the train.

By the time they had pressed through the crowd and arrived at the baggage coach, the porters had already begun unloading.

This was one thing Nye had given no thought to since boarding the train in Amarillo. He felt the biting edge of panic. He hoped Brockman wouldn't ask him how many pieces he had checked. Nye knew that every piece of luggage had to have a name tag in plain sight. He just hoped however many pieces there were would be placed together.

As the luggage was being placed on the depot platform, Dick Nye tried to disguise his nervousness. What if Brockman asked him to point out the pieces of luggage?

Relief came when a man drew up and said, "John Stranger! How are you, sir? Delbert Harrington. Remember me? Raton. Three years ago."

"Oh, sure!" said John, gripping his hand. "How's your family?"

"They're fine, Mr. Stranger. Of course, I wouldn't have any of them if you hadn't saved them from that Comanche attack!"

From there the conversation led to inquiries about each member of the Harrington family. Then Harrington's attention went to the badge on Brockman's chest, and John found himself giving an explanation about becoming chief U.S. marshal.

In the meantime, a tense Dick Nye moved about the luggage as it was being placed on the platform. He spotted a small trunk with the name *Danfield* painted in block letters on the lid. Seconds later, an identical trunk was set down beside it.

Nye's heart lurched when Brockman's deep voice came from behind him. "I see two pieces. How many more do you have?"

Nye had to take a chance. "Just these two, Chief."

"All right. I'll get a porter over here to put them on his cart and bring them out to the parking lot."

The porter was procured, and the two trunks loaded into the rear of John's buggy. Nye breathed a secret sigh of relief when they pulled out of the lot and onto the street.

As the buggy picked up speed, he stole a look at the man next to him and felt a thrill rush through his chest. He was going to kill the famous John "The Stranger" Brockman, and get paid for it!

While Brockman drove the buggy toward the federal building, he told the impostor about Duke Foster's gang trying to kidnap Chester McCarty, and why. He explained about the shoot-out in the Westerner Hotel, saying that as soon as the shooting started he had killed Duke Foster's younger brother, Chick, and a gang member named Layton Patch.

"I see," said Nye. "Got those two right away, eh?"

"Mm-hmm. Wounded another one, but two of the gang

members pulled back into the room where they were waiting for McCarty. Locked the door and got away through a window. It was on the second floor, but they used a balcony outside the window to drop to the ground. By the time I could get down there, they were gone. No doubt they went running to wherever Duke was holed up. I didn't get a look at either of their faces."

"So what about the wounded one?" Nye now knew it was Jim Felton who had given Brockman the information on the hideout at Monarch Pass.

"His name was Jim Felton. He was dying, and he knew it. I persuaded him to come clean as the decent thing to do in his last moments. He named Duke Foster as his leader, and the two dead ones as Chick Foster and Layton Patch. He also named the two who got away—Dick Nye and Pete Dawson. All of them were wanted for robbery and murder. I had Wanted posters on each one, with vague descriptions, but no photographs and no artists' drawings of any of their faces. In coming clean, Felton told me where Duke's hideout is located in the mountains."

"Oh, really?" Nye was cursing Felton under his breath.

"So your first assignment, Deputy Danfield," said John, "is to go with me to the Foster hideout and help me take Foster and his remaining gang members by surprise. Together, we'll take them into custody and bring them in for trial. I understand this kind of work is your specialty."

"You got that, Chief," said Nye, chuckling. "I really want to be an asset to you on this new deputy's job."

"I have no doubt that you will be," said John. "You come highly recommended by Chet McCarty. Hate to put you to work without a good night's rest, but you and I are leaving on horseback just as close to three o'clock as we can. I want to get a good start before sundown."

"Sure. Whatever you say."

"We'll put your trunks in a storeroom at the federal building. I want you to meet the man who was my predecessor."

"Solomon Duvall."

"That's right. He's filling in for me while we go after Foster and his gang."

Nye laughed inwardly as he said to himself, *If you only knew this will be your last time to ever go after outlaws, Stranger! I'll be comin' back to collect my pay at Harold's house…but you won't be comin' back at all!*

19

PETE DAWSON TURNED off the street and hurried down the alley. He saw the curtains move at a window of Harold Sheetz's house as he entered the yard.

Duke Foster opened the back door and looked at him expectantly.

"Yep, Dick has done the job, boss!" said Dawson as he passed through the door. "He got off that train wearin' Danfield's badge, just as planned. I think he's even wearin' the man's gun belt. At least the one he's wearin' ain't his old one."

Foster laughed. "So, was Brockman there to meet him?"

"Sure was! They shook hands, and Brockman was all smiles."

Duke smacked a fist into a palm. "Great! I knew Dick would pull it off. So Danfield's dead, and Brockman's gonna be!"

"I can't wait to see Dick when he comes back from killin' Brockman, boss."

"*You* can't? Hah! How about me? When he comes back and tells us Brockman's as dead as Danfield, we're gonna have us a celebration!"

John Brockman paused in the hall of the federal building and asked two janitors to carry the trunks from his buggy and put them in the storeroom. Then he and Palmer Danfield entered the U.S marshal's office and found Solomon Duvall going over some papers at the desk with Billy Martin. Brockman introduced Danfield to the two men.

After shaking hands, Duvall said, "Your name was brought up just about every time I had contact with George Frame, Danfield. You have quite a reputation."

"I've tried to maintain one, sir," said Nye.

John looked at the new man. "Well, Deputy Danfield, we'd better get moving."

"John, you be careful," said Duvall.

"I will," the tall man replied, starting for the door. "We'll be back in a few days."

"Nice to meet you fellas," said Nye, following Brockman out the door.

As they climbed into the buggy, John said, "I've rented you a horse at the stable down the street. My horse is already there."

Ready to take you on your last ride, thought Nye. Aloud, he said, "I noticed the gun rack in the office, Chief. Maybe we should go back and get me a rifle."

"You've already got one in the saddle boot on your horse."

Nye looked at Brockman with a sly grin. "You seem to be a well-organized man."

"I try," said John, chuckling.

John guided the buggy up in front of the hostler's office and pulled rein. The hostler came out and greeted the chief U.S. marshal, then grinned at Dick Nye, saying, "So this is the new man who's ridin' after the Foster gang with you, eh, Chief?"

"That's him," replied John, stepping out of the buggy. "Eddie Bascom, shake hands with Deputy U.S. Marshal Palmer Danfield."

As Nye shook hands with Bascom, he thought, *If you really shook hands with Danfield, pal, you'd find his fingers a little stiff.*

Bascom opened the gate and led the two men across the corral to the barn, then led them inside to the horse stalls.

When Ebony saw his master, he whinnied and snorted. While John was petting the gelding's neck and speaking softly to him, Bascom pointed to the horse in the next stall and said, "Here's the one I picked out for you, Deputy. You'll like him."

Nye opened the waist-high door of the stall and eyed the black-and-white piebald gelding. "Looks like a good animal. Does he have experience in the mountains?"

"Plenty."

Dick Nye eyed the bedrolls, camping gear, canteens, and stuffed saddlebags on both horses. "Looks like we're ready to ride, Chief."

"Let's do it," said Brockman, leading Ebony out of the stall.

Nye followed, leading the piebald.

As both men were mounting their horses outside the barn, Brockman said, "Just one more stop, and we'll be on our way."

John bid Eddie good-bye, saying they would be back with the Foster gang in a few days.

As they entered the broad, dusty street, Nye said, "So what's our stop?"

"The hospital."

"Hospital? You not feeling well?"

John chuckled. "My wife is a nurse there. I want to tell her good-bye."

"Don't blame you for that."

When they rode up to the hospital, John guided Ebony up

to the hitching rail and said, "Would you like to come in, Danfield?"

"No need, sir," replied Nye. "I'll just wait here with the horses."

Brockman swung his leg over the saddle, touched ground, and said, "I won't be long."

As John turned away from Ebony, there was movement at a window on the second floor, which caught his attention. It was Dave Taylor.

He waved back and said over his shoulder, "One of my deputies, Danfield. Got shot up pretty bad."

"Oh. Too bad," said Nye, smiling at Taylor and waving to him. "He going to be all right?"

"Yes, thank the Lord. But it will take a while."

John's mention of the Lord reminded Dick that John "The Stranger" Brockman was also a preacher. He hoped there wouldn't be any preaching on the trip. He grinned to himself as he thought, *I won't have to listen too much, anyway. Dead men can't preach.*

Brockman greeted Mabel Trotter as he passed through the lobby. When he turned into the hall, he saw Breanna come out of a room just as another nurse was passing the door. The two nurses spoke to each other, then Breanna spotted her husband and hurried toward him.

"Did your new man arrive all right, darling?"

"Sure did. And we're ready to go." Looking around, he said, "Isn't there a closet or something where we could find a little privacy?"

"There's a storage room right down there," she said with a mischievous smile.

John took her by the hand and led her inside. Then he took her into his arms, kissed her lovingly, and said, "I'll miss you."

"I'll miss you, too, darling," she said, laying her head against his chest.

"It'll just be a little over a week."

Breanna pulled her head back and looked into his eyes. "I…I still have this strange feeling about this trip. I'm uneasy about it. I wish you weren't going."

"I'll be fine, honey," he said, cupping a hand under her chin. "Duke Foster and his gang are menaces to society. They must be brought to justice. Palmer Danfield and I are going to do just that. We'll bring them back to face multiple charges of murder and robbery. They'll hang for sure."

Breanna laid her head back against his chest, put her arms around him, and held him tight. He circled her body with his strong arms, kissed the top of her head, and said, "I know your prayers are with me. The Lord will keep me safe in His hand."

He could feel her head nod against his chest. She squeezed hard around his waist and said with a quiver in her voice, "Oh, John, I love you so very, very much. I…I just wish I could shake this feeling."

"It'll go away, sweetheart," he said, kissing the top of her head again. "I love you so very, very much, too."

As they stepped back into the hall, John said, "I will be back, honey."

"You carry my heart with you, darling. Don't forget that."

"How could I? God gave me the most beautiful and wonderful woman He ever made. I could never forget that she loves me."

Breanna stood in the hall and watched him walk away. When he reached the lobby door, he stopped to wave, then disappeared.

As she headed toward a room where she needed to tend to a patient, she whispered, "Dear Lord, I don't know what it is, but

I fear for John's life on this trip. Please keep him safe, and bring him home to me alive and well."

In his room on the second floor, Deputy U.S. Marshal Dave Taylor sat in his chair at the window, watching for his boss to come out the door and rejoin the new deputy.

When Brockman came into sight, he was walking swiftly. He literally vaulted into the saddle, and the two lawmen rode away.

Dave wondered who the new man might be. He had never seen him before.

John Brockman and Dick Nye rode due south out of Denver, skirting the foothills. Wanting to cover as much ground as possible before dark, John kept Ebony at a steady gallop, and Nye made his horse keep up.

When the sun dipped behind the mountains to their right, John slowed Ebony to a walk and said, "We'll ride another half hour, then find a good place to camp. We've come about thirty miles, and I'd like to pick up a little more before we stop. That will put us just about halfway to Colorado Springs."

Nye had made the trip many a time, but playing ignorant, he said, "I assume we'll turn west into the mountains at Colorado Springs."

"Right. Then we're looking at close to three days to reach the summit of Monarch Pass. It's rugged, mountainous country all the way to the base of the summit, then we've got a real climb up the pass. It tops out at 11,300 feet."

"Guess we do have quite a ride ahead of us," commented Nye.

They rode till twilight was coming and stopped when Brockman spotted a clearing alongside a meandering creek that came down out of the mountains and flowed toward the eastern plains. The area was surrounded by cottonwoods and elms.

John built a fire, using limbs from a fallen tree. While twilight deepened into night, the two men sat on the ground and ate hot beans, along with hardtack, and drank strong black coffee. While eating, John pointed out another campfire upstream in the dense woods. Others were taking advantage of the ideal spot for camping.

When they were finished, they washed their tin cups and plates in the creek, then Nye sat down beside the fire again. Brockman went to his saddle, which now lay on the ground, and took his Bible out of a saddlebag. Nye watched him as he returned from the shadows and sat down on the opposite side of the fire, angling himself to let the firelight glow on the pages.

John could feel the other man's eyes on him as he read. Twice he paused to toss more wood on the fire, then went back to reading.

Nye sat in silence, wondering what people got out of reading the Bible. To him it was old and outdated.

When John finished reading, he closed the Bible and sent a glance to his partner. "Wonderful Book," he said, smiling. "Have you read it, Danfield?"

"Uh...no, Chief. I've heard some Bible stories here and there, but I've never read it."

"You don't know what you're missing."

"Maybe someday I'll take time to read it."

"You need to read it and heed it," John said. "This Book is God's only way of showing you not only how to live this life but to prepare for the next one."

Nye did not comment.

As John rose to his feet, he said, "You do realize there's a next life, don't you—that your existence doesn't stop when you take your last breath on this earth?"

"Yeah. Something deep inside a fella tells him that."

"Right," said John. "And God put it there." With that, he turned and put the Bible back in the saddlebag.

Brockman and Nye had tethered their horses where there was plenty of grass to graze on. They took a few minutes to lead the animals to the creek and let them drink, then laid out their bedrolls on opposite sides of the fire, using their saddles for pillows, and settled down for the night.

John lay with his head on the saddle, thinking of Breanna and missing her.

Dick Nye lay in silence, pondering the task before him. The man so long known as the Stranger was a mild, gentle man, but Nye knew that under the gentleness, the man had a fiber of steel. Nye would have to be very careful when the time came to send him into the next life. He would have to pick just the right place and time, when he was sure there were no people anywhere nearby.

A soft wind fanned the fire, blowing sparks, white ash, and thin smoke into the black night.

John broke the silence, saying, "I understand you're a widower, Danfield."

Nye told him he was, and he made up a story about how much he loved his wife and how it hurt to lose her. John didn't press for any details but wanted his new man to know he was interested in him.

Both men were becoming drowsy when a wild, mournful howl came down from higher country. It was not the howl of a prowling beast, but the wail of a lonely wolf, crying out the meaning of the mountains and the night.

⚔

Dr. Matthew Carroll was going over a patient's records at his desk when a knock came at the door.

"Yes?" he said. "Please come in."

The door opened, and he recognized the face of one of the young messengers from the Western Union office. "Good morning, Bryan. I hope you have a telegram for me from New York."

The straw-haired youth smiled and stepped in. "Yes, sir. I do."

He handed an excited Carroll a slip of paper to sign, then gave him the sealed yellow envelope. The doctor reached in his pocket, pulled out a silver dollar, and laid it in Bryan's palm. "Thanks."

"Thank you!" said the messenger, and hurried away.

Matt ripped open the envelope and unfolded the sheet of yellow paper. Soon his brow furrowed, and his countenance sagged. Shaking his head as he finished reading, he folded the sheet and stuffed it back into the envelope.

He left the office and headed down the hall. Mary Donelson wasn't in her office, so he proceeded on to the nurses' station. Two nurses were there as he drew up. "Ladies," he said, "I know Mrs. Donelson has Natalie working other patients than Dr. Rawlins today. Is she on this floor?"

"Yes, she is, Doctor," said one. "That way she can pop into Dr. Rawlins's room from time to time to check on him. I believe you will find her with Mrs. Watkins in room 8. If not, she'll be in room 10 with Mr. Baldwin."

Carroll thanked the nurse for the information and hurried down the hall. When he reached room 10, he found the door open. Natalie was giving patient Aaron Baldwin a cup of water.

When she looked up, she saw Carroll looking at her through the open door. "Is there something I can do for you, Doctor?"

"I need you to accompany me to Dr. Rawlins's room as soon as you can."

"Certainly," she replied, noting the strange look in his eyes. "I'll be right with you." When her patient finished drinking, she excused herself and hurried from the room.

As she walked alongside Carroll down the hall, she said, "Is something wrong, Doctor?"

"Yes. I have to tell you and Dr. Rawlins something, and I want you together when I do."

When they entered room 4, Rex was lying flat in the bed. He looked up at them watchfully.

Natalie moved close to the bed and took Rex's hand, saying, "Dr. Carroll has something to tell us, Rex."

Matt's face pinched as he said, "I have some bad news. I just received a telegram from Bellevue Hospital in New York. Two days ago, Dr. Cusing was performing the surgery on the police officer I told you about. He collapsed in the middle of the surgery and died moments later. Heart failure."

A shocked silence followed this announcement. Then Natalie said, "I'm so sorry to hear that."

"Me, too," said Rex. "The medical world has lost a great surgeon."

"This takes us back to where we started," Carroll said glumly. "Now I don't know what to do."

"I do," spoke up Rex. "I want you to perform the surgery on me, Dr. Carroll. I have already told you I have the utmost confidence in your knowledge and skill as a surgeon. Sure, you're not a specialist, but I trust your good judgment. Will you do it?"

Carroll looked at Natalie, then back to the patient. "Dr. Rawlins, I'm glad for your confidence in me, but I'm not a Hallet B. Cusing, nor anywhere near him. I've read some of what he has written, and I have studied other books on spinal surgery, but my experience in the field is quite limited. Maybe I should try to find a doctor in one of the larger cities back east who knows more than I do, and is more experienced in spinal surgery."

"My swelling has gone down, Dr. Carroll. The surgery should be done right away. You and I both know that if it isn't done soon, whatever is wrong in there is going to get worse. Damaged disks could fuse together. Cartilage could deteriorate. The time it would take to find a better-qualified surgeon could nullify what he can accomplish. Am I right?"

"Yes, but—"

"Then I would rather have you do the surgery right away than to wait maybe weeks before we can locate the better-qualified man and get him here."

"But what if I blunder because I'm not knowledgeable enough for what I find when I get in there? What if my lack of knowledge and skill should make it so you will never walk again?"

"If you wish, Doctor, I'll sign a paper stating that I will not hold you responsible if the operation is a failure."

Carroll turned aside, rubbing the back of his neck as he wrestled with his decision. After a few moments, he turned back and said, "All right, Doctor. I will do the surgery. But a signed paper is not necessary."

A smiled spread over Rex's face. "Thank you, Doctor. Thank you!"

"Yes," said Natalie. "Thank you!"

Laying a hand on Rex's shoulder, Carroll said, "I'll begin

making preparations right away, and I'll do the surgery tomorrow morning. Let's pray together. I'm going to need all the help I can get from the Great Physician."

After praying with Rex and Natalie, Dr. Carroll excused himself and left the room.

Natalie bent over Rex and kissed him, then said, "I have to get back to work, darling."

"I'll miss you."

"I just know the Lord is going to let you walk again. I just know it!"

Rex smiled. "Keep it up, Natalie. Your faith will help mine."

"And when you're well, we can—"

"Please, honey. Let's talk about the future when we know more about the present."

"As you wish, Dr. Rawlins," she said, tweaking his nose. "See you later."

With his heart heavy over the famous surgeon's death, and feeling the weight that now lay on his shoulders, Matt Carroll began forming plans for the surgery he would perform the next morning. He had certain medical professionals he wanted at his side when he did it. Two of them were somewhere in the hospital at the moment.

When he drew near the nurses' station, he said to the nurse behind the counter, "Wanda, do you know the whereabouts of Mary Donelson and Breanna Brockman?"

"I believe Mrs. Donelson is in her office, Doctor. I don't know where Breanna is, but I will find her for you."

"Thank you. Ask her to come to my office as soon as she can."

Wanda left the station and headed the other direction.

Carroll moved toward Mary's office. The door was closed, but he could see her through the window, talking to one of the orderlies. She noticed Carroll through the window and said something to the orderly, who got up and opened the door, greeting the doctor before leaving.

"You wanted to see me, Dr. Carroll?" said Mary.

"Yes. I've sent for Breanna, too. I need to talk to both of you at the same time. Wanda's trying to find her. When she arrives, join her in my office, please."

"Sure will, Doctor. Oh! Have you heard anything from Dr. Cusing?"

"That's what I want to talk to you and Breanna about. See you shortly."

Less than five minutes later, both nurses entered Carroll's office and were asked to sit down.

"Ladies," he said, leaning forward, placing his elbows on the desk, "I received bad news from Bellevue Hospital. Dr. Cusing collapsed while performing surgery on that New York police officer day before yesterday. He died shortly afterward from heart failure."

After Mary and Breanna had adjusted to the shocking news, Carroll said, "Dr. Rawlins has asked me to go ahead with the surgery. I don't mind telling you, I'm nervous about it. I will do it first thing in the morning. I want both of you at my side. And I'm going to ask Dr. Goodwin to be here, too."

"I'm honored you want me in there with you," said Breanna.

Mary nodded. "That goes for me, too."

"You two are the best," he said. "It will help me a great deal to have you assisting me, and to have Dr. Goodwin there to give advice when I need it. I'm going to need all the support I can get."

"Dear brother-in-law," said Breanna, "you will do fine."

"Breanna, I appreciate your confidence in me, but to be perfectly honest with you, I feel very much inadequate for this."

"That's how Zerubbabel felt, too," said Breanna.

"Hmm?"

"I said that's how Zerubbabel felt. You know, when he had the task laid on him to rebuild the temple in Jerusalem. With all the opposition facing him, he felt very much inadequate for the task. It looked like an impossibility. But do you remember the message God sent to him through Zechariah?"

Matt nodded. "God told Zerubbabel that he would get the job done, but not by his own might or power."

"Correct. 'Not by might, nor by power, but by my spirit, saith the LORD of hosts.' Well, Dr. Matthew Carroll, did the temple get rebuilt?"

"Sure did."

"Praise the Lord," said Mary.

"Yes," said Breanna. "Then, dear brother-in-law, let's pray about it right now. You tell the Lord about your inadequacy, then let's ask Him for success in the surgery on Dr. Rawlins, by faith, claiming the Lord's own words in Zechariah 4:6. Where you come short, Dr. Matthew Carroll, let the Spirit of God take over. It will not be by your might or power, but by the Holy Spirit."

"All right," said Matt, "but I would like to have Dr. Rawlins and Natalie in on our prayer time."

Breanna asked Mary to go get the Bible she kept on her desk, and the two nurses left Carroll's office with him. They found Natalie caring for a patient in a room at the end of the hall. They waited until she was done, then took her with them to room 4, explaining that they were going to have prayer about tomorrow's surgery.

Rex was surprised to see the doctor and three nurses come into the room.

"Dr. Rawlins," said Carroll, "I am having Mrs. Donelson and Breanna assist me when I do the surgery in the morning. I am also going to ask Dr. Lyle Goodwin to be there."

"That's good," said Rex as Natalie drew up to him on the opposite side of the bed. "I'll be glad to have each of them there."

"I was telling Mrs. Donelson and Breanna about how inadequate I feel for this surgery, and Breanna came up with something from Scripture that has encouraged me. She's borrowed Mrs. Donelson's Bible to read it to you. Then I want all of us to pray together."

Natalie gripped Rex's hand and smiled at him. "It's going to be all right, honey," she said. "I just know it."

Breanna told the background of Zechariah chapter 4, then read verse 6 to Rex and Natalie. When she finished, she said, "Dr. Rawlins, Natalie, we're going to ask the Lord for success in the surgery, claiming this verse for God's help in a special way beyond Dr. Carroll's surgical skills and experience."

"We have a powerful God," said Rex. "Let's trust Him to do it."

Heads bowed as Matt Carroll led the group in prayer, quoting the verse to the Lord and claiming it by faith. When he closed the prayer, everyone said amen, but Rex Rawlins's amen was the loudest.

20

HAROLD SHEETZ PUSHED back from the breakfast table. "Time to get to work. Pete's right, Duke. You need to calm down. Dick's going to handle the job."

"I wouldn't be nervous at all if Dick was ridin' with anyone else, plannin' to kill 'em. But the more I think about Brockman's history of comin' out on top in countless situations where the average man would have gone down, the more I worry."

"Dick will handle it, boss," said Pete. "Palmer Danfield is lyin' dead somewhere, and it was Dick who did it. Danfield's record, from what we've learned, was pretty impressive. But that didn't stop Dick from arriving at the depot wearin' Danfield's badge. Granted, Danfield didn't have the reputation for bein' as hard to kill as Brockman, but Dick's a sharp fella. I'm tellin' you, there's no sense gettin' ulcers over this. Relax. It'll be all right."

Duke rose from his chair and reached for his cane. He limped about for a bit, then turned and said, "But let's say Dick does muff it, and Brockman gets the upper hand on him. Dick's got murder charges hangin' over his head. Brockman might be able to dangle a life sentence before him instead of a noose if he will lead him to us."

Sheetz took his hat from a peg by the kitchen door. "Duke, I agree with Pete. You're going to have ulcers if you're not careful. Dick's got a good head on him. He'll do the job."

Duke made a half turn on his cane to look at Sheetz straight on. "You're dead sure that only Dick rode out for Monarch Pass with Brockman?"

"Yeah, I'm sure. Like I said, both Billy Martin and Sol Duvall told me that just the two of them were traveling together. Both Martin and Duvall expressed their concern that there weren't more men with them."

"So you see, boss," said Dawson, "everything's fine. Won't be long till Dick comes walkin' in here to tell us Brockman's as dead as Danfield, and we're gonna have that big celebration you were talkin' about."

Duke chuckled. "Okay, okay. So I'm nervous and worked up over nothin'. Yeah! We're gonna have us a celebration! A big celebration."

"Now, that's what I like to hear," said Sheetz, opening the back door. "I'm off to work. See you later."

At Mile High Hospital, the talk of the staff was the surgery about to take place in operating room 2.

Rex Rawlins lay on the operating table, watching Dr. Matt Carroll making final preparations for the surgery with the help of Mary Donelson and Breanna Brockman. Natalie Fallon stood beside the table at Rex's head to give him support before the surgery began. She would leave when Breanna administered the ether.

Dr. Lyle Goodwin stood at the foot of the operating table, looking on, while Mary arranged the scalpels, forceps, and other necessary items in proper order on the cart next to the operating table.

When all the instruments were in place, Breanna picked up the ether bottle and nodded to Dr. Carroll.

"All right, Dr. Rawlins," Carroll said, "we're ready. We won't turn you over on your stomach till you're under."

Rex nodded. "Thank you again, Dr. Carroll. I'm glad it's you doing the surgery."

Matt smiled, then ran his gaze over the faces of his assistants and said, "Let's pray."

Matt claimed Zechariah 4:6 before the Lord, and as before, when the amen was said, it was Rex Rawlins who said it the loudest.

Natalie leaned down and planted a kiss on Rex's forehead. "Time for me to go, darling. I'll be praying continually while the operation is in progress."

"I love you," Rex said.

Mary and Breanna exchanged glances, smiling.

"And I love you," breathed Natalie, then rushed to the door before he could see her tears.

Breanna poured ether into a heavy square of cloth and said, "Good night, Dr. Rawlins. Sleep tight. We'll see you later."

When Rawlins was under, Drs. Carroll and Goodwin carefully turned him over.

Taking a deep breath, Carroll said, "Okay, team, let's go to work."

When Dr. Carroll's scalpel had opened the damaged area, he studied it for a long moment, then said to his team, "It's what I feared the most."

Mary, Breanna, and Dr. Goodwin waited for him to continue.

"He's paralyzed because there's pressure on the spinal cord from collapsed vertebrae. The disks are out of place, and the ligaments are damaged."

Dr. Goodwin leaned close and examined the exposed area through his half-moon glasses. "Mm-hmm. The paralysis will disappear if you can realign the vertebrae, which will relieve the pressure. It won't be easy, Doctor. The hard part is—"

"Getting it all back in place firmly so the pressure will be gone once the swelling from the surgery goes down," Carroll finished for him.

"I wouldn't want to try it," said Goodwin. "But you've been into the spinal system more than I have, Doctor."

Sweat beaded Carroll's brow. Breanna mopped it for him and said, "Zerubbabel and his laborers had to go as far as their knowledge and experience would take them, Doctor. The success of the task came from God. Do what you know to do, and leave the rest to Him."

Matt nodded, took a deep breath, and went to work.

Two hours later, Carroll was almost through as he connected two pieces of broken cartilage together, which was meant to ease the last of the pressure from the spinal cord. Breanna administered more ether.

Matt handed Mary an instrument, let out a shaky breath, and said, "It's up to God now. I hope I did it right, but it's in His hands. Let's stitch him up."

Dr. Goodwin remained at the foot of the table, praying all the while under his breath.

Forty minutes later, as Carroll was tying off the final stitch, Dr. Goodwin gasped.

"What's wrong?" Carroll said.

"Nothing wrong! His left foot moved!"

Mary's eyes widened. "Doctor, are you sure?"

"Yes! It was just a slight twitch, but it— Look! It did it again!"

This time they all saw it.

"Oh, praise the Lord!" exclaimed Breanna.

"It's a good sign," said Carroll, "but we dare not let ourselves get too excited yet."

"I understand," said Breanna, "but I can't help getting a little excited. That's the first time he's moved anything below his waist since the day this horrible thing happened."

"We need some time to see if the pressure is really gone," Carroll said. "We'll know one way or the other in a couple of days, when the swelling goes down."

"Doctor, are you going to tell Natalie about the foot movement?" Mary asked.

"Yes. I'll have to caution her not to get her hopes up too much, but on the other hand, she deserves to know. After all, he did move that foot. Twice!"

Natalie was at the nurses' station on the first floor when she saw a tired-looking Dr. Carroll coming toward her.

He motioned to her and said, "Come into my office, please."

Natalie hurried from behind the counter to catch up with the chief administrator.

As Carroll closed his office door behind them, he said, "Natalie, I have something good to tell you, but please understand that we can't go into euphoria yet. Okay?"

"Okay," she said, finding it hard to breathe.

"Just as we were finishing up on him, his left foot twitched twice."

Her eyes grew wide. "Oh! Oh, praise the Lord! It's a good sign, isn't it?"

"Yes, but it'll take a couple of days before we know if the operation was a success. And if it was, it will be because the

Lord took over when I guessed at how to do what needed to be done."

"Rex is in His hands, Doctor. You've done all you could. We'll leave the results up to the Great Physician."

Matt drew a shaky breath. "I...I sure want that young man to walk again."

"I believe God does, too, Dr. Carroll. I am so grateful to you for going ahead with the surgery, even though you felt inadequate."

"I hope you still feel that way forty-eight hours from now."

Natalie smiled and said, "I'll be staying after my shift to be with Rex for a few hours, Doctor, if you don't mind my being in his room past visiting hours."

"Not at all." He paused, then said, "As an observer, I would say things are working out between the two of you."

"They are, sir. Rex hasn't wanted to talk about our future, because he didn't know how it was going to be after the surgery. I haven't pressed him to talk any more about it, but he loves me, and I love him. It's going to work out. The Lord wants us together. I know that."

"You're both fine Christians, Natalie. I want to see you together and happy."

"You will," she said. "And thank you for caring."

"Natalie..."

"Yes, sir?"

"I probably won't be there when Dr. Rawlins wakes up. It's best that you don't tell him about his foot."

"I understand, Doctor. I won't tell him."

Rex Rawlins had stirred and opened his eyes several times as the hours passed, but it wasn't until almost sundown that he awoke and found Nurse Lynette Fraser checking his pulse. She had been his nurse on every third shift since he had entered the hospital.

He attempted to focus on her face.

"Dr. Rawlins, it's Lynette," she said. "Are you in pain?"

He ran his dry tongue over equally dry lips. "No, but I am thirsty."

A familiar voice from beyond his line of sight said, "I'll give him a drink, Lynette."

Rex's languid eyes found the lovely face of the woman he loved as she left her chair and moved up beside the bed. "What time is it?" he said in a groggy voice.

She poured water into a cup from the pitcher on the bedstand. "Almost seven-thirty."

"You should be home by now, Natalie."

"Not on the day the man of my dreams has surgery," she said, raising his head slightly to give him the water.

"I'll be back in a few minutes," said Lynette.

When she was gone, Rex swallowed the last of the water in the cup, and as his eyes met Natalie's, he asked, "What's the prognosis?"

"Dr. Carroll says we won't know anything for sure until your swelling goes down. Couple of days."

"He said no more than that?"

"No. He's been checking on you every hour since the surgery, but he really didn't expect you to be awake until after he had gone home. He'll see you first thing in the morning."

Rex blinked in an attempt to clear the slight blur in his vision. "But he feels he did what was needed?"

"Other than saying it would be a couple of days before we know anything for sure, he said if the operation is a success, it will be because the Lord took over where he was no more than guessing at how to do what needed to be done."

"But he didn't say what it was he guessed at?"

"No. I'm sure he will fill you in on the details tomorrow."

Rex closed his eyes. "That's probably best. My brain is a little foggy right now, anyway."

"I'm sure that's why he didn't wait around till you woke up. Your mind will be much clearer in the morning. Are you in any pain?"

"No, but I'm sure it will come when the ether gets out of my system."

"Mm-hmm. Lynette will give you a sedative to help you sleep."

Still trying to clear his vision, he blinked and said, "Natalie, I…I—"

"What?"

"I just felt something. I—"

"You felt what?"

"A tingling in the toes of my left foot."

Natalie's heart leaped in her breast. "Are you sure?"

"I think so. It sure felt like it."

"But it's gone now?"

"Yes. No! It just did it again!"

Natalie went to the end of the bed, pulled the covers loose, and exposed his feet. "Still feel it?"

Rex's countenance fell. "No. It's gone."

"See if you can wiggle your toes."

He closed his eyes and concentrated for several seconds, then said, "Can't do it. There's no tingle. But, Natalie, I felt it. I really did!"

As Natalie tucked the covers back in place, she squeezed his toes without saying anything. When there was no response, she figured he had simply imagined the movement. But maybe not, she told herself. He did say it was his left foot, and it was the left one that twitched earlier.

The door opened. "Me again," said Lynette, carrying a tray with a steaming bowl on it.

"What's that?" Rex asked.

"Broth, Doctor. I'm supposed to get as much down you as possible. Doctor's orders. You know about that, don't you?"

Rex made a face. "Yes. But I hate broth."

Natalie giggled. "On that note, I think I'll head for home." She kissed his forehead and headed out the door. While walking down the hall, she pondered the tingling Rex had felt…or thought he had felt.

"Dear Lord," she said in a whisper, "if You have done Your miracle, it is quite possible he would have feeling somewhere below his waist already. Please let it be so."

John Brockman and the killer posing as Palmer Danfield had left Colorado Springs just before noon. Just as the sun was going down, they were deep into the Rockies.

After climbing for hours, they reached a rolling meadow fringed with aspen, birch, and conifer. A small brook bubbled along the meadow's edge. In the meadow itself were isolated trees here and there on the carpet of green grass. Colorful wildflowers added to the beauty of the scene.

To the west, the floor of the meadow rose in smooth grassy banks to great towers of jagged rocks five hundred feet high. A mile or so beyond them, taller crags rose up to touch the golden sky. As the sun disappeared behind the crags, shadows stretched eastward, and between them streamed a red-gold light.

"We'll camp here, Danfield. Plenty of grass and water for the horses."

During the day's ride, John had talked to his partner some more about the fact that life on earth was only temporary, and that sinful human beings were responsible to their Creator for violating His Word, which included the Ten Commandments. John had pointed out there were actually hundreds of commandments in Scripture, and there did not live on earth a man or woman who wasn't guilty of breaking them.

Taking just the Ten Commandments as given by God to Moses at Mount Sinai, John listed them one by one, showing how people broke them in one way or another. When he had covered all ten, Danfield readily admitted his guilt as a sinner before the holy God of heaven. With this established, John carefully explained how God's only begotten Son came into the world to suffer, bleed, and die on the cross of Calvary. His death provided the way of forgiveness and salvation, so that sinners could miss the flames of hell and eternally enjoy the bliss of heaven.

John had not mentioned the subject for several hours. He had wanted to give the Word a chance to sink into Danfield's heart and mind.

As they were heating their beans and coffee over the campfire, John said, "Danfield, have you considered the things we talked about today?"

Dick Nye kept his eyes on the skillet in his hand as he stirred the beans. "Some."

"So what do you think?"

Nye took his time answering, "Well, I can't dispute what you've told me, but there are a lot of religions in the world. How can we know which one is the right one?"

"There is no right religion," John said. "What I'm talking to you about is not religion. Men invent new religions every day. What I'm talking about is salvation. Religion can be found anywhere, but salvation is found only in one place: the Lord Jesus Christ. If you have Him in your heart, you have salvation and forgiveness of your sins. You will go to heaven when you die. If you do not have Him in your heart, you will go to hell when you die. The Bible says hell is a place of everlasting fire and torment."

Nye did not comment.

While they were eating, John quoted several Scriptures on salvation, the horrors of hell, the wonders of heaven, and the love of God for sinners.

Nye commented, "You've really memorized a lot of that Bible, haven't you?"

"Quite a bit. I work on memorizing more all the time."

Nye wanted to get Brockman off his back with the salvation theme, but knew he must conduct himself with the show of respect that a deputy would have for his chief. "Well, Chief," he said, "I admire a man who knows what he believes and stands by it, but I have my own beliefs, and I'll stick to them."

John eyed him across the flickering fire. "But where will your beliefs take you when you die? Without Jesus Christ, God's Word says it's a burning hell."

Nye felt uncomfortable and nervous with the Scriptures John had been quoting. Trying to come up with a satisfying retort, he reached for the coffeepot, which sat on a couple of small flat rocks in the fire pit they had hollowed out earlier.

His fingers closed around the handle, and he got the burning sensation a moment after picking it up.

"Ow-w-w-w!" he hollered, and dropped the coffeepot into the fire. He shook his hand as if to throw off the pain, and almost resorted to profanity, but caught himself before it came off his tongue.

Brockman used a stick to lift the coffeepot out of the fire

and set it aside. "Burn it bad?" he asked, trying to see the afflicted hand.

Nye's thumb and first three fingers were bright red, as was a strip on the palm.

"Good thing it's not your gun hand," said John, rising to his feet. "I have some salve in my saddlebags. Be right back."

While Brockman was going for the salve, Nye cursed under his breath as the pain throbbed in his hand. He, too, was thankful he had used his left hand to pick up the coffeepot. He'd need his gun hand to shoot Brockman and send him into eternity.

Brockman returned and hunkered down beside his partner. While applying salve and wrapping Nye's hand loosely with a bandage, he said, "A little lesson, here, Danfield."

"What's that?"

"You're in a great deal of pain from a burn on your hand. It will stop burning in a short time. Think about going to hell and burning all over—body and limb—and never having a moment's relief from it…ever."

Nye ignored Brockman's words and said, "Thanks for the salve and bandage."

Later, when both men were in their bedrolls and a wolf was howling somewhere in the mountains, Dick Nye was deeply disturbed. His hand burned, but the disturbance came from deep in his soul. He tried to shake his thoughts from the torments of hell by forcing himself to concentrate on the reason he was traveling with John Brockman. The right time and place would come to kill him. They had better than two days before they would reach Monarch Pass.

On the first day after the surgery, Dr. Matt Carroll was at Rex Rawlins's bedside at sunrise. Nurse Lynette Fraser was with him. Rex had rested quite well during the night and was awake when the pair came in.

"Your color is good, Doctor," said Carroll. "Lynette told me she had to give you very little medicine for your pain."

"Yes, thank the Lord," said Rawlins. "So, Dr. Carroll, what did you have to do to me?"

Carroll explained in detail the damage Rawlins had suffered, and the work he had done to repair the vertebrae, disks, and ligaments.

"I have to say that the last part of the procedure I used was done almost blindly. I had to guess, because I wasn't sure what to do. I'm sorry, but—"

"No, no. Don't be sorry. I'm the one who asked you to perform the surgery. And we committed it to the Lord, asking Him to take over where your knowledge and experience ended, didn't we?"

"Yes."

"Then the results are in His hands, and I believe He has done what we asked Him."

Carroll's eyebrows raised. "What do you mean?"

There was a gleam in Rex's eyes. "Last night when Natalie was here in the room with me, I felt a tingling in my toes."

"In both feet?" asked Carroll.

"Just the left one."

Carroll recalled that it was the left foot that had twitched shortly after the surgery. This was encouraging, but he also knew that sometimes patients thought they felt pain or movement, even in limbs that had been amputated. It was called phantom pain syndrome, or phantom movement syndrome. That might be what Rex Rawlins had experienced.

"Have you had any tingling since last night?" Carroll asked.

"I think maybe there was some when I woke up once before

dawn, but I'm not sure. It might have been what woke me up, but it was gone by the time I realized I was awake. I could have been dreaming."

Carroll nodded. "Well, let's see what happens today. I'll look in on you later."

"Dr. Rawlins, I'll be going off duty in a few minutes," Lynette said. "I understand Mrs. Donelson is assigning Natalie to your room again today, so you'll have her popping in quite often."

"That's good news," said Rex. "And thank you for such good care."

"It's a special pleasure to look after one of our own in the medical profession," Lynette said.

The chief administrator and the nurse left together.

In a few minutes the door opened, and Natalie came in, smiling. "Good morning, darling. Lynette said you had a good night's rest."

"That I did."

"I'm so glad. And Dr. Carroll said he just explained the surgery to you."

"Yes. I like the man, Natalie. He's as honest as can be."

"And very humble for a man of his stature," she said.

"He wouldn't have the stature without the humility."

"I agree. Any more tingles?"

"Maybe. I'm not sure. I either dreamed that I had some, or I really had some just as I was waking up before dawn."

"If you get any more, please tell me, won't you?"

"I sure will!"

"Well, darling, they've got breakfast cooking in the kitchen. Are you hungry?"

"A little."

"All right then, let's take care of it. I'll be right back."

⚡

That afternoon, when it was time for the shift change, Natalie came into Rex's room.

"Before I leave for home, I just wanted to tell you that I love you," she said. Tilting her head and studying him, she said, "You look happy, Dr. Rex Rawlins. What is it?"

"I had another tingle in the toes on my left foot. Just a few minutes ago."

Natalie frowned. "Are you sure?"

"You think I'm imagining it, don't you?"

"Rex, I want to believe it's real. I really do, but—"

"Phantom movement syndrome?"

"Well, possibly. I just—"

"I understand, sweetheart," he said, taking her hand in his. "You don't want me to get my hopes up, then be disappointed."

"I have the utmost faith in the Lord, darling. I believe He is going to let you walk again. If the tingles didn't start until late tonight or even in the morning, I'd say they were genuine. As yet, it may be too early. You understand what I'm saying."

"Yes, I do. Let's just leave it at that, and see what happens by morning."

Natalie wanted to make her little test again. Pulling the covers loose at the bottom of the bed, and lifting them up to expose his toes, she said, "Let's just see if there's reason for celebration. Can you work up a wiggle for me?"

Rex closed his eyes and concentrated on trying to wiggle his toes, but to no avail. "Can't do it."

"Well, let's give it till morning when the swelling in your back is down some more. Maybe you'll be able to move them then."

As she covered his feet again, she gave a hard squeeze on the toes of his left foot. Rex gave no sign that he felt it.

Leaning down, she said, "I've got to do some shopping before the stores close. Mom's out of some things she needs. I'll see you in the morning."

Rex reached up, placed his hand on the back of her head, and pulled her face down to his, kissing her soundly. "I love you, sweet Natalie. Thank you for being so concerned about my morale."

"That's because I love you so much, darling," she said softly. "You will walk again, but only in God's good time."

They kissed again. When she stood up she saw him grinning from ear to ear. "What are you grinning about, Rex?"

"You need to go. I'll tell you tomorrow."

Natalie giggled. "Come on now. What are you grinning about?"

"I love you, Natalie. Go on. Take care of your mother."

She tweaked his nose. "All right. I'll wonder all night what the grin is about, but you promise to tell me tomorrow?"

"Promise," he said, raising his right hand as if he were taking an oath.

"And promise never to stop loving me?"

Repeating the same sign, he said, "I promise."

She kissed him again, then hurried from the room, giving him a little wave as she passed through the door.

21

MARIE FALLON LOOKED at her daughter across the supper table and said, "So what do you really think about the tingle in his toes, honey?"

"I'm not sure, Mom. But seems to me that if Rex can feel a tingling in his toes, he ought to be able to feel the pressure when I squeeze them."

"Honey, let's say the Lord would choose not to give Rex his legs back. Do you think he will really let his paralysis keep him from marrying you?"

"Not if he loves me like he says, Mom. And I know he does. I realize he was experiencing a great deal of trauma when I tried to talk about our future together, but if somehow the Lord willed it that he should remain paralyzed, I believe He would still bring us together as husband and wife. The love is there between us, whether he can walk or not."

She drew a deep breath and sighed. "However, I have this peace down deep inside. I know it's God's peace. And it tells me that the man I love is going to walk again. I believe the Lord wants Rex to carry on his practice in Empire, and that he wants me to work as his nurse—a husband-and-wife team."

Marie smiled. "I can't see it going any other way, honey. The Lord didn't let the two of you meet and fall in love just to let you be torn apart and live your lives separately." She paused, then said, "Rex is such a fine young man. It will be nice to see him again."

The first shift was just getting started the next morning when Mary Donelson and Breanna Brockman entered Dr. Carroll's office. Dr. Goodwin was already there. Greetings were exchanged, then Carroll said, "All right, team, we're going to Dr. Rawlins's room together. I've advised you of the tingling he says he has felt in his toes. I wanted the three of you in the room when I work on him to see if there is any feeling anywhere below his waist.

"If the surgery has been any success at all, there will be some sign. The swelling was down considerably when I examined him early yesterday afternoon. It has to be almost gone by now."

Lyle Goodwin laid a hand on Carroll's arm. "Dr. Carroll, however this turns out, you did all that could be expected of you. Please keep that in mind."

Matt nodded and said, "Let's go."

When Natalie entered Rex's room, he was sitting up with his back against a pair of pillows.

"Well, what have we here?" she said. "Sitting up, are you?"

"Mm-hmm." He was wearing the same grin she had seen the evening before.

She leaned over, kissed him, and said, "All right, Dr. Rawlins. You made me a promise. What's that cat-that-swallowed-the-canary grin about?"

"You really want to know?"

"Yes."

"Will you marry me?"

Natalie's mouth dropped open. "Will I marry you? Of course! But...but what brought this on?"

"I love you, that's what! You will be my nurse at our office in the small town of Empire, won't you?"

"Yes! Oh, yes! But what about—"

"My paralysis?"

"Yes."

"Think back to last evening. You were skeptical as to whether I really had a tingling in my toes, right? You know...phantom movement syndrome."

"Well..."

"Honey, it was so sweet of you to squeeze my toes before you left."

Natalie's eyes widened. "You felt that?"

"Yes, I did. That's what I was grinning about. But you needed to get to the stores before they closed. I didn't want to detain you, and I probably would have if I'd told you I felt the squeeze."

"Oh, praise God!" she exclaimed. "You have feeling in the toes of your left foot!"

As she spoke, Natalie threw herself at him, wrapping her arms around his neck.

Rex and Natalie shed tears of joy as they clung to each other.

"Natalie, that isn't all."

She pulled away to look into his eyes.

"Pull the covers off my feet."

She moved quickly, tugging at the covers with trembling hands. When she lifted the sheet and cover, the toes on both feet were wiggling.

"Oh, darling! Both feet!"

Natalie broke down and sobbed for joy while Rex kept wiggling his toes.

Rex was about to say something else when the door opened, capturing their attention. Natalie dropped the covers over Rex's feet and wiped tears as Mary and Breanna entered with Drs. Carroll and Goodwin behind them.

"Honey, what's the matter?" Breanna said as she dashed toward Natalie. Then she saw Rex wiping tears from his face with the corner of the sheet. "What's happened? What's wrong?"

The other three were closing in as Natalie said in a broken voice, "Nothing's wrong! Everything's right! Rex can wiggle his toes—on both feet!" As she spoke, she lifted the covers and said, "Show them, darling."

The doctors and nurses were stunned as they observed ten toes wiggling with life.

"Glory to God!" cried Mary.

"Yes!" gasped Dr. Goodwin. "Glory to God!"

"God is the only one who deserves the glory!" Matt said in a choked voice. Then he said to Rex, "When did you discover you could wiggle your toes?"

"Before I went to sleep last night. But that's not all."

"What? There's more?"

"Yes! Watch!"

Rex set his jaw with a determined look, braced his hands on the mattress, and lifted his left leg about an inch off the bed. While the team was looking on in awe, he lowered the left leg and showed them he could raise the right one, too.

Shaking his head in wonder, Matt Carroll laid a hand on his patient's shoulder and said, "Doctor, there is no question about it. If you can do that, you will walk again!"

Rex reached around Natalie and extended his hand to Matt. "Dr. Carroll, you had the courage to attempt the surgery. Thank you, my friend and Christian brother. Thank you! I give the glory to the Great Physician, yes, but I also give my thanks to you. Without you, I would never have walked again."

"And without the Lord's wisdom imparted to me while I did the surgery, you still would never have walked again," said Matt, gripping his hand firmly.

Rex then took Natalie by the hand and said, "It's time for an official announcement."

They all stared at him, waiting.

"Natalie and I are announcing our engagement. It'll be a little while before I can get her a ring, but we're going to be married! We are going to work together as a team at the office in Empire."

Breanna wrapped her arms around Natalie and wept happy tears with her, and then it was Mary's turn.

Rex set admiring eyes on the lovely blonde and said, "Breanna, that day in my office when I told you of my love for Natalie and said that I probably would never marry because I could never love a woman like I love her, you said you were going to pray the Lord would take control of the situation and bring the two of us together. Remember?"

Breanna nodded, wiping tears.

"And I said it would take a mighty big miracle to ever bring Natalie and me together."

"Yes. You didn't think Natalie would budge from her position about not marrying you because you were a small-town doctor."

"And you said to me, 'Doctor, our God is the God of miracles...mighty big miracles.'" Rex's lower lip quivered. "God let me hit that tree, Breanna, and He let you find me lying beneath it paralyzed from my waist down. You brought me to this hospital. Natalie was here because God brought her to Denver.

"And…and now, not only do I have my wonderful Natalie, who is willing to marry me and be the wife of a small-town doctor, but I'm going to be back on my feet shortly so we can get married and go home to Empire. Praise the Lord!"

"It's a miracle, all right," said Mary. "The surgery and the bringing together of you two wonderful young people—not by the might, nor the power of man, but by the Spirit of God!"

The good news about the success of Dr. Rex Rawlins's surgery spread quickly through the hospital, and there was much rejoicing. Hospital staff members of the first shift visited him one and two at a time during the day to share in his joy.

The next morning, Natalie, Breanna, and Mary gathered in room 4 with Dr. Matthew Carroll.

Breanna told Rex that she had stopped by the Western Union office on the way to the hospital and was told they expected to have wire service to the mountain towns restored within two to three days. She left a message to be sent to Isabel Mullins as soon as possible that Dr. Rawlins would keep in touch with her about when he would be returning to Empire, and that he would be bringing his new bride with him.

Dr. Carroll stood over his patient, who was sitting up on the bed, and said, "All right, Dr. Rawlins, let's get you on your feet. You're going to walk right now."

"I'll do my best," said Rex. "Let's try it!"

Without help Rex swung his legs over the edge of the bed. Matt put an arm around him for support and inched him down till his feet found the floor.

The three nurses watched with their hearts in their throats as Rawlins stood on shaky legs. Carroll eased his strong grip on Rex's body, allowing him to support himself.

"Oh!" squeaked Natalie, clapping her hands together. "He's standing on his own!"

Rex smiled at her, then said, "Okay, Dr. Carroll. Here goes…"

With Carroll ready to keep him from falling if he started down, Rex took a faltering step, then another. He looked at Natalie and said, "If you've got a hug for me, I'll walk to you."

Natalie was no more than eight or nine feet away as she opened her arms and said, "Come on, darling. Your hug is waiting."

Breanna choked up, and tears filled her eyes. Mary was having the same problem.

Matt Carroll stayed with his patient as Rex took each careful step, having to hesitate a couple of times to keep his balance. When he reached Natalie, Carroll supported him from behind to allow Natalie to enfold Rex in her arms.

The young couple wept for joy together, and in spite of the audience, enjoyed a brief kiss and mingled their tears.

Everyone else applauded.

It was midmorning when Breanna entered Deputy U.S. Marshal Dave Taylor's room and found him sitting in his chair, looking out the window. She set the tray she was carrying on a small table near the bed. "Time for your medicine, Dave."

"Good morning, Breanna."

"How are you feeling?" she asked, pouring powders into a cup.

"Quite well, thank you. I should be getting out of here in another week or so."

"Won't that be good?"

"Sure will. I heard the good news about Dr. Rawlins."

"Wonderful, isn't it?"

"Sure is."

Breanna added water to the powders, stirred the mixture vigorously, and handed the cup to him. "All right, Deputy Taylor, drink your medicine like a good boy."

When Dave had downed the bitter-tasting liquid, he handed her the cup and said, "Is Chief Brockman back yet?"

"Not yet. He and Deputy Danfield won't be back for probably another four or five days."

Dave frowned. "Did you say Deputy Danfield?"

"Yes. Palmer Danfield. He was sent here from the Amarillo office to join John's staff of deputies."

Dave's face turned gray.

"What's the matter?" Breanna asked, leaning down to look him in the eye.

"Breanna, when Chief Brockman came here the other day just before riding out, he had a deputy with him. There was camping gear on their horses. Did you see the deputy?"

"No. He stayed with the horses while John came in to tell me good-bye."

"But the man who was here at the hospital with him, and who rode away with him, is supposed to be Palmer Danfield?"

"Why, yes. Why do you ask?"

"He's not Palmer Danfield. Palmer and I worked together for several years under Marshal Jake Gibbs in Kansas City. We're good friends. I knew he was working out of the Amarillo office. If that man with Chief Brockman says he's Palmer Danfield, he's a liar! Breanna, something's wrong, and I don't like the looks of it."

Terror filled Breanna's heart. "Dave, if the man John is riding with in the mountains isn't Palmer Danfield, who could he be?"

"I don't know, but he's an impostor, and he can only be up to no good!"

Holding her dress ankle high, Breanna turned the corner on Tremont Street and ran toward the federal building.

Billy Martin looked up in surprise as Breanna rushed through the door, panting. "Mrs. Brockman! Is something wrong?"

"Terribly wrong, Billy! Is Chief Duvall in John's office?"

"Yes," he said, starting to leave his desk.

"It's all right, Billy, I'll announce myself." With that, she opened the door and stepped inside, still trying to catch her breath.

"Breanna!" Solomon Duvall rose from his chair. "You look frightened! What's the matter?"

"Sol, that man who's riding with John to the Foster hideout is an impostor! He's not Palmer Danfield!"

Spilling the words rapidly, Breanna told him what Dave Taylor had said.

Duvall's features were like granite as he picked up a yellow sheet of paper and said, "Breanna, I just now got this telegram from the Washington office. They found the body of Deputy Palmer Danfield late yesterday afternoon in a thicket alongside the railroad tracks in southern Colorado. He had been stabbed to death and thrown from the train. His gun belt, badge, and identification papers were missing. It took the authorities a while to identify the body."

"Sol, I had a strange feeling about John going on this trip into the mountains. I told him about it. Now I know why.

Whoever is riding with John, he killed Deputy Danfield. This means he passed himself off as Danfield to John! Why else would he do that than to kill John?"

"I can come to no other conclusion myself," said Duvall, his voice quivering.

"I'm going after them!" Breanna said, whirling to leave. "I'll see if I can get Curt Langan or Steve Ridgway to ride with me. Maybe I can find another man to go with us."

"Breanna," called Duvall.

She paused at the door and looked back.

"You mustn't do this. It's too dangerous. I have one deputy who returned from an assignment last night—Pat O'Rourke. I'll send Pat with Curt or Steve, or by himself, if neither of them can go."

"One man isn't enough, Sol," she argued. "I know Pat, and he's a good man, but there should be at least two. I'm sure that since John's life is in danger, Curt will give us Steve if he can't go himself."

"Now, don't you try going, Breanna," he warned. "Like I said, it will be dangerous. Besides, they'll have to ride like the wind to catch up to John and the impostor."

"Nobody has seen the horse yet that can outrun Chance, Sol. On him I can keep up with anybody."

"Such a venture is not for a woman, Breanna. Please stay here and let Pat go. If Curt or Steve will accompany him, fine, but don't you try it."

"That's my husband out there with a killer at his side, Sol. I'm going! You tell Pat I'll be right here at the office in half an hour. I rode Chance to work today, so he's at the barn behind the hospital. I can borrow camping gear from Curt or Steve. See you shortly."

Duvall looked at the lavender and white nurse's apron she

wore. "You can't ride in that dress, Breanna."

"I rode to work in it. Besides, there isn't time to go home and put on a split riding skirt." With that, she was out the door.

Thirty minutes later, Sheriff Langan and Breanna Brockman rode up to the federal building. Solomon Duvall and Pat O'Rourke were standing beside O'Rourke's horse at the hitching rail. Breanna had removed her apron and let her hair down. It lay on her shoulders in golden swirls, highlighted by the sun. Bedrolls and camping gear were tied to their horses behind the saddles.

"Ready to go, Pat?" Breanna said.

"Sure, but I think you should stay here, Breanna."

"That's what I told her," said the sheriff.

"Me, too," said Duvall.

There was a stubborn set to Breanna's graceful jaw. "Now that all three of you know that what you say doesn't count, can we ride?"

Solomon Duvall watched the three of them gallop away. Chance was already pushing ahead of the other horses.

Breanna's long hair streamed behind her as they vanished from sight.

Breanna knew the route her husband was taking to Monarch Pass. As she and the two lawmen rode hard for Colorado Springs, she moved her lips in prayer. "Lord," she said while the wind caressed her face, "I'm trusting You to take care of John, and to somehow keep that impostor from harming him." Her mind went to Zechariah 4:6. "John is not aware of the danger he's in, Lord. Keep him safe…by Your Spirit."

⚓

When Dick Nye awakened at dawn on the morning of the third day, the aroma of hot bacon met his nostrils. He opened his eyes to see John hunkered beside a blazing fire, skillet in hand. His back was toward Nye.

Why not now? thought Nye. Sitting up quietly, he pulled his boots on and rose to his feet. His gun belt lay beside the bedroll. He leaned over and slipped the revolver from its holster.

Suddenly there was a high-pitched screech overhead, and Nye saw a huge bald eagle swooping down from a craggy cliff nearby. The screeching continued as the eagle came down and swerved to Brockman's right, quickly catching his attention. At the same time, Brockman saw the impostor in his peripheral vision and turned to get a full view of him. "Some bird, eh?"

Nye slipped the gun back in the holster and made it appear that he was simply picking up the gun belt to strap it on. Looking up, he said, "Yeah. Some bird!" He cursed under his breath. He would have to wait for another opportunity.

While they ate breakfast, John once again talked to Palmer Danfield about his need to be saved. Nye was getting irritated at the man for preaching to him, but dared not show it. He told himself that before the day was over, Brockman would be dead. Then he wouldn't have to listen to any more of this salvation stuff.

When breakfast was finished and everything was packed up, the two men swung into their saddles. As they headed higher up the trail with the sweet scent of pine in their nostrils, John said, "We'll reach the summit of the pass by sundown, and camp there. In the morning we'll drop down on the west side of the pass and head for Dead Man's Canyon. Foster's cabin is supposed to be close to the canyon. Once we get the cabin in sight, we'll plan our approach."

Nye laughed to himself, thinking what a surprise it would be to Brockman if he found out that only four men were at the hideout and the man he wanted most was in Denver at Harold Sheetz's house! But Brockman would never find it out. A bullet would plow into the back of his head before this day was over.

After being on the trail for about three hours, John said, "We're coming up on a stream. Let's stop and water the horses."

Nye was thinking this might be his opportunity until he saw two riders off their horses at the stream, letting their horses drink. Brockman was headed straight toward them.

The riders greeted both men in a friendly manner, then elbowed each other when they spotted the badges, quipping that they were glad they were ranchers and not outlaws, or they'd be in trouble. They told the two lawmen that they were from Colorado's western slope and were on their way to Denver on business.

Brockman introduced himself and Palmer Danfield, but didn't divulge what their trip was about.

"Need to keep a sharp eye, gentlemen," said one of the men. "There's a renegade band of Utes on the rampage in these mountains. Killing whites at random."

Brockman knew the Utes had villages spread along the west side of the Rockies from the base of Monarch Pass all the way south to Durango. "Have to be renegades," he commented. "The Utes have been peaceful with whites for years."

"We were told it's a subchief called Wolf's Eye," said the other man. "He's developed a burning hatred for whites and is leading his band of renegades on a killing spree. Just keep your eyes peeled."

Brockman thanked him for the warning, and soon he and his partner were climbing higher.

It was nearly ten o'clock in the morning when they stopped

at a bubbling spring along the side of the trail to water their horses and fill the canteens.

As Nye dismounted, he scanned the area, looking back along the trail and into the deep shadowed pockets among the pines. They were alone.

This was the moment.

He let Brockman kneel at the spring to fill his canteen and felt his heart quicken as he dropped his hand to the butt of his gun.

Suddenly, both horses whinnied shrilly, rearing up and pawing the air. Nye's horse bolted and ran, but Ebony stayed close to John, pounding ground with both hooves and whinnying.

John whirled to see what had frightened the horses, putting Nye in his view, and saw a shadow moving in the woods. A massive male grizzly appeared in the dappled shade at the edge of the trees. He growled menacingly and took a few steps that carried him into the clear sunshine, then paused and growled again. The silver tips of his cinnamon-colored fur glistened in the sun.

Nye froze to the spot, his white face mirroring sudden terror.

John stood perfectly still and said, "Don't move, Danfield. Maybe he'll decide to leave us alone."

The huge beast stood erect and let out a bloodcurdling roar. The grizzly was no more than thirty yards away.

Ebony's eyes bulged, and his entire body trembled, but he refused to bolt and leave his master behind.

The massive beast roared again and dropped to all fours, mouth drooling, muscles bunched. Small dark eyes flashed fire, nostrils flared, and the huge beast charged, propelling his bulk with shocking speed.

"I was wrong," said John.

Brockman's Colt .45 Peacemaker was in his hand quicker than the blink of an eye, and he fired from the hip the same as he would if he were facing a challenge from a gunfighter. There was no time to pause and take careful aim.

The slug tore into the charging bear's brain—a direct hit squarely between the eyes. The impact dropped him to his belly, but his momentum caused him to roll several feet before coming to a stop less than five paces away.

The grizzly let out a death cry, shook his head, and tried to get up.

John took careful aim this time and put another .45 slug in his head. The grizzly roared again, fell flat, and blew out a gusty breath as life left his body.

While Dick Nye stared at the dead grizzly, John holstered his gun and took hold of Ebony's bridle, talking in soothing tones, trying to calm him. He glanced at Nye and said, "Your horse is down there in the woods by that stand of birch trees, Danfield. See him?"

"Yeah." Nye nodded, his heart still banging his ribs. "I'll go down and get him."

When Ebony saw no movement from the grizzly, he settled down quickly. John patted his neck, saying, "It's all right now, boy. He's dead."

John pulled his gun, punched out the two empty shells, and replaced them with live ones from his gun belt.

When Nye returned, leading the nervous horse, his face was sheet white.

"You all right, Danfield?" asked Brockman, preparing to mount Ebony.

The impostor was actually shaken about two things. The charging bear had given him a jolt, but seeing the speed with which Brockman had drawn his gun and his deadly accuracy were frightening. If there had been no bear, but Brockman had happened to turn just as Nye was drawing a bead on him, it would have been Nye who took Brockman's bullet.

There was cold sweat running down Nye's back as he said, "I'm okay, Chief. That charging grizzly had me a bit scared."

"Yeah," said John. "Me, too."

As they pressed the horses up the trail, Dick Nye made his decision. He would wait and shoot Brockman in the middle of the night. Catch him while he slept. It was the only safe way.

22

ON THE SECOND day since leaving Denver, Breanna and the two lawmen slowed their pace as they rode into a small settlement some twenty miles west of Colorado Springs. Towering mountain peaks surrounded the level spot where the settlement lay nestled amid wind-ruffled pines.

A group of people were standing to the side of the road next to one of the larger shacks, watching the three riders approach.

"Howdy, folks," said Curt Langan. "I'm Sheriff Langan from Denver. The lady next to me is Mrs. Brockman, wife of Chief U.S. Marshal John Brockman, and this gentlemen is Deputy U.S. Marshal Pat O'Rourke. We're trying to catch up to Chief Brockman and another deputy U.S. marshal who are headed for Monarch Pass. They were planning on taking this route. They would've been through here a day or two ago. Did any of you see them?"

"Might've," said a middle-aged man with a moon-shaped face. "Is one of 'em real tall and rides a black horse just about as big as the one the lady is ridin'?"

"That would be Chief Brockman," said Langan.

"They was through here day before yesterday. Me and Ma both noticed they was wearin' badges."

"Much obliged," said Langan. "We just wanted to make

sure they had taken this route as planned."

As they rode out of the settlement, Breanna felt a measure of relief. At least the impostor had not shown his hand nor tried to harm John this far into the journey.

The next day, in higher country, they came upon another small settlement along the trail and found that some of the people there had seen the two riders who wore badges. One was quite tall in the saddle and rode a large black horse.

The bold world of jagged, snow-laden mountain peaks loomed up before John Brockman and Dick Nye, some of the peaks topping off at well over 14,000 feet.

It was midafternoon as they reached the base of Monarch Pass. The sky ahead of them was a brilliant blue, with shafts of sunlight shooting down from behind a huge bank of puffy white clouds.

A cool wind drifted down from the lofty crags, plucking at their hat brims, as Brockman said, "Six miles to the crest of the pass, Danfield. The trail is plenty steep, but we'll make it over the top and find a spot to camp before nightfall. In the morning, we'll pull our little surprise on Duke and his boys."

"That's what we came to do," Nye said.

Touching heels to the horses' flanks, they started the steep climb. About an hour later, they slowly came around a bend in the trail and quickly drew rein.

Two bearded men, easily identified by their rough attire as fur trappers, were off their horses and standing in a shallow draw beside the trail. Two burros laden with pelts stood by the horses.

The trappers were standing over the bodies of four men sprawled near the bottom of the draw. Feather-tipped arrows protruded from their lifeless forms, giving mute evidence that they had met up with hostile Indians.

Noting the approach of the mounted men with badges on their vests, the trappers raised their hands in a friendly gesture.

Nye followed suit as Brockman left his saddle. Together they descended the gentle slope to the bottom of the rock-covered draw.

Three of the dead men lay face down, while the fourth one lay on his back with an arrow buried six inches in the center of his chest.

John introduced himself and Deputy Danfield, and the trappers identified themselves as Ed Payton and Paul Fleenor from Laramie, Wyoming.

Gesturing toward the dead men, Fleenor said, "These poor fellas no doubt met up with that renegade Wolf Eye and his bunch. They been slaughterin' whites all over these mountains from what we been told."

"That's what we hear," said Brockman. "You've seen no sign of them?"

While the trappers were saying they had seen no Utes, Dick Nye's line of sight strayed to the dead man who lay on his back. There was a sudden tightening of his throat as he focused on the face. It was Acton Huxley! His face was twisted in death, and its hideous expression put a cold chill down Nye's backbone. A wave of nausea swept over him.

Nye shot a glance at the man who lay closest to Huxley.

Even though only a part of his face was visible, Nye recognized Mel Skinner. It was the same with the other two. He knew they were Web Crispin and Isaac Gerton.

His heart sank. For some reason, the four men who had remained at the hideout had been riding on the east side of Monarch Pass. He heard Ed Payton say that apparently Wolf

Eye and his band had taken the dead men's horses.

"Maybe we ought to search the bodies," said Brockman. "If we can find out who they are, we can notify their families."

"We sure ought to do that," agreed Fleenor.

Each man picked a corpse to search. While Nye was searching Web Crispin's body, he knew there would be nothing on any of them to identify them or link them to the Foster gang. It was an unwritten law among outlaws that no one carried anything on his person to identify him.

When nothing was found, Brockman said, "Well, at least we can bury them so animals won't eat their bodies." He looked around for a minute and then said, "Even if we had shovels it wouldn't do us any good. This ground is too rocky to dig through. All we can do is pile stones on the bodies to protect them from scavengers."

The bodies were laid side by side on the lowest part of the draw.

While Dick Nye helped carry heavy stones from around the area, his thoughts ran to what Brockman had read to him from the Bible about men dying in their sins and going into eternity without Jesus Christ. He thought about his four partners in crime who had been sent into eternity by Wolf Eye and his band of savages. If what the Bible said was right, Acton Huxley, Mel Skinner, Web Crispin, and Isaac Gerton were now in that awful place of everlasting fire.

A nagging fear plucked at his mind. Fitting a stone into place between two others at Mel Skinner's side, he stood up and shook his sagging shoulders to rid himself of the horrid concept of hell.

When the bodies were sufficiently covered, Brockman and his deputy bid the trappers good-bye and resumed their climb toward the summit of Monarch Pass.

As they rode away from the crude rock grave, Nye thought about how Duke Foster would go berserk when told that his four men had been massacred by the renegade Utes. Maybe Duke wouldn't take it quite so bad since he would learn first that John "The Stranger" Brockman was also dead.

Brockman and Nye had been back on the steep trail only a few minutes when they noticed dark clouds forming ahead of them, beyond the jagged peaks.

"Rains up here on the Continental Divide just about every day in the summertime," said John. "Looks like today will be no exception."

"Must turn to snow above timberline," commented Nye. "Here it is August, and those high peaks are still snowcapped."

The horses whinnied and snorted, catching the scent of the impending storm. Soon, a mass of inky clouds came prowling over the highest peaks like angry beasts. Forks of lightning flashed like daggers of white fire, and, like the roar of an avalanche, thunder followed.

"We'd better take cover," said John, heading toward a rock ledge that jutted from a sheer granite wall.

The ledge formed a cover some ten or twelve feet in depth, and was high enough to allow the horses to take shelter beneath it. The rain came down in torrents only seconds after they had reached the natural refuge. The wind whipped beneath the ledge, spraying water on man and beast, but it was better than being out in the downpour.

John was stroking Ebony's long mane and talking to him in low, soothing tones when lightning cracked in a long series of bolts. John could feel the electricity in Ebony's mane, and it tingled through his hands and up his arms.

Thunder clapped, seeming to shake the very foundations of the mountain.

Dick Nye watched his intended victim, wishing he could get the task over with, but there was no way he would try it with Brockman looking at him periodically over Ebony's back. *Tonight,* he told himself. *Tonight.*

Again lightning came, spreading brilliant crooked branches across the black sky, then reaching like deadly tentacles toward the mountains. Thunder boomed along the peaks, reverberating in the canyons, then rumbled away into silence.

Almost as fast as the storm had come in, it went away. Soon the rain stopped, leaving behind a fragrant pine perfume.

The clouds broke up, the wind died down, and the sun sent its slanting rays over the land.

Having lost the time it took to help bury the four dead men and wait out the storm, Brockman and Nye were not yet to the summit of the pass when the sun disappeared behind the lofty peaks above them, leaving behind orange streamers of clouds that hugged the highest elevations.

"Guess we'll have to camp on this side of the crest," said John, looking around for a level spot.

They could hear a stream gurgling somewhere off to the right. "Let's check back in there," said John, pointing with his chin.

They weaved among towering fir and pine trees, leading the horses. Soon they found the stream, which was a bit swollen and foamy along its banks. The air was quite cool at this altitude.

When the horses had been allowed to take their fill of water, the bedrolls and other camping equipment were removed and laid on the ground. While Nye was removing his saddle, he ran his gaze over the flat area where they would build the campfire and lay out their bedrolls. He picked the spot he wanted, which would give him the best advantage to shoot Brockman.

As soon as Nye laid the saddle on the ground, he picked up his bedroll and unobtrusively plopped it on the chosen spot.

Brockman had released the cinch under Ebony's belly and was about to remove the saddle, when over Ebony's back he saw movement in the shadows among the trees. His eye caught a vertical feather under a headband, and his reflexes went to work. There wasn't time to voice a warning to his partner.

Brockman pulled out his gun and leaped to the side in order to clear himself from Ebony.

Nye saw Brockman's swift move and heard the Colt .45 roar. The slug struck the Indian a split second before he released an arrow, spoiling his aim. The deadly feathered missile hissed past Nye's upper body, clearing him by a foot.

Nye was clawing for his gun when a series of wild whoops cut through the forest, and Brockman's gun roared again. Another Ute went down at the edge of the trees.

Suddenly, others were coming from off to the left. Nye and Brockman unleashed a series of shots at them. Arrows cut through the air but missed their marks.

John emptied the Peacemaker into the shadows while Nye was shooting a few feet to the left of that spot.

In one smooth move, Brockman holstered his revolver and grabbed his rifle from the saddle still on Ebony's back.

He dived behind a small boulder for cover and began pumping .44-caliber slugs at the Utes, who were all on one side of the stream. Nye had reached his rifle and was behind another boulder, taking aim and firing.

Gunsmoke permeated the air. Arrows whined, some thunking into the trees behind the two white men. Two more Utes had fallen when suddenly one of them broke from the shadows off to Nye's right side, wielding a tomahawk. It was raised for the kill, and the warrior gave a deadly cry.

Dick Nye stiffened, expecting to receive the blow, but Brockman's rifle cracked and the Ute went down, dropping the tomahawk. His momentum carried him into Nye, but the bullet in his head had killed him instantly.

Nye threw the lifeless form off him and joined Brockman, who was already unleashing relentless, deadly fire against the others.

John had no idea how many Utes were back in the trees, but he knew if there were many more, he and his partner were done for, unless... At that moment, the eagle eye of the man known as the Stranger caught sight of a bronze-skinned warrior wearing a long headdress. Wolf Eye!

He knew that if he could take out their leader, the others would turn and run.

Nye was still firing as arrows rode the air.

Brockman saw another Ute go down, and when he fell, directly behind him was Wolf Eye, half exposed behind a tree. The renegade leader was furiously notching an arrow to his bow.

John's Winchester .44 thundered, and Wolf Eye dropped like a rock.

There was a high-pitched cry from a few feet away, followed by a string of panicky words in the Ute language. Suddenly no more arrows were flying, but the Indians could be seen running deeper into the forest.

Sudden silence prevailed.

Both white men rose to their feet.

"You got Wolf Eye," said Nye. "They won't be back, will they?"

"No."

"Whew!" gasped Nye, wiping sweat from his face. "That was close! How many do you suppose were in the band?"

"Hard to tell. You never know about Indians. Could have had some in reserve. I doubt it, though. Usually their leaders will not get involved if they can stay out of it. We must've taken out enough to lure Wolf Eye into the fight."

"Glad we did," said Nye. "Otherwise we might have been the dead ones lying here." Nye looked toward the body of the young renegade leader. "Why do they give up the fight when their leader goes down?"

"Indian culture," said Brockman. "When a man becomes a chief, or even a subchief, in their eyes he is a god. As long as he lives to lead them, they will fight till they drop. But when he dies, they believe they have no god to lead them, which means certain defeat and certain death. So they run from the fight."

Together, the two white men dragged the bodies into a low spot back in the trees.

By the time John had the fire going, darkness had fallen and the cool, rising night wind was tossing sparks into the air while it stirred a faint silken rustle in the boughs of the trees.

As John stirred the beans in the skillet over the crackling fire, he was thinking of Breanna. His lonely heart yearned for her. Silently, he thanked the Lord for sparing his life in the battle with the Utes. Soon he would capture the outlaw gang with Palmer Danfield's help and go home to his sweet Breanna.

Even as his mind stayed on her, and he thought of how lonesome he was for her, the lonely howl of a timber wolf came on the wind. *Lonely for your mate, too, ol' boy?*

Brockman noted that Danfield was unusually quiet while they downed their beans, hardtack, and coffee.

Smiling at him, John said, "Fighting grizzlies and savages isn't quite the same as fighting outlaws, is it, Danfield?"

As if his mind had been a million miles away and suddenly returned, Nye looked at him in the light of the flickering fire and blinked. "I'm sorry, Chief. What did you say?"

"You seem a little shaken. I said, fighting grizzlies and savages isn't quite the same as fighting outlaws."

"Oh. Ah…no. It isn't."

Brockman cocked his head, deep lines running across his brow. "You all right, partner?"

"Sure. Why?"

"You're awfully quiet."

Nye studied Brockman's pale gray eyes for a moment. "Been quite a day. Lots to think about."

"Oh. Well, that's for sure."

When the meal was finished and the tin plates and cups had been washed and put away, John went to his saddlebags and pulled out his Bible. He sat down close to the fire as he had done every night since they had been on the trip, opened the sacred Book, and began to read.

Without a word, Dick Nye left him there and walked into the deep shadows outside the circle of fire. He stood on the bank of the small stream and watched the stars dance on the dark surface of the water. Turning around, he looked back at the tall man who sat on the ground and said to himself in a whisper, "It has to be done. Might as well get it over with."

Moving like a shadow, Nye pulled his gun from its holster.

John's mind was on what he was reading in God's Word when Dick Nye's voice cut into his thoughts from behind. "Chief Brockman…"

John looked around, and by the firelight he saw Nye's gun in his hand and a strange look in his eyes. He closed the Bible and rose to his feet. He let his gaze drop to the revolver, then raised it to look the man square in the eye. "Yes?"

Nye's voice was on the verge of breaking as he turned the gun in his hand butt first, extended it to Brockman, and said, "I surrender."

"What did you say?"

This time, the killer's voice cracked. "I...I surrender. You can take me into custody." As he spoke, he gently pressed the gun into Brockman's hand.

Perplexed, John said, "Danfield, what's going on?"

Nye choked as he tried to speak, then tried again. Tears filled his eyes as he said, "I'm not Palmer Danfield, Chief."

Stunned, John said, "What? You're not the man George Frame sent me from Amarillo?"

Nye swallowed hard, wiped tears from his eyes, and said, "My name is Dick Nye."

The name instantly rang a bell in the chief U.S. marshal's mind. "The Dick Nye who, along with Pete Dawson, made an escape through a hotel room window the night I shot it out with Chick Foster, Layton Patch, and Jim Felton?"

Nye's features were like old stone. Nodding, he said, "The same."

Brockman held his gaze with his own for a long moment. "Where is Deputy Danfield?"

"I killed him."

John felt as if he'd been kicked in the stomach by a mule. He stared at the killer while stuffing the man's gun under his belt, then said levelly, "Tell me about it."

In a faltering voice, Nye told Brockman why Duke Foster wanted him dead, and how he had sent him to kill him on this trip. He explained in a dismal tone that Foster had an informant who worked in the federal building and had supplied him all the information he needed to set him up for the kill. Brockman was shocked to hear that Harold Sheetz was the informant, and that Foster and Dawson were presently at Sheetz's house in Denver, waiting for him to return and tell them he had killed Brockman.

At this point, Nye explained that it was Sheetz who had alerted Foster that Chet McCarty was coming to Denver so Foster could get revenge for ten years in prison and the crippling of his leg.

Nye went on to tell how he had gone to Amarillo, made himself known to Palmer Danfield as Denver merchant Ambrose Benson, and lured him onto the dining car platform. He had stabbed Danfield to death, taken his gun, badge, and identification papers, then thrown his body off the train. He followed that by confessing all the other murders he had committed on his own, and as a hired killer for Duke Foster.

He then told Brockman how he had come close to shooting him in the back, but was hindered once by the eagle, and again by the grizzly.

John could see God's hand in both incidents.

"I was gonna shoot you in the back of the head after you went to sleep tonight, Chief," Nye said with a crack in his voice. Again, John shook his head, thanking God in his heart that it wouldn't happen now. He thought of Breanna telling him she had a strange feeling about this trip, and that she wished he wasn't going. Now he understood why she had felt that way—the Spirit of God was speaking to her heart.

"I also need to tell you," said Nye, "that those four men we buried, who had been killed by the Utes, were Foster's men who lived at the hideout. Besides me, Pete Dawson is the only gang member left."

John shook his head, as if it all seemed too incredible to be true. "You're just full of surprises, Nye."

"You really didn't suspect anything, did you?"

Brockman sighed and said, "I had some misgivings when your reaction to the grizzly incident and the Ute battle seemed out of line for a lawman with Danfield's reputation, but this is a total shock. Now tell me why this sudden surrender and confession. Why didn't you go ahead and shoot me in the back of the head tonight as you planned?"

Dick Nye's lower lip began to quiver, and tears filled his eyes. "I came plenty close to death twice today, and you saved my life both times. And...and when I stood over the bodies of my four outlaw friends, I thought about them burning in hell."

He swallowed hard and went on. "Ever since you started quoting Bible to me, it has kept me upset. It made me want to kill you even worse. But...but..."

"But what?"

"I couldn't shake it, Chief. It just kept needlin' me down deep inside."

"The Word of God will do that, Nye. It's quick and powerful, and sharper than a two-edged sword."

"I kept thinking of hell, Chief, and of Jesus dying on that cross. While we were eating supper tonight, I knew I had to do it. I had to surrender to you and confess the whole thing. Now I have one big question to ask."

"What's that?"

Nye drew a shuddering breath. "Would Jesus save a man like me? Would He save a murderer?"

John smiled. "First Timothy 1:15, Dick. 'This is a faithful saying, and worthy of all acceptation, that Christ Jesus came into the world to save sinners.' You're a sinner, right?"

"The worst."

"Romans 5:8 and 9: 'But God commendeth his love toward us in that, while we were yet sinners, Christ died for us. Much more then, being now justified by his blood, we shall be saved from wrath through him.' Second Peter 3:9 says that God is 'not willing that any should perish, but that all should come to repentance.' Wouldn't you, as a murderer, be included in 'all sinners' for whom Jesus died?"

"Yes."

"And if God is not willing that any should go to hell... wouldn't that include you?"

"It has to."

"Then are you willing to repent of your sin and, by faith, to ask Jesus to save your soul and wash away all your sins in His blood?"

Tears glistened the killer's face. "Yes. Oh, yes!"

After shedding tears of repentance, and receiving Jesus Christ into his heart, it took Dick Nye several minutes to bring his emotions under control.

Wiping tears from his face, he said, "Chief, thank you for caring for my soul."

"That's part of being a Christian, Dick," said Brockman. "I'm supposed to care where other people spend eternity."

"I've been around other people who said they are Christians, but they never showed any interest in my eternal destiny."

John nodded silently.

"Do you realize, Chief, that if you had not cared for my soul and quoted Scripture to me, you would have been killed in your sleep tonight?"

Again John nodded silently, knowing it was true, and thanking the Lord in his heart for bringing Dick Nye to Himself, and in so doing, saving John Brockman's life.

Nye stared into the crackling fire and said, "I realize I must still face the law for my crimes, Chief, which means I will hang. But when I die, I will die in peace, knowing that I've been saved from the wrath of God through Jesus Christ. Instead of going to hell, where I was headed, I will go to heaven."

"You sure will, Dick," said Brockman. "Thank God for His mercy and His grace."

23

THE NEXT MORNING, as John Brockman and his prisoner headed back down the trail, John quoted many Scriptures, assuring Dick that all his sins had been washed away in the blood of the Lamb of God.

John wished that his new convert would not have to hang, but the law was the law. And Dick Nye had blatantly broken the law. Though God had forgiven him for his crimes, society had not, and Dick must pay his debt to society on the gallows.

John was both pleased and amazed at the peace Dick had, knowing he was riding back to Denver to face the noose. The man had believed and obeyed the gospel, and Paul had called it the gospel of peace in Romans 10:15.

They rode without speaking for a while; then Nye broke the silence by saying, "I know Duke and Pete will hang, Chief, but what will happen to Harold Sheetz?"

"I'll arrest him for aiding, abetting, and harboring men who are wanted by the law. He'll also face charges of conspiracy for passing on information to Duke Foster that he gained in my office as a trusted federal employee. The information he gave to Foster was for the purpose of assassinating Chester McCarty, and resulted in the death of Palmer Danfield so that you could impersonate him and be in a position to kill me. Mr. Sheetz is going to prison for a long time."

Nye thought on it for a moment, then said, "Man's a fool to buck the laws of society, Chief. And you're looking at one of the greatest fools who ever lived."

"I agree that it takes a real fool to be a criminal, Dick. But there is one difference between most outlaws and yourself."

"What's that?"

"Most of them live and die as fools. You've lived as a fool, but you will not die as one. You will die as a child of God—the wisest decision you've ever made."

"Yes, sir. You're right about that."

The hours passed, and in late afternoon they came out of dense forest where the trail was quite steep and rode onto level ground where a beautiful lake glistened in the sunlight. The water was clear as crystal, and the tall pines and colorful wildflowers that fringed it were reflected magnificently in its calm surface.

A massive mountain loomed on the far side of the lake, its rocky peak a jagged finger piercing the sky. Snow glistened from the deep pockets of its rugged shoulders, and its surface was scarred and gouged into a tangle of snow-filled crevices and ridges. The peaks and snow pockets were streaked with fire in the wash of the lowering sun.

Brockman heard his prisoner gasp and say, "Chief, look at that!" as he pointed to the lake and the mountain. "What a magnificent sight!"

"You didn't notice it when we came by on the way up?"

Nye ducked his head. "No, I was too caught up in trying to figure out how to kill you without endangering myself in the attempt." Running his appreciative gaze over the scene, he said, "Isn't that something! You can even see the mountain reflected in the lake!"

Both horses nickered at the scent of water.

"Let's give them a drink," said John, guiding Ebony toward the flower-strewn shore.

While the horses were taking their fill from the clean, clear water, and Nye was looking around at the awesome handiwork of God, he saw three riders emerge from the dark shadows of the dense forest. "Riders, Chief," he said, pointing in that direction.

It took only a second for Brockman to recognize Chance and to identify his rider. Breanna had spotted them and was forging ahead of the other two riders at a full gallop, her long blond hair looking like windblown flame in the red-gold light of the setting sun.

"It's a woman on the big black," commented Nye.

"Yes," said John. "I know her."

"Oh?"

"She's my wife." Focusing on the two riders behind her, he said, "One of the men is Sheriff Curt Langan, and the other is Pat O'Rourke, one of my deputies."

"And I suppose they're looking for you."

"I would say so."

As Breanna thundered in, Ebony lifted his head and gave off a loud whinny.

Skidding Chance to a stop, Breanna said with urgency in her voice, "John! That man with you isn't Palmer Danfield! He's an impostor!"

John reached up and took hold of her, lowering her to the ground. "I know, sweetheart," he said, holding her close. "It's all right. You will notice that he has no gun in his holster, and no rifle in his saddle boot. Both of his weapons are in my bedroll."

Langan and O'Rourke drew rein and quickly slid from their saddles.

Keeping his arms around Breanna, John said, "Welcome, gentlemen. Everything's under control. How did you find out this man isn't Palmer Danfield?"

"Dave Taylor told me," said Breanna. "He saw you ride away from the hospital with this man. When I happened to mention that the new deputy's name was Palmer Danfield, Dave was quick to tell me that he and Danfield are old friends, and he didn't know the man riding with you. We both knew then that whoever you were riding with was an impostor, and he was up to no good."

As she spoke, Breanna's eyes flashed fire at Nye. He looked away, unable to bear her gaze.

She went on. "I ran to your office to tell Sol what I had just learned, and only minutes before I arrived, Sol had received a wire from Washington, telling him that the body of Deputy Danfield had been found alongside the railroad tracks in southern Colorado."

"I know all about it," said John. "This man is Dick Nye, a member of the Duke Foster gang. He was sent by Foster to kill me."

"So what's happened here?" asked Langan.

John told them the story of how he had witnessed to Nye on the trail, and how the Holy Spirit had done His work in the man's heart. He gave them the details of how he had saved Nye's life twice the day before, and of Nye's handing him his gun, confessing who he was and why he was there, and saying that he wanted to be saved.

There was rejoicing in Nye's salvation and in the way God had spared John's life.

Nye told them of the two times he was about to shoot John in the back but was kept from it by the appearance of an eagle the first time and a grizzly bear the second time.

Tears were streaming down Nye's face as he said, "Chief Brockman unknowingly saved his own life by giving me the gospel and trying to get me saved."

"Praise the Lord!" Breanna cried. "John, darling, you faithfully witnessed for Jesus, and by using the Word to convict Mr. Nye's heart and bring him to salvation, the Spirit of God was your Protector!"

John agreed, also giving praise to the Lord.

The group decided that since the sun was setting, and they were standing on a level piece of ground, they should camp there for the night. When John had Breanna's gear and bedroll off Chance's back and had laid his own next to it, he said, "How's Dr. Rawlins?"

Breanna's eyes lit up. "Just wait till I tell you!"

"How about taking a little walk along the edge of the lake while these gentlemen build a fire. You can tell me all about it."

"Okay!" she said, smiling from ear to ear.

John removed his hat, hung it on his saddle horn, and led Breanna away, saying over his shoulder, "We'll see you guys in a few minutes."

When they were some thirty yards from the campsite, Breanna told John about the Swiss surgeon's sudden death in New York. She explained about Matt's performing the surgery by Rex's request, and how at one crucial moment of extremely difficult surgery, the Lord performed a miracle with Matt's hands.

Smiling happily, Breanna said, "John, Rex Rawlins is already walking again, 'Not by might, nor by power, but by my spirit, saith the LORD of hosts'!"

Breanna then told him the story of the love between Rex Rawlins and Natalie Fallon, and that they were now engaged to be married.

"I like to see the hand of God in action," John said. "I'm glad for both of them."

He folded Breanna in his arms, and when she laid her head on his chest, he pressed his chin tenderly against her head.

The wind rose, and twilight was beginning to replace the light of day.

"I've missed you terribly, darling," Breanna said in a whisper.

"And I've been awfully lonely for you, sweetheart," John said softly.

From somewhere across the lake came the lonesome howl of a timber wolf.

The publisher and author would love to hear your comments about this book. *Please contact us at:* www.multnomah.net/notbymight

OTHER COMPELLING STORIES BY
AL LACY

Books in the Battles of Destiny series:

☞ *A Promise Unbroken*

Two couples battle jealousy and racial hatred amidst a war that would cripple America. From a prosperous Virginia plantation to a grim jail cell outside Lynchburg, follow the dramatic story of a love that could not be destroyed.

☞ *A Heart Divided*

Ryan McGraw—leader of the Confederate Sharpshooters—is nursed back to health by beautiful army nurse Dixie Quade. Their romance would survive the perils of war, but can it withstand the reappearance of a past love?

☞ *Beloved Enemy*

Young Jenny Jordan covers for her father's Confederate spy missions. But as she grows closer to Union soldier Buck Brownell, Jenny finds herself torn between devotion to the South and her feelings for the man she is forbidden to love.

☞ *Shadowed Memories*

Critically wounded on the field of battle and haunted by amnesia, one man struggles to regain his strength and the memories that have slipped away from him.

☞ *Joy from Ashes*

Major Layne Dalton made it through the horrors of the battle of Fredericksburg, but can he rise above his hatred toward the Heglund brothers who brutalized his wife and killed his unborn son?

☞ *Season of Valor*

Captain Shane Donovan was heroic in battle. Can he summon the courage to face the dark tragedy unfolding back home in Maine?

Books in the Battles of Destiny series (cont.):

☞ *Wings of the Wind*

God brings a young doctor and a nursing student together in this story of the Battle of Antietam.

☞ *Turn of Glory*

Four confederate soldiers lauded for bravery mistakenly shoot General Stonewall Jackson. Driven from the army in shame, they become outlaws…and their friend must bring them to justice.

Books in the Journeys of the Stranger series:

☞ *Legacy*

Can John Stranger bring Clay Austin back to the right side of the law…and restore the code of honor shared by the woman he loves?

☞ *Silent Abduction*

The mysterious man in black fights to defend a small town targeted by cattle rustlers and to rescue a young woman and child held captive by a local Indian tribe.

☞ *Blizzard*

When three murderers slated for hanging escape from the Colorado Territorial Prison, young U.S. Marshal Ridge Holloway and the mysterious John Stranger join together to track down the infamous convicts.

☞ *Tears of the Sun*

When John Stranger arrives in Apache Junction, Arizona, he finds himself caught up in a bitter war between sworn enemies: the Tonto Apaches and the Arizona Zunis.

☞ *Circle of Fire*

John Stranger must clear his name of the crimes committed by another mysterious—and murderous—"stranger" who has adopted his identity.

☞ *Quiet Thunder*

A Sioux warrior and a white army captain have been blood brothers since childhood. But when the two meet on the battlefield, which will win out—love or duty?

☞ *Snow Ghost*

John Stranger must unravel the mystery of a murderer who appears to have come back from the grave to avenge his execution.

Books in the Angel of Mercy series:

☞ *A Promise for Breanna*

The man who broke Breanna's heart is back. But this time, he's after her life.

☞ *Faithful Heart*

Breanna and her sister Dottie find themselves in a desperate struggle to save a man they love, but can no longer trust.

☞ *Captive Set Free*

No one leaves Morgan's labor camp alive. Not even Breanna Baylor.

☞ *A Dream Fulfilled*

A tender story about one woman's healing from heartbreak and the fulfillment of her dreams.

☞ *Suffer the Little Children*

Breanna Baylor develops a special bond with the children headed west on an orphan train.

☞ *Whither Thou Goest*

As they begin their lives together, John Stranger and Breanna Baylor place themselves in danger to help a friend.

☞ *Final Justice*

After Silver Moon's Cheyenne village is destroyed, she lives for revenge. Can Breanna's compassion bring about a change of heart in time to prevent further tragedy?

Books in the Hannah of Fort Bridger series (coauthored with JoAnna Lacy):

☞ *Under the Distant Sky*

Follow the Cooper family as they travel West from Missouri in pursuit of their dream of a new life on the Wyoming frontier.

☞ *Consider the Lilies*

Will Hannah Cooper and her children learn to trust God to provide when tragedy threatens to destroy their dream?

☞ *No Place for Fear*

A widow rejects the gospel until the disappearance of her sons and their rescue by Indians opens her heart to God's love.

☞ *Pillow of Stone*

After the death of her husband and the theft of her inheritance, Julianna LeCroix heads west to start a new life—only to be kidnapped!

Books in the Mail Order Bride series (coauthored with JoAnna Lacy):

☞ *Secrets of the Heart*

Kathleen O'Malley Stallworth is a young widow, and now her wealthy in-laws have taken her daughter from her, claiming she's not fit to be a mother. Can Kathleen find faith and forgiveness as a mail order bride?

☞ *A Time to Love*

After her fiancé deserts her on their wedding day, Linda Forrest travels west to find the life—and the love—God has chosen.

Available at your local Christian bookstore